PRAISE FOR *THE BR*

"A startlingly original novel that dizzyingly keeps erasing and redrawing the distinction between magic and science fiction as it takes apart what it means to belong or not belong. A story about reparations, necromancy, and college cliques, and about the way in which the world, in being made and remade, remains both incandescent and deadly."
—**Brian Evenson, Shirley Jackson Award-winning author of** *Song for the Unraveling of the World*

"*The Bridge* has one foot in dystopian darkness and one foot deep in a mythology that feels both new and subconsciously familiar. All at once beautiful and terrifying, this is horror that hits close to the heart and close to home."
—**Sarah Read, Bram Stoker Award-winning author of** *The Bone Weaver's Orchard*

"Casts a dark, mesmerizing, poetic spell."
—**Kaaron Warren, Shirley Jackson Award Winner**

"A twisting tale of what it means to live with the scars of your survival that crosses the territory between Shirley Jackson and Emma Cline. The world of *The Bridge* is as harrowing as it is expertly realized, demonstrating once again that J.S. Breukelaar is a talent to be discovered. Utterly captivating stuff."
—**Helen Marshall, World Fantasy Award-winning author of** *The Migration*

PRAISE FOR *COLLISION: STORIES*

Shirley Jackson Award Finalist, Aurealis Award and Ditmar Award Winner

"All 12 stories hit the same surreal nerve despite their sometimes vastly different plots, making the transition from one story to another feel like entering an entirely new world. The only predictable element is the collection's overall strangeness, which is something that never gets old."
—***Booklist***

ALSO BY J.S. BREUKELAAR

American Monster
Aletheia
Collision: Stories

"Breukelaar's delectable prose draws in the reader, and I frequently found myself in that perfect hypnotic state where I forgot I was reading—the highest honor one can bestow on an author, in my opinion."
—**Kris Ashton,** *Andromeda Spaceways Magazine*

"*Collision* is a wonderful collection of complex tales that cross genres in ways that are never fully expected at the beginning but always fully realized by the end. The boundaries between different styles are as porous as the boundaries between worlds, but each aspect is precisely organized and elevated by Breukelaar's versatile and vital techniques. It's no stretch to say there's something for everyone here, but we can go further and say there's something for every version of everyone, even as they shift and change."
—*Hellnotes*

"Breukelaar's stories are fueled with gorgeous darkness, often thematically heartbreaking and always nothing short of amazing."
—**Shane Douglas Keene,** *Inkheist*

"I immediately felt captivated by J.S. Breukelaar's evocatively descriptive style, her convincing observations of human behavior and the incisive quality of her dialogue. At times it felt as though her characters, and the worlds they inhabited, were leaping off the page, demanding my full attention. Although each of the stories is very different, what remains constant throughout the collection is the author's skill in drawing her readers into the fantastical worlds she is describing. Yet these are worlds which, albeit in slightly distorted ways, are often all too easily recognizable, possibly because there is always an element of people struggling to make sense of, and adjust to, the world they are inhabiting."
—**Linda Hepworth,** *NB Magazine* (**5 stars**)

"The stories are ruthless, nothing is safe—even the child who offers a lollipop and loses a wrist to the Clint Eastwood dog. Breukelaar experiments with the Gothic and queries the queer. Bedded within the tales is a voluptuous energy that turns pages. Tables pirouette in a blink and, before you know it, the story is eleven shades grimmer."
—**Eugen Bacon,** *Breach Magazine*

ALSO BY J.S. BREUKELAAR

American Monster
Aletheia
Collision: Stories

THE
BRIDGE

J.S. BREUKELAAR

Meerkat Press
Asheville

ISBN-13 978-1-946154-44-6 (Paperback)
ISBN-13 978-1-946154-45-3 (eBook)

Author Photo by Guy Bailey
Cover Design by Luke Spooner

Printed in the United States of America

Published in the United States of America by
Meerkat Press, LLC, Asheville, North Carolina
www.meerkatpress.com

For Eric and Marvin

Weave the weird dance,—behold the hour
    To utter forth the chant of hell,
    Our sway among mankind to tell,
The guidance of our power.
Of Justice are we ministers,
    And whosoe'er of men may stand
    Lifting a pure unsullied hand,
That man no doom of ours incurs,
    And walks thro' all his mortal path
    Untouched by woe, unharmed by wrath.
    But if, as yonder man, he hath
Blood on the hands he strives to hide,
    We stand avengers at his side,
Decreeing, *Thou hast wronged the dead:*
    We are doom's witnesses to thee.
The price of blood, his hands have shed,
We wring from him; in life, in death,
    Hard at his side are we!

—Aeschylus, *The Furies*

CONTENTS

Chapter 1: Tower 1

Chapter 2: Horns 6

Chapter 3: Twisted Sister 18

Chapter 4: A Good Beginning is Hard to Find 36

Chapter 5: Kill Zone 52

Chapter 6: Notebook 63

Chapter 7: FiFo 73

Chapter 8: Dirty Bert's 80

Chapter 9: Real Deal 93

Chapter 10: Sister-Act 101

Chapter 11: Win-Win 112

Chapter 12: Planned Obsolescence 122

Chapter 13: Gatherum 128

Chapter 14: Chimera 136

Chapter 15: Fresh Meat 142

Chapter 16: Stinky Sister 154

Chapter 17: Big Made on Campus 161

Chapter 18: Which Witch? 165

Chapter 19: Sweeney's 172

Chapter 20: The Bridge 179

Chapter 21: Drowning 185

Chapter 22: Last Call 190

Chapter 23: Sweet Sixteen 194

Chapter 24: Three Way 198

Chapter 25: Last Supper 203

Chapter 26: Lost and Found 213

Anamnesis 225

Acknowledgments 229

About the Author 231

CHAPTER 1
TOWER

I was raised by three sisters—one a witch, one an assassin and the third just batshit crazy. By the time I left our home deep in the Starveling Hills, I'd met the middle one, Tiff, once, but I never told the others. She'd run off or something, and they didn't talk about her much, and maybe it was for that reason that she was my favorite—her ghostly absence having as big an impact on my growing-up as the others' larger-than-life presence. When I finally came to live in the Hills, carrying my own dead twin in my arms, Tiff was already gone, leaving behind nothing but bad blood and a trunk filled with old clothes from across the ages. Among them were a pair of Roman sandals that fell apart in my hands, some rusted crinolines, a moldy cat-o'-nine-tails, some concert T-shirts and even a notebook from her days at the Blood Temple with the Father—bound in the skin of one of her victims, for all I knew. The pages were scribbled in with illegible symbols which set something humming inside me, convinced me from day one that "Aunty" Tiff wanted me, and only me, to find her.

I was good at finding lost things, Kai always said, and they were good at finding me.

In time Narn, the eldest sister, sent me away to Wellsburg college, ten thousand miles away and on the other side of the planet. To the ends of the earth, may as well have been.

I had arrived at the campus just before the start of the semester and was soon sick with one of my frequent chest infections. I lay awake in the Tower Village dorm room, feverish and snotty, too ill to go to the first week of classes, forgetting why I was here. The damp pillowcase chafed my cheek. The weary thwack of a campus security pod overhead tangled in the jerky drum of my heart, and I tried to push thoughts of the Father's birds away, couldn't help wondering how far I had really come from all that—Narn and her crazy sisters and my sister Kai, buried under a bloodwood tree, high in the Starveling Hills. I tried not to think. I tried not to ask myself if it would ever be far enough.

My pajamas, blue plaid with pink elephants, were damp with sweat. They insistently nudged between my legs. I shifted on the mattress, trying not to think of the downy young shearers who drank at the pub in the nearest town to our hut—a twenty-kilometer drive in Narn's truck, but worth every pothole. I was nineteen and Kai would be too—my better half as Narn called her, not joking. Narn never joked. Maybe that's why Kai had been *her* favorite from the beginning—law of opposites or something. My sister *always* joked, even when she lay in the Blood Temple infirmary covered with sores and the Father already sharpening his scalpels for the unmaking.

Even then.

The door opened with a click. I squeezed my eyes shut, hoping my roommates, Lara and Trudy, would leave me alone. Their laughter subsided when they saw me still in bed, but they continued their conversation in whispers—something about an urban myth of a ghost of a fur hunter from the 1800s who crawled out from under the bridge after being pushed to his death by a witch.

"Yes, but don't most old colleges in the Slant come with *some* kind of scary story?" Trudy was saying. "In orientation they told us . . ."

I couldn't resist. Partly because in the mostly bedridden week that I'd been at Tower Village, I'd barely spoken or been spoken to, but also because long before I'd even gotten here, Narn had versed me in the history of witches' rights. "He jumped!" I croaked. "Probably. They had to blame somebody. Why not witches?"

"Know-it-all," Lara said beneath her breath.

No, Kai was the know-it-all. Always had been. My cheeks burned with fever, but there was no stopping me now. Kai always said how just a sniff of threat was enough to make me see red.

"Witches got the blame for the fur trade drying up in Upper Slant," I continued. "People said they poisoned the game—even after the Apology it wasn't safe for them here."

The air in the dorm room was stale. My nose was blocked with congestion so I drew it in as best I could through my mouth, watching Trudy dart through the shadows like a bottom feeder through lakeweed, for a moment the meds and the fever telling me that it was Kai. That my twin was not dead after all and I was home in the Starvelings and the Father had not found us as she always said he would. But then Lara flicked on the light and I blinked into the reality of what I'd lost.

Lara moved to check her roots in the mirror for telltale regrowth. Like all Mades, her hair was course and dull, but she'd applied conditioning treatments and lightened it to a chestnut brown, had it cut into a curly bob that suited her. "It stinks in here," she said.

"Anyway, what do you care about myths?" I propped myself up on a wobbly elbow. "We have enough problems with reality."

Lara and Trudy were made on the Blood Temple's mainland property but the Father's synthetic reproductive protocol was the same there as it was in Rogues Bay, where I was from. Their teeth looked ultraviolet in the blue-stippled light from the bridge outside our window. Their forms were limned in a milky afterglow which seemed to slow their movements one minute, speed them up the next, silvery jetsam shredding in their wake. Or maybe it was just the meds.

"The counselor in pain clinic said we shouldn't fixate on the past, Meera," Trudy shivered mechanically, "if we want to belong to the future."

I wanted nothing less.

"Well, we *can't* fixate on the past," I said. "It's not how we're, um, *made*."

It was something my sister would do—hiding good intentions behind a dark pun, an offhand joke—but I sucked at reading the room, something Kai never let me forget. Instead of admiring my cleverness, Trudy's eyes brimmed and she reddened in the shame of our shared congenital amnesia.

"Myth or not," Lara turned defensively from the mirror, fastening a chain around her wrist from which dangled a rose-gold feather, "they've put a curfew out now that semester's started. The bridge is off-limits after ten."

"Why?" I asked.

"To keep us where we belong," Trudy sniffled. "Especially after dark."

They moved about, preparing for the night. Later they would come home smelling of beer, faces bleached in the light of their program-issued phones, and fall immediately asleep dreaming, I imagined, of a new tomorrow.

What I really felt like was a drink, but before I could ask them to wait while I dressed, Lara reminded me that today, Thursday, was the last day to sign up for our second-choice electives. And that we needed these for credit point requirements to complete our transfer program in the specified time of eighteen months.

"The sooner we complete the program," she said, "the sooner we can get out of here."

"I almost forgot."

"You did forget," Lara eyed my pile of snotty tissues. "And you need to get *up* now, Meera, or you never will."

I hacked phlegm into another tissue. My nostrils were chaffed and there was blood in my snot. Unlike most of the Redress Award recipients, including my roommates, who *had* followed the award recommendations and arrived during the summer, my body had not had time to build up the required immunities. Nor had my brain gone through the regulation mnemonic and behavioral reconditioning. The dormitory pulsed black and blue in the light from the illuminated bridge. It wasn't much different from how my eyes would open into the half-light of the little room I shared with my dead sister in the Starvelings, before closing once more on the shifting optics of a digital dream.

Unfamiliar constellations pricked the alien September sky. I looked through the window high up in my Tower and thought how I wanted to be here—didn't I? Yet a part of my consciousness did not. Some part of me—my mind—remained in South Rim where, beneath Crux and the Jewel Box, blossoms would be blowing across my twin sister's grave beside the bloodwoods. Where Mag would be cleaning their gun and Narn would be peeling potatoes while she stirred a cauldron of beans on the stove—she was a terrible cook of everything but sweets and libations, and even from here, I could taste the burnt scum from the bottom of the pot, smell the lemon myrtle in her velvety pudding and the stinking hellebore in her soup.

But my heart could not.

The walls spasmed in another flash of electric blue. I closed one eye. Through the window of the high dorm, saw a shadow haltingly separate from a row of unintegrated shapes on the bridge and unfurl what looked like fleshy wings before drawing them once again into itself and settling hunched in the cold blue light. When I opened my eye, it was gone.

The medication I'd stolen from the bathroom made my head fuzzy. In my footlocker I kept some of Narn's *A. sarmentosa* tea for pain, but I couldn't recall the sorcery required to activate it. The words were written down somewhere—Kai had seen to that—but ink in the hands of the dead tends to ravage the paper it's written on.

The Regulars called us survivors—although none of us saw ourselves that way: we called ourselves Mades. The Father made us by inserting a soluble microscopic implant laced with his Forever Code into a human female zygote in vitro, birthed from a surrogate we would never know. I was raised along with thousands of others in the Blood Temple, which flourished in remote Southern Rim camps for just shy of three decades, although the first years were much less productive than was hoped. According to our Father, Mades, by virtue of our... virtue, would be the bridge to lead man back into the Paradise from which he'd been so unjustly expelled. It made perfect sense at the time. We understood the Father. He made us feel his pain as if it was our own.

It *was* our own.

My roommates went out, leaving me alone with nothing except a reminder of my own amputated singularity. Lara *was* right. I needed to get out of here and the sooner the better. I crawled from the bed to Trudy's bunk and helped myself to two pills from one of her many bright jars purchased from the pharmacy. If they knew I was stealing their meds, they didn't say. They brought me things sometimes—cough drops and once, some soup. My throat was on fire, and my nose so congested that I'd dreamed last night of drowning, of hanging, of a hand across my face.

I heard a snuffling under the bed, that cheap-carpet drag, and slowly lifted the sheet, my breath coming quick. I was maybe expecting the spotlit eyes of a lost flying fox, like once back in the Blood Temple—dragging itself by its broken wings, it had looked more insect than mammal—but there was nothing. Each night since arriving in Upper Slant, I'd had the same dream, or different versions of it. Kai and me playing on the lichen-striped outcrop even though I am already too old for games and Kai is already dead. She taunts me through lips black with rot, teeth hanging by ropy gums in her still beautiful face. In my dream the shadow when it first appears is both distant and too close, a shadow without a shadow, erect as a monument, the ravens circling overhead with their iridescent wings and their sad-baby cries, Kai rank and rotting beneath a sky too high and never high enough. "He'll always find us," she gurgles. "We'll never be free."

In my dreams it was Kai the guilty survivor instead of me.

CHAPTER 2
HORNS

"Native hair," they call me at the Blood Temple, and occasionally "pube-head." Sometimes a Made punches me in the stomach to watch me gasp for breath or throw up. The Assistants summon me to the laboratory and make me take off my clothes, walk around me scratching their chins. No one sees me lurk weeping at the edge of the playground where a little girl waits behind the bins, a girl I never see in the bunkroom or in class. She is lank-haired and red-eyed. I watch her lick her lips like I am what she's waiting for. She has a snake around her neck and another around her waist and holds a bunch of them in her hands like a bouquet (or a cat-o'-nine-tails) and she smiles as one by one, she bites their heads off—blood running down her chin. Chew, swallow, repeat.

She speaks to me, this headless snake girl, and I am lonely enough to listen. Of course it's not a hiss. That would be something that someone with no imagination would come up with. By now I am tortured by the guilty secret that my brain does not work within the same constraints as the other Mades. *I* have imagination to spare. The headless snake girl smiles a pointed-toothed smile at me and she says in a baby-raven voice,

"Truth or dead."

"You mean, truth or dare?" I say.

"Suit yourself." When she shrugs, the snakes sway around her head like headless, sexless dancers.

"Are you Tiff?"

At that she howls in furious mirth, and her red eyes narrow to slits and she puts a finger across her lips and it is the wrong size for her, this finger, swollen and pale and stiff, and she holds it across her lips long enough for me to pee my pants, and then she is gone.

I look around to make sure no one sees the pee running down my legs, and across the playground, Kai is staring back. Narn has not yet told us that we are real sisters. And that it is she, as much as the Father, who made us.

The Father and his business partner in Silicon Alley once shared two huge chunks of South Rim, enough Paradise in any man's language. There are many barracks in the Blood Temple, spread across land the Father owns in the Rim, depending on if they are for Littles, Middles, Bigs, or Males. The Rogues Bay property where I am made, is the biggest. It is thousands of acres in a shallow plain ringed by a mountainous ridge to the south and to the north, the black straits of the bay. There is a weapons testing facility somewhere to the west. Paddocks stretch all around littered with drought-starved sheep carcasses and rabbit droppings, and where feral dogs howl and yap and will drag a stray Made off and eat her alive. The Father's ravens are there to protect us, to ensure we don't stray. There are caves nearby painted with long-legged people the color of pus and short-legged animals the color of blood, the floors littered with petrified thylacine bones. Except for scheduled school excursions, the caves are out of bounds. The ravens keep it that way. Beyond the caves is a field where slate stones lie scattered among the kangaroo grass and sheep droppings. We have heard that surrogates are buried there when the Father's incinerators fail. Even the Blood Temple has its myths.

There is a town too, and a school, and there is a community of First People on the other side of the wide lagoon—they are elongated shimmers along the shore. The noise from their pub carries across the water, the crack of footballs and the smell of their cooking fires. Their songs populate my dreams and I wake up with them on the tip of my tongue. But the Father owns it all now after his business partner was found murdered , and the First People keep well away.

On dreaded assembly mornings, the Father's Blundstone boots echo down the hallway. Silence follows in the wake of his footsteps. The silence, like the noise of his passing, is multiple—he has many Assistants. Most of them are scientists. He also has a robotic surgeon who implants the source code into our brains in vitro, but we have never seen it. All we know is that it came from the weapons testing facility outside of the property. In return for the robot, the Father sometimes lets the officers from the facility take *his* Mades for what he calls a "test run."

Silence is not the only thing that marches in the wake of the Father. Mades follow in neat, silent lines toward the asphalt play area. The ravens croak at our approach, flap their rose-tinged wings, so we know they are watching. Mades from all the other Middles Bunks assemble too. The school was abandoned years before the Father found it—Matron says that the townspeople fled after contamination from the weapons testing facility. Itinerants and meth-cookers and possums and families of brown snakes took over, until finally something even more lethal came along.

The Father.

The Littles are on another part of the property. The high school and the Bigs and the Malemades, are somewhere else entirely.

Matron stands to one side of the Father before the whitewashed brick wall, and on the other side, the head Assistant rocks on his heels. Matron lifts up a jar in which floats a shriveled pink thing with two long curly ears. She announces importantly that it's a lady-bit.

"You all have them," the Father says, making a triangle with his hands near his crotch. He wears jeans and a battered Akubra over long braids. We know that he is very rich. Remnants of a silky Upper Slant accent cling to his tongue.

Kai stands too close to me. I don't yet know that we are twins, for all that I feel a connection to her that shames me—I salivate in her presence, think I might faint. I am obsessed. I feel her flinch when the Matron holds the glass jar up high. Unlike me, Kai is beautiful with long black hair that ripples like the heat aura of a bush fire. Tall and fierce, she is no more my champion than she is any of the other ugly runts, but I take it nonetheless. Even better though, is when she ignores me to the point of marking me out for a special kind of indifference—I feel that she has already given me my life simply by being someone to love more than myself.

"What if Matron," we both whisper at the same time, "drops the jar?"

She turns to me with a joker grin. Her mouth is too big and her teeth are too small.

My heart is in my mouth. Matron jiggles the jar with the lady-bit floating in it. It bumps against the glass like a fish in a tank. Like it wants to get out.

"That there womb," the Father is saying in his funny accent, his *r*'s gone all squishy, "is a bad 'un. Cut it from a faulty Made after her unmaking. *All* the bad cooches"—the Father uses that word to describe us, and other words beginning with *c*—"are removed for scientific study."

We know this. Unmaking is either chemical or surgical—what the Father calls the "Final Cut."

"Science never sleeps," the Father continues, taking the jar from Matron and letting it fake-slip. We gasp and the Father laughs at his own joke, just like a real dad.

"Had you there," he says.

No one answers and we begin to fidget. We want to hear more about the lady-bits. The Assistant rocks impatiently on his heels and clears his throat. The Father raps the glass with a long manly finger. Tappa-tap-tap. The pink thing in the murky liquid jumps and its ears wiggle sluggishly. "What does this here bad lady-bit look like to you, Mades?"

"An elephant!" yells out a Made. "A rabbit!" says another. "With wormy ears!" We are all warming to the task.

"A raven," Kai abruptly brays. "With its feathers plucked."

I am mortified. Not for her too-loud cracked voice but for my own gutless silence. Of course, I also saw a plucked blackbird (baked in a pie), but was too scared to say it, to even think it. If I live to be a hundred, I will never be half the Made she is. That only makes me love her twice as much.

Up until recently, Kai has been the Father's pet. Kai is a boardgame queen. Five-card draw, Scrabble, backgammon, Word Whomp, checkers—and the Father loves nothing better than to summon her to his rooftop quarters after she returns from picking up his pharmaceuticals from the witch. They play for stakes mostly. Smartees sometimes. Sugar packets maybe, or teabags, both of which Matron must confiscate later because Mades are not allowed caffeine. And the sugar packets attract ants.

"I opened with a two and a one, split my back runners—risked the blot but I had a total of twenty-eight ways to cover it and make the five point," she'd bragged one evening, her mouth smeared with chocolate. "So I did. The Father didn't know what hit him."

Maybe not at first. And by the time he does, it is too late.

And now after Kai's outburst, the assembly has gone uncomfortably silent. Mades have no self-control—that is the reason for the Forever Code, but it works better in some of us than in others and is in occasional need of adjustment. Matron jots a note in her book, not a good sign. We lower our eyes to the ground and our shoulders slump. We get anxious when one of us is in trouble, especially someone as beloved as Kai.

"Think before you speak, Made." The Father holds the jar in one hand and points to the thing inside it. "Those twisted appendages are not wings, but clearly, horns. Like on a goat. Matron, why don't you tell us what they are?"

"Fallopian tubes, Father."

We shift on the asphalt. The cicadas have gone silent.

The Assistant beams at us. "Why do they look like goat horns, Mades?"

Maybe because no one answers, or maybe because she can't help herself, Matron primps and says, "Because the goat is Satan's Beast, of course."

"Satan's Beast," we intone with relief. Our memories tell us it's a phrase we know, but our memories have more holes in them than Cook's breakfast damper.

"Bingo," the Father says. "The mark of the beast, horns and all, inside each and every one of you. Until I came along and saved you. Thanks to me, this is what you have now." He turns to the Assistant, who holds up the other jar. The liquid is less cloudy, less the color of piss, and the lady-bit inside it has no horns or wings, but instead what looks like small amputated little ears at the side of the heart-shaped "head." If the bad lady-bit looks kind of like a goat, the good one looks a lot like a man.

"Women are an accident of nature," our founder continues, "and therefore, unnatural as hell. If men are made in the image of God, women are what ended up on the cutting-room floor. Scrap, waste for the devil's dustbin—" The Father falters for a moment, but the Assistant beams encouragingly at the Father's overreaching metaphor.

"—from which he pulled you out, being the scavenger beast that he is," he continues in his slippery-slidey accent. "Took a big old bite out of you and tossed you back on the junk heap of history. Where you've stayed. And stunk. And foulness has bred inside you and out."

Kai and I avoid each other eyes.

"For centuries men were confounded by the impossibility of removing the mark of the beast from women," the Father says, "The mark that kept us men, by association with it, out of Paradise."

Mades have short lifespans. The oldest are not yet two decades old and Matron says even with improved protocols, our generation'll be lucky to make it to fifty.

I think even then I knew Kai would be taken from me.

A murder of ravens bursts from the tin roof, bleating out their sad-baby cries. I am hungry for breakfast, but I am always hungry. I think of Tiff munching on her snakes and my mouth waters.

Finally the Assistant steps in. "Through our, um, combined efforts—known as ART—which stands for?"

"Augmented Reproductive Technology," we answer as one.

"You have been remade according to another kind of image," he says.

"Without those pesky fallopian tubes, you have at least a passing chance of a new Paradise right here in Rogues Bay, through which you may re-enter at the Father's will. It's a tricky thing known as restriction protocol that none of you will ever understand, but basically it means no more horns as it were. You're free at last."

"Free my ass," mutters Kai, and I feel a cold finger at the base of my spine

But the Father isn't finished. "No longer do you carry the mark of the Beast. No longer can he draw you into sin in his name. Amen to ART," the Father says.

"Amen," we intone.

The Father's genius with ART is the reason we are here.

The blind pink womb bobs around like a puppet. The Father aims a playful finger-gun at the assembled Mades and says: "Bottom line, thanks to my carefully assembled experts"—he nods curtly to the Assistant—"and at significant expense, you are now remade at the level of blood and circuitry to be sterile."

The Assistant fake-claps his pale grabby hands.

"One day, of course, that will change, and you'll be able to reproduce, to couple, such as it is, with my source code—"

"Until which, it is safe behind a firewall so thick not even the Devil himself can butt his way through." The Assistant laughs and smooths his mustache and Matron smiles uneasily at the nerve of the interruption.

"Meantime," the Father says. "Not a cooch among you that can bleed, breed or carry a human seed."

Bleed, breed, seed.

By now all up and down the line, Mades have their hands to their bellies, praying that their bits look like a deaf god rather than a horny beast.

The assembly is almost over. My stomach is growling with hunger. The Father spreads his arms out wide, palms up, as if taking ownership of the sky itself. "The Devil lurks beneath the bridge, Mades. Under the arches he waits—not for the saved but for the fallen, those who linger in the crossing. These he will undress with his eyes from which there is no possibility of self-defense—mark me—and his diseased nostrils will quiver at the smell of their unhealed wound and his clawed hand will snatch at them and they will not weep like you, or fear him as you do. They will laugh, and spread their legs to the Darkness, and beg for its seed, only to be torn asunder by their own monstrous hungry issue. I saved you from this. Without me you are lost. Fear not, because I will always be with you."

And also with you.

This is what passes for sex ed. in the Blood Temple.

* * *

The windows of the Tower were double glazed, the sensory deprivation of the dormitory interrupted only by elevator tings, the occasional shuffle of feet past the door. The minutes ticked by. I found myself missing Rogues Bay, just a little. Especially Middles Bunk where the call of the bats, the yap of feral dogs looking for ghost sheep and the smell of the night guard's cigarettes leaked through the high, rattling windows and into our dreams. Here the only smell was my roommate Trudy's lotion, and music leaking from Lara's earbuds where she'd left her phone behind, the only sound. They were survivors too—raised in the Blood Temple—yet it was as if they were doing everything they could to forget, when all I wanted was to try to remember.

Because I hated the Father and I loved him. I couldn't help it. He made me love him. Even after what he did to Kai. He impregnated all of us with love, with submission. He wiped our memories. His were enough, he said. His code cured us of imagination, a monstrous appendage and prone to corruption. Reality was enough, he said.

"I have healed your wound, Mades," the Father had said. "You're welcome."

After my escape to the Starvelings, Narn tried to rebuild my faulty memory as best as she could. She had a pile of tattered Golden Books and told me to read them. All of them. She babbled at me in that discordant pidgin of hers, which I could barely follow, but somehow absorbed after the fact, the taste of her words on my tongue, the feel of them in my heart.

I knew she didn't love me. I knew she did it for Kai.

Slowly, through Narn's spells and charms and silly songs sung in her perfect pitch, clicks and glottal and crimson tears, and also through her libations and bitter teas, oblivion gave way to patchy recall. My memory was never as good as Kai's, and Narn and I fought bitterly over my slow progress. It was only later, much later, that she would begrudgingly acknowledge that Kai's one weakness—an imagination irreparably damaged by the Father's code—was my own monstrous strength.

It was the nicest thing she ever said to me.

The low, opaque sky wrapped around the window like a dirty bandage. The Father made us for a different climate, a different sky. High up in this Tower, worlds away from everything I knew, *Redress* had all the treacherous finality of déjà vu. Redress? At nineteen, and getting sicker by the day, I knew well enough not to trust such a word. I had welcomed the chance to leave the Starvelings, be free of Narn's disappointment in me, but balked at the last minute. Who would collect the rare golden-eye, *telochistes chrysophtlamus*, that had just begun to bloom across Kai's gravestone? Who would get drunk with the thylacine—my leaving would kill him, I protested. And even Narn had seemed to have second thoughts. But we both knew that I had to go. The truth had already begun to eat us alive.

I shivered. September in South Rim was spring, a time of new beginnings, of the first fragrant breezes blowing in from the East, swelling bellies of heifers in the paddocks all the way to Norman. I tried not to imagine how, at every moment, Narn would be moving slowly about the little hut I had left behind, folding up into quarters, eighths and then sixteenths the lying Wellsburg brochure with images of castellated ramparts, firelit rooms and moonlit fountains. I could see her holding for a moment in her weirdly unblemished hands, the crisp white release documents from the South Rim Redress Scheme of 2014 (updated in 2019):

~ *Which fully acknowledges that many young women, and young men, were genetically abused in the cult known as the Blood Temple*
~ *Which unconditionally recognizes the harm caused by this abuse*
~ *Which holds the Blood Temple and other participating institutions accountable for this abuse, including but not limited to participating institutions such as the Upper Slant and Lower Rim military, and various Silicon Alley media consortiums, social media conglomerates and cryptocurrency investors (see below for a full list of participating institutions)*
~ *Which will aid survivors in gaining access to counseling and educational services, a direct personal response and monetary payments*

Would she toss the documents in the fire? Linger over Kai's botanical sketches, an old snapshot of me—a stunted kinky-haired shadow glancing over her shoulder at a space, an absence that filled the frame with its presence? Would she gather up the bundled muddy clothes I wouldn't be needing any more, with all the dread and hope of a beloved guardian on the day her grown ward leaves for college?

The very thought of it brought on a renewed fit of coughing. Because that was in a different time and place. And because I wasn't really Narn's ward and she was a shitty guardian. She wasn't even a real witch any more than her little sister Mag was a tattooed goth or the other sister, Tiff, was a rock chick. These were just disguises to mask their true forms, but once when I asked Kai about what they really looked like she just said, "Pray you never know."

Night came slow in the northern hemisphere autumn, an attenuated bridge of time between half-light and full-dark that I wasn't yet used to. Trudy, Lara and I were on the nineteenth floor. Shelves divided the space into roughly equal thirds. My roommates and I each had a bed, a desk, a narrow closet. Lights winked and refracted across the window from the ancient campus town across the river. The livid glow of the bridge pulsed and faded like the breaths of a giant blue beast, a dinosaur or Golden Book dragon. It seemed foreign, unreal yet familiar—a reminder, or a marker of something hidden in plain sight.

For a long moment I lay in the electric glow, just another particle of light. It was a kind of ecstasy.

Or course Lara was right about the missing elective—but I felt so ill. I'd been plagued by a sensitive throat and bad lungs since adolescence—compromised immunity one of many symptoms of the Father's experimental IVF media. Back in the hut tucked deep into the Starveling Hills on the other side of the world, Narn and I—the blind leading the blind—had poured together over the Wellsburg College Integrated Bachelor's Degree Diploma. It was a bridging program tailored just for Blood Temple survivors, and it focused on our rehabilitation, reintegration and transition back to the real world. No one said, "dehumanization." At least not to us.

So without giving it much thought, I'd chosen Biology, of course, and then just for laughs, Computer Science and Geography. I signed the form and Narn cosigned as my official guardian, then gave it to Mag to run to Norman to make the five o'clock mail. But on arrival in Wellsburg, there had been an email waiting for me saying that Com-Sci was not on offer until second semester and I would need to select something to replace it. The email repeated the stringent conditions of the Redress Scheme—that until we successfully completed our first eighteen months based on a B-plus average, we were only eligible for a limited number of non-core arts electives.

Now, on a program-issued tablet, I searched the electives available this semester and three came up. Spanish, Music and Technology and one by the strange name of Fictional Forms. Spanish was held in the Tower Village campus, where all my other classes were, but the other two were across the bridge, in Wellsburg. Both offered "limited availability" to Redress students. Both were evening classes. I looked through the window. Two weeks—a minute—since the shuttle had sped through the winding cobbled streets of the old university town with its gargoyled windows and bell tower sleeping in scaffold. Two weeks—a lifetime—since my hopes fell as the electric engine whined across the bridge and through the blue arch toward the deathly Tower Village. The program I'd signed up for was called Made for Tomorrow, but the closer we got to safety, the stronger my conviction that safety was a future free from fear for which I, at least, was never made.

I stared at the slouching façades across the river and I saw a story about something that I couldn't remember, a codified itch impossible to scratch.

There were no prerequisites for either class, beyond competence in a musical instrument in the one, and basic literacy in English (not necessarily as a first language) in the other. Doubting my language skills and lacking in any musical ability, I chose Fictional Forms. Mainly because the reviews said that it was an easy three credit points. Focusing on storytelling, and open to a quota of Redress Scheme participants, it encouraged people from diverse and margin-alized backgrounds to "write their own truth."

The line struck me as funny. It reminded me of how Kai, vicious after death, had tried to tell me something. Something that wasn't funny after all.

Truth or dead.

I woozily fumbled the combination to my footlocker and found among the powders and herbs and charms and candle stubs, the packet of starchy *Alectoria sarmentosa* filaments that would clear my head, and had the extra benefit (at least to her) of keeping Narn and me telepathically bound.

"We have our phones," I'd reminded her when I caught her fretfully smug-gling the tea into my luggage.

"Witch-hair shroom works for when words don't." By which she meant that, brewed with the proper incantations, the tea worked on my brain in ways that kept us connected—enough of her in me and me in her to belie the fact that we weren't blood. I muttered what scraps of the hex I could remember—Kai had inscribed it somewhere—as I sprinkled the tea over a mug of microwaved water. Almost as soon as I drank it, I felt a jolt of clarity, my thoughts unmud-died, my vision sharp.

Sipping on the tea, I submitted my application for the elective, feeling awake for the first time since my arrival, a ripple of life in my veins. A memory surfaced and immediately retreated, but not before I caught it by its tail—an argument with Narn about her Tiff and my Kai. A promise made and broken. Remade from memory, but remade wrong.

Because memory lies like the devil.

An automated reply came in from the Office of Writing and Culture. It advised me that applications would remain open until seven o'clock tonight for physical copies, and that there would be an administrator there to process the forms. The Office of Writing and Culture was on the other side of the bridge. On the old campus, the Wellsburg side.

I stared at the email, balking at the thought of leaving the dorm as I had balked at leaving the Starvelings. It was one thing to want, I knew, another thing to get. The effort of the application had already weakened me close to tears. I had not been out of my pajamas for over a week. My hair was bushy. My head too large, my neck too thin. My eyes puffy from crying and fever and bad dreams. The misery of homesickness had reminded all the other miseries to return—even I couldn't fail to remember all that I had lost. Narn had lost a sister too, but at least Tiff was somewhere—Kai wasn't even a ghost anymore. She wasn't anything.

I wanted to hear Narn's voice, and through her, Kai's. But lack of privacy and bad reception in the dorms made it difficult to talk. I decided now to wait until after I'd been successful signed up for the elective so that I'd have something to look forward to when I returned from it. Lara and Trudy would be out until late.

I began precisely, mechanically, to undress. The Father created us to have no more conception of our own nakedness than a dog, or a monkey. How then did we feel shame under the gaze of his Assistants—why did the memory of their touch never wash away? Waves of illumination lapped at the edges of the dormitory room, washed my skin a livid blue.

I splashed water on my face and rummaged for a pair of jeans. The rough denim grated like sandpaper on my feverish skin. Narn had persuaded me to buy a new college wardrobe—jeans and bright, cheap skirts and cropped jackets—from the carer's subsidy she received from the Redress Scheme. It was her way of settling the argument, because by then we both knew it was as much for her as for me.

I had mostly worn hand-me-downs my whole life—shorts and T-shirts from older, bigger Mades in the Blood Temple, and in the Starvelings, cast-offs from Kai. As self-conscious as any teenager ashamed of her shabby appearance, I'd ransacked "Aunty" Tiff's trunk to twirl a soiled G-string in my fingers, wobble in her platform boots—each item shimmered with the missing sister's terrible failure to win the time war. Unable as I also was to move past the grief and guilt of living with the unlivable, I deeply connected with this failure. Tiff was a hot mess. And I was just a mess. I'd buried my fingers in the folds of the vodka-spattered bikinis and the absinthe-stained ruffles and I called to her, and maybe I prayed a little too. Alone and uncoupled, I hoped that it would be me to find her one day, this fallen sister, and that in return, she'd give me back my life.

A sister for a sister, we'd finally agreed. Lost and found.

I smoothed my hair with water, stepped out into the hall and into the elevator. After a swift descent, it lurched to a halt. The doors opened and the lights of the lobby snatched my shadow away. I paused on the threshold and stepped through just in time to avoid the doors closing on me, a stray strand of hair caught and quickly freed. I swung around, taunted by my split reflection. I saw me as *they* would see me in Writing and Culture—two halves of an impossible whole, from my stunted body (I could pass for fourteen) to my mismatched eyes—to everything else the media said about us. Compliance bled into survivors at the neurological level. Human-digital hybrids, mutants for the New World Order. Would fuck for food. Would fuck for anything.

That part of course was true.

CHAPTER 3
TWISTED SISTER

When I finally get the guts to ask Kai, she says Narn is not a witch exactly. Not like the witches that the 1880 Apology was talking about, the priestesses and Gnostics and Fairy Queens addressed in order to:

~ *Honor the ancient rite of witchcraft, the oldest continuing practice in human history.*
~ *Reflect on their past mistreatment, including but not restricted to the centuries-old slandering, shunning, and mistaken association with the demonic or the deranged.*
~ *Reflect in particular on the false trials and institutionalized hangings of innocent women and girls accused of witchcraft, this blemished chapter in our history.*
~ *Turn a new page by righting the wrongs of yesterday and so moving forward with new confidence to tomorrow.*
~ *Apologize for the laws and policies of governments that have inflicted so much suffering, loss and grief on our fellow citizens of the fair sex.*
~ *Apologize especially for the accusations of demonic worship that led to the removal of mothers from their families, daughters from their mothers, and sisters from each other.*
~ *Take this first step based on tolerance, respect and resolve to recognize the peaceful practice of witchcraft, with a stake in shaping the next chapter of the history of humanity.*

Narn is no Fairy Queen, Kai says. But she isn't a witch, either. Kai would know because she has had the special task of calling on the old crone to collect ingredients for the Father's ART. We are in the lavatory in Middles Bunk and Kai is sitting on the toilet. She looks unwell and she smells much worse.

"What is she then?" I ask.

"Maybe some other kind of sorcerer," she stands and pulls up her bloomers.

"She told me that where she was born it was always night, and the air was, like, filled with blood and screams."

I don't know what gives me the courage finally to approach the charismatic, popular Made, the Father's favorite. It is some days after the assembly when she angered him with her heckling, and rumor has it that he has begun the chemical unmaking for her sins.

She stands at the stained mirror. "He said that it will hurt him much more than it will hurt me."

So I know that it is true. I drop my head and study my ugly bare toes, slate blue and scrawny as a hatchling's. Why wasn't it me who blurted out the line about the plucked ravens? What more punishment for my gutlessness than to witness the unmaking of my goddess? The Father favors Kai, and for all the wrong reasons. Her noncompliance is what he loves about her, but he must cure her of it, or accept that there is something lacking in his ART, which he cannot do. Harder for the Father to accept his own failures than to lose the daughter he never had, who always was, he admits, too smart for her own good. Her "exuviates" will beat his "ejaculate" at Scrabble, but it will be her undoing. I can see it in his small eyes when she doesn't know he's looking at her (he never sees me). The way she flings her hair, her swagger, her way with words. He waggles his finger. He tries to fix her. But first, he must break her. In the usual way, with drugs. Pills she must swallow under the supervision of Matron and the eye of the ravens. She pretends to change, but this only convinces him further that she's rotten to the core. A bad apple. He has made us without the capacity for pretense. We are damned either way.

He invites her to his library room for poker and she raises him with a pair of sixes. She's too smart. What has gone wrong? The Father blames her lady-bits—not his poor poker skills—for the easy bluff. Although he's engineered us all without devil horns, there is another factor that he calls "whore-moans" which are a little more difficult to control. Unable to be sure, the best bet is chemical hysterectomy. He increases the pharmaceuticals.

I pray that the chemical cure works, and fast, and that her body will expel her lady-bits and keep the Father happy, without him resorting to surgery. Those who survive the chemical removal have every hope of living a full and productive life, Matron says. Those who don't, were never meant to be.

"What's Narn's hut like?" I ask, to change the subject. "Is there, like, a boiling cauldron and a broom?"

She turns around, pale as chalk. "Nah, but there's a black cat and a dead janitor, the one who shot himself in the head after he got caught perving on the netball team in their dressing room when this dump was still a regular school."

She crosses her arms and legs, and her socks bunch over her scuffed school shoes.

We are twelve. Lately I've been feeling strange. There is something wrong with me. And not just because of the pictures in my head that shouldn't be there, but also because beneath one of my nipples is a hard sore swelling, and I'm ashamed of how I try and get the seam of my shorts to rub between my legs, imagining it is . . . imagining that I am not alone. We are not meant to see with our mind's eye. That eye was gouged out when the Father genetically engineered us from our wombs to our brains. We barely even dream. It is the kind of thing I would have liked to ask Kai, but one of the other girls calls for her and she is gone, leaving me alone with her stink.

Over the next few weeks, things return to normal, almost. Kai's condition improves. I listen everywhere for the tap-tap of her brown shoes. She appears in the playground at exactly the right moment to deter some prowling bully, dumps her share of bread pudding onto my tray. Plays one of her practical jokes—some green dye in the shower, a cicada shell on my pillow. Plants a dry kiss on my cheek. I collect Kai's kisses like abandoned bug shells, a chalice for my love. Even before I know she is mine and I hers, I move in her shadow, and her grace. Her justice, her belief in all that is fair in love feeds her indignation at all that isn't. Even before the realization of our shared DNA, and before the suspicion that our genetic connection is a worm in the Father's apple, I feel it burrowing in my heart. My exaggerated sense of shame feels like the sentence that her overdeveloped sense of injustice tries to finish and vice versa. She is tall while I am short. Her skin is porcelain while mine is sallow. Her neck that of a swan, mine a heron. What's opposite about us feels, at least to me, more like mimicry than mockery.

Why should the Father suspect that what's wrong with Kai is that she's a twin? Even in the unlikelihood of a twofer slipping through the protocol—or Narn's miscarriage potions—the chances of a multiple's survival are almost non-existent. The Assistants see to that.

"No twofers on my watch," the Father says and by his watch, he means the ravens and we know why. Twins are the Father's nightmare. Multiple births are a bitch—the only thing that can uncouple themselves from the Father's code, twist it and recreate it anew. Into what? That is what keeps him awake at night, pacing his rooftop aerie alone except for the ravens.

Even before I know this, I see myself in Kai's speech and in her actions. In her shadow I see my own being flung against the wall. Kai flutters her hands, and I grow wings. I love her, even if I don't know yet why, and she loves me, even if she does.

Because Narn tells Kai first.

She has to. The old witch in the janitor's shed gives, has been giving, Kai potions, spells and charms to fight the Father's drugs. And it works for a while. Until it doesn't.

It all ends with the Assistant. And after what Kai does to him a month after the lady-bit assembly—the Father calls it "The Incident"—he has no choice but to send her to the infirmary. The drugs he gives her there are different. They're stronger. It's the last step before surgery, he says, holding her hand and sitting at the end of her bed. Be a good girl, he says just like a real dad.

When he gets up, he leaves a deep indentation in the coverlet from where he sat.

Kai is hooked up to a bag of liquid pain. She has broken out in sores and her voice is weak, her blue eyes cloudy. She didn't have to summon me—I've been haunting the sick room like a ghost. Waiting for the other adoring, worried Mades to disperse for Kai to finally acknowledge my presence. She beckons me over, my heart swells. When we are finally alone, she tells me what we are: Sisters. Nonidentical twins.

I nod because I know. Was, after all, born knowing. We are a twofer. The old witch told her, she said.

"Why?" I ask. "Why did she tell you now?"

"Because she has to save us," Kai says. "Or else."

She makes a slitting motion across her throat. Twins are cursed, the Father's bane, his nemesis, she says—an eight-letter word she gave him at Word Whomp. Let him think he had her there.

"What's a nemesis?" I say.

"Mortal enemy, you idiot. How are we even twins?"

"I don't know," I say seriously. "How did it happen?"

But Kai just sags back onto the pillows. She reminds me how, before Narn retired to the shed, she was head midwife at the Blood Temple. The in vitro lab was hers. Filled with her plant-based IVF solutions, antibiotics compounded from lichen, and for her mainstream obstetric equipment. Not even the scientist Assistants had access to Narn's lab back then.

"Secrecy is how she did it," Kai says. "And smarts. Abracadabra! But if anyone finds out, we're dead meat."

I don't want to be dead meat.

Kai tells me to rummage under the mattress for the healing powder that Narn gave her on her last visit, a powerful chemical protection against spontaneous hysterectomy.

"But what if the Father cuts you open?"

"You're my twin," Kai smiles darkly. "You're not going to let that happen, are you?"

I shake my head, no. So this is why she has finally told me. She needs me. Me, Meera the runt, who nobody has ever wanted or needed, ever. I blush.

"No matter what?"

My heart is too full to answer, and anyway, it isn't really a question. Instead I watch her try and mix the powder in a glass of water, before I ask, "What's it made from?"

"It's lichen," Kai says. "Its protection will buy us some time."

That is the first time I have heard the word, *lichen*. I have grown up with the Matrons' whispers of Narn's "hocus-pocus" and how her botanicals work better, are safer and with a lower mortality rate on surrogates and babies, than any synthetic potion that the Father's scientists have been able to devise. I like the word so much that it is only later that I remember Kai said, not *me*, but *us*. I am no more an ordinary Made than the unmade twin into whose lips I am spooning some foul-smelling medicine. Because of that I instantly realize that, whether or not Narn is a real witch, the Father's *belief* that she is, has made her indispensable to him. Even more important, it has bought her his protection.

That word.

Protection is how she leverages privileges like her own shed away from the prying eyes of the Assistants. The Father's protection is how she gets away with not being buried out in the paddock with the other failed surrogates.

It occurs to me with a shock: the Father is scared of Narn.

The words come pouring out of Kai in a hurry. She says that Narn came to the Blood Temple not looking for Paradise but for her lost sister.

"She disappeared around here," she says.

"Where?"

"Rogues Bay. Narn disguised herself as a witch and worked her way into the Father's good books to buy time to figure out what happened."

"Has she?"

"At first she thought maybe her sister drowned in the bay. Maybe *an accident* like the Father's business partner. But now Narn says she may be hiding out in Upper Slant. Narn told me Tiff was lonely in the Rim, waah." Kai plays a tiny violin with two trembling fingers. "Never 'found herself' here."

"But if she went to the Slant looking for herself—why didn't Narn follow if they were both looking for the same thing?"

"What a way with words you have," Kai grins feebly. "*Now* I can see the family resemblance."

Narn couldn't leave, she explains. Couldn't abandon her twins to the Father's bad intent, just to look for a trashy sister who probably didn't want to be found anyway. The point is that Narn is stuck here, same as us.

"*Her* twins?"

"She is going to save you," Kai says.

"I'm not the one who's sick."

"That's why," she says.

None of this is sounding right.

"And whatever you do," Kai says, squeezing my arm with all the strength of a kitten, "don't call her a witch."

* * *

I was glad, stepping out onto the Corso now, that I'd swiped Lara's scarf. Would I ever get used to this northern wind? I hacked into the fragrant Lara-smelling folds. Mica glittered along the curved avenue that connected the residential Towers, "learning hubs," administration offices, cafés, bars, a gym and a long low modern library pretentiously called the Bibliotheca. From the windows at the end of the hallway in my dorm building, I could see the large circular park ringed by the Corso. Playing fields, a reservoir hollowed out of waste dumps where ducks now swam and water lilies grew and where we—the survivors—were encouraged to meander for the good of our mental health.

Mades milled in twos and threes, shivering in their mass-produced coats and itchy tights and chattering about Happy Hour at a bar called Dirty Bert's. If any were from Rogues Bay, we didn't recognize each other, partly because of our unreliable memory but mostly because none of us wanted to be remembered from there anyway.

The narrow sulfurous Lott's River bisected the entire campus—the old buildings of Wellsburg on one side, and Tower Village on the other. Spanning the river, and linking old with new, was the revolutionary-era Blue Bridge with its quaint arches and futuristic light shows. But the connection, like so much else about Wellsburg, was deceptive—blue being the color of division, less conjoining than a severing, an uncrossable sea between *them* and *us*. Regular and Made. Real and Artificial.

Tower Village was purpose-built for the Redress Scheme in order to meet requirements for substantial grants and fiscal rewards offered to participating institutions like Wellsburg. Here, on reclaimed swamp and landfill along the old Lott's River fur trade routes, Wellsburg was able to erect an innovative new campus to meet the needs of cult survivors like us. From state-of-the-art amenities to its "Assimilation-in-Place" model of rehabilitation, and its rigorous bridging programs (not only for Mades but for other transfer and foundation students), Tower Village had everything necessary to equip us for the "real" world.

I saw rare Malemades among all the females, blinking in the neon glare. I stayed in the shadows. Maybe it was because I was one of two, a twin, an anomaly in the Blood Temple and now also here, at home at the edges of things. Or maybe it was because here, in the Tower Village, I'd never felt more alone, and never less like counting myself one of them—the fake-it-till-you-make-it Mades with their hoarse laughter and sideways mincing walks. More like show ponies than real women.

Either way I was grateful not to blend in. Skinny and plain and inches shorter than anyone else, I moved against the tide of elbows and swinging satchels all intent on a different direction. The bridge loomed above the river and disappeared into emptiness, but I was at home with emptiness. I hurried toward it, jostling students veering back to the Towers around the guardhouse, or streaming through the archway, anyway they could to get back to where they belonged. But not me. I pushed against what I was told to *be*, pulled toward Wellsburg and to the smell of the river—to where I *wasn't*—toward the hunched outlines of the old town, which transformed at my approach with an instantaneous parting of the moon-obscuring clouds, into a jagged smile with yellow teeth.

All we Mades had to do in return for tomorrow was sell off a part of today. That part of ourselves that we should never have had anyway. The unnatural part. The artificial layer of our makeup that made us repulsive—especially to ourselves.

That made us Mades.

The Made for Tomorrow scheme would make us better, assuredly. But I didn't want to be better. Unlike the scented-candle sterility of the Tower Village, the broken outlines of the old town promised a kind of breakage that I felt in myself. My heartbeat drummed with all the possibilities that I thought had died along with my sister: what *if*, what *if*, what *if*? As I stepped under the cobalt-streaked shadow of the western arch, my feet in Kai's shoes tapped across the ancient boards, and it was almost as though she was with me. For the first time since I could remember, Narn's magic and Mag's lies and all those bird-shit-and-bad-hair days fell away like a ribbon caught in the breeze, a brief flutter of hesitation before being sucked out of sight.

What I really wanted was a drink.

Dark silhouettes of passing students parted to let me pass. I expanded into the role of ugly duckling—Narn's favorite Golden Book. I fluffed my bushy hair up and reveled in the way Kai's shoes pinched my toes. Blue-lit miasma curled up over the edges of the bridge. Someone murmured something about the curfew. A lighter flared. Cigarette smoke plumed and burned my nostrils. Blocking my path, as if out of nowhere, was a student who wore a loose gray beanie and tinted specs.

It was a Malemade.

"Ten o'clock sharp!" he said, drawing an imaginary knife across his throat.

Narn's trippy tea was still in my system so for a moment I imagined that his thumbnail slicing horizontally across his neck was an actual blade—vapor, veined red in the sunset plumed in the wake of the gesture. But I realized, after a cough, that he was talking about the curfew. He took a drag on his cig and I felt the blistered ash flare inside me like an open sore. I muttered something about being late to sign up for an elective, hid behind Lara's scarf and ducked out of his way.

"Thursday is half-price Martinis at Dirty Bert's," he called after me. "We'll be expecting you."

And then I was walking away from him and as fast as I could. Away from the landscaped safety of the Tower Village riverbank and toward the eldritch chaos of something that beckoned to me with all the promise of truth.

My truth.

The scent of Lara's scarf, a remembered fragrance, made me think of Kai. The bundle of star jasmine and lemon myrtle under her pillow barely masking the old-bone reek coming from her pores.

"Narn is one of three," she'd said. "Not a twofer like us."

"There's another sister besides the lost one?"

I'd felt her pointy chin dig into my scalp so I knew she was nodding.

"What are their names? The sisters."

"Not allowed to say them. Anyway, they have different names now."

That was when she told me that one sister still lived with Narn in the shearers' shed.

"And if you think Narn is weird," Kai'd said, "wait till you get a load of this one."

The recall came out of nowhere and took my breath away for a moment, but I welcomed it. Kai's scent caught in the back of her throat, her voice back in my head. It had been too long.

"You know what they say," she'd added. "Third time's the charm."

Inscrutable conifers and age-spotted birch crept up the riverbank, over which the jagged façade of Wellsburg perched like a fairy-tale crown from the stories Narn hoped would override the Father's code. As if in stony defiance of the eroded river and the season-ravaged banks, the tiny college town held its ground with all the stern permanence of a love-addled knight, braced to protect a damsel within—long dead and lost to time—a sad, forgotten place.

But it remembered me.

That was the main thing: that it remembered. Stepping off the arterial no man's land of the bridge, the feeling I had entering Wellsburg was that I'd walked here before, was still walking here, had never left. I felt my arrival less as a return—it wasn't that—than as a continuum. Darkness gathered. The worn soles of Kai's hand-me-down shoes slid on the wet cobbles beneath the mist, and not being able to see my ugly feet, I could convince myself that I couldn't feel them either, and was gliding through the streets, inhaled like a homecoming queen into the very heart of the place.

The toothy angles of stone turrets and prickly spires had grown soft in the dying light. The bell tower wrapped in a skeletal scaffolding soared above the slate roofs while hawks swirled around the attic windows open to the last scraps of summer dusk. Cut off by the river on one side and by a high ridge behind it—the coastal city of New Dip a day's drive to the south—the town floated above the mist, a timeless place, and all the more authentic and more emphatically *present* than anything in the Tower Village. Belonging neither to the river nor the woods, it hinged between them, self-made and autonomous—neither living nor dead, modern scrambled with ancient and the whole conjured, it seemed, from a fever dream.

The three sisters conjured themselves out of godjizz. That came back to me now—it was one of Kai's stories she'd bring back from the old crone to entertain the Mades in Middles Bunk. Someone had piped up that they didn't know that gods had jizz, and Kai'd said, all men have it, and gods are no different. It's what Narn and her sisters did with it that made everyone so mad. It was how they used the god's waste—blood from his castrated man-thing—to create themselves anew as goddesses.

I remembered wanting and not wanting to hear any more. I remembered wondering if she was making it all up, and how I'd die for her. It was as if stepping into the self-conjured world of Wellsburg, I could . . . suddenly remember.

A pair of students walked ahead of me—Regulars, I could tell, not only because their voices weren't cracked but also because of the natural way they moved, not the needle-skidding-across-vinyl drift of the Mades. My augmented hearing picked up that they were heading to a pub called Sweeney's Landing and it was with a sense of relief and longing that I watched them veer north as I continued south toward the campus. I felt ungainly in my synthetic sweater and badly fitting jeans, my untamable frizz attributable to a double-yolker harvested from an anonymous womb and fertilized by ungodly seed (so many *uns*) and laced with corrupted code. I tried to tidy up using the beveled window of a milliner's shop as a mirror, something gaunt and savage in my mismatched eyes easily attributed to my chest infection, even though I knew better.

The streets of the campus itself, when I turned into them, were more brightly lit than the town. In the distance I heard the murmur of water and discordant halting music of a band practicing in the Music and Technology building. I moved stealthily along the sidewalk from tree to tree. This was a street of narrow, balconied buildings, centuries-old dorms, and administration offices, maybe. I saw a sign saying, *Classics.* I smelled burned meat—a group of students were barbecuing at the front of a building, strains of violin practice wafting from an upper level.

I concentrated on walking smoothly, on being seen for what I could be and not for what I was. Willing myself to keep going, to lean into whatever had to happen next. Because whatever it was, I needed it more than it needed me, and I told myself over and over again that it was the right choice. That the further I got from Tower Village, from the so-called safety of my shared room—where connectivity was a trap and total conformity was a real and present danger—the better.

And I remembered more. Out of nowhere, a word from Kai's notebook: *abe[cedar]ian*. Kai had placed "cedar" in square brackets, and scribbled "nested word" above it in pencil. It was a tattered exercise book with a red and black cover that she'd stolen from the classroom and jotted in every week in preparation for her Wednesday evenings with the Father. Obscure words—palindromes or anagrams—a chess move she'd read about, a backgammon strategy she planned to try, columns from which she memorized dice or card combinations. Looking back, the Father must have known about this mnemonic aid—there was no place to hide from Matron—and maybe it helped him feel better about her unmaking. Maybe he told himself that she wasn't so smart. Not enough to live, anyway.

Abecedarian, I remembered, was a word for someone who is just starting out. A newcomer or novice.

I picked up my pace, turning through the main gate at the end of the street and across a lawn through an arched passageway and into the Quad. This was an area the size of two or three of the Father's paddocks, surrounded by dorm rooms, a student cafeteria, a bar, a coffee shop, classrooms—all in age-defying granite. Unlike the paddocks, the grass here was lush and green, dappled shadows from the gaslight lamps playing across its surface. At the center a fountain played. At both the eastern and western ends of the Quad towered a giant maple. Students—Regulars—stretched out on the grass on blankets, or mingled around the fountain. A girl strummed a guitar with slender fingers that looked carved from marzipan. I hid my own bitten fingernails, still swollen from gathering wood and skinning rabbits back in the Starvelings. My sinuses knifed. My hair threw a monstrous shadow like a grotesque elongated crown. I could taste the fresh ground coffee at the back of my throat and feel the perfumed air on my skin—want *made* me real even if my shadow mocked me.

I was tempted to join the line at the coffee cart and order hot chocolate maybe, drizzled with hazelnut syrup and served with a slice of orange cake—I watched the staff slice it into dripping triangular chunks. As if my scholarship stipend would extend to such luxuries! One slice of that cake, frosted in candied peel and almond praline and sprinkled, according to the chalkboard menu, with edible flowers—would probably cost as much as two drinks at Dirty Bert's! A cup of coffee was half the price over in Tower Village, and donuts were a Made's sugar-fix of choice. Besides, there was still the ordeal of handing in my application.

Fictional Forms, whispered that mocking shadow before me. "Kai?" I said, but my shadow fled, leaving me to enter the building alone.

A clock on the stone wall in an empty hallway said six forty-five. Beneath it was a bulletin board bristling with fliers and notices. I smoothed my hair, refused to look at my reflection in the glass panel of an office door that said, *Writing and Culture*. My nose chafed with blowing and my lips blistered from the wind.

The door opened to an altogether different vision. "You must be Meera."

Mades didn't have surnames.

"Pagan Case."

She was pale, slim like a dancer or a Golden Book princess. Her heart-shaped face and high forehead were capped with a glossy dune of hair. She wore a dark green blouse, her pale arms extended like those of a stone saint. Her smile quivered with the careful stillness of nectar in a cupped petal. She sashayed on long legs swathed in high-waisted trousers to her desk and ushered me into the opposite chair with a choreographed diffidence, some sense of being watched, or judged—or even mocked—but not by me. Conscious of not being the audience that she played to, or feared, I looked around the room expecting someone else to be there, but in all the homey clutter of the Writing and Culture Office, there was only us.

She gestured for me to sit. Her eyes were amber, but without amber's warmth—a lens to capture her worldview and preserve it, keep it intact. While she leafed through a pile of folders, my brain looked around, but I fixed my gaze on her.

A potter's wheel stood in one corner. Books everywhere. Framed portraits of famous poets, a gaming station. There was a souvenir print of the Witches' March of 1879, a poster commemorating the Blood Temple riots of 2010—the protest that led to our final freedom.

"Some extreme shit, right?" she said, the fiery images in the poster setting her eyes alight. "Ironic how witches once flocked to the Rim—your part of the world—to escape, quote, *persecution*, only to find themselves hounded to death by those Paradise fiends."

There was a framed poster of the documentary film about the Blood Temple: *Made to Break*. Another flier advertising a guest speaker from the

Board of Studies: "University Quotas and their Discontents." Notices about book readings and sculpture exhibitions, a cork board on which was pinned information about conferences, writers retreats and grants, yellowed and curling with age.

But out of all the bewildering chaos, it was the trashcan against the desk to my right that held my attention. It was filled with scrunched paper on top of which had been tossed a slice of orange cake on a paper plate. There was a single bite taken out of the cake. The plastic fork still stuck in its pale flesh. Edible flower petals lay sprinkled in the garbage. My mouth watered.

What a waste, I could hear Kai say at the same time as Pagan Case opened her mouth to speak—as if my sister were talking through her—and I started. Pagan reddened and began to flip through some sheets of paper. Her fingernails were varnished not quite black and not quite blue. I sniffled into the scarf and didn't know where to look.

"Tell me something, Meera," she said. "Why did you apply for FiFo and not one of the other electives? There are plenty on offer in Tower Village. Day classes, where you'll be among your own kind."

They're not my kind. But that wasn't the right answer. I tried to think of what was, to read the room as Kai could. In the end I went for the truth. "I like it here better."

"In Wellsburg? Hundred percent understandable. Another thing." She paused, as if not quite knowing what to say. "You do understand that it's a night class, right? I mean, don't you survivors do better in the day?"

The put-down made me flinch. Memory made the pain come again. How, back in the Blood Temple, the Assistants powered us down at night, at least where our vision and sensory input were concerned, all the better to lead us blindly into a dream we'd have forgotten by the morning.

But not entirely.

"I understand," I said. "I take medication for focus." Never mind that it was Narn's special libation. The main thing was that it was true.

She held up her hand, smiling. "Who doesn't?"

She made a note on a pad with her pencil. I sat mesmerized by her waxen fingers whose caress I felt at the back of my neck.

"You mention in your application that storytelling is, quote, *in your blood*?"

I blushed. Lara had put on her application that fashion design was "in her blood," so I'd decided to copy her. And it wasn't as far from the truth as it could have been—Kai with all those stories she brought back from Narn's shed, stories that were more than the sum of their parts—Kai was my blood if anyone was.

"What kind?" She passed me a box of tissues.

"Of blood?"

"Of stories, Meera. Were they true stories, or what?"

The plaintive notes of some wind instrument came to us from a distant classroom. My mind played back to Kai on the top bunk surrounded by wide-eyed Mades drinking in her words from which she conjured worlds—forbidden castles and genies and enchanted trees and slavering wolves.

"*Made*-up stories," I said.

What a way with words you have! Now I can see the family resemblance.

It was all coming back now, that rapt gaggle of dusky, coarse-haired girls clustered around Kai with their too-big eyes and crooked noses, their cracked stage whispers and balance so poor, they would randomly drop out of the bunk without warning, like hatchlings from a nest. "Conjure tales," Kai had called them, and the Mades around her had leaned longingly into any "what-if" that didn't kill them, any "once-upon-a-time" that didn't slam a door in their face. I was beginning to remember, but try as I might I could not attach the flickering form of the memory to the substance of the tales themselves. Hard as I tried, I could not conjure their content.

Something like a shutter opened in Pagan's cold eyes, narrowed in on the empty space behind me. I turned, almost expecting to see Kai against the wall with her collapsed socks and one scuffed shoe crossed over the other, so keen did I feel her (unwelcome) presence. Pagan's voice brought me back to reality and I shamefully shivered with relief. "Stories somewhere between oral poetry, folklore and fairy tale," she was saying, more to herself than me. "A veritable *cadavre exquis* and all the more powerful for being that."

Someone giggled on their phone out in the hallway, but she seemed not to have heard. I felt Pagan's voice like the tip of a tongue on a spot somewhere between my nostrils and the base of my skull. She reached over and turned on the desk lamp, her poison-berry fingernails looking good enough to eat.

"You'll have to excuse me. I did a paper on the Blood Temples and Rim history for my sociology course."

"You sound like you know a lot," I said. "More than me." She smiled, and honey dripped.

"Anyway, Meera. Super-cute name by the way. Actually, the quota is full, but we *are* intrigued by *you*."

She waggled a finger at me and I almost cried. No one in nineteen years had ever been intrigued by me, unless you counted an imaginary friend I'd had at the Blood Temple with snakes in her hair.

"You say you're from, let me check . . ." She flipped through some sheets on her desk. "*Starving* Hills?"

And just like that, as if a stricken ship, the slice of orange cake sunk deeper into its sea of trash. Had I heard her wrong? My breath caught in my throat and I tried not to cough. My face grew hot. She flipped the page around and showed me where I had, along with Narn, clearly written my address care of the post office in Norman. But it had been inked over, a blot of indigo, and above it someone had carefully written the forbidden word, butchered yes, and missing two letters, but still, forbidden. I peered at it some more, and a nauseating realization washed over me: I had no memory of blotting out the word "Norman" and replacing it with the other, forbidden one.

Had I? And if not me, who . . . and why?

"Fearsome name," Pagan said. "It caught the eye of my superior immediately. Anyone from a place called Starving Hills *has* to have some stories to tell," she said. "Which as it turns out, is correct, right?"

I flinched just to hear it on her lips. I stared at the word. Written not in the cheap ballpoint pen that Narn and I had used, but in blue-black ink in clear but ornate handwriting.

Starving Hills.

Missing letters or not, Narn would never have allowed it. We were not to speak the name, nor to write it. It existed on no map that I knew of. I registered the mistake—*Starving* instead of *Starveling*—and as I did, the walls inched closer.

Pagan steepled her fingers together. "I'll take that as a yes. Mades can't lie, can they?"

What the Father did to us at the genetic level—hobbling our memory, lesions in the hippocampus, whatever—was so well known that I may as well have been carrying a sign, "Made to Break."

"No," I said. "But—"

I tried to stand. To leave. My feet couldn't get enough purchase on the floor to push myself off the chair.

"Can they?" Her brow wrinkled and doubt, even fear, flickered across her amber eyes. "I mean you didn't make it up, did you? Starving Hills?"

Please stop saying it.

"I don't remember," I said in a small voice. The walls inched closer—blank now of posters and decoration—Pagan's desk floating away from me on a sea of spilled ink. She leaned back in her chair and exhaled softly. There was a sheen of sweat at her temples, the first human flaw I'd noticed since being here.

"Hundred percent. The source code thing. I get that at the genetic level, and at the endocrinological one, your kind is made without the capacity for higher-level cognitive function," she extended a hand across the desk, but stopped short of taking mine. "Never mind. FiFo is a safe space for your truth. I think you're going to love it."

"Can I think about it first?" I said. "I didn't realize you'd be wanting, you know, stories from my life. The whole memory thing—it's painful."

She looked taken aback. Withdrew the extended hand to check her watch. "While I totally understand, Meera, it's a bit late for that, I'm afraid. Failure to comply with the credit point requirements for the Redress Award typically results in immediate dismissal."

The story of my life.

"I know it's a lot," she said, "after everything you've been through. But honestly, what's there to think about? We're like a family in FiFo. Sasha is going to love you. Hundred percent. Look at those little ringlets of yours—must have taken ages to style."

The concave walls curled around me like a fist, or a womb, geometry of enclosure. And at that moment I did feel like a bird in the hand of fate. Except I didn't believe in fate—Narn raised me not to. If only I could remember how I got in its false grip, I could remember a way to get out. I held the edge of the desk with my too-small hands. I felt my belly cramp, a drip from my nose. Pagan looked at me with barely disguised revulsion. And that was when I could have stood up. Should have. The chance I had to walk, to fly far away. To find a crack in the fist of destiny and burst out, broken but free of both the bad sister who couldn't be found and good sister who I couldn't escape. Was it the panic that immobilized me—over who (if not me) scrawled out "Norman" and wrote "Starving" (not "Starveling") in that bleeding ink? Or was it the promise in Pagan's rough-smooth skin, her lips slightly parted and her quickening breath?

I touched my hand to my hair. "Thanks," I said. "But I was born this way."

Narn always warned that choices make us, and they are not always our own. I knuckled the drip off my nose. The floor heaved and burped me up against the desk, the edge digging into my ribs.

Pagan said, "So, you'll give FiFo a try?"

"I just have one—"

"Wait. You're worried about those pesky trigger warnings?" She sat back against her chair with a satisfied nod. "Sasha thought you might be."

I opened my mouth. She put up a hand.

"Sasha Younger—she's the course co-coordinator. I know the Redress info pack makes a big thing about triggers—it's all this sensitivity hoo-hah. The college has to cover its ass. But try not to get too caught up in it."

"I don't know what a trigger warning is," I said, struggling for breath between the chair and the desk.

She lifted her lovely head and laughed outright, that mesmerizing angle of jaw and throat. "Delicious! You are going to be a hit. I just know it."

The chair wobbled on the sea of ink. I caught my breath. Those stories Kai brought back from the witch—they wrapped us all in their protection. They kept us safe. From the Father, from his wants. They opened a door, and we could imagine walking through it. The problem was that I couldn't remember them. How could I? If I enrolled in this ridiculous course, how and where would I get the stories expected of me, and even more important, how could I protect them from appetites that up until now, I had no idea existed?

At that moment, Pagan leaned in conspiratorially and said in a low voice, "You don't really have to remember the exact details, Meera. It's not really your truth we're interested in. And I mean that in the nicest possible way. I like you. I do. Really. Sasha will too."

I nodded. A hundred percent.

"The whole Blood Temple thing? The actual reality? All unvarnished and preachy?" She shook her head, and her floppy quiff trembled. "Nope. Nope. We want you to turn reality into art. Art is sexy. We want you to show us the abyss. We want to imagine it, feel it, without actually having to go there ourselves. Because you're there. And we're not—never will be. We want stories to reassure us on that point, think you can manage that?"

"I don't . . . it's just . . ."

"It's just vantage," Pagan said. "The abyss is sexier from a distance—right? Not too far away though, not so that we can't feel the, quote, *frisson*. Like from a cute bar near the edge, drinking sneaky spritzes and wearing brand new shoes. I'm probably not making much sense . . ."

"No." But I nodded again. "I get it." And the moment that I kind of did, I heard a rustle in the trash can. When I looked down, I saw that the slice of cake was gone. The paper plate was still there, some crumbs and a smear of frosting. But no cake.

"Are your eyes actually different colors?" Pagan asked. "Were you born that way too?"

"Not exactly, but . . ." I began.

"The truth is boring, remember?" She pressed her lips together and then that smile was back—not exactly mocking, not quite sincere—like it didn't quite know what it was. "You'll be fine."

The walls finally receded and I could see islands of exotic carpet through all the spilled ink. There was a keyboard in one corner and a mixing deck. Framed art prints. Three dimpled, curvy women dancing naked in a circle beneath a flowering bough. It was just a picture, but the women, with their imperfections, their flab and mismatched nipples and pink toes, looked more alive than the real girl sitting in front of me. The one in the middle of the picture had her back to the viewer, her arms extended to embrace the other two.

"Rubens," the girl said, "*The Three Graces*. They're all sisters. The one in the middle is Aglaia who represents brightness, the one on the right is Euphrosyne who is joyfulness and the one on the left is Thalia, whose name means bloom. Related indirectly but not to be confused with the Furies who were three very, quote, *different* sisters."

I found myself standing up on steady feet, wiped my hand and extended it to her.

She stood and took my sweaty fingers in her cool dry ones, then withdrew them as quickly as she could.

CHAPTER 4
A GOOD BEGINNING IS HARD TO FIND

I emerged into the Quad, emptied now and silent except for the murmur of the fountain. Indistinct clouds hid the moon, and the maple trees agitated in the cold wind coming off the river. My sweat-drenched clothes felt sticky against my skin, and my back ached from hunching over Pagan's desk. I loosened the scarf from around my neck. My chest rattled with every breath.

It felt like I'd been in the Writing and Culture office for hours, but it was just eight o'clock. The arachnid eyes of the Towers across the river pulsed their twenty-four seven glare, yet over here in the old college town, darkness fell early. Stars pocked the horizon like moth holes. I was shaken from the interview—especially by that change on my application form that I had no memory of. Partly because of that and partly because of my terrible sense of direction (in this I was like every other Made), in moments I was lost.

The campus gave way to unfamiliar Wellsburg streets. Neat professorial homes and walnut trees. Streetlamps were few and far between and curtained windows glowed a warning yellow. Go back, they seemed to say. Nothing to see here. But I knew with a quickening of recognition that this was a lie. False was attracted to false and this impression of end-of-day was no more than a trick of the light. A ruse to repel the interlopers as Wellsburg waited to return to its true form. I didn't know what that was yet, but I heard it calling to me, rumbling beneath the cobbles from my feet right up to my mismatched eyes. Lurking in these stone-still streets was everything I needed to find. Everything I needed to be.

Everything I needed to remember.

That inkblot on the Redress Form flashed on my retina. Kai's brown shoes struggled to gain purchase on the unfamiliar sidewalks. Back in the Rim, the seasons eased gently one into the other, but here, the chill of autumn was definitive and had a ragged finality to it, like someone had broken a piece off the end of the year and frozen it in time. A road sign pointed to Founders First Presbyterian Church and Cemetery. Because the sign indicated the edge of town, away from where I wanted to go, I turned back into a lane where I saw lights burning. I hoped I was heading in the right direction finally, and my mind raced back to the interview. Why had I pretended that I would be able to conjure the kind of story that they wanted—impossible stories about a truth they'd never have to live—when I had only unreliable scraps? Fragments of Matron, the way her apron smelled of cigs and instant coffee and the smear of her cherry lip gloss on the cup, of the Father's muscle T-shirts, and how his braids flicked around his broad shoulders like the legs of a tarantula? Flying lady-bits and a blind girl with a bouquet of headless snakes . . . the interview with Pagan triggered—that word—memories I didn't know I had, and the more I tried to follow them, the further they took me off the path. I stopped in my tracks under a streetlamp wondering where I was.

No one wanted those truths. Pagan said as much. But what else did I have? How could I render my reality as their fantasy? How could I empower them with my powerlessness? And why did I want to?

Because . . . *Starv ing Hills.*

Because . . . I needed to remember.

In the beginning, when she first came back from the dead, Kai and I would curl up in my narrow bed and she'd tell me a story, one that she'd reassembled from Narn's weird tongue. "How did you know what the words mean?" I'd asked. She told me it didn't matter. The words knew themselves. "They come out all right in the end," she said. "It's the beginnings that are hard. Starting something from not nothing, but from something you can't see. Or something you can feel but no one else can. It pushes against you. It wants to come out. Beginnings hurt."

Lamp light fell across a stone bench. I felt something in my shoe and sat down to remove it. Racking my brain, I hoped to remember one of those self-told stories, but nothing, not a shred of any of them returned to me. Except these pictures in my head, useless crumbs of the past that led nowhere. Where did they, or I, end and another begin? The shadows cast stains across my bare foot, thick pools of memory between my misshapen toes (Kai always had such pretty feet). I wriggled them and the heavy shadows danced.

Suddenly it came to me: "*The sole confessor of my tale of dread has passed. No one knows that once . . .*" I froze on the bench with one shoe in my hand. *That* was how Kai always began her stories, like a joke. Except it wasn't. It was to cover up the hurt—the words were a bridge for the broken beginning to crawl onto.

The stains of liquid light between my toes were still there. I pulled my sock over them and they were gone. I laced up the shoe, rose and began to weave my way down the narrow street. But behind the gossamer veil of cobbles and ironwork balconies, all I could see was Kai holding court on her bunk. Small hands of many colors clapped over groggy giggles, the eyes of the other Mades— brown, blue, round, oval—wide with suspended disbelief, wider with love. A love that even the Father couldn't unmake because Narn's twice-told stories promised no less than a chance of survival itself. Such was the power (chemical or alchemical) of those tales—and the teller. The stories made them multiple, conjoined their brains in a way the Father couldn't fathom. Kai gave the Mades a reason to live. No wonder they would die for her.

"No one knows that once . . ." I said out loud, the words echoing down the empty street.

How did she say that with a straight face?

"The soul confessor of my tale of dread . . ."

Kai had no imagination—she couldn't have made those words up. She must have stolen them from a book—I couldn't remember which one—as a bridge maybe between Narn's gibber and the hungry ears of her listeners. And then it came to me. Kai may be gone, but Narn wasn't. And I had found a bridge of my own.

Kai had said that Narn told her about finding space to move in power's blind spot. And power always had one. Maybe Pagan was right. It wasn't the *what* of Kai's twice-told tales that gave us our safe space. It was the *how,* how they had the power to stop time. How they gave both teller and listener a place to imagine another one. It was the stories that had our back, not the teller. The stories lived separately, grew and changed over time—so that *we* could.

I would ask Narn for a story for FiFo. Taking a leaf out of Kai's book (the pun brought up a giggle, like a burp), I'd find a way to make them what they needed to be for the Regulars. Buy my own brand of protection. After all, I thought with a lick of jealousy, if Narn did it for Kai, why not for me?

I thought of the beautiful Pagan, and I hoped, with a different kind of lick, that the stories would buy me my own brand of love, too.

A sudden breeze blew up and rifled the leaves and there was the bridge over the quaint rooftops. I smiled at the ghostly blue glow ahead of me. I wasn't lost anymore. I quickened my pace, almost running. I stumbled in my sister's shoes. The gargoyles turned away and the narrow doorways receded at the gimpy haste of the interloper. In their place I saw an old sheep paddock and at its edge, a shearers' shed that had not seen enough rain.

It should have been me.

* * *

It should be Kai going on the Father's errand to pick up the compounds and pharma from the old crone. But Kai is in the infirmary and insists that I volunteer in her place. A glitter returns to her dead-sea eyes as she becomes more and more agitated by my reluctance. If anyone gets it wrong, she reminds me, he'll be ropable. Everyone knows what the Father is like when he's ropable. My sister is more convincing even at the edge of death than I am alive.

Lying beside her in the infirmary, I am shocked at how weak her grip is on my wrist.

"You owe me," she says. "If it wasn't for me you'd be . . ."

Truth or dead.

Because there are no words for my shame. The shame of what the Assistant wanted from me. The shame of Kai bursting in on it. Her fine face distorted in rage. And then it became something else, beyond embarrassment, beyond memory's reach—only *him* lying on the ground, gore where his man-thing should be and Kai's brown shoes slick with blood. Blood in her hair. Kai grabbing the Assistant's handkerchief from his pocket to wipe it off. Passing it to me with an urgency that robs her of grace. She jerks toward me, pulls me out the door with bloodstained hands. The call of the ravens outside.

Wash your feet.

She saved me and I *do* owe her. It should be me lying in the infirmary instead of her. So when Matron comes marching down the hallway with Father's errand list, looking for a "volunteer," I am front and center. Matron looks down at the barefoot runt, trying to place me. There are so many of us, and we all look the same to her. Doubtfully hands me the scrap of paper and a small white cooler bag emblazoned with a red cross. She begins to give me directions, but I am already gone.

I don't know the way but I force my mind back to the times I watched Kai swinging that medical bag across the dusk-slanted fields toward the witch's shed. Her black hair melting into shadow one moment, an inky flash against the weak sunlight in the next like an on-off switch, ones and zeros. How I'd wait for her to safely return with powdered lichen compounded into antibiotic solutions for the embryos, tree-fern bundles for luck, henna for the Father's hair (his pride), poppy seed pods for kicks, a myrtle cake for the midnight feast—and a story. *No one knows that once . . .* Demon lovers and lonely highways and gingerbread houses. Dragons and damsels and ragged mountains. Stories with the twin powers to conjure and protect.

The shed nestles in gangly Tallow woods that rain blossoms on its roof. Tongues of shadow unfurl at my approach, and stones dig into the soles of my bare feet. Mades only get shoes if there are enough to go around, and my feet are too small to fit into most hand-me-downs. The sky behind the trees is fiery and the Father's ravens track my progress. Even if we were made with any desire to escape, which we were not, our Father's bird's-eye view of all he has created, is more of a deterrent than any fence.

Look! Looo-ooook, the ravens cry, *at what the ca-aaat dragged in.* I limp across the small yard, bird shit in my hair.

The digital layer of my brain snaps into overdrive—details are stark. Colors blinding. I visor my free hand above my eyes. The shed is up on low joists, blooms of corrosion on scrap metal strewn in the crawl space. The old crone stands on a veranda under low eaves. She wears guano-spattered gum boots and a coarse smock, her face in shadow except for agate eyes bright in a slice of setting sun. She beckons me forward. I hesitate. The hut passed from shearers to the pervy janitor who shot himself dead. But here he lounges in plain sight, on a squatter's chair with half his head missing and the gun held loosely in his liver-spotted hand. Blood and brain matter have soaked the canvas and drip through the boards of the porch and onto the subfloor where a huge silver-gray cat laps at the pudding-like puddle.

Following my gaze, the crone makes a sign in the air and the janitor disappears leaving nothing but stained canvas and splintered pine.

"Him has the Dead-See?" she says, pointing a bent finger at me. It will take me some time to get used to her catch-all *hims, thems,* and *its,* unable for some reason, to get her tongue around *she, her* or *you* or *me.* And never *I.* It will take me some time to get used to never knowing, with Narn, where the act ends and *she* begins.

From under the shed, the cat glares at me resentfully, pawing at her bloodied whiskers.

"What does crappy twin want?"

I think that I want to be anywhere but here. How did Kai stand it? But I am on a promise. "I have a list from the Father."

"Where's other one?" the crone asks. "Better twin?"

I swallow. "How did you make us?"

"Ah. No time for questions."

"Tell me. How?"

"Narn wanted one," she says, pointing to herself. "Got two—a crappy twin and a good one." She points a crooked finger at me, and another one at her heart. "Special words needed to make double-yolker using code and two eggs." She holds up two fingers. "Long story. Hard work. Plenty shrooms, special words—danger everywhere."

A magpie warbles sadly. I clutch the medical bag. "How did you hide us, what we are, from the Father?"

"Boss only saw what him wanted to see." She shrugs, and even then I guess that I will probably never know the whole truth. "Shrooms helped. Magic helped more, even false magic. Problem was two surrogates needed—only one be real, and other fake. One alive, one dead."

A dead surrogate?

"Many dead surrogates. Narn picked a fresh one."

Helpless tears of horror prick my eyes. "But the ravens?"

"Too many questions."

I am insistent. "Didn't they see what you were doing?"

Her sigh is like sandpaper on rough wood. "Special words for ravens too. Ravens be Narn's children. Special words for Assistants made him see nothing but themselves."

I think she's telling me all this because she's going to kill and eat me like the witch from the last story Kai told at midnight on the morning before she kicked the Assistant in the thing. The witch lures twins—a boy and a girl—away from their father to her cottage made of candy and cookies in the woods, to fatten them up and eat them. "The Father will be waiting for his delivery," I say, holding the bag out in front of me.

But now she acts like she doesn't hear, and her eyes have gone an earthen red as if she is looking nowhere. "One surrogate dead with him baby dead inside. Narn pulled dead baby out and throws him away. Then put crappy twin"—she points to me—"up instead, shove it up real good and then did C-section. Boss likes knives. Knife made Boss see what him wanted to see. Narn said many magic hoo-hah words to keep Boss happy. To make Boss believe."

"You hid me in a dead surrogate? And her own dead baby—you threw away? The real one?"

"Trash baby." She beckons, and I start to walk backward instead of forward. "Many babies in trash back in them Temple days."

Narn half-turns toward the front door. The orange light behind her hut grows surly, making the shearers' shed seem to move forward, move toward me, like if I won't come to it, it'll get me anyway.

"You put me in the belly of a dead mother?"

We aren't meant to call them that. They aren't our mothers, or anyone's. They serve the Father. Never ask about the surrogates. Which ones are . . . which? Because it doesn't matter. The eggs are harvested at random and implanted in the same way. And the witch knows I'm not asking about that . . . about the surrogate. I'm asking about the eggs, the double-yolker conjoined by the same bridge of broken code.

"Tried to throw crappy twin in trash too—but good twin cried himself almost to death. Made Narn save him sister."

And she jabs that finger at me again. And then she cackles. And it's nothing like the fairy tale. At all.

* * *

The shearers' shed fragmented into Wellsburg bars and cafés. They oozed a cozy menace with fashionable patrons raising painted eyes as I passed. I stayed on the road to the bridge. It throbbed overhead like a broken vein, and the guard stepped out to watch me pass, to make sure I joined the rushing student throngs eager to be across and in the safety of a world made just for them.

I had planned to call Narn, but now that I knew what I had to ask from her, it all seemed too hard. How would I explain it—without one drink at least? Booze helped me deal with Narn, always had. Dirty Bert's, the Malemade who'd stopped me earlier—I'd been too sick to go to any of the bars in Tower Village, swore I never would, but for some reason now I wanted the company of my own species, almost as much as I felt like a drink. Normalcy beckoned. The promise of swift conformity and bland disappointment—all the trappings of the civilized world—seemed all the more precious now that I'd knowingly and willingly exiled myself from it.

Except, when I finally pushed through its swinging double doors, I hesitated on the threshold. The only pub I'd ever been to was the Five-Legged Nag in Norman. Dirty Bert's was not the Five-Legged Nag. Instead of drovers and shearers, Dirty Bert's thronged with digitally augmented survivors of a Paradise cult, hefting identical plastic pints with shutter-stop enthusiasm. Or maybe just disbelief in their own existence.

Dirty Bert's was about as phony a dive bar as its name suggested. If I'd been this desperate for a drink I could have gone up to my room, gotten soused on some of the moonshine—also good for sore throats and warts—that Narn had slipped into my luggage.

"Like immigrants finding themselves in a rich capitalist country for the first time, willingly seduced by a game they know is rigged, telling themselves they have soul to spare."

I turned to the voice behind me. It was the Malemade from the bridge. What I'd thought was a gray beanie was a shock of hair gone prematurely silver, and behind tinted glasses glistened round, mournful eyes, upturned like a cat's, with dilated pupils that narrowed in the light. Suspenders held his trousers up over a cheap crumpled shirt. I recognized the affectation for what it was. A bid for differentiation, a wave, or a prayer, to the ravening wolf that here be no ordinary sheep.

He said his name was Marvin. I followed him to the bar. Many of the other Mades acted like they recognized him, laughed at his jokes, drawn like me to how comfortable he seemed in his own skin. If I looked closely, I could almost see their mouths move along with his, as if they were putting his easy dialogue through new software, memorizing it for a rainy day. Or if—and this was just as likely—their augmented cortical stack was communicating with his, and they knew what he was going to say before he did. But I hadn't had those weeks to repurpose my processing power, and I could not see myself in the laughing faces and unsmiling eyes, the fast fashion and hair gel. I could not see Kai there either, or Narn. But above all what drew me to Marvin was how, between being charming and clever, he would sometimes turn his gaze to one side as if to listen to someone who wasn't there, or only he could hear. And see. A ghost?

Either way, it was another thing we had in common.

I complimented him on knowing his way around, or seeming to. He told me he'd started his program last semester, had been at the Village since just after Christmas last year and stayed over the summer. He was from the Father's property on the mainland, and raised separately with the other Malemades in its furthest northern edge. There, bordering the desert, Masters were charged with overseeing the selective breeding program that grew into a lucrative side-hustle. Chemically neutered a year after puberty, the Malemades would soon become an outsourced concession to marginalized tastes and specialized travel services.

"You had Matrons. We had Masters." Marvin said. "Any stepping out of line and we were dangled over the crocs. Legs were lost. Among other things."

He looked away then—it was awkward. Above the bar, screens played reruns of hit TV shows that I did not recognize, but other Mades laughed and clapped and mouthed the punchlines. There was a poster on the wall showing a wizard looming over a quaint little town like Wellsburg, and below it the words, *Our shadow's taller than our soul.*

"Maybe best not to talk about it," I said. "The past I mean. Our memories could be false."

He asked if I learned that in orientation and I explained that I'd missed that week, but got the gist of it from my roommates.

"It's what they want us to believe. That memory is a curse. They're right. But it's a weapon too," he said, "even false memory. Why else do you think the Father cut it out of us?"

I followed his gaze around the happy forgetful crowd. Plain and pretty, fat and thin, black, brown and white—yet all with the same careful mincing movements and cracked laughter, slurping as one their sweet cocktails, a candied cherry here, a twist of lemon there, sold out wholesale for a life free of fear.

"So it's okay to just make it up?" I said. "I mean in terms of its power? But what about the whole thing of not being able to lie, even to ourselves?"

"You're asking about Fictional Forms?" he said gently. "If you'll be able to fake it?"

I cocked my head at him, feeling too warm in the overheated room.

"You told me," he said. "On the bridge."

I shook my head. Had I?

He leaned in. "See?" he said. "I see your amnesia and raise it and you have no way of knowing if I'm bluffing or not."

He sat back and shrugged. "On the bridge you mentioned how you were rushing to sign up for an elective. Knowing the limited offerings to Mades, and that even most of the places are gone, *and* seeing that you were heading to Wellsburg instead of staying in the Towers to sign up for Spanish—well, I put two and two together and guessed Fictional Forms."

"Great detective work. Annoying but impressive."

His laugh came out as a jubilant purr. "Plus you don't look like the musical type."

The extra time he'd been here had not only allowed Marvin to know his way around the system better than anyone should, but also explained his hybrid accent, part Upper Slant but still with some Rim drawl to it. It reminded me a little of the Father's but less squishy. Marvin's major was criminal psychology—plenty of opening for that in Upper Slant, he said—he was six months away from completing his program.

"Sounds like you've got it all figured out," I said.

"Honestly, I don't remember much about . . . before either," Marvin said. "The shtick just fills in the blanks, or cuts them out and sticks the broken bits together."

Starv ing Hills.

I'd never met a Malemade in the flesh, but had seen the footage on the small TV at the Nag when the pods came in and airlifted them out of the desert, the screen filled with their drugged and blinking faces.

"We just called our amnesia the Forever Code. It was unbreakable, the Father said."

Marvin thought about it. "Coded neural mesh implants laced with memory-suppressing proteins can be tough to override. But one day they'll hack it, whether we want them to or not."

"Who?"

"The real scheme behind the Redress Scheme," he said, yawning.

"Who? What?" My head was spinning, and my feet ached from walking.

"There's this database called Skillzone . . . you're on it. We all are."

It was hard to get drunk and process so much information at once. I chose the first option. Once I came back from the bar with another round, I said, "So once all this is over . . ."

"You ain't never going home, Dorothy. Not intact. None of us are."

Dorothy, like *The Wizard of Oz*? "I get it. You had your share of Golden Book Therapy too," I said.

There was a fetching slyness to his smile. "Pretty much an essential prerequisite for acceptance into the Redress Scheme, wouldn't you say?"

"Why do they do it?" I said. "Go to all this trouble to fix us?"

He explained that the Scheme was less about rehabilitation than a way to beef up enrollments in a failing Liberal Arts College.

"And ongoing," he said, "to fatten a dwindling Upper Slant labor force. And keep in mind that the data of every living Blood Temple survivor—the retrievable code on our neocortices—is recorded on numbered and named files for research."

"What kind of research?" I asked.

"Research that doesn't rely on live test subjects." One of his suspenders was a little twisted. "Everything from brain labs to the military to the history of witches."

"Witches?"

"Wellsburg having a great deal invested in that old chestnut."

I said: "Come on. Why would anyone want to study us, Marvin?" His name dropped easily from my tongue, as if I had said it many times. "We're just a bunch of broken toys."

"It's the Forever Code they want," he said, pointing to his head. "If they can hack it, they can cut it out. And if they can cut it out, they can replicate it."

The room lurched.

"Back in the Blood Temple," I said, "it wasn't our brains they cut out."

In my mind's blue eye the Father was tall and rangy, going soft in the belly. In my brain's other eye, the brown one, he was nimble and effete as a spider.

"Paradise doesn't come cheap, Dorothy." Marvin cocked his head to one side—reminding me of Kai. "You honestly think any of *us* were going to get in?" I could see slow fatherly fingers as they hovered over a bone-white doubling cube. My sister on the other side of the backgammon board deliberating whether or not to take or drop—and damned either way.

Marvin took out his phone and brought up a video and passed it to me. I watched ants forming a bridge of their bodies for other ants to cross over. I watched as the ants below were crushed by the weight of the bodies they supported to get to the other side.

I passed it back coldly, my heart pounding. "No one is hacking *me*. And I'm not an ant." I got up to leave, but he coaxed me to stay with the promise of one for the road. He didn't have to coax me very hard.

"I gather you met the delicious Pagan?"

I sipped my fake martini. "She was . . . delicious. I guess."

"Except for the bad taste she left in your mouth?"

"She'd thrown a whole piece of cake in the trash." I slowly spun the glass in my hands, avoiding his eyes, thinking about that treacherous inkblot, the unspeakable broken word. "I think I got in under false pretenses."

"I gave FiFo a try last semester," he said. Inflamed circles below his gray-green eyes that made him look older than he probably was. "It wasn't for me."

I didn't ask why because I figured by now that he'd tell me if he wanted to.

"Fictional Forms is one of the electives that agreed to the quota. Tokenism with intent. So some survivors attend. We're the new ground zero. Below zero, actually."

His arms were ropy. His Adam's apple fascinated me. His imagination—his way with words—these were some of the things that drew me to him.

"Yeah but why tokenism with intent?" The more I drank, the more it tasted like Narn's *Islandia* brew. And Marvin's voice, mannish and purring, helped the medicine of memory go down.

"There's always an agenda behind tokenism—exemplification if nothing else. The singular as a demonstration of the multiple. Did you know that the word demonstrate comes from the Latin verb, *monere,* which means to warn, the noun form of which, *monstrum,* means 'an evil omen'? *Monstrum* eventually became *monstre* in Middle English and then monster in modern English."

"Fun fact."

And for the first time since arriving in Upper Slant, I *was* having fun. "What does that have to do with . . . us?"

"I guess I just didn't want to be the token monster."

I wanted to tell him the rest, about the inkblot, the half-lie on the form, but something stopped me. I think I wanted, even then, to protect him from me. "Seems like the Regulars want to get off . . . on our pain?"

"Cult porn is the new fakelore, and we're the new fakes." He spoke quickly but annunciated carefully. I had the impression that he'd thought none of this through.

"They can't get enough of it. AIs gone wrong and atrophied uteri, boy sacs fed to the pigs, lab technicians with their fingers up nonconsenting orifi. It makes Regulars wet and it makes them wild in a bland new century where a good skeevy is hard to find."

"What's a bad skeevy?" I said.

"This." He waved around the room.

And he was gone, looking off to one side like someone had stepped up beside him and distracted his attention away from me. Away from now and from here. And then he was back. Shaking out his silver hair, he reached in his pocket and pulled out what looked like a joint.

"Is that what I think it is?"

According to Redress Scheme literature, drugs were so contraindicated for our augmented brain that to be in possession could mean instant expulsion.

"Let's get out of here," he said.

We walked down to the landscaped track above the riverbank, sat down on a bench that looked into fog. The bridge arced above us.

"My problem in FiFo was that I couldn't remember what was real and what wasn't," he said. "They wanted stories of damnation that made the lucky feel double-happiness blessed, their exceptional worthiness confirmed by being spared, or even better, having daringly defended themselves against the inevitable, clever clogs. Proof in the pudding and whatnot. My stories weren't convincing enough I guess, because they were too real." He held a match to the joint, drew it in, and said: "No one can believe us, Dorothy. That we went through what we did and survived. The suspension of disbelief is just too much to ask, is my two cents."

"So we have to conjure a suspension that doesn't ask as much. Something abyssal and sexy. I get it."

"And maybe slip a mickey in, you know. Beware Mades bearing gifts."

"Meaning?"

"A seed of truth in the fiction, the poison in the potion and vice versa."

I swallowed my drink the wrong way. Took a few minutes to cough into my elbow, Mades glancing around in disgust. Finally I managed to say, "There *was* an old woman who lived at the edge of the Rogues Bay camp. She told stories. Not to me, exactly but—"

He smiled at me quizzically, one corner of his mouth lifting beneath his stubble. "But you'd eavesdrop, Nellie No-Friends, from your sad little spy hole of boogers and voodoo dolls?" He passed the joint, leaned back and draped an arm across the back of the bench.

I laughed uneasily. "I thought you said you had no imagination."

"I don't. But I was a Nellie-No-Friends, too."

I tried to explain how the stories the witch told had a life of their own. "There was something between the lines, I guess—an image, or sound, or thoughtform—that tangled with the Forever Code. Imparted some kind of neural protection."

"Or psychic maybe." He played with his suspender, and that ghost of a sly smile played at his lips. "Sorcery either way."

"I never quite figured it out, to be honest."

"You will, Meera." He raised an eyebrow as I expertly held the smoke in my infected lungs with all the finesse of a Five-Legged Nag regular. "If anyone can."

I was glad the light was too dim for him to see me blush at the compliment. At the sound of my name on his lips.

"Problem is I can't remember them," I said behind the swirling smoke.

"Can you get more stories from her? Who was she?"

I couldn't tell the whole truth—I wanted to, but it was buried too deep— that unscratchable itch. And yet I couldn't lie.

"She rescued me—got me out and raised me. She had been a midwife for the Father. Well, more than that. A scientist, really. She knew how to compound lichen and fungi to stimulate ovulation and make the IVF media work better and faster. The natural antibiotics and coagulants helped keep the surrogates safe. And reduced the chances of birth abnormalities."

If the Assistants let them live, it was only as specimens. Or worse.

"Well," Marvin said. "I guess a little conjure goes a long way, especially in the belly of the beast."

Kai had been an insufferable know-it-all. Marvin—so present, so completely in himself—reminded me of her, but it was painful. Because Marvin wasn't Kai.

"How do you know about conjure?" I asked slowly.

"Everybody knows about the witches in the Rim. Even, well especially, the Regulars. No wonder Pagan wanted you if she clocked that was in your background."

I remembered the altered word on my Redress Form.

"Honestly," I bristled, "my guardian may have a trick or two up her sleeve, but her real stock in trade is an encyclopedic knowledge of plants and their healing properties—analgesic, antibiotic, sedative, even hallucinogenic. She's kind of famous in what passes for a survivor underground where I grew up." I heard the brag in my voice, and felt that I had said too much, not as cheap a drunk as other Mades, but cheap nonetheless.

"She passed this on to you?"

"Let's just say that I know the difference between wolfbane and witch's hair."

He blew the joint back to life, cradled it between sensitive fingers. The round green orbs of his eyes swimming with light from the bridge. "Is it true what they say about the power of botanicals to corrupt the cult's memory blockers?"

"That and Golden Books," I smiled. "And you know, smudge sticks and candles and a necromanced thylacine. The usual."

"She's a witch then?"

I studied my hands. "Not a fairy-tale witch though."

Marvin shifted on the bench, which caused one suspender to slide down his shoulders like some kind of strip tease. I felt a heat between my legs. Our fingers touched, and the heat intensified. I was starving.

"Fairy tales have left the building," Marvin said, looking at me closely.

I froze with the joint halfway to my lips and the smoke bringing tears to my eyes. I felt his seeking mind. I tried to power mine down. But I was too stoned to really care if he'd started to read my thoughts, too buzzed to care that this may have been his intent.

"You never know," he said. "You might be quite good at it."

"What?"

"Conjuring. Maybe you remember more than you think."

Later, standing in line on the Corso for pizza, he told me how after the helicopters came in and lifted the inmates out of both the mainland and Rogues Bay properties, he went to the city for a few years and lived with a foster family—"cue Golden Book Therapy," he said—until he took up the Redress Scheme. He asked about me, and I told him about the Starvelings, even though I did not say the name.

"Look," he said. "FiFo is intense. If you're going to survive it you'll have to remember this: our pain is their breakfast of champions. You'll need to figure out a way to fake them out."

"Mades can't lie," I reminded him.

"No," he said. "But witches can."

A good beginning is hard to find.

"The bridge has the best reception." He grew serious. "Near the middle. But be careful. The bridge has eyes. And ears."

I smiled up at him. "Of course it does."

"Wait. Tell me something: it was just the two of you? Back in those hills?"

I knew he was probing, gently. And that he wouldn't be doing it if it was unwanted. But still I hesitated. "Narn has . . . two sisters. One of them ran off. The other one wears black from head to toe and has tattoos all over their face.

Oh, and the one with tattoos, they're mute. Something went wrong with their tongue."

"Something went wrong with all of us."

I blundered on. "And there are lots of ravens. And Eric . . ."

He waited.

"My thylacine."

"*Your* thylacine. And?"

He really had the saddest smile. And the kindest eyes.

And it was too late to lie, even if I could. "And Kai. For a while . . ."

"Until?" He pointed to his eyes.

I shook my head, no.

He nudged a lean shoulder against mine. The unfamiliar physical contact made the Corso spin around me, all fake neon and cheese whizz.

"I guessed there was a twin. The mismatched eyes are the giveaway." He paused as if considering what to say next. "I ate mine."

I put one hand over my sister's blue eye. "No."

"In utero," he continued. "Or what passed for utero in the Blood Temple. Absorbed her." He paused. Gathered himself. "It's called vanishing-twin syndrome. Like you with your different colored eyes, one from her, one from you. I have a man-thing, F.Y.I., but also the same kind of cute little atrophied uterus like most Mades have. They discovered it through imaging and so on after I moved to the city. Not all Malemades are like that. But the good thing is that, unlike the other Males, I didn't have to be made sterile once my sperm was banked—Meera, I *was* born this way."

He pulled my hand gently away and held it in his, and a current jumped between us. "But they're never really vanished, right? More like, our twins are just in hiding. Inside us. Waiting for a chance to come out."

I lurched on the mica. Managed to push him away just in time to throw up onto my twin sister's old brown shoes.

I woke up sometime the next afternoon to a text from Marvin.

It was the first text that I'd ever received that wasn't from the university or the Redress Scheme. I read it wound in rumpled sheets and through blurry eyes. It asked how I was, and said that after I'd thrown up, he had managed to locate my roommates who were at a film screening nearby and they got me to the dorm, where I'd passed out.

I remembered none of it.

I should have felt something. Gratitude. Maybe even love. I know now that it's too late, but back then, all I could do was burn with shame. I didn't want to need anyone here. Was "needful" the only thing a Made could ever be?

I checked the time. It was after four o'clock. A headache needled at my right temple, but apart from that I felt miraculously lighter in my chest than I'd felt for days. I was hungry too. I found some peanut butter and crackers that belonged to the roommates, and I washed them down with Coke from the vending machine, thinking as I sunk back into sleep about Marvin eating his twin and if he ever regretted it. If he ever wished it had been the other way around.

*　*　*

Kai's hair is unsettlingly black against the white pillow, like spilled paint. I have taken her sweaty hand in mine, and she doesn't remove it.

The other Mades attending to their fallen hero, have left for now. With no more stories they are unsure, once again, of where to direct their love. We are alone in the infirmary apart from a sick Made across the aisle, hooked up to an IV. A slow cramp creeps across my pelvis. This thing that the Father said he bred out of us when he clipped the wings of our lady-bits—this ability to *imagine*—hits me with a sense of physical pain. A picture emerges in my head, a picture of . . . time. Not Narn's time before time, but her time that is also *ours*. Kai's and mine. A time of protection, and vice versa.

For the first time I imagine time and protection as conjoined, and how you can't have one without the other. For the first time, I see time as my friend—if only I knew what a friend was.

Kai is watching me carefully. "Sometimes," she says, the milkiness in her blue eyes clearing, "sisters just don't want the same thing."

"I want us to be together forever," I say. "Don't you want that too?"

"Be careful what you wish for."

"Why is the Father unmaking you?" I ask, taking a strand of her long hair and winding it around my stubby fingers.

"Because he loves me."

"But you're too smart?"

She closes her eyes and the lids are darkly webbed with veins. "Because I don't need him," she says. "And that scares him."

I concentrate on twirling the black tendril around and around. "Can't you . . . pretend?"

She opens her eyes and looks at me dully.

"Like in the stories you tell. The conjure tales the witch gives you. Where people pretend to be what they're not—like frogs and wizards and good queens."

"They're just stories, idiot. The Father isn't stupid like Mades. He knows I'm not stupid like them either. He just doesn't know why. I try and pretend, but I suck at it. Obviously. I let him win when I can. I try not to let him see all the words I know. I take his doubles and I lose a game of backgammon, but then I win at stupid checkers with a basic bridge defense, and I take all his dumb sugar packets and he doesn't know why." She finds a sudden strength and leans forward, her face inches from mine. "And you can't let him find out. Promise?"

I must go to dinner. Her hair has left red welts around my wrist. "Will it hurt?" I ask. "The unmaking?"

"Like hell," she says.

I come back as soon as I can, with some overripe grapes that she sucks. "Good," she says with her mouth full. And then she throws up. Fleshy, milky bile with streaks of blood through it.

Once I get her clean, she says, "Anyway, according to the Father, what doesn't kill me will make me stronger." She weakly slices a thumb across her belly like a knife.

I grin at how strong she'll be when she gets better. "You're already strong. Stronger than I'll ever be. The Assistant never saw you coming."

I clap my hand over my mouth.

"So you do remember?" she says slyly.

"No."

But I do. How when Kai burst in on where he had me on the block like a specimen, he'd looked up from his magnifying glass and beamed. *A twofer!* he'd said. *My lucky day.*

"It wasn't his lucky day." Kai turns and fixes her stormy blue eyes on mine. "You're stronger than you look. Remember that. The Father will see that too, the way he saw that I was smarter. Did you clean yourself up?"

She tries to peer over the bed at my bare feet—too small for the older Mades' cast-offs and too big for baby shoes. I nod.

The Assistant was right about the twofer even if he didn't know it. Twofers, threefers—multiple births are a bitch, the Father says. Double-trouble—a nightmare. Split and multiplied, the noncompliant ovum corrupts the source code, weakening its defenses and allowing hell to seep into the cracks.

"How long will I have to hide it for? Being strong?"

"The witch will tell us," my sister says. "The witch knows even more than the Father."

* * *

I woke after a nap, and had an early supper of more crackers and peanut butter and two of Trudy's headache pills swallowed with a slug of cold witch-hair tea. Then I dressed and went to the bridge to make my call. Mades with nowhere to go on a Friday night huddled into phones against the blue-lit rails, keeping their cracked voices to a gravelly hum that rose and fell as I passed. I found an empty space somewhere in the middle.

"Narn?"

It would be dawn in the oasis of bloodwood and bamboo with the sun yellow between the branches and I could hear the *ah-aaaah-aaaaaah* of the ravens.

"Who?" Narn's voice was strong but huskier than I remembered.

"I enrolled in a new class yesterday." I was trying not to yell. "It's called Fictional Forms. It's a writing class—and it's held every Wednesday evening on the Wellsburg campus."

There was a clunk and chittering at the other end as if Narn had put her phone on the table under the bark awning and gone to set something on the stove. I could hear the tap of Eric's paws on the boards and I inhaled sharply.

"What kind of writing?"

"Stories." A few faces turned in my direction. "Made-up stuff."

She asked what happened to Computer Science, and I explained how the electives worked and how this was my only option unless I wanted to be stuck in the Tower Campus for the rest of the program. I told her about the quota of survivors in FiFo.

"Tower Campus all right for other Mades," she sniffed.

"Yes. Okay. But not for me. Being in Wellsburg is the only way I can get through the program. And I need to survive to get back to you. And Eric. To get back to . . ."

"Shhhh!" she hissed. "Mustn't be spoken. Stay with own kind. Safer that way."

"They're not my kind," I sighed. "You know that. I feel lost there. In Wellsburg I stand out. People see me, and I can hide behind that. With all the other Mades . . . we disappear. And it's terrifying. That's what the Regulars want—to make us disappear."

"Safety in numbers," she said, and the ravens flapped in agreement.

"I know, I know. Find room to move in power's blind spot," I said. "But it's not as easy here."

"Not easy anywhere." Down in the bushes below the bridge, an owl began its gallows chortle.

"I'm scared all the time here, Narn. I live in a tower with hundreds of other strangers and none of us will survive intact and I'm lonelier than I've ever been in my life."

And worlds away in the Starvelings, a lonely thylacine sighed and lay down at the feet of a pretend witch with time on her hands.

"Choose different class, then. Why be telling tales with them stinky skanks?"

"Not all of them are stinky," I said, brightening up. "The girl in the Writing and Culture Office had skin like the petals of a swamp lily."

The guard barked something at some rowdy Mades thronging past the gatehouse.

"Her name is Pagan. And she threw a whole piece of cake in the trash. And I met a Malemade, too. An autodidact—he wears suspenders to hold up his soul."

"Fetch him trash-cake," Narn barked into the speaker. "Cut off a piece and cook in a pot with a club foot and some wood shavings and three drops of monthly blood . . ."

I coughed painfully, partly from the rotten-egg vapor from the river, and partly because of the infection roaring back into my lungs. My hands looked blue as a corpse's in the light from the bridge. "Thanks Narn, but I don't need that kind of spell this time."

I tried to keep my voice even. Narn wasn't a morning person and she hated anyone to startle her birds. She called them her children because they were the only real ones she'd ever have.

"What kind, then?"

The bridge was emptying and a Made further along against the rails palmed her phone and headed back toward Tower Village where she belonged. Where we all belonged.

"The story kind," I said, cupping my hand over my mouth. "Like the ones you gave to Kai."

I could see Narn shaking her clown head, holding onto her cap so it wouldn't fall off. "Good twin needed stories to keep Blood Temple sisters safe. Make them love her more than Father—dead now. No need for conjure stories, and dangerous in wrong hands—crappy twin has no memory for stories."

And there I was, where I'd always been. Up against her dismissal of me.

"Kai remembered them and still got them wrong. I'll just fill in the blanks. Make up what I don't remember."

"Make-up lets the conjure in," Narn warned.

"Isn't that the point?" I said.

"Mades be bad liars," she reminded me. "Even twofers."

"Making-up isn't lying exactly, though, is it Narn?"

"Wouldn't know," she said cagily.

"Well, lying," I said, thinking about it, "is falsifying with intent."

"How is making-up different?" There was suspicion in her question which I knew I deserved. A test maybe.

I gathered my answer together, letting the twinkling lights from the town assemble themselves into a discernible pattern. "Make-up is invention. Configuration. Fabrication—over a framework that is already there." I lowered my voice. "Like how you and your sisters made yourselves up, but not out of nothing." I ignored her ragged shushing—we'd rarely spoken of such things. "It can also be a compensation for failure, Narn. Like to make up a test you've missed, or failed. Or have been unable to face." I was drawing from knowledge I didn't know I had, the kind of pedantry that Kai reveled in. I felt for a moment a vertiginous impulse to climb atop the railings and jump off, see if I could fly.

There was a pause while Narn lit a stick for smudging—a little early for that I thought, but perhaps there was need for it. I could almost smell its damp, bitter heat, thanks to my drinking the telepathy-enabling tea. But for some reason, instead of being a comfort, the reminder that Narn's smoking bundle of sage and wattle and guano and who knew what else, could reach across worlds and hold us both in its protection, made the hair rise on the back my neck.

"What does crappy Made want from rich bitches?" Her voice deeper now, and stronger too.

"Protection. The same as Kai wanted."

"Protection from what?"

The Father is dead. Long live the Father, the owl hooted.

"Something else is here," I said carefully, forcing the truth—my truth—to the surface, where it pierced and hurt. "Maybe the Redress Scheme is not what it says it is. Maybe it doesn't want to make us better."

"Unmake instead?"

I didn't hesitate this time. "*Re-*make Narn. And I don't want that either."

"Why not?"

"I'm already Made." I waited. "Aren't I?"

"Rich bitches want Mades in story class. Otherwise why quotas? Why do what rich bitches want?"

I had the feeling she was testing me.

"It's not Mades they want," I said, as if she didn't know. "It's the stories. They don't care about us."

"Why?"

Because we're just trash, baby . . .

What then?

Once they're done with me, maybe they'll want to throw me away.

"But with your help, Narn, I'll survive the Scheme. Come back home to you. Come back to the Hills where I belong."

I no longer knew if we were talking or just reading each other's thoughts. But out of nowhere came a memory of the dead thylacines back in the Rim, how the settlers exterminated them by baiting sheep carcasses with wolfsbane. I tried to breathe through the panic induced by Narn's capacity to conjure memories into my brain, even across ten thousand miles and half a dozen time zones.

"The old bait and switch," I said.

"Dangerous game." Again reminding me with her thoughts, how, back in

South Rim, the wolfbane-baited meat made it into more than a few settlers' stews, although Narn swore that was never her doing.

"Apparently the Regulars love to be scared, Narn," I said, "Pagan said that they see us like barmaids from the abyss. Don't tell me you didn't slip a mickey into those conjure tales you told Kai."

She scoffed. "Them rich bitches eat Mades for breakfast. Barmaids too. Power don't love scares. Power just loves itself. Gobbles up strength from weakness."

Four and twenty blackbirds baked in a pie.

"Fakelore, it's called. And yes, that's the bait: our weakness is ourselves. Mades, witches"—I felt her flinch at the word—"every weird story that was born from the Blood Temple. It's all fakelore."

There was a long pause, during which I listened to her quickened breath. "What's the switch?"

Finally, we'd come to it, sooner than I thought. My heart skipped. Most of the bridge callers had gone back to where they belonged, so I could speak more freely now without fear of being overheard. "You said stories conjoin love and fear, Narn. What else can . . . do they join? I mean any opposites, right? Life and death, maybe, too?"

"Get to the point," she snapped impatiently. "Rich bitches take big bites from each one. Twin truths be trash food for hungry power."

"You're not listening," I said very slowly. "The switch is what if I . . . we . . . were able to bite back?"

The silence stretched out on the other end. Even the ravens held their tongues.

"No," Narn said. "No biting back. No more blood vengeance."

What I said next took us both by surprise. It wasn't what I'd planned to say, but the words came, out of nowhere, from the mist swirling at my feet. "Okay, not vengeance. But justice. They took your sister. Tiff. I mean something did. You deserve to know. She flew the coop in Rogues Bay. Last heard of in Upper Slant and then nothing. Maybe I can find her."

I heard her breath stop. The phone felt hot against my ear.

"Crappy twin wants to be bait? Let rich bitches chew on fake stories, wet panties with scares while crappy twin sniffs out lost sister?"

"In a nutshell," I said. "Might need some fine tuning, but yeah."

Narn said a little hoarsely. "Maybe lost sister doesn't want to be found. Maybe too lost.

"Maybe. But at least you'll know. There is justice, not vengeance, in that."

The bridge was half-empty. The blue railings stretching to either side. A streak of light left in the sky. Everything below in darkness.

"Think about it, Narn. The stories you gave Kai conjured protection. They made the Mades love her more than they loved the Father. They would have died for her, and that love protected them, enabled them to survive the unsurvivable. Whatever code you conjured, or conjure you coded—what if you can do the same for me? What if you can conjure love to not only protect me, but give you back your sister, too?"

What if, what if, what if went my heart. I had no idea what I was saying. It was as if the words, the ideas, were coming to me from somewhere, someone else. Kai? I felt like a means to an end, the bridge between the thing and the word.

"Stories made sister dead meat," Narn said quietly, and I could hear the unhappy shriek of her cooking pot scraping against the hob.

"That was me, Narn. I made Kai into dead meat."

Hadn't confusion dogged me my whole life? Her lost sister, and my found one. Her living one, mine dead. Hers bad, mine good. Me crying beside Kai's grave, while Narn, thirteen moonshine sheets to the wind, sobbed over the disappeared Tiff, stumbling to her cave and emerging days later, smeared with shit and bleeding from the scourge hung on the rock wall by a hook fashioned from a pig's snout. When the Redress Scheme was offered, I had been ashamed of wanting to leave all that confusion and sorrow behind, to leave Narn and the mutilated Mag, and yet here I was, between something and nothing, making it all up as I went along. Afraid not so much of what I was asking for but how, and why.

The whole flock of Narn's ravens were awake now, and I could cup their sad-baby song in my hand. Narn had begun to growl, a grinding snore. Eric whined.

"The sooner I complete the program the sooner I can come home," I said as gently as I could. "And then you'll know about your sister. Maybe. It's the least I can do for you. You and Mag."

She snorted, but I suddenly knew that I meant it. More than I'd ever meant anything in my life. Because she would never know how desperate I was to prove that she was right not to throw me away.

"Crappy twin really doesn't like living in castles?" she asked sharply.

"It's not your fault. We couldn't know—the pictures on the brochure were fake. It's not a castle. This is a prison. And we're just test subjects—models made to break for their tomorrow, not ours. If I stay here too long, it'll be me who's lost."

There was a long silence. I wanted to hear that she didn't want to lose me after all. But she didn't speak. Into the pregnant pause, I said: "Narn? All of our brains are on a database called Skillzone."

"Kill what?"

"And there's a ghost," I said more to myself than her. "Some witch-hunter who jumped off the bridge."

"Them bitches not scared of hunter?"

"No, but we are," I said.

"Kill Zone?"

"It's some kind of hack, I guess."

"*Daaa-ata. Haaa-aack,*" the ravens cried.

"Like lady-bits?"

"Yes, but this time it's our brains." My eyeballs prickled. "I don't want to be in another temple, Narn. I won't survive this one."

Along the bridge, as if on cue, the remaining Mades hung up their phones and wiped their eyes, our grief contagious. Narn's droning continued, a breathy wheeze like a motor in a piece of obsolete machinery.

One of the guards called out, reminding anyone planning to go into Wellsburg of the curfew.

"Who's that?" she said sharply.

"A guard," I said it too loudly.

"How many?" her voice sounding too close and never ever close enough.

"Two. One on either side."

"Regulars?"

I nodded, and her droning grew louder, no longer a backdrop to her voice but the other way around.

"What else?" She wasn't a real witch and I was a shitty Made and we'd never really seen eye to eye, but she knew when I was trying to hide something, and that I sucked at it.

I said, in the lowest voice I could—I felt my tongue mouth the words but couldn't hear them above her incantations: "Someone, maybe me, crossed out where we'd written Norman on the Redress form. They spilled ink on it, and put something else. Something that made me look ... more interesting than I am."

"Interesting to who?"

"I have no idea. Maybe to some Regulars with the power to select the right students for the course, I suppose. Marvin, the Malemade, says that there are Regulars in Wellsburg who are worried that the Redress Scheme threatens their way of life. They want to make courses like FiFo sexy again, and boost enrollments . . ."

"Stories are sexy?" Narn's humming reverb rose to a crescendo and then abruptly quit.

"Fear is sexy."

Suddenly I heard Eric leap to his feet and begin that sibilant keen peculiar to the thylacine, neither dog nor cat. "Shhh," I said into the phone. "I love you too." I wiped my eyes. "The spelling of the word on the form was wrong."

"How wrong?"

"Not wrong enough." There was another, longer pause. Some nocturnal thing moved on the riverbed far below. The pause stretched out, longer even than the last one. Had she forgotten me? It wouldn't be the first time.

And then, slyly: "When is class?"

Next Wednesday, I told her. Between six and eight.

"And then?"

"Depends on the story, I guess."

"Hah." She barked out a laugh. "Narn has a story that will scare the bark off the trees. Make them rich bitches shit him britches."

Leaning against the rails, I coughed wetly and painfully and then I let the sweet cut of her gibber slice into my ear, my brain, my heart, and cut open my treacherous memory like an artery, and worlds away, the ravens shut their eyes.

When I hung up the phone minutes that seemed like hours later, or vice versa, my spine was still tingling, a cold sweat across my skin where the goose-flesh had subsided. At either end, the guards had retreated into the safety of their watchhouses. Three or four steps along in the direction of the Towers, I halted, unable to comprehend what I was seeing: a distorted hand—more a claw—reach up from under the bridge, and grasp onto a rail. The hand was blacker than the night, sharp against the glowing blue of the railing, putting everything around it into a greasy soft-focus. Five segmented phalanges joined by another set, creeping over the lower edge feeling blindly for one of the glowing blue spindles. I forgot to breathe, my heart in my throat. The claw was both animal and human, with pointed talons at the end of grappling fingers. The fingers scrabbled like a spider's legs. My stomach rolled. I imagined the rest of it dangling over the river. Or suctioned onto the underside of the bridge. *I imagined.*

Suspended in fog between the winking leer of Wellsburg and the panopticon gaze of the Towers, the darkness was shot with red strands of vapor that webbed around my own ankles and lashed me to the spot. I struggled against what I clearly saw—the monstrous hands—and against nineteen years of loneliness, an unreliable witness to my own life, because there *was* someone there, not just beneath the bridge, but, horrifyingly, also behind me. A meaty perfume made my throat close up. My vision grew cloudy. I tried to tell myself the fog was real but its hold on me was not, and that the rank breath at the back of my neck was molecular, nothing more, and wanted nothing, asked nothing from me except for my . . . fear. Yes! A small price to pay, I could give it that—enough left from the Blood Temple to last me a lifetime. Forgetting everything else—the walls of the Culture and Society Office closing in on me, the humiliation of Pagan's bullying, never another punchline to that old joke, the shipwrecked cake and the broken word on the Redress Form—forgetting nothing and imagining everything, I gave the fog my fear. Not all of it but enough to make it recede and open a door back to the beginning. To where the worst of what slithered in this place waited for me, and I would meet it halfway, if I could. In the glare of my fumbled phone light, the claws grew still against the thrown shadows that a moment later would become their camouflage, and for the first time in my life, I screamed.

CHAPTER 6
NOTEBOOK

At my scream, the guard emerged from his gatehouse. He took two steps toward me with his night stick out before I stopped to mumble an excuse about how I'd "seen something." He sent me on my way, giving me curt advice to stop by the infirmary on my way home to get medication for my nerves. Mades had bad nerves. Everyone knew that.

The guards hated us.

I spent the next Saturday in the dorm trying and failing to remember the gist of the story that Narn had told mostly in a language—part words, part sound, part thought—that I didn't know. I wished Kai were here to remind me. In the Starvelings, after she came back from the dead, I would seek out new places to play, unclassified forms of lichen to introduce to her. I made up games for us, and characters—for her, for Eric, for me—and she would remember it all, come home and scribble it down in Narn's notebooks so that we wouldn't forget.

But that part of me was gone now.

The memory of those hands clawing their way over the edge of the bridge blurred with Narn's syllables. Transforming the lost tongue of the ancients into modern words—much less a coherent story—defeated me. Why hadn't I written it down? How many times had Kai lectured me on this, sternly supervising my jotting down of every new potion or charm in Narn's tattered grimoire, so I wouldn't forget? And as always, even in death, Kai was right. But Narn's glottal singsong babble scrambled my thinking. I couldn't remember anything more than that nightmarish fog that had lashed me to the bridge, and a feeling, more than anything else, of creeping talons inching toward my heart.

I tried to scribble a sentence here or there, but the *implications* of the recall were lost to me immediately, like that headless snake girl back in the Blood Temple. How had Kai managed to extract meaning from Narn's madness? How did she know what was the beginning, middle or end?

How could Kai's listeners understand what she was saying when she herself did not?

I blew my nose. Kai's dainty nostrils had run with black goo when she came back from the dead. I was constantly wiping it away with paper or rags that I tossed into the stove, a rotten-eggs smell the origins, the implications, of which I tried not to imagine. But the more I tried *not* to imagine it, the more clearly I could.

"The female imagination," the Father had preached, "is single-handedly responsible for opening the gates of hell—what crawled out is your fault, my pretties, and for your sins, it will chase you to the ends of the earth. That is the curse you brought down upon yourself, upon the world, and this is the only cure." He raised a scalpel. "You'll thank me later."

We already did.

The Father showed us the petri dish in which we were made. Made us watch footage of the egg fertilized by the fast-swimming sperm. The development of the blastocyst, the laser insertion into the gonad cluster of a mesh of electrodes, mesh thinner than a wavelength of visible light, onto which the algorithm of our "artificial" intelligence was coded. We watched on jerky film as the implanted embryo was then placed into a special IVA medium—a combination of the salts and sugars, buffers and cell volume regulators extracted by the Assistants, along with the human albumin of which there was an endless supply from his donor surrogates. This last came with a high risk of contamination, which is where Narn's botanicals came in. From her lichen, she compounded a genius brew of antibiotics—her plant extracts provided essential vitamins and amino acids to protect the zygotes *and* the embryos from disease. She added to this a secret concoction—a growth factor perhaps? Magic? Whether science or sorcery, she refused to divulge—and the Father was so convinced that it was the latter, that it made him, in Kai's words, the "witch's bitch." But Narn was bound to the Blood Temple or lose the Father's protection—and that made her a prisoner just like the rest of us.

Or in other words, it was a mutualism from hell.

Eventually all physical sign of the mesh filaments disappeared across the blood-brain barriers. And there we were. The fast-action absorption into the developing brain of the coded filaments was so smooth that they literally became us, directing our actions, augmenting our behavior, deforming our cognition, compromising our immunity. On top of that a restriction protocol designed by a team of geneticists stunted our embryonic brains in sections of both the occipital and hippocampal regions, where imagination and memory are activated, respectively. For their efforts, the assisting geneticists were recompensed with offshore bank accounts, chunks of Rim property, and even a Made or two of their own.

My legs were still heavy and my head foggy from flu. I flopped down on the bed, exhausted. Lara and Trudy were out, and the dorm, with its high double-glazed windows overlooking the river, was silent as the tomb.

I shivered, the disremembered claws creeping over the edge of my heavy eyelids. That too-long thumb. I tried to nap but those spidery black fingers pulled open my eyes and kept them stretched grotesquely wide. I tried to close them, pressing them shut with my hands as I had with Kai's after she died. And like hers, mine flew open as soon as I took my hands away. Thoughts teemed. Terrors gathered. Tears ran. When I checked the mirror, a new array of baby crow's feet had imprinted at each eye. I rubbed some of Lara's eye cream on them but it did no good.

The day was getting away from me.

It was time to admit it. That the Father was right, again and always: the imagination is monstrous in the wrong hands—I knew those claws.

* * *

The first thing Narn does when I enter the shed is pour me a cup of thick, slow-steeped tea from a pot on a high table. She tells me to sit at a stool. I put the cooler bag on the table and sneeze in the musty air—oils from all the wool that had once piled in the shed, a ferrous whiff of blood from the backs of the sheep overlaid with other smells, the funk of moss and fungus piled high on the table, the sharp reek of cat piss—but I stay standing. On the floor beside the wood stove is a cat bed. I sneeze again. The old woman's hair is more like a clown's than a witch's—as orange as if she's ripped off a shred of sunset for a wig. Her skin is seamed and there are black streaks of grime in the leathery folds, but she regards me steadily from eyes once again filled with agate light, red and copper and a galactic green. They are the eyes of someone much younger—for a moment I get a glimpse of a ripe, pubescent nymph instead of the ageless hag before me.

"How bad is it?" she says.

I tell her it's bad. I tell her the Father gave Kai medicine to make her better but it just made her worse.

"Good twin loves too much."

"Loves me?"

Narn clucks disparagingly. "Who else?"

It's all my fault.

"Kai said your stories were her protection," I begin.

"No protection against a sister's love," Narn mutters. "No protection on earth."

"Well where then? There must be something!"

She reaches for her pestle, sniffs the powder and licks it off her nose with a tongue dry and forked as a lizard's. "Truth is only protection."

"I can't remember," I say. "I can't remember the truth."

"Can't? Or won't?"

I sit down on the stool, my short legs dangling above the greasy floor. I feel cheated. Imagine how different life would have been if I'd known from the beginning that I was a twofer. I would have had someone to tell about the snake girl behind the tree. Someone to teach me word games. Teach me how to deal with a witch. Now all I have is someone to save.

I unhappily gulp the tea. It smells terrible but tastes sticky and sweet. It makes me relax enough to focus, more than I really want to. A single bulb from the ceiling casts a queasy cone of light. Beneath it details pop, leaving the edges of the room in darkness. Through the shadows, I make out the angles of a camp bed. But my eye is drawn to the table. Scattered across it are brown paper scraps crawling with names—I register the words *betony* and *ocedar*—and scribbled equations, and liquid in beakers and chunks of resin in glass jars. The light picks up bones on a shelf above the stove, a dingo skull and an infant's crooked spine. Glimmering in the bad light is a bone-handled knife that I will later learn is a boline. There are containers filled with muddy powders, baskets of rubbery lichen whose names I have yet to learn—lurid curls of snot green, amber lobes and flat scales that look like flakes of rust. The huge gray cat comes in, dugs dragging on the floor. She leaps nimbly up onto the table and sniffs at a bowl in which float pustules of midnight blue. Her teats sway heavily.

"*Strigula nitidula*," the crone says. "Good shroom for bad blood."

"Are you a witch?" I say. "Or a goddess?"

Narn shrugs, her thin lips curved grimly downward: "Same difference."

"Why did you come to the Temple?"

She shakes her head and her agate eyes glitter. "Looking for bad blood."

"I know about that. Your sister, I mean. Did you find her?"

"Not yet. Maybe him not ready to be found."

I already hate the way she writes her own linguistic rules. I hate the way she talks in riddles. How she makes herself deliberately misunderstood, playing word games, playing with my head. My knuckles are white, and I want to hit something. I want to leave, at least. Get what I came for and be far away. But somehow I know that's no longer possible. "What will you do?"

"Pretend to be boss's bitch." She tops up the tea. "Boss lets witch stay, buy time to look for lost sister. Boss thinks good witch Narn will get him to Paradise with secret shroom and conjure words." That stomach-lurching eye-roll. "Narn not real name—Boss doesn't care. Boss says 'witch' like a sex-word. But Boss is witch's bitch." Her laugh is free, unsettlingly girlish. "Babies and mothers dying, only sexy witch can save babies and mothers too. Fewer graves to dig . . ." She dissolves in an unintelligible mutter that makes my spine tingle.

"Do you think your sister—the one who ran off—do you think she's still alive?"

She shakes her head—the stiff orange frizz gives off a golden syrup smell. The room is getting dark and I am shivering.

"Alive but not alive," she says, topping up the tea.

"Do you think the Father knows where she is? Is that why you stay?"

I know I'm asking too many questions and that there will never be enough time to find out everything I want—need—to know. The old woman shrugs miserably, looking more like a sad clown than a mad witch.

"Boss made sister wicked."

"Maybe she was wicked already." I am thinking of the snake girl in the playground, and when I look up, Narn's blood-clot eyes are fixed once again on mine.

"Crappy twin doesn't know what it doesn't know. Anyway, have to save twofer now." She rises from her stool.

"Both of us—Kai and me?"

"Wanted one, got two instead. One is a blessing. Two a curse."

Which is which witch? I gulp more tea, and more and more. A piece of myrtle cake has suddenly appeared on a plate. I take a big bite. I think I have the answer.

"If you save my sister," I say with my mouth full, "I'll tell you where I've seen yours."

"Sister gone." She shrugs, picks up a cup to take to the basin. My mouth is too dry to swallow the big bite of cake I've taken and my cheeks bulge. "Crappy twin has bitten off more than it can chew."

Dead candles litter the hut. Crumbling wax mountains and stunted melted glaciers frozen mid drip. The shroomy funk is everywhere and I feel it in my very veins. Narn is glancing at me sideways through the floating spores and half-light. My scalp itches with thoughts of the headless snake girl.

Chew, swallow, repeat.

"Honestly, I can show you," I say excitedly. "I'm good at finding lost things."

Even then I think I knew that I was exchanging a life for a life.

"Too late." She goes to open the stove door, nimble as a ferret. She shoves in some kindling and closes the door without lighting it. Her motions jerky, fast-forward. I watch the piled sticks burst into flame through the stove window. She holds the boline up to the light. "Crap twin or good twin. Make choice."

Horrified, I somehow manage to get to my feet. The floor feels spongy. "No way. No choice. I'd never leave Kai. Ever."

Narn nails me to the spot with her pointed finger. "Maybe *good twin* leaves crappy twin instead." Her voice catches, an airless, chalk-on-blackboard scritch. "Sisters don't always want same thing."

"Shuddup, witch! Save her! I'll do anything!" Shame washes over me. I see myself standing before the Assistant's prying eyes, his poking fingers, how I said I'd do anything—just make it quick—and Kai bursting in, and then no more. "Kai saved me from the Assistant. It's my fault. It should have been—"

"—trash baby," Narn whispers.

Me.

* * *

The doubled memory of the claws came to me halfway through that gray Saturday afternoon trying to make something out of the nothing of Narn's story. Suddenly I knew where I'd seen them before. On the high edge of the windowsill of Middles Bunk the first time Kai told her conjure tales, and every time after that. Hanging on, I imagined—I didn't yet know why I could imagine, only that I could, and did—several feet above the asphalt below. I never told Kai. I knew that if I did it would make them real. Those neither-in-nor-out, both-human-and-monster claws that were both fingers and toes—terrifyingly all the same length, nauseating. How I'd stared up at them, drooling, from my lonely bunk. I never told Kai because what I would have had to admit to was fear *of* and *for* anyone with the power to conjure them. My love for her became my wound, not just because it was greater than the love I had for myself, but also because even then I knew there was no protection from it.

However I tried to resist them, Narn's conjure tales worked their magic on me too.

By the Wednesday of the next FiFo class, my memories of Narn's story had taken on the sly, patchy quality of nightmare. Scraps of black feathers, the velvet of soiled ribbon and the taste of pennies—nothing that I could assemble into a beginning, middle or end. I nibbled on some vending machine pretzels. My cold had come back with renewed violence. My head was thick, my throat on fire. I doubted everything. I cursed everything, especially my memory. A broken, starving thing.

I had desultorily attended classes during the week. These included a biology lecture with a lab afterward, mainly showing us equipment I already knew how to use, and a geography class where we listened to a presentation on glacial river formation in Upper Slant. I thought of the vast terminal lake outside of Norman, thirty miles long and almost as wide, but less than a meter deep depending on the time of day. Formed millions of years ago when the earth's crust rose, blocking drainage from myriad river systems, it filled and emptied over hours and no one knows why. Evaporation and the wind blowing the water back on itself, maybe. Herds roamed across it, sheep and kangaroos. Flocks of black cockatoos nested in the trees at its edge. Brown snakes lurked in the shallows. I came back to hearing the lecturer saying something about icy claws carving great ridges out of the world. His world, not mine.

It was getting late. FiFo was in just over two hours. I had all but given up trying to make sense of Narn's story—didn't know whether to be more disappointed in her or myself. I had attempted to paint my nails, and chipped one of them on a drawer. I would not cry. I did cry. Blotting my mascara, I chose one of the dresses Narn and I had ordered together. I remembered the two of us taking a strange, sad pleasure in the bright colors and fashionable textures—she said the clothes reminded her of Tiff. "Cheap," she said, "but cheerful." I stepped into the sturdy brown shoes I inherited from Kai, the ones she used to unman the Assistant. They fit snugly because her feet were always a couple sizes bigger than mine. By the time she died, she was a head taller than me, too. Maybe that's why she could never meet my eyes.

The opaque sky hung low over the slate roofs of the old campus nestled behind the dippy tips of hemlock and spruce. The NyQuil I'd chugged made my hands shake over the keyboard. It was already four o'clock and I'd barely written a page.

The bridge by day was a flat military blue, like Kai's eyes when she was caught in a lie, even by omission. The Father's algorithm, his Forever Code, was supposed to make it impossible for us to lie, like a computer. But his fear of multiple births was that repetition would corrupt the compliance with which he'd impregnated us, and Kai was, as Marvin would say, the proof in the pudding. To be clear, it wasn't that she'd been caught in any lies. Nor had I proof beyond the exchange in our glances that she too could see the little snake girl in the playground. But there was something about how Kai *made herself* into more than she was that drew me to her, even before I knew she was my twin. Her acting out indicated a second self that she didn't know what to do with, just as my furtive yearnings and forbidden playmates betrayed memories not my own.

I think that the Father knew that she was a bad Made, just not why. Why some lady-bits refused to relinquish their horns, no matter what genetic pyrotechnics he performed on them. He took the unmakings badly. They cost him a pretty penny, the Matron said, although *pretty* probably wasn't the right word.

Kai's unmaking hurt most of all. Kai was the daughter he never had. The only Made who could beat him at his own game. Who managed to find words like "pyroxilic" and "abrogator" in word puzzles or on her tile rack, and who he loved for the very autonomy he had to kill her for. Testing her at everything from chess to crosswords, hoping (he said) to prove himself wrong. Seeing (he said) himself in her, the brilliance of *his* ART made manifest in *her* staggering potential to think on her feet. Such a waste, he said, to have to throw it all away. The Father hated waste.

But had no choice.

"This will hurt me a hell of a lot more than it will hurt you, you little bitch," he said, not at all like a real dad.

I actually pitied him.

What could I have done to stop it? Wobbling around the darkening dorm in Kai's old brown shoes that I grew into and never out of, I thought that even if I lived to be hundreds of years old, like Narn, it was a story I could never tell. And I had no other.

I scraped a brush through my knots. I hadn't turned on the lights in the room, and in the dark reflection my hair looked like one of the birds' nests the thylacine would bring home, back in the hills, bucket-shaped and knit with shit and dirt and purloined feathers. Over the crackle of the brush and through blocked ears, I suddenly heard a faint reverberation, a kind of drag on the carpet outside the door. But then a ghostly stain edged into the corner of the mirror, grew a little larger and stayed there. Slowly, gooseflesh prickling, I turned to see what it reflected. Someone had pushed something under the door. The light in the room was dim and I banged my ankle on one of Trudy's dumbbells. There, on the floor lay a notebook, slim and slightly smaller than an exercise book. I picked it up and leafed through it. The pages were blank. The fleshy cover smelled pungent and had an unpleasant feel to it. I opened it—in the watery light through the window, I saw indentations—as if some sheets had been written on and torn out, leaving their delicate imprint.

Scribbled in a jagged left-slanting hand across the front page were the words, *I hope this helps you find your story. M. p.s. No strings attached.*

This must have been the notebook Marvin used in FiFo before dropping out. I held it at arm's length. A gift? Gifts were new to me, and I didn't trust the whole proposition. There was even a pen ring on the back cover with a chewed-up pencil. Did I really want to inherit someone else's failure? Hadn't I enough of my own?

The pale blue pulse of the bridge washed across the paper with its strange ghostly marks. I went to my desk, took the pencil out of the pen ring and scratched it lightly across the first page. I could feel the ridges of Marvin's heavy hand beneath the feathery line that I drew and the sensation was immediately calming.

"I have to tell you something," Kai said before she vanished for good. *"Stop crying and listen. There is something that you need to remember."*

She'd been dead for months, clawed herself out of the earth with intel I didn't care about, didn't want to know—it would cost more than I could pay. I held the notebook, feeling the weightless scrawl of Marvin's soul in my hands, for which he'd asked nothing in return. A gift—no strings attached? I opened it and I began to write. And when I looked up two hours later it was almost dark, and I was ready for class.

I did not read my story over once I'd written it. Looking back now, I should have—everything would have been different. I think it was partly wanting to get out before Lara and Trudy got back. But mainly, I was so relieved at having written anything, that I didn't want to risk any further obstacles to my actually getting to FiFo. Something waited for me there, I knew. Something that was . . . everything.

I felt as nervous and excited about seeing Pagan again as Cinderella, I imagined, going to the ball. I ran water through my hair, pulled the wet tendrils into a frizzy bun at the top of my head. It made me look taller. And my mismatched eyes more noticeable. I stole some of Lara's makeup—armor, she called it—and smudged eyeliner into smoky black wings.

I opened the footlocker beneath my bunk with the secret combination. From a tattered purse I drew out a black feather tinged with red and tucked it between the leaves of the notebook. The tip of my fingers brushed against something warm in the purse (*a bird in the hand*) but I wasn't ready to take that out. Not yet. The scent of eucalyptus and dirt and unwashed blankets and urine and cheap lotion filled the room. The reek of the ravens. The smell of sisters.

Of bad blood.

CHAPTER 7
FIFO

I can hear the Father's ravens call from outside—Mades are not allowed out after dark. Narn's witchy way with pronouns is making me half crazy. There is a revolting cadence to her mutters, a rise and fall that finds its way from my ears to my bowel to my throat, addling thought. I can make out the syllables but not what they mean—they make my belly cramp and suddenly, when I look down, there is blood on the crotch of my shorts.

I yelp, and wipe drool from my lips. It can't be. The Father clipped our devil horns so we wouldn't bleed . . . there! The terror! The Father's ART must not have worked on me—the shame! I freeze, the blood tracing a roadmap under my shorts and down my thighs: I have a bad womb!

And then it all makes sense, and Narn's dirt floor lurches and I have to hold onto the table so I don't fall. Because if Kai and I are twins, she must have a bad lady-bit too, and what made her kick the Assistant in the thing was the devil himself!

The beast: it's in us both!

Without meaning to I begin a shrill high whistle at the back of my throat. The Father will kill us, bury us in the paddock, feed us to the wild dogs! Narn has begun loading glass vials into the bag's pouched compartments. Her head turns at my cry and her gaze drops to the darkening stain at my crotch. She drops the jar. It smashes on the floor. The cat hisses.

"Double-trouble," Narn says, stepping over the mess. "Boss's ART won't work on double-yolker."

She quickly rummages in a drawer and comes up with what looks like a white bullet with a string, and she tells me to push that all the way into the hole between my legs. She makes a shoving motion with her finger.

"Kai too?" I say.

"Same-same."

She points in the direction of the outhouse, tells me to wash up and that I'll find a change of clothes there.

"But we're not meant to be out after dark." I feel like I'm swallowing my own voice. "The ravens will tell the Father."

"Ravens won't tell."

She clicks her teeth and an inky face appears, hooded, in the window frame. Beneath the hood are bloodshot eyes raw as meat.

Narn inclines her head at the creature and waves a crinkled paper bag for me to bring back the dirty clothes.

Miserable with shame and nausea, I shuffle to the door, sticky streaks down my thighs, dripping everywhere, clots between my toes. I am too ashamed to cry. Too scared of the pain and color to worry about the creepy hooded person outside. I walk across the porch, not looking to the right or the left and aware of those sores of eyes at my back, mindful of the tread behind me. Up close the creature is bigger than I thought, and broader and more human too, their shoulders sharp jaunts of bone beneath the voluminous hood. Even in my misery, my flesh crawls. I feel a clinging kind of awe, a curiosity as to the actual shape of it.

Is this—could it be—the other sister?

The path jumps in my eyes in the deceptive light of dusk. I follow it to the outhouse behind the shed. I close and lock the door, checking for spiders. The whitewashed boards are scrubbed and swept and beside the toilet is an upturned wooden crate with a pair of my sister's underpants and her shorts on top, both freshly washed and folded as if waiting for me. My heart sticks in my mouth at the thought that she went through the same thing, has been bleeding all along, bearing the shame and fear alone, no one to share it with. I would have taken her pain if she'd given it to me—I would have made it mine. I begin to cry. Why didn't she tell me?

To protect me, or herself?

I wash as best as I can. I finger the plug into my hole with a shudder, wash the blood off. How am I even doing this? I step into the fresh underpants, feeling the secret unfurl inside me. With every cramp I feel a surge of strange power, Kai's strength flowing into me. I pull her shorts on, and they smell of sun and eucalyptus, and the tears flow anew. I'm not doing this. I am. Big baby tears. I will tell her when I get back. Look, I will say, we're the same. Different from everyone else except each other.

I *will* save you.

I put my soiled clothes in the paper bag. Outside the ravens roost heavy-lidded in the branches, tatty wings limp. The weird sister's hooded head swivels to follow my passing, down the path beneath an indigo sky sprinkled with dim stars. Through the window I can see the old woman lighting the candles. But when I get there, the inside of the shed is darker than the night outside. The huge gray cat snoozes in a bed by the fire. The stove is pulsing heat and in a blackened steel pot, something bubbles. Instead of fungus, now the whole room smells like burnt baked beans.

"How did you make the ravens sleep like that," I ask, "if you're not a witch?"

"Love," she says.

"Who is that? Your other sister? What's wrong with them?"

She has removed the cloth cap from her hair which is matted and tousled, a pallid echo of the flames in the stove. "Don't ask," she says.

But she is busy. Without the cap she looks younger, capable and strong as a farmgirl. Her garnet eyes fix on me and she holds out her hands for my clothes, opens the stove window and throws them on the fire. She passes me the insulated bag filled with the Father's order. "Give to Big Boss. Not to little boss, not ever." Then she presses a small vial filled with powder into my hand. "Take this much"—she indicates the top knuckle of her thumb—"in water every day. Make the bleeding stop. Tell no one."

She gives me a paper packet. "Tea for sister's pain."

"Will it stop the unmaking?"

She looks grim. "Slow him down, maybe."

"The Father will know about the blood—he always knows."

She gives me three more of those white plugs. "Bury away from dogs and pigs."

I wonder where Kai hides the medicine to stop *her* blood. Where she buries her plugs. My belly cramps and I buckle, darkly elated that the Father's code didn't work on us. Kai and I can and do lie and imagine and tell secrets because . . . we are different from everybody else.

Except each other.

My mind is racing. Later I will learn that the tea activates a dormant (or damaged) part of my brain unused to asking questions and that questioning does unpredictable things to our artificial layer. It puts it into overdrive and my mind, riding shotgun in my runaway brain, calculates that the hollow tubing of my metal bed frame will do nicely for a hiding place.

Narn takes the thumb that she used to measure my medicine and makes a slicing motion across her throat, leaving a vapor trail of sparkles that float away toward the ceiling.

"But—"

She shoves a black stump of candle at me. "Burn in the window when it's time."

"*Taaa-taa*," the ravens call.

"You have to get us *both* out of here now." I steady myself. "Us. Not just her, not just me. Us."

Behind her the cat sits up in its bed and starts licking its ass.

"Burn candle," Narn says. "Don't forget."

* * *

After I wrote the story in Marvin's notebook, I wound my hair into a bun, pulled on a skirt and my thin coat and raced toward the bridge. I balked at the spot where the spiked claws—neither human nor animal—had crooked themselves around the rail. They were not there now—but I knew better than to trust either my faulty imagination or my crappy memory. Best just to pretend they never were. My feet kept moving and if my racing brain calibrated two dark smears at the lower edge of the railing, it stored the image for a rainy day.

I did not slow until I got to the other side.

A velvet mystery hung over the cobbled streets of Wellsburg, and it wrapped around me like a cloak. My whole being leaned into the history lurking around the corners, behind the walls, the listing road signs. My soul dipping into a cool clear stream of a reality that I could steal and make my own. I breathed in the *truth* of this place—smells of coffee and expensive perfume, and sounds of music and peals of laughter—and felt the cracks inside me fill with possibility.

I smiled.

Backlit water tumbled in the fountain at the center of the Quad. It was warmer on this side of the river, similar to September in the Rim, balmy yet with an edge to the breeze. The fickle nature of the weather had revved up my cough, and a few people looked up as I passed, curious maybe about what kind of weak constitution could be unwell on such a night as this? One look at me, at what I was, told them all they needed to know: cult survivor—endangered species. *Their* faces glowed with health and flawlessly applied makeup—lipstick that never smeared, mascara that never ran. Their expensive, casually assembled couture clung like a second skin. I felt like a plucked bird, a bad joke with my war paint and kohl-black wings, and I kept my head down.

There were some others like me. Mades and other special-program students from the Tower Village, dancing clumsily to and from electives or from jobs they had in taverns and shops, keeping to the shadows, insisting on their own planned obsolescence.

I didn't want to be a bad joke.

I passed under the maple and through the granite arch to the Writing and Culture Office. Pagan had said that she would be in class. I was counting on that. Walking through the streets of Wellsburg had jangled my nerves and mixed up the words of the story in my head. I wanted to make Pagan believe in me—see that I *was* real enough to keep. Invisible in the Blood Temple behind Kai's larger-than-life protection, only half real in the Starvelings where Narn never forgave me for being the wrong half—all I wanted was to dangerously *imagine* myself through the gaze of another. To prove that Narn was right, after all, not to throw me in the trash.

Distant music played from the Music and Technology rooms. Someone was practicing a strange diminished chord over and over again. I climbed some stairs and passed a landing illuminated by a huge leadlight window that depicted Eve leading a shamefaced Adam from Eden. Laughter tickled down from the level above and I balked. Kai's ugly shoes echoed on the stairs. The laughter turned to something else. A moan. The stunted arpeggios from the music room quickened. Adam buried his face in his hands.

I wandered down a wide hallway lined with sconces. The ceiling receded into shadow. I smelled expensive weed, and the moan turned to a sob, getting louder as I neared the restroom. I kept walking. Room 225 was to my left. The door was ajar and I stood on the threshold looking into a small classroom dominated by an oaken table which students sat around with typewritten sheets and note-books like mine. The walls were of age-defying stone and a stern old-fashioned clock hung behind the instructor, the second-hand juddering. I identified two other Mades, but otherwise it was all Regulars. Pagan lounged with her friends, a gaggle of swans with long necks and lush feathers that caught the light. I sat down facing a high window against which the maple branches flung themselves in the rising wind. Sweat pooled at the small of my back.

The instructor was a nervous Made a few years older than me, with emer-ald streaks in her hair and a small fierce freckled face. She wore a department store Bohemian skirt and earrings that jangled. She nodded at me, checked my name on the roll, and explained the workshopping process for the benefit of the "latecomers." We would read from our work, she said, and the class would offer their critique, beginning with the student to her left, and concluding with feedback from Jacinta herself. The other two Mades and I avoided eye contact. There was a quota, but I didn't know how many places were left, and I wondered if they did either. Were we all competing for the same thing—protection? I felt something in me rise to the ugliness of the game.

There were only females in the class. No males. My heart sunk. Was there no damn place in this whole campus where one could meet a nice young drover, take him upstairs into a room with faded wallpaper like in the Five-Legged Nag? Unbutton his jeans before he knows what you are?

Someone read a chapter from the start of a novel about the end of the world. Another student read a poem about antique tools. The instructor made notes in a yellow pad and everyone commented on the pieces, lies mostly, how much they enjoyed it and how they couldn't wait to read more. The Regulars were looking aggressively bored or were on their phones, and even then I knew that Jacinta couldn't have stopped them if she tried. Everything about their attitude suggested that they were less students than paying customers, with a line of credit as long as their necks—she served them. We all did. This was the tomorrow we were being re-Made for. I felt my hopes plunge, my power drain.

Pagan had not acknowledged me. The readings were muffled beneath the roaring in my ears. I was rigid with anxiety. A few Regulars read stories about bad dates and true detectives and dead mothers, none of which we Mades knew anything about. I was to read last, and by then Pagan was asleep with her head on her hands and her sandy quiff flopped over her eyes. I almost felt a sense of relief. At least this way, she couldn't laugh at me. If she laughed at me, I thought I might die.

I didn't know whether to stay sitting or stand up. I stayed sitting, kept my eyes on Marvin's notebook, without really seeing it. At first when I began to haltingly read, nothing happened. I knew my lips were moving, but in my anxiety I could hear no sound. Faces turned to me, pale and tense. I was making no sense. It was all just mumbo-jumbo, a bad joke after all. I heard a titter, saw someone swiping the screen of their phone. I stopped rushing. Tried to slow down to make space for the out-of-joint meaning.

Once I asked Kai what we were, exactly. What the fragments of our being amounted to. "Tell me and we'll both know," she'd said.

The story I read was and wasn't the same as Narn told me on the bridge. It was both more than that, and less . . . There is a man with a raven's head pulled over his own like a mask. He uses his beak to peck the faces off little girls in their sleep. They wake up every morning with something missing—a-tongue-a-tooth-an-eye, and every night the man-raven returns one thing—a nose haphazardly affixed to an earhole, an eyebrow ripped away and replaced with an upper lip—only to take something else instead.

"Their eyeballs," I finished very slowly, "squish like grapes between my beak."

Silence slammed down on the room. The clock stopped ticking and it was no longer a clock but a map. Across the map, place names—*Demos, Kokylus, Akheron, Elysion*—materialized in symbols I didn't know I knew. The play of moon-cast shadows through the maple branches bounced the map across the faces in the room, refracted contour and form-lines with no earthly reference, the blur of tongue-twister toponyms, impossible sea levels and nightmarish elevations—a shifting restless map showing directions to nowhere. Pagan smiled in her sleep. Another student rushed from the room and there was a bang of the lavatory door, moaning that I suddenly realized I had not so much heard as foreseen. Jacinta, her freckled forehead sheened with sweat, jumped up from her chair and the markings were stark across her face.

"Stop!" she cried.

A door banged again. Open or shut. Giant wings flapped past the window casting the room in sudden utter darkness, and when they passed in the blink of an eye, the map had gone. The clock was just a clock. The faces of my classmates just pale, stunned faces.

"Why should we listen to this?" Jacinta asked, trembling.

"If someone lived it," Pagan answered without raising her head. "We should at least be able to listen to it."

CHAPTER 8
DIRTY BERT'S

The night of my disastrous reading at FiFo, a Made was mauled on the Wellsburg riverbank and was now in the hospital fighting for her life. Everyone in Dirty Bert's the next day was talking about some ragged blade that she never saw coming. In response, bridge curfew had been moved forward to nine p.m.

Marvin was already slurring his words, "You're drawn to lichen because it's not a single organism, but a symbiosis."

"Also, the longest living thing on earth," I said brightly, trying not to spill the drinks I'd ferried through the nervous crowd. "It can grow on anything. Soil, ice, steel, plastic, air. The bacteria element—the photobiont—takes energy from the sun, which it provides for the fungus element—the mycobiont. And in return the mycobiont gives the photobiont a place to live. It's speciating without reproduction, see, a two-way deal."

I'd managed while talking to place our drinks on the table, and to slide along the booth opposite him.

"Mutualistic as fuck." Marvin gave me a sideways smile. "And this Narn of yours concocted potions from lichen to enable the Father to make his Mades? Whose side did you say she was actually on?"

"The actual word is compounding. And the lichen didn't enable the Father. It just fed the fantasy that he was creating his own species—without the need for actual women. And while he was distracted with that, Narn sowed the seeds of his destruction."

"Bwaaahaaa. But he still needed actual eggs," Marvin said. "From women."

"Maybe not for long," I said. "He had his Forever code. And he had . . . the ravens. Or Narn let him think he had."

I had not thanked him for the notebook. I didn't know how. I wanted to tell him I didn't need it now. I wanted to tell him I'd failed FiFo. Failed him. Failed myself. But I was worried that, like Narn, he wouldn't be surprised.

I ordered fries which were terrible, but he ate them anyway. His stubble was darker than his hair, which would have turned white from shock well before puberty. His flirty smile did not match the deep sadness in his eyes—they ratcheted open in the dimly lit bar, the pupils black as pitch.

"Honestly? I don't think I can ever go back there," I said. "To FiFo. But I can't see myself lasting here an extra semester, either."

He licked some ketchup from his patchy mustache. The TVs played their silent gags, and the edgy crowd was overly boisterous and spilling drinks and yelling in each other's ears. The weather had turned nasty. A cold rain fell, and I regretted not bringing a coat—my chest rattled every time I breathed. "Was it dreadful?"

I shivered. "The worst. People freaking out, running to the bathroom. Others laughing like it was a joke. Or that I'd started a war."

"Maybe it was. Maybe you did."

I told him about the hellish map conjured from the innocent wall clock. I didn't tell him about the dark wings flapping at the window.

"The psychology major in me suggests that might have been a shared illusion. Like collective hysteria."

I fiddled with my straw.

"The South Rim native in me suggests something else," he said. "That the map was conjured by some spell your Narn wrote into the story. Or that you did, unconsciously."

"Unconscious or not, the TA accused me of triggering the more vulnerable classmates, the survivors."

"I told you there's a quota, Meera. Everyone's fighting for the same spots."

"She warned me to balance my artistic freedom with the appropriate sensitivity next time. But Pagan liked it. I think."

"Well then." He sat back against the booth. "You got in."

"What do you mean?"

"The Regulars are all that matters." Marvin downed his shot. "The end."

I thought of the poor Made weeping in the bathroom, and saw that smile playing across Pagan's mock-sleeping face. The end?

"All of the TAs at Wellsburg are Mades," Marvin explained. "Not the deans and professors of course—our memory issues naturally disqualify us from tenure-track positions—but most of the lesser teaching jobs, not to mention all of the admin staff. That's the same on both campuses. Everyone serves the Regulars. Do you really want to get into this, is the question you need to ask yourself. Or are you better to leave FiFo alone, and stay another semester at the end of the program? There'll be others like you."

I looked around the soulless bar, the streamlined hell of the Corso through the window.

"There's no one here like me." A boisterous caravan of Mades trundled past.

He pointed a finger at his ear, shook his head.

"You said do I really want to get into it," I yelled. "Get into what?"

"The struggle." He leaned in closer. "The struggle between those Regulars who are for the Redress Scheme because it provides labor, cannon fodder, funding, test subjects—and those against it because it lowers the tone, muddies the water, threatens the status quo. Transforms a remote campus down into . . . this." He looked around the room, blew a strand of silver hair off his eyes. "But it's a pretend struggle. Just to distract us while the real power tightens its grip."

"The scheme," I said, "behind the scheme."

"Bingo."

I just wanted to get drunk. How did Marvin keep up? I watched as a DJ took her place in a corner of the bar. Her movements betrayed her as a Made but her get-up was a pretty good imitation of the bespoke style favored in Wellsburg—a black crepe mini-dress embroidered with sequins over silk stockings and a garter belt, platform boots. She had pink hair fringed with black. Within minutes she was obscured by strobing hands waving in the air.

My head hurt. "I can't even remember what my story was about."

He lifted an eyebrow. "You wrote it down though, right? In the notebook I gave you? That's important."

"Yeah, yeah. Because of the memory glitch. But what came out was different. Like it had a life of its own. But it wasn't real, Marvin. I never lived that. How could I—and still be here?"

I realized with a start that was the point. He watched me. Waited for this to compute. And just in case it didn't, he said, "Either you lived it and survived, which you say is impossible. Or you lived it and didn't survive, which means you're not here. When you clearly are. Or . . ."

"Or . . . it didn't happen."

"But it could have," he said, "which is all that matters. Like pornography, kind of. Want makes it live. Want makes it wet."

I thought of how Narn's stories conjoined love and fear, life and death—impossible twins or twinned impossibilities or some obscenity in between. Neither existence nor nonexistence, but a bridge conjured between the two.

Be careful what you wish for.

I said that I didn't know if that's what Pagan had in mind.

He smiled a catty smile. "I guess you'll find out soon enough."

And then he was off in his thoughts, wherever he went, leaving me alone. Sitting beside him, but he wasn't there. Until he was.

"Let's get out of here," he said like he always did. His silver hair flashed white in the strobing light as I followed him from the bar. We walked back to our Towers along the thronging Corso.

"Where do you go?" I asked. "When you slip away like that?"

"Where no one can find me, I guess."

"Well, I'm just wondering who's got your back."

He smiled and draped a heavy arm over my shoulder. The longed-for physical contact was like an electric shock. "I'm there but I'm not there," he said. "The me that stays and the me that goes. We keep an eye out for each other."

Maybe he told me because he knew I'd understand, and maybe I did.

We stopped in a no-man's-land between two of the Towers, and he rummaged in his satchel, his face lit blue as the Aspergillus mold that would grow on Narn's dried lichen during the rainy season. "Listen and learn, Dorothy: if enrollments improve across all the electives, Wellsburg will soon be able to reassure its investors and the governors that it doesn't need the Redress Scheme, in which case it might get shut down, or moved to a different institution. Meanwhile, the Regulars are dependent on it for funds to restore the clock tower, build a new gym behind Old Dorm Hall, the geeky graduates they've been trying to lure to their computer labs—there is a worry among some factions that the Redress Scheme is making Wellsburg and all it stands for, dependent on it."

"So?"

"So, a Wellsburg dependent on the Redress Scheme is a Wellsburg dependent on . . ."

I stared at him. "Us?"

"Bingo. The horror! And while some factions are okay with that, others are not. Surly counter-revolutionary forces for whom mutualism—economic or natural—is an anathema, especially if it also benefits the great unwashed."

"Mades."

He had a glass pipe this time and drew on it quickly. I inhaled the heady bite of cheap hashish. "They don't want us here, Dorothy. The Pagans of the world. However they act as though they do, it's a lie."

"Not even our stories? Not even fakelore? She said . . ."

"FiFo is the brainchild of an alumna called Sasha Younger—she's part of the Writing and Culture faculty but more important, she's founding family. She has no intention of sitting back and watching Wellsburg, with its history and patrons and secrets, become a decrepit snooze town hooked up to Redress oxygen. We're a quick fix, Meera. Just so long as you know. When they're done with you, you'll be . . ."

Trash baby.

"Dead meat," he said. Thanks to the Father, obsolescence is built into our system, he said. They needed us now but they wouldn't always, "by which time we'll have been seamlessly repurposed, Amen."

"Hacked, you mean."

"Gone either way."

The mica glittered and we skirted lines around the food chains. We walked beneath the fake Zen sign above the twenty-four-hour yoga studio. The rain had lightened but it was still freezing. We slowed, and at the side of my eye I noticed vertical cuts on the inside of his arms. I thought of those snapping crocodile jaws, what he'd had to forget, but how the shame would snap at him as long as he lived.

"What's your plan?" I asked.

We'd arrived at my building.

"Survival," he said. "Where there's life there's hope and all that snappy crap."

"What if this isn't it?" I hesitated, searching for the right words. "I mean I get that what Mades want right now is a life free of suffering and they'll do anything for it. But I have no intention of being dead meat, Marvin. And I know you don't either."

He made that snapping motion with his hands. "My idea of survival—"

He held the pipe out to me and I shook my head, surprising myself.

"—and yours, are different. Just be careful, is all I'm saying. Make sure that your stories are as smart as you are."

No one had ever said I was smart before. I invited him up to my room. "You haven't lived until you've tried Narn's shroom brew."

"Another night," he said, turning to go.

"Wait," I held his arm. "Marvin, someone accessed my Redress application form and altered it. I have to find answers before they find me."

There were raindrops on his eyelashes. "The answers already know where you are," he said gently. "Answers always do."

I trembled a little, knowing he was right. That didn't stop me wanting, wishing I could magic us both back to the Rim, back to not where it all began, but somewhere in the fleeting safety of the middle.

"Let's just get through this and get back to South Rim where there is a life waiting," he said, entwining his fingers in mine. "A life broken but not beyond fixing, and *made* for us."

"When will that be?" I said. "In ten years or more, you'll be stuck. You'll be a hard-drinking social worker in some Upper Slant prison."

He nodded, deadpan. "With debts and an incriminating dating app profile to stop me from going into politics."

"You'd be a terrible politician, Marvin."

He dropped my hand. "Maybe. Stay in the blind spot. Out of trouble. And if it doesn't kill us, we may just get home again."

The rain grew heavier. Maybe that was one time I should have kept my mouth shut, but Kai always said I could never read a room.

"Do you know why the Father had to have a robot to insert the almost invisible neural mesh laced with his code into our embryonic brains?" I asked, trying and failing to keep the urgency out of my voice.

"Rhetorical question?"

"The human brain pulses with the beat of the heart, Marvin. Badoom. Badoom. All those blood vessels pumping blood through the brain make the neurons jump around like tree branches in the wind." I paused to tighten the scarf around my neck like a noose. "Before the bot, the Father's most skilled human surgeons couldn't track the movements of our brains sufficiently to prevent bleeding on insertion of electrodes less than 350 nanometers in diameter—that's the diameter of the wavelength of visible light, Marvin. *Insertion killed us at the gate.* Or later in utero, when our brains would hemorrhage and we'd die, killing the surrogates along with. Or even later, the nurseries filled with brain-dead babies, no use to anyone. The Father all but bankrupted, was never getting back to Paradise, not without that robot."

Marvin was smiling sweetly, too broadly. Tears glistened on his cheeks.

I kept going, long past my best-before: "You . . . you talk about the power of blind spots, Marvin, of betting a piece of our soul on some kind of running game. But how can we find room to run in the blind spot of the world when it is never in the one place?" I felt my cheeks grow hot with tears, too. Stupid baby tears. "When every time we think we have found a place to insert ourselves, to replicate and thrive, we find ourselves drowning in the tears of the brain?"

He shoved his hands deeper into his coat pockets. "*A*, tears aren't in the actual brain, and *B*, I don't have your courage, Dorothy."

I shook my head and stamped my foot at the same time and he lifted one corner of his mouth in mock surprise.

"It's the opposite of courage, Marvin. It comes from the same place as the broken word on my Redress Form. *Fear.* Isn't that why I'm here?"

* * *

The machinery from the military base is quiet. The launch pads look like gaunt giants with their arms raised to the purple sky. A bat swoops, chasing food. I run all the way back to the Temple, flanked by the awakened ravens. I take the shortcut across the edge of the old town near the school instead of around it—and the ravens shriek their disapproval. It's a ghost town, an artificial place made for a purpose and abandoned when that purpose no longer mattered. I regret going so close to the town, this close to the weapons facility where we are forbidden to go, especially after what Kai did to the Assistant's man-thing. The Father is worried that word will get out and it will be bad for business. My heart races and sweat runs into my eyes. The devil's horns butt against my insides like a goat. The dead janitor lurches out of the doors of the abandoned pub, the top of his head missing.

He looks right through me.

When I finally get back to the Middles Bunk, Matron emerges from her office to make a mark against my name for breaking curfew, but I tell her the "witch" made me wait. No one makes a mark against the name of the witch—because that's what the Father needs to believe she is. I get that even the Father needs someone to believe in, except what he mostly believes in is himself. It is his own power he worships, his place at the center of things—alone in the Paradise of his own skull—where calling Narn a "witch" is just his way of erasing her.

And her way of letting him think that he has.

Matron doesn't question my story, because she believes that we are made without the capacity to lie. Matron doesn't know that I bear the mark of the beast deep in my belly—which I confirm to my shame, by lying to her by omission.

Maybe I am learning. Already Narn's potions, her words, are making me into something else. Or maybe it's because I bleed.

She goes back into the office to make a quick call and when she hangs up, she tells me that the Father is waiting for his delivery, and I must take it to him before I'm allowed to see Kai in the infirmary. But first I have to clean myself up. She points at the bird shit on one shoulder and the feathers in my hair. "You're a disgrace," she says.

If she only knew.

She sends me to the showers and on the way, I duck into the bunkroom. It is empty—everyone is at dinner. I quickly shake some of Narn's powder into my mouth, skipping the dissolving-in-water part. It burns going down. My eyes water. Matron has left a cup of tea on a shelf and I quickly swallow the dregs. She's left her matches and cigs there too. I swipe both. She'll never suspect any of us—noncompliance unthinkable in a Made. She'll just think she misplaced them somewhere.

It's amazing what you can get away with in the blind spot of the world.

In order to slide my vial of powder up into the metal tubing of my bunk I need to lift the whole thing, which is not as hard as I think it is going to be. Mades are born weak, but I'm no ordinary Made. I quickly lift one corner, tuck the glass vial up into the hollow frame and it's done. In the shower, I wash myself and change the plug. There is nowhere to bury anything away from the gaze of the ravens, and I can't risk having the evidence on me, so I hold the used plug under the hand drier until it dries enough to burn, at least until it is nothing but a charred pile of goop, and I flush that down the toilet. I light the cigarette and wave it around to cover the smell—one of Matron's underlings will get in trouble for smoking in the shower room, which is strictly forbidden—passive smoke plays havoc with our delicate respiratory systems.

I am now ready to see the Father—as ready as I'll ever be.

The Father spends Wednesdays in the library. It is accessible only via an overpass between the science and the art block. No one is allowed through unless they have business with him, and Kai has been back and forth many times. Letting my connection with her guide me, I climb the stairs and make my way through the empty art rooms, their wide windows boarded over or shattered. Paint spatters the floor. Clay figures crumbled beside a kiln now home to rats. I start at a naked man at the edge of my eye. A ghost. I bite my tongue. But it is only a plastic life-size skeleton with "Yorrick is a cock," written across its forehead.

The overpass is at the top of a landing where I should have emerged if I'd taken the stairs I was supposed to take. I am already out of breath. I hesitate at the opening, my hand sweaty on the handles of the cooler. It is in almost total darkness. Stars flicker dimly through begrimed high windows along the length of the walkway. I take my first step across the threshold. I want to move quickly but I am mesmerized by the walls—scrawled with so much graffiti that they look three-dimensional, as if some of the images, finding no room on the surface, have had to float above it. There are names everywhere—Emily and Nadia and Lou and Cam and Ollie and Angus—in hearts in circles in thought balloons. Messages about love and hate and homework and parents and priests and cats. There are curses: *Eat Shit and Die, Emily. Rot in Hell. C U in my dreams.* There are luminous floating faces, and breasts and skulls and giant eyes and man-things. By the light of the stars, I make out the word, *Help!* and another that says, *Eternity.* The floor below my sneakers is covered with debris. A transparent numbat minces past as if I wasn't there. Am I? I watch the numbat with the feeling of being slowly blown apart. Cigarette butts and glass pipes, and bottles and condoms, a number of decaying backpacks, water bottles, paperbacks, a stroller and a toilet bowl filled with the dried black corpses of kittens. I am in a sweat by the time I get to the other side, my belly knifing. Maybe my blood will overflow and the devil will smell it and I'll never get back to save my sister like I promised.

I push through double doors that say *LIBRARY.* They open into a large circular room with a high reception desk painted across the front with *LI AR.* A gum-chewing Assistant moves out from behind the desk and reaches his hand out for the pharmaceuticals. I want nothing more than to shove the bag at him and run, but Narn told me not to give it to any of the little bosses. So I shake my head, and this must be something he's used to because he blows a limp bubble and tells me to follow him.

I have heard about the library and I glance behind me but all the shelves are empty. There are piles of books tumbled on the floor, their pages crushed and spines broken. The Assistant takes me through a door behind the reception desk and leads me up some stairs, then stops at a landing. He points at another flight leading up.

"Roof," he says, moving his gum wad across his open mouth. I begin to climb, feeling his eyes on my bottom.

I step through a bright light and onto the roof. It's a hot summer night, and Crux is stark in the sky, white nails on a starry cross. The smell of guano bites at my throat, and I smell cologne too. My eyes adjust to what is unmistakably before me. A vast cage as big as the bunkroom crowded with ravens. One of them lazily stretches out long ragged wings, giving me a glimpse of crimson.

"*Corvus,*" says a squishy voice and when I turn, it is the Father. Oh my Father. I squint against the blue glow of his T-shirt, his big white teeth. I hold out the medical bag, but he doesn't take it. My heart is beating like a train. I might faint.

"*Corvus* being the crow genus, and *coronoides* meaning crowned or corolla-ed, referring to the neck ruffle that sets apart the species."

He steps into the rectangle of light from the door. He is very tall, over two and a half meters, with ruddy skin and dun-colored braids that he nourishes with Narn's rosemary and henna solution. He isn't smiling, although with his rugged bush clothes and the Akubra he holds in broad hands, he looks like he should be.

"Until now *Corvus coronoides*—the Rim Raven—was the smartest bird on the planet. But what you see here is a new breed I created—*Corvus chimaeralis*—a passerine-AI hybrid, genetically engineered using an Augmented Reproductive Technology similar to what we use on you lot. Implanted with neural mesh much less complex of course, a fraction of the electrodes, and controlled using sensor technology—couldn't have sentience in an unmanned aerial vehicle now, could we?"

I shake my head. Feathers rustle.

"Still, there are some pivotal differences with standard UAV capabilities that I'm rather proud of. For a start they allow for discrete, like pretty much silent monitoring—no motor on these birdies. Secondly, they're capable of extra-long flight times—no batteries required either. Three: easy to train, because, well, they're so fucking smart. Four: real-time monitoring and coordination due to the hermetically sealed motherboard that enables a direct data transfer to me here." He points to a screen on his watch. "Five: tough in any weather, well you'd think that of course. And six: payload flexibility, which is the kicker because we can strap any kind of ordinance or what have you, onto the birdy, so to speak, and they wouldn't miss a beat."

My mind flies back to Narn putting a whole flock of ravens to sleep with a click of her tongue. What did that look like, I wonder, on the Father's watch? Did it go all staticky while I was running around in the dark, with telltale blood down my legs? Did Narn replace that image with another? Maybe some fake footage from a musical or a bible cartoon like we're allowed to watch sometimes on Sunday afternoons after the sermon.

But no, probably not a cartoon.

What I get is that the Father thinks of the birds as an extension of him. His eyes and ears, and even his brain. And maybe even more than that. His soul. His seed. One thing is clear to me, even at twelve years old: without the ravens the Father would be utterly alone. Without the birds, his kingdom would be like a terminal lake, sloshing in his skull with no way in or out.

Narn loves the ravens like a mother. The Father needs them more than God. That's the difference.

"Pound for point, these lovelies pack more neurons in their tiny brains than primates." He turns to the cage, puts his hand through the bars and a huge ruffled raven—looking more like a chimp than a bird—lands on his furry arm and turns her head so that she can regard me from one eye, and so that I can admire the light-eating curve of her beak.

"This is Dani," the Father says. "My best girl. Aren't you, Dan? She has a brain structure that's analogous to the mammalian neocortex, the part we use for higher order functioning like conscious thought, sensory perception, spatial reasoning and language. In the wild she can not only spot a carcass from half a klick, but also communicate its location to the flock. And that's without the implant."

Dani fluffs her wings, angles her head at me. A breeze blows a big black feather into my hair. I pluck it out, tuck it in my pocket. The Father absently frowns.

"There's some rufescence in their feathers that we can't account for, and that we can't seem to breed out, bit of a shame about that. Something unnatural about magenta, pink, what have you? Something a little womanly."

I desperately jiggle the bag so that the vials and bottles jangle in their pouches. The huge bird starts, ducks her head and plunges her beak into the Father's arm.

He screams, pulls his arm out of the cage. "Holy fuck!"

She floats onto a dislocated tree limb in the giant cage. "Ah-ahhh," she cries. "Aah-aah."

"You scared her!" he says, turning on me. A squiggle of bright blood writes something illegible across his forearm.

My lips quiver in reply.

"Speak, Made!"

"I have your delivery, Father," I say, hearing my voice crack below the rustling of feathers.

He looks down in surprised recognition at the bag of meds in my hand. "You're the one they sent instead of the Unmade? She's taking a hell of a time to expel her bits—knew she would, unruly little bitch too big for her boots. I brought you cunts in. I can take you out. And that's a promise."

He gestures to the table for me to put the delivery down and then he turns away as if I don't exist and never have.

* * *

The Corso was freezing. "What's the notebook really for?" I said, trying to change the subject. "The cover feels gross. Like skin."

"It's vellum," Marvin said. "Calfskin. Fake of course, but you'd never know."

"Even grosser." My teeth chattered.

"Did you notice the markings on the pages themselves?" He moved closer to me, sharing his warmth.

"The indentations, you mean? From your stories? I can't make them out."

"*You* can't," he said, almost in my ear. "But your brain can. At least the digital layer can. And they're not words, Meera. It's code. Maybe it'll form some kind of firewall around the part of you that's human. That's the plan anyway."

"Protection?"

"Where you're going you'll need all you can get."

I wanted to thank him. And I wanted to hit him. Marvin's kindness confused me and I didn't know how to take it. The drovers and shearers I had led upstairs at the Five-Legged Nag back in Norman—that was mainly about friction. I had no experience with boyfriends, or with friends, period, unless you counted the thylacine.

The Father's chip in our brain was a world unto itself. Converting his coded constraints to action potentials, spikes that sent messages to our cortex, a different message depending on the shape of the neuron for which the code had on-chip detection. The organic film substrate made of a substance exactly like tears. We knew what we were—but it was a knowledge that gave us the opposite of power, whatever that was.

"After I read my story, Pagan said something like if I had lived something, then everyone should be able to listen to it. But what if it was all a lie, not because I hadn't lived it, but because I couldn't remember it?"

"Or didn't want to? You don't have to, Meera. None of us do."

"I have to try," I said. "For my sister's sake."

He put his hands on my shoulders. "What happened in the Blood Temple stays in the Blood Temple."

I could smell the wool of his sweater. I had to crane my neck to meet his pussy-willow eyes.

"You know that's not true. We both know that."

"Good night, Meera."

He bent to kiss me on the forehead, like someone twice his age, an uncle or the big brother he'd never be, but I moved my face at the wrong moment, so the kiss landed on my mouth. It was an awkward moment between us. I waited until I was inside before I wiped it off.

CHAPTER 9
REAL DEAL

At two on Monday morning a text came in from an unknown number. I looked across at my sleeping roommates, fearful that the notification had woken them. The rule was that all phones had to be on silent in the rooms, but I had gotten so few texts and none at night, so I hadn't bothered to switch modes.

The text said: *Hi this is Pagan, from class. *Loved* your story. Meet me in the Quad tomorrow at noon?*

I stared at it, disbelieving.

It wasn't a question. So what was it? Pagan had no reason to question my compliance. I was a Made after all. What did she care that I would have to ditch a meeting in the library with my geography group about some presentation I was already behind in? I got up for some water and high on the wall, a blue square of projected light from the bridge grew bright and then dimmed. Lara snored and Trudy lay flung out on her bed as if she'd been dropped there, her eyes open and watching me. The room reeked of booze and for once, I was as responsible for the stink as they were.

"Do you think they'll ever crack our code?" Trudy whispered. "And when they do, what'll happen to us? To me and Lara and . . . you?"

Outside, the mist swirled thicker than usual so that it looked like the bridge was boiling in acid. The indigo sky hung low over the quaint roofs of Wellsburg on the other side, a few lights winking sleepily. But I knew better. I peered closer and noticed a hazy glow cast by a building along the river, the glamorous, infamous Sweeney's Landing—invitation only—no Made had ever been on the List. The clock tower in its scaffolding cage rose above the mist, and a shape on the bridge jumped into the edge of my eye. I stepped back and peered out from the edge. I probably needn't have worried. It wasn't as if my window could be differentiated from the hundreds of identical ones in the Tower, each with a lonely Made standing in the frame—but better to be safe than sorry. From my hidden vantage point I watched a crouching figure materialize on the railing. As its outlines sharpened, I saw what looked like wings drawn around its body.

Its head was shrouded in shadow but surely angled toward my window, and at this distance and beneath the folds of its starlit hood, I looked into a face that was a void into endless night. I shivered and couldn't stop, my insides filled with the coldness of that hole.

Trudy had turned onto her side, still watching me. I realized with a shock that I liked her. And that brought warmth back into my body. I stopped shivering. "Nothing will happen to us," I said. It was less a lie than a prayer—was there a difference?

"But they, the governments or whoever, they see something in us. They pretend we're just sad useless cult victims that need their help, but I don't know. It's like . . . they're afraid us or something."

"Maybe they are." I turned away from the window, tried to unsee that black hole of a face.

"Do you really think they're going to hack us?" she lowered her voice to a whisper. "Lara says that's just an urban myth."

"Lara is just trying to make you feel better," I said.

"I can *hear* you," Lara mumbled from her bed, groping for her earphones. "We just have to stick together is all. I heard of places in Upper Slant cities, and in New Dip and the Wastes too, where Mades congregate, watch out for each other. And there is this counter-hacker out there called Made2Break who's trying to get to our code before anyone else does. Which may also be a myth, but whatever helps us survive is good enough for me."

I thought of Kai's stories and the way they gave the Mades something to live for, to live and to die for.

Lara said all of this with her eyes closed and her earphones in, and the blue light played across her face, and Trudy said, "And then what? What will we be then?"

"Free, maybe," Lara mumbled. "Fingers crossed."

Trudy smiled at me and held up two sets of crossed fingers. Then she turned to the wall and in minutes was asleep.

It took me a while. The excitement about Pagan's text was overshadowed by the shame of having dismissed the two Mades whose lives were intertwined with mine whether I liked it or not. The figure on the railing of the bridge seemed to be gone but I knew better than to believe that, so I texted Pagan back.

I'll be there.

When I finally slept, Kai was in my dreams again. She walked up to a giant crocodile and began to recite to it from a notebook bound in Malemade skin. Her blue ribbon had slipped so it lay across her eyes like a blindfold, and her hair bristled with black feathers. The crocodile was the size of a small mountain, like one of the Starveling Hills, and its tail formed a glittering escarpment that dropped into the abyss. I couldn't see the drop but I knew it was there. Kai began to cry, black tears seeping beneath the ribbon. The huge jaws of the croc opened and I could see down its abyssal throat. The jaws opened wider and Kai began to move toward it and there was nothing I could do to stop her.

When I woke the pillowcase was soaked and the sheets reeked of sweat, but my illness had finally broken. I got in the shower, trying to wash off the sadness of the dream. The girls had gone to class, leaving their cheap scents behind them. Trudy's bed was all hospital corners and fluffed pillows and Lara's a tangle of sheets and shorty pajamas, with a charging cord wrapped around the leg of a teddy bear. I spent half an hour in the shower, scrubbed my skin raw. Washed my hair and braided it wet into a high coiled basket on top of my head. I helped myself to my roommates' makeup and watched a video from a Wellsburg blogger to learn to apply it.

Maybe I was already hacked. Already corrupt. I couldn't have resisted Pagan if I tried.

At eleven thirty I set out across the bridge. I ignored the guards, kept my arguing eyes on the prize. Gargoyles leered in the weak sun. The leaves were turning gold, and the narrow, terraced buildings shimmered on the wet cobblestones. Rot from the river wafted in the air. The coffee crowds spilled onto the pavements, standing on the curbs smoking cigarettes and sipping from keep-cups. I spotted some bonny lads who reminded me of the drovers at the Nag. But by the time I got to the Quad, where students clustered around the fountain, I had begun to lose my nerve. Maybe the Regulars were right. Maybe the whole thing—the Blood Temple, Starveling Hills, everything—had all been a dream, but the kind from which there was no waking, because maybe it had dreamed me instead, and Kai too.

"Her eyes pop like grapes between my beak?"

I turned to see Pagan dressed in white jeans and flat shoes. A suede fringed poncho hung over her shoulders. She wore sunglasses and no makeup, the angles of her face gleamed like marble.

"I think I upset the TA," I said. "I didn't mean to."

"Trigger warnings are the first step to censorship. This is a free country last time I looked. I like your makeup." Pagan's lips pulled back in a gargoyle's grin. "Jacinta won't last. They never do. What's with the flesh-eating bird? Is that a thing?"

"Yes and no. *Corvus chimaeralis*, they're a hybrid introduced by . . . one of the cult scientists. They're good at finding things. The birds, I mean."

But she was reading a text, smoking a cigarette I didn't see her light.

"Listen," she said. "There is a reading series you should check out. I think it could appeal to your, quote, *aesthetic*."

My heart flipped. I forced myself to hold my ground, to refrain from sniffing.

"What happens at a reading series?" I asked.

She needled smoke from delicate nostrils. "Right. I always forget that you wouldn't have had much exposure to culture in the, quote, *conventional* sense. Our little series is called Fearsome Gatherum. Look it up online to get an idea of our vibe. It's kind of a protest group, actually."

I nodded enthusiastically. "Against?"

"Against the fear of fear, of course. The taboo against terror." She raised both hands in mock-horror. "Because of, well, you . . . survivors. Out of respect for what you went through. The Blood-thingie cult and all that."

All what?

"Everyone has to be so sensitive all the time now," she continued. "But if you're always tiptoeing around other people's, quote, *feelings*, then where do you find your own truth?" She composed herself. I imagined that for the likes of Pagan, life *was* a series of poses and the challenge was simply in holding them. "Everyone has the right to take truth where they find it. That's what, quote, *fearsomeness* is about. "

"Fearsomeness?"

"Yours feels very lived in, Meera," she dimpled. "Please tell me that you have more where that one came from?"

I began to shake my head. Cannot lie. Mustn't lie. "I don't want to get in trouble."

She held her cigarette in still fingers. "You're killing me," she said.

"Maybe I should go."

"Look. There's that psycho on the loose now." Her forehead crinkled in irritation. Maybe boredom. "People make their own happy endings, Meera. The Fearsome crowd are good people—we protect each other. Like sisters. You need friends in a place like this."

I swallowed. "Why me?"

She dropped the butt in the fountain, checked a text and then she looked up. "I told Sasha Younger about your crow story. I said it was the real deal. So that was enough for her."

"Ravens," I said. "They aren't crows, despite being in the *Corvus* genus."

"Hundred percent detail-driven. I like that."

I remembered the name from Marvin—Sasha Younger, daughter of a founding father. Well, at least we'd have something in common.

Pagan stepped away to talk to some unsmiling guy with a camera slung around his neck. I sat back down on the fountain edge listening to it lapping at itself, and the voices all around. Pitched high and low, melodic and percussive—none of them with our peculiar crack, splintered and brittle as bone. A cluster of Regulars spoke about another attack on a Made over the weekend The victim survived, they said, but only just.

"God. Talk about being in the wrong place at the wrong time," someone said.

"She crawled to safety. Said something scared her free. A noise that startled her attacker."

"The Hunter?"

"That's what they're calling him over there—you know how they love their fakelore."

"There is meant to be an actual ghost of that jumper in the 1800s, the one who killed a bunch of, quote-unquote, witches."

"Or who was pushed."

The click of cigarette lighters, the ting of text messages.

"Who knows? The attacks are breathing new life into the myth, whatever. Rumors of a black hunter's cloak—a long leather duster—will have something to do with it. But could just be talk—you know how superstitious the survivors are."

Their voices were filled with rapturous schadenfreude.

"Imagine being a . . . I can barely even say it."

"I know, right? The word, 'survivor' is totally ironic and not in a good way."

"The Blood Temple. Sheesh. Created with AI protocol and human flesh and real wombs and embryos—my God. What could be worse than being sentient enough to know what one isn't?"

"What could be worse than being *almost* human?"

"Like, with enough exposure to the real world, you'd blend right in. But you'd always know."

"Hundred per cent."

The air filled with the sultry aroma of high-class weed—different from Marvin's dirty leaf. Infused with hints of berry and chocolate.

"I wonder if our pets would love us like they do if they knew they weren't the same as us."

"Gypsy would love me no matter what. You love God, even though you know you're not like Him."

"I wouldn't call it love," someone else said, as they moved off toward the coffee stand. "Fear maybe."

"Fear totally."

By the time Pagan came back, my mind was made up. I don't know if it was the talk of the victimized Mades or the Hunter. Or if it was just her promise of protection—*you need friends in a place like this*—or something I could not yet define. But I told her I'd give the reading series a try.

"A trial, actually," she said. "I mean we're giving *you* a try, not the other way around. You get that, right? Like an audition, kind of." That dimple.

"Trial by ordeal, I get it."

She nodded absently as if she'd expected nothing else. "A tip? Just make sure that your story delivers beginning to middle to end. No cliff-hangers. It's a reading series, not a sitcom—Sasha's rule. The audience wants to dream the dream and then wake up. A different dream next time. Got it?"

But then her eyes traveled from my stained brown shoes to my hair. "There *is* a dress code, by the way, even for the trial. I'd hate you to get it wrong. I'll have some clothes sent over."

I assured her there was no need, but she insisted. "Don't want you to waste your money buying an outfit just in case … well, fearsomeness isn't for everybody."

Once, after a game of backgammon with the Father, Kai had bragged about how she'd started bearing off before he was even out of his inner board. He had been so busy racing to the end that he'd forgotten to keep his eye on the beginning.

"I'm not everybody," I said.

"No kidding." Pagan narrowed her eyes against a shaft of late afternoon sun, and blew me a stone-cold kiss, and I was gone.

* * *

High in his aerie on the roof of the Blood Temple, the Father says that we Mades would lose our heads if they weren't screwed on. I turn away from the caged birds and start down the stairs, holding my breath. But I must have missed the door that led into the lobby. Instead I just keep descending, flight after flight. The fire stairs seem endless—at each landing a locked door. I panic and start climbing back up, trying to keep count, but when I get to the lobby level, or what I think is the lobby, the door is locked. I turn the knob in a growing panic then start back down, sweating and spitting sobs, four, five, six, ever downward. Finally there are no more stairs. I am at the bottom. I push on the door, not wanting to think about what if it too doesn't open, and I imagine scenarios of having to sleep there and leave my sister without her healing tea, without me to sponge down her forehead, to whisper in her ear how I'll never leave her.

The door finally opens at my shove, and I burst through it stumbling. I am in the school basement—there is a metallic underground smell from the earth but also something chemical—contaminated ground water from the weapons facility. There is a wide dark hallway with rooms leading off to the side and crinkled heating pipes with the silver coating peeling off, and pipes running along the ceiling. It is unlit of course, but there is a glimmer at the end and when I get to it, I turn into another hallway, narrower and lit from above by sputtering fluorescent tubing whose illumination stops about halfway down. My heart is pounding. I try not to panic. There are doors along it, signs saying *HAZCHEM* and *CLEANING* and I realize that the smell is that of a hospital, and that this is below the infirmary and the birthing rooms and some of the pathology labs. A sign to my right says "Morgue" and through the glass panel I see metal gurneys and a big lumpy oblong shape on one and a smaller lumpy shape on the other.

Glass crunches underfoot. I hear distant voices—the cheerful authority of the Assistants and a Matron, and I cannot breathe. I can't feel my feet—I grope the walls, freezing. If I am caught, I am dead, and if I die, then Kai is dead meat, and I can't let that happen. I need to get to her. Surely this hallway will lead to an exit. My thoughts are like chewing gum. Kai looked so ill before I left. I think of her waiting to be chemically unmade in the infirmary and how much she knows about everything and how little I know about anything. I don't want to live without her, because without her I am lost. I need to save her to find myself and I need to save myself to find her.

I wish my head would clear, like in Narn's hut—what I would give for some of that tea. I think of the ravens, how they are connected somehow to Narn's magic, which is different from that of a normal witch. Zigzagging blindly along with my arms waving in front of me, I wonder if maybe I can be unmade in her place. My hands grope the darkness. Maybe I can start taking the Father's unmaking drugs instead of Kai. I will make some fake pills from the soft insides of our dinner rolls like Kai did for our dolls when we were little, and I will give them to her, and I will swallow her real pills, the ones for unmaking. But the thought of losing my horny lady-bit, now that I have found it, just makes me feel like crying.

My flailing arms steer me toward a room that ripples with self-generated light from a half-open door, like an opal. I move toward it urgently, my mind elsewhere—but then the door opens further at my touch, and I am in the shimmering room. Refracted light from the liquid in dozens of jars on dozens of shelves. Each jar contains a single pink lady-bit suspended in liquid dark as ink.

I am all eyes. Only eyes.

The lady-bits have curly horns or ears like on a sheep or a goat, just like the Father said, so they must have belonged to Unmades—twins or liars—bad Mades who didn't turn out as the Father intended. Mistakes. My butt clenches. Each jar has a faded number and a name. They're dusty, an irregular harvest. I back away, the frigid air cuts my skin. I won't look at the names, refusing to let my brain record any of them. My hips collide with a steel table on wheels, and something smashes on the floor. I pivot into a crouch and glimpse beneath my feet the broken jar, and on one fragment of glass, a number and a name handwritten in Sharpie. The name is not faded like the rest but dark and glossy and still wet.

I run.

CHAPTER 10
SISTER-ACT

The abrupt seasonal change literally took my breath away, and although my infection was mostly cured, October found me with a persistent bronchial tick that made it hard to talk. Or at least that was my excuse for not seeing as much of Marvin as I should have. The real reason of course was that I had a story to come up with—this time for Pagan's reading series—held most Sundays except for session breaks. Sasha had been keen, she said in a follow-up text, to "trial" me at least once before Halloween. Fearsome Gatherum? I could barely say the name—I wished Kai were here—she'd die laughing. I texted Marvin a sick face, and frittered away the hours until I could call Narn. I couldn't do it without her. When I had tried, after meeting with Pagan, to come up with a story on my own, my imagination deserted me. If memory was Kai's strong suit and imagination mine—our symbiosis complicated by the Father's Forever Code—then why was the triangle that defined us failing me now?

A drift of leaves dropped at my feet on cue. The wind blew wads of sulfuric frost up from the river. Above me bare branches spasmed then grew still. The shop windows were strung with pumpkins and rubber spiders. Halloween wasn't a big celebration in South Rim out of respect for witches, but here it was as if the Apology never happened. A wart-chinned manikin cackled at me outside the front door of the yoga studio.

I'd managed to get to one more FiFo, where because of a twenty-minute power outage midway through, we ran out of time for me to read. Jacinta ignored me and Pagan and her crew of Regulars snuck away before the lights came back on. After that I virtually stopped going to other classes too, glomming what I could from discussion boards or from recorded lectures, telling myself I could catch up later. I knew that Marvin would disapprove, as if he had some kind of claim on me by virtue of us both being nonvanished twins. But no one could make that claim. I belonged to no one except Kai. Still I had to admit that because he once shared his DNA with another, and his code was potentially as corrupted as mine—as broken—maybe one day we could help each other. Except I'd failed so utterly the last time I'd tried to help anyone.

I told myself I didn't need a friend. And I didn't need a boyfriend. I'd had plenty of those upstairs at the Five-Legged Nag. They never lasted, which was how I liked it. I kept thinking about Pagan's invitation, both attracted and repelled by the promise of being severed from all I knew. From the double that I was.

* * *

I don't remember getting back to the bunkroom. I remember voices and pounding feet in the wake of the noise of broken glass, and then nothing.

I somehow manage to brew Kai's tea using a paper cup and hot water from Matron's kettle when she isn't looking. Because of the Father's ravens, security is lax in the Blood Temple. They have no reason not to trust us, and no one knows that I share my twin sister's noncompliant brain and her code-corrupting womb. No one knows that I should be the one slated for unmaking, that it is *my* horned bits that should be cut out and my name on that broken jar, as much as hers.

But *I* know. I'll always know.

I wake up in her bed in the infirmary. Kai pulls me toward her in sleep. The bag drips painkillers into her veins. Unmaking hurts. I butt my head hard against her collarbone and sweat-soaked nightgown and the terrible smell of her breath. It is a few heartbeats before I remember that we are in the infirmary. Across the aisle is the Made hooked up to a blood bag—a common enough sight, but Kai and I don't share the trait of anemia common to the Father's creations.

"I have to get up and burn a candle," I mumble. "The witch is going to get us out of here."

"Don't call her a witch."

"I made her a promise," I say. "If she saves you, I'll . . . I'll . . ."

I've forgotten.

"Idiot." But she hugs me closer. "She is going to get us to the Starvelings. Shhhh."

"The Starvings?" That doesn't sound like anywhere I want to go.

"It's where shlee lives, where her slisters live too, used to." Her words slide into each other from the medication. "We aren't meant to say it because it's a secret place."

"She blindfolded the ravens, Kai. Even the Father can't do that. And she looks like a witch."

"She was something else, before." Her words float from the fog of the drugs. "And you couldn't look at her then. She was too horrible."

"Before Starving Hills?"

"Shhhh." Kai puts a finger to her lips and then tells me how, before that Narn came from this place in hell called Dungeon of the Damned. "They flayed sinners there. Sometimes they ate them."

"Why?" I ask.

"Because that's what they wanted."

"The sinners?" To my shame, I can understand sin. What it's like to want to be eaten.

"People who did bad things to their family. Murdered their mothers, or fathers, or hurt children, or sisters."

"I'll never do anything bad to you, Kai."

"The sisters flew after the bad person with their scourge."

I nod like I know all about scourges. And flying.

"They had wings then, big black wings. And claws. And the scourge—it's like a whip made of snaky ropes that rip your flesh down to the bone." Kai's voice is weak but warms to the tale-telling. "Another word for scourge is actually bane which means curse or death or ruin."

I shiver, snuggle closer. "Do they still do that?"

"They're not supposed to."

"If the sisters are that old, how come they're not dead?"

I am distracted because across the aisle, something strange is going on with the Made hooked up to the blood transfusion. Her eyes fly open and she begins to pull at the cords. Kai is so taken up with the story of the sisters from hell that she doesn't notice.

"They take on new forms when the old one falls apart, so they can live as long as they need to. Not forever, but near enough."

"No, wait!"

Because the Made across the aisle pulls the needle out of her arm with a yank, the blood spurting from the bag.

Kai is rabbiting on about how Narn and her sister called Mag recycle themselves, parts of themselves, attach the old bits to new forms over hundreds of years, thousands even.

The Made lowers her bare legs to the floor.

"Mag?" I think of that hooded being skulking around the shearers' shed in that huge black sweatshirt, dwarfed by the massive hood. "The one with the tattoos?"

"That whole silent goth thing is not their original form."

"Back in the dungeon, you mean?"

The Made is still across the aisle. She squats on the floor. I flick my eyes away from her bits. Her hair is in white-blond braids.

"But it's not like being a goth couldn't be Mag's truth, in some way. Like the shoe fits, if you know what I mean," Kai mumbles.

"The middle sister who is lost," I ask without taking my eyes off the abominable Made, "did she run off because she didn't want to change?"

But abruptly, Kai has now noticed what's going on in the opposite bed. The Made, deathly pale, squatting on the floor with her gown pulled up. Blood spurts from the transfusion bag and pools in a puddle around her.

"Wait?" Kai says, craning. "What?"

"It's nothing," I say, trying to distract her. I don't want to get in trouble.

The Made is playing in the blood, the hem of her hospital gown turning crimson.

"Stop!" Kai tries to sit up but she is too weak. I am crying. I don't want this dirty Made to tell on me, to get me in trouble. I know who she is, and Kai will be angry. Angry at me! The Made gets up and her mouth is covered in blood and her teeth are white and pointed and her white braids are ghost snakes that writhe around her head. Big white snakes with ruby eyes and shimmering scales.

I stand up on the end of Kai's bed, wave my arms at the snake girl. My voice is shrill. "I don't need you anymore. I *have* a sister. I don't want you!" I turn cold when I see what she has been doing in the blood. Not playing. Writing. *S-T-A-R-V-*

She is writing with her finger in the blood.

"Go!" My voice is that high whistling keen again, a broken fingernail against a blackboard. "Away!"

And just like that, she does.

Kai has clapped trembling hands on her ears and is breathing through her mouth, looking at me with horror—I don't yet know that it is also the look of love.

"What language were you speaking?" she finally asks in a little voice.

"Go to sleep," I say. "You've had a bad dream."

Later that night, an irritated Matron returns to the infirmary with the anemic Made caught sleepwalking near the lavatories, but her teeth are no longer pointed and there are no snakes in her hair, and she quietly submits to being hooked up to a new bag of blood and to straps around her wrists to ensure she doesn't wander a second time.

I never see the snake girl again in this place. But I never forget the power of those words I spoke in a language I didn't know I knew, and is lost to me as soon as it leaves my mouth.

"Tell me another story about sisters," I say when we are alone again. "A story just for me."

She closes her eyes and tells me how when the three sisters got out of hand with all their blood vengeance and fury, another goddess stripped them of their power and made them leave the dungeon and go up top to make the world a better place instead of a worse one. They weren't allowed to be assassins anymore—but they got some other skills. And a new name.

"Seems like a strange punishment." I snuggle closer, eye the sleeping Made in the other bed, her wrists compliant in their straps.

Kai's voice slows to a sluggish rasp like a wasp against a window. "It was a punishment, because the middle sister didn't want to change."

"I was right."

"You were right. She didn't want to make the world a better place. She thought her sisters were selling out. 'We're not kindly,' she said. 'We're filled with fury and blood rage—that's our power.' She tried to tell her sisters that if they gave it up it would be the end of the world as they knew it. Blood crimes would go unpunished and chaos would reign. But mostly it was because the middle sister didn't want to die."

I say, "That's the biggest change of all."

"The oldest sister tried to reassure the middle one that they'd still be goddesses, except now their job was to protect the people from *injustice*, not to enforce justice, and that knowing that you're going to die, even if it's after a really, really long time, keeps you true. And that went down like a turd in the punchbowl"—one of the Father's expressions, maybe—"with the middle sister. She liked killing and scourging, and she liked the taste of sin, and she didn't give a rat's ass about the truth.

"'Goddess, shmoddess,' she said. 'There will be crimes of sister against sister, child against parent, of blood against blood—don't talk to me about justice or the law. The only way to get anything done in this world or the next is to live forever You'll be a couple of invisible old hags and I'll be a rock star.'

"'Something else will take our place,' the big sister said. 'Justice must prevail.'"

Kai's blue ribbon has slipped down drunkenly over her eyes, and I must adjust it. It burns from her fever. Her breath is vile. She continues her story about the sisters, how the old one said that change was natural, and that it would be against nature not to go with the times. Eternal life is what's not natural, the big sister said, and who wants that anyway?

She is a natural storyteller and I'm drawn along by the misremembered tale. It is firing up parts of my brain I didn't know I had. Beginnings, middles and ends.

"What happened?"

"They had a big fight about it. So the middle sister ran off. Kept on killing people if their enemies paid her to do it. She got rich and infamous. She had clothes and men and women, angels, devils—anything she wanted. And the other two sisters missed her. They loved her. But they had to make do. Find a way to survive their grief and adapt to the new world. Protecting, not punishing. And it changed them."

"How?"

"The older they got, the younger they got. The more they learned, the less they knew. The more they grew, the fresher they stayed. They just kept borrowing bits of themselves, remade them as their truths changed on the inside and out."

"And the middle one? Tiff?" I lick my lips, tasting Kai's bitter sweat.

"She loved herself too much to change. She loved herself more than God. She killed people and stole their bodies, threw them in the trash when she was done. But she stayed the same, just growing older, until she just . . . kind of died inside. And then . . . she began to rot. And the rot seeped through and infected everything the bad sister touched."

Kai pants from exhaustion. I try to help. "So the other sisters became and . . ."

". . . just kept rebecoming. Remaking themselves from scraps of . . ."

". . . their souls . . ."

". . . a good witch, a skinny goth . . ."

". . . but the middle one unmakes herself . . ."

". . . from what she can never be . . ."

I have lost track of who is saying what, or maybe we are both just thinking the same thing. My heart is so full that I don't care.

"What happened in the end?" I try and get comfortable on the crumbs of myrtle cake that sprinkle the bed.

"To be continued." Her voice is barely a whisper.

The security lights come on in the playground, wash the infirmary in their wakeful glare.

"There's a jar," I say.

"Shuddup." She smacks her mouth against mine.

And then she falls back on her pillow and I listen to the other Made in the infirmary cough in her sleep. My sister's breathing sounds different. Shallow and labored.

I drift a little. I come to and she's staring up at the ceiling. Her eyes are cavernous in the darkness. "Just promise me you won't let the Father hack me. Promise me that?"

"I'm going to save you."

"Promise."

I do.

"Meera," I sense her smile.

"Kai," I say. "I saw the birds."

There is no answer at first. I nudge her sharply in the ribs. They stick out like the bars on the Father's aviary.

"You meet Dani?" she whispers so softly I have to lean in to hear.

"She bit the Father."

She wheezes out a laugh, but then begins to leak a greasy, rank sweat. I kneel up in the bed, reach for the washcloth and dip it in a bowl of water. I wipe the snot from her face and the tears. Her lovely hair is lank against the pillow and I try to cover the bald patches on her scalp.

"Go light that candle," she says. "It's time."

And when I wake up in the darkest hour, I am curled up beside her with the hooded Mag's leathery hand over my mouth, and my sister is dead.

* * *

I knew it was time for me to turn up at another FiFo. So I went. It was the second week in October. It wasn't my turn to read, and I needn't have bothered. Jacinta wasn't there and neither was Pagan. A grad student from the music department tried to run the workshop but gave up in the end, and we all made it home well before the curfew.

I spent the rest of the week anxious about coming up with a story for Fearsome Gatherum. On the Thursday before the weekend, with the session break upon us, I had nothing, and went down to the bench in the shadow of the bridge beside the running track. Wrapped up in a deceptively thick coat and false memories, I waited for dusk so I could call Narn, although I wasn't sure how I'd explain what a reading series was to her, having only the faintest idea myself. My imagination failed me. I shouldn't have been surprised. Even Kai's mnemonically noncompliant brain, untethered from the Father's code, had betrayed her in the end.

The Father showed us pictures once, projected on the whitewashed brick wall of the playground, of broken children. The drawings were from medical books hundreds of years old and had captions like on the jars in the womb room, rather than the actual names of the children, if they'd had them. One little girl was called "The Hairy Virgin." She was born covered in hair because, according to the doctor, her mother was obsessed with a saint in his bear coat rather than her own husband. "The Boy with the Upside-Down Face" was a child born with no forehead, the spitting image of a print of another saint seared on the mother's imagination while her husband was on top of her, "trying his bloody best," the Father reminded us, to "give her a son." Instead of looking at him, the mother gazing the wrong way up at the saint resulted in *this* upside-down abomination, the Father said, because women have no idea which way is up. There was another drawing of a crippled teenage boy with his limbs contorted in agony. The Father said that the child was born that way after his mother went to a public execution instead of staying at home where she belonged.

"Study after study has shown that females can't tell the difference between what's real and what's not. Between real memories and images created from nothing. Your adulterous imagination is as slutty as you are," the Father said, "and monstrosity its only issue."

Mades, the good ones, couldn't bear children. For there to be more of us, we needed the Father's code. For there to be less of us we just needed time.

The sky hung in low clouds heavy with clotted tears that blew in my face As I sat on the bench, talk of the latest victim of the Hunter wafted by from bikers and joggers. There was a giant chessboard paved onto the ground beside some tables, and I watched pigeons shit on the pawns. At dusk I followed the other lonely Mades back onto the bridge to call home.

"I feel like I'm falling," I said when she picked up, worlds away.

I think I meant to say "failing," but what I meant to say these days, and what came out seemed to be less and less connected.

"How many credit points for fearsomeness?" Narn said, when I told her about it.

"None. It's the belly of the beast," I said. "That is its own reward."

All along the blue railings, blue-washed Mades perched like birds on a wire. Midsession breaks were a lonely time for us, a reminder of how we had nowhere to go, Wellsburg parties to which we weren't invited.

There was a doubtful pause. "Tiff said the same," Narn said. "But hungry beast must eat itself."

"I'm not Tiff," I said.

Narn clicked her teeth.

"If I'm lucky," I said, "it will be the stories they eat up, instead of me."

"Mades aren't lucky."

"It'll buy us time. Even more than FiFo. This is the real deal," I said, echoing Pagan.

"Time is hungry," Narn said. "Middle sister lost to it."

"This is the only way we'll find her," I said. "You gave me one story. Just a few more. The semester won't last forever."

"Hunter still hunting?" she asked.

"I think he's just getting started, don't you?"

The ravens answered for her. "Mades always in the wrong place at wrong time. Boss man fixed them that way."

"The stories are a way to move beyond those constraints, if there is one. Someone knows I am here—the broken name on the Redress Form proves that. So maybe for once, a Made is at the right place at the right time."

"Who?"

I sighed. "Me," I said. "Meera."

"Takes two," her voice was both needy and dismissive.

"Maybe, but one is better than none, witch. Just like three is better, maybe, than two?"

There. It was said. I didn't know where it came from. I waited for her wrath—the gnashing of her teeth, the whine and retreat of the thylacine. Had I gone too far?

"Never want to lose sister. Rule of threes." Narn's voice was a monotone, more terrible to me than any of her rages.

"Depends on the kind of rule, from what I've heard. Either way, remember my promise, to find your sister if you saved mine?"

"But good twin *wasn't* saved." She sounded defeated, suddenly. Old and confused.

"That was me, Narn. I was the one who wasn't saved."

"All this because crappy twin just wants to save itself? That's what whole story is about?" Narn said. It was harsh, but I was prepared for her bluff, and came back with a winning move—the truth. Did I have a choice?

"Kai died for me. And a part of me never came back. The good part. I owe you, Narn. I owe you my life. But mostly, I owe you a sister."

It worked. For a moment she seemed to be foundering for an answer, another excuse. I felt bad. "No," she said wearily. "Sister is too lost now, too old. Too angry." She'd hang up on me soon if I wasn't careful. A flock of Mades and Malemades walked past passing a bottle between them. "Truth or dare . . ." began one.

I peered down at the opposite bank—what had caught my eye? Nothing.

It began again, that dreaming sound, the song of her hexing. "Double-double."

Callers along the bridge were hanging up and heading toward the safety of Tower Village. They moved with a new urgency. Far off I heard, *Truth! No, dare! No truth . . .*

"What if Tiff is the key? To everything. If she went to Upper Slant, then this is our chance." I said gently: "Isn't that why you let me go, Narn? Isn't that the real reason why you didn't throw me in the trash?"

The two of us living a lie for so long. I heard Eric lap at his bowl—pictured him laying his elongated marsupial face on his paws. I had left him—would I ever see him again? Who could I count on to explain it to him? Between a dead twin, a demented witch and a tormented mute, that didn't leave many options. But I was beginning to see that you had to suffer into truth, wherever you found it, or it found you. It hurt because you never knew the whole of it. It hurt because the truth was always broken, always missing a piece.

"Conjure tales' power is old. Older than sisters'. Older than time. Angrier too. Teller must bend to its will, won't bend to teller's," Narn warned.

A new silence took shape between us. I knew it was a shape that wouldn't hold. Was made to break. But it was all we had.

"I saw Kai bend to it. She didn't break—"

But before I could finish, a scream from across the river tore the air and people turned and started running toward the Towers. At the edge of my eye I saw black wings outstretched, the tips so sharp they cut the sky. Someone called my name. It sounded like Kai and my heart leaped. But when I turned and it was not Kai, but just my roommate Lara, I felt so full of rage I could have choked her with my bare hands. Her open mouth a rictus of fear, one hand gripping the arm of the dusky, tearful Trudy, the other extended out to me.

I didn't hear what Narn said next because Lara grabbed my hand, squeezing so hard that I felt something pop. Babbling in her high, rasping voice about the Hunter, they dragged me away, half sobbing, half breathlessly laughing back to the Tower, where we belonged.

CHAPTER 11
WIN-WIN

Swinging each of my hands in theirs, Lara and Trudy had told me about a costume party in one of the Tower dorm rooms on the weekend. An anti-Halloween, party, apparently. A chance to get dressed up in costume without being disrespectful to witches, because the real Halloween was still weeks away. I thanked them but said I couldn't come. That I had homework to catch up on. And besides, I said, three's a crowd.

"Just for one drink," Lara had said, the rose-gold feather trembling on her bracelet. "How can it hurt?"

"You'll meet people—our people," Trudy had added, like it was a good thing. "It's not called a village for *nothing*."

Her creaky voice braked sharply to avoid making it sound like a question. It made me wonder if maybe Marvin and I weren't the only ones who felt endangered in Tower Village—caught in a war between those who wanted to make more of us, and those who wanted to make less.

I said I'd think about it.

Survival of the fittest, the Father said, that's why I've made so many of you. It takes a village to make Paradise. The protocol by which he inserted his coded commands onto our fetal limbic system, in order to remake us in the image of a Lilith for the New World Order was literally ART, he joked. Think of ART, haha, as a chance to press "rewind" on the Fall.

> ~ *Think of your digital layer, he said, as mankind's augmented action potential.*
> ~ *Think of yourselves as the bridge between heaven and earth.*
> ~ *Think of the female imagination, he said, as a vestigial tail.*
> ~ *You will never sin again, he said, simply because you won't want to.*
> ~ *I alone have found a way to make men without the aid of women, he said.*
> ~ *I will always be with you. You are the bird in my hand and in the bush—there is no end to my protection. Not even death can separate us.*

~ You'll thank me later, he said.

But we already did.

"It takes a village," Lara fluffed her hair, "to make a future."

It wasn't that she meant to parrot the Father. She just couldn't help it. "Or an aviary," I said. But no one laughed.

"If you come to the party, we'll help you catch up on your homework," Trudy said. "You probably need it."

She had me there.

The party was boisterous and boring. There was a cauldron of some apple liquor and cheap wine made into a punch. Candy bugs floated in it. A Malemade wandered around with a plastic axe sunk into his head. Mades moved stiffly against the wall in nurse makeup and white suspenders. Someone came dressed as the Cowardly Lion from *The Wizard of Oz* and with her was a half-naked Malemade painted silver from head to toe, his modesty protected by silver Speedos. It was the Tin Man, who turned out to be Marvin. I was surprised. He hadn't mentioned a girlfriend. I felt the old rage, that old unchanging sense of being sidelined. Was that how Tiff felt when her sisters left her out of the deal they cut with the goddess? When they signed up for it anyway, assuming it was all for one and one for all? Maybe it was that which turned her against them. Not the deal itself, not even how they accepted their repurposing as demigods in return for a place in the modern world. But how they went ahead without her. As if she wasn't there.

Narn always hated how I took the lost sister's side.

I drank a lot of punch and kept seeing the silver flash at the edge of my eye but Marvin and I avoided each other until well after midnight.

"Didn't expect to see you here," he said. "Thought you'd be beavering away at your overdue homework."

One night in Middles Bunk, soon before the Father began her chemical unmaking, Kai had bemoaned how the Father refused the beaver and dismissed her from the backgammon table in a sulk. I remember being frightened for her and asking what a beaver was, and how the whole Middle's bunkroom erupted in laughter, hers the loudest of all, and how my face burned from my chin to my hairline, and how I hated her at that moment even more than I hated myself.

"As it happens," I said, "Pagan's invited me to read at a series called Fearsome Gatherum."

His silvered brow knitted in a frown. His nose-cone had begun to slip.

"Didn't the Dean outlaw the Gatherums? There were complaints, if I recall."

"Just jealous 'cos they weren't invited," I slurred. "There's someone called Slasher Younger behind it."

He laughed. "Seriously? Don't you remember? Queen Bee if ever there was one. And Pagan is hand to the Queen if ever—"

"Blah blah." I ladled some more punch into our cups, accidentally on purpose slopped it over the bulge in his Speedos.

Marvin swayed, and I could smell his body paint. "You're not worried about risking your scholarship? Might be a challenge keeping your grades up with the extra pressure. Not to mention your soul."

"Is that crotch on your punch, or are you just sleazed to be me?"

"Come on. You really want to throw it in with a bunch of women's college narcissists, Meera? Maybe just put a neon rinse through your hair, start an exfoliating blog and be done with it."

I decided I one hundred percent loved anti-Halloween.

"Everyone who gets mixed up with the Gatherum crowd comes off worse for wear." His irises looked like mirrors—his pupils dilated as a cat's in which I saw myself times two.

"I'm already worse for wear." I looked around for someone drunker than he was, but not as drunk as me. There were rosy stains of punch on Kai's brown shoes. "Who's your date?"

We both looked to where the Cowardly Lion and a black-wigged Dracula were sucking each other's faces off. I was leaning against a window which looked north over the brightly lit parklands and the rest of Tower Village. In the very far distance a vaporous blur indicated a large city. The stars hung bleached and indifferent above all this light. I asked him how he was going with his term papers, and he told me that he was working on a really difficult assignment about criminal profiling.

"It's called mind-hunting," he said.

The room began to spin.

"Really what it comes down to is learning, through imitation, to empathize with the criminal's motives, to understand how they think by putting yourself in their place."

"So in order to find the criminal, you have to see yourself as guilty?"

Glass smashed from the kitchen.

"Pretty much. My face is up here, by the way."

Reluctantly I lifted my eyes from his Speedos to his sad silver face.

"Did you hear those screams across the river a few days ago?" I said.

He put his punch glass down. "Just partiers at Sweeney's. The usual mid-session hijinks."

"Hijinks sound good," I said. "You look amazing, Marvin."

"I'm the Tin Man. Steadfast and true."

I touched his arm. My fingers came away slick with silver paint. I smeared it across my mouth.

"We're not going to have sex," he said.

* * *

There is a wooden boat with a high curved prow, and a covered cabin on the deck where Kai and I lie curled in a nest of blankets. A rope coils in one corner. Blankets. Fresh water in squat steel canteens. The bony hooded being pilots the craft. We are crossing the black straits of Rogues Bay for the first time, heading for the mainland to the sisters' home in the Starvelings, where Narn is waiting for us.

I tend to Kai. I won't let the hooded creature near her.

When they came for her, I'd tried to scratch them, and opened my mouth to scream when they tried to pull me away. I refused to leave without her. I hissed like a lizard. I spat and kicked the bony tattooed sister. Kai would not be a name on a jar. She would not be a caption for one those horny devils in Father's womb room.

"Both of us," I snarled, "or neither."

And because in the end they took us both, I knew that one was better than none—and that we were both important to Narn in ways that I had yet to understand. But back then all I knew is that I may not have been the twin she wanted, but I was the one she would get.

I hold Kai's head in my lap. I brush her black hair and keep the flies off. Her nightgown is filthy. I try to close her eyes but they spring open as soon as I take my fingers away. Her face still contorted from the agony of the unmaking drugs, her body growing colder by the minute but safe from the Father's knife. And from his jar.

"I got the lady-blood too," I tell her. "It hurts."

I show her the feather I pocketed from Dani's wing. I trace my finger along the rosy iridescence, a faint blush at the edge of the oily black.

"Have you ever seen anything so beautiful?"

I believe she can still hear me. I have to believe in something. I try not to cry. I do cry. Sometimes I have the sense that the hooded sister steering the boat up and down the swells is listening. Their painfully angular form makes them lean into the wind like a collapsing tent. They wear baggy leggings and black high-top sneakers. I wonder what they are trying to cover up. I remember what Kai said about how Mag and Narn were born as monsters from spilled man-thing blood and how in order to keep going they must remake themselves in the image of their own truth. I wonder about this bony, sneakered body tattooed over every inch of visible flesh—what about its suffering rang so true to Mag that they literally became it? They never let me see their face, but sometimes look back over a humped shoulder and scribble seethes deep within the folds of their hood.

The passage is rough. The boat climbs up a mountain of slop and falls down with a sickening lurch that makes me reach for the bucket that the sister-creature empties for me. They bring me fresh water—warm and rank but I am grateful for it. Seabirds alight on the rails and huge bat-like wings chase them away.

"Bats," I say. "A long way from the mainland."

But I know better. I know that bat-like and bats are not the same thing.

Outside on the deck the first night, when it's calm, a hot blue Crux wheels across the sky, and the bright scattered Jewel Box hovers like withheld tears. Dolphins play beside the boat. I see their humped backs and fins on the inside of my eyes when I close them to sleep. On the second night there are Right Whales, their flippers dipped in moonlight as they breach. The whales breach the surface of my dreams and I wake up tasting salt. Transport pods move like beetles through shreds of clouds. On the third night there are lights to starboard, distant ships carrying endangered timber to the mainland.

What wakes me on the morning after the third night, is birdsong. Not gulls or terns but a magpie's warble and the whistle of a shrike. Yellow light ripples against the rough-hewn wood of our cabin. It's warm and I am dry. I can even hear a small waterfall and I tell myself none of this has happened. That it's all been a dream. My sister is awake, and is already playing in the waterfall, cleaning off the stink.

A heart-stopping dread gets me to my feet. The boat is anchored ten meters from a messy bank thick with waterlogged willows and mosquitos in its depths. Naked corymbia branches brush the dome of sky. Beneath one stands the sister-creature clutching the end of a rope. They do not know I watch. Their hood is dropped back from a skeletal face, the bones of their nostrils upturned and foreshortened. Inky tears flow from their eye sockets. Mouth hole moving in soundless refrain. From a fleshy tree limb, my dead sister swings stiffly in the morning breeze. A makeshift noose tightens around her neck. Her nightgown looks freshly scrubbed and dried, the hem brushes ankles mottled with yellow bruises. Her hair, banded in the blue ribbon, has been washed and brushed so it gleams like black ink. Her dead eyes stare.

Narn's ravens flap around her face. They ruffle tainted wings with an air of penance, of great resignation.

I am splashing through the water and up the bank at a dead run. I am running out of my body and out of my mind. I ram the cloaked abomination with both fists, knock them down like a pile of sticks, and I am up the tree and unwinding the looped rope, ravens exploding from my sister's eyes.

I cut her down. Find a dry place on the bank. One eye is a bloody hole. The other is hanging by a rosy strand of muscle. Finally I become hysterical.

"She died intact!" I foam at the mouth. "And now look what you've done!"

I scream blue murder. I cry for death, for bloody vengeance. I am thirteen years old today.

* * *

Marvin and I didn't have actual sex. But I would be lying if I said I didn't wake up covered in silver paint, either.

I'd be lying if I said that we couldn't help ourselves.

Guests were not allowed to stay over in the dorms. Lara and Trudy had gone to Sunday breakfast, leaving behind a fragrant cloud of hair spray and judgment. Someone had put a bottle of aspirin on my bedtable on top of a Post-it note with a winky-face drawn with a Sharpie. I made instant coffee and looked over my timetable and the syllabus for each class, and I figured out that with help catching up, I could still get minimum grades to pass the program even with juggling FiFo and the reading series.

I just had to get Narn to agree. There was something about Fearsome Gatherum that I wanted as much as (Pagan said) it wanted me, and maybe that was why. What or who'd ever wanted me, who wasn't already dead? The coffee burned. The truth hurt. I had to make Narn understand that I wanted to find her sister not despite the fact that she lost mine, but because of it.

But Marvin was right. I had to keep up my classes, at least the eighty percent required to meet the demands of the scholarship. Biology had gone from basic to bewildering. The last lecture I'd attended was on the nature of science compared to nonscience. After that was a lab in which we were meant to learn the care and use of the microscope, various cell sizes and their properties, including osmosis and diffusion, and the difference between plant and animal cells, tissues and organs.

The homework schedule was daunting. I had already missed two reading assignments on cell division, mitosis and meiosis, and there was a DNA quiz in two weeks. The only microscopic life I had seen was my own. I would need all the help from Lara and Trudy that I could get, even if it meant attending the Thanksgiving "Feastaroony"—which they were already trying to rope me into.

I finished studying on Thursday and I exited the overheated Bibliotheque and lifted my face to the lavender dusk. I went straight to the bridge, keeping my head down. Narn picked up on the first ring like she was waiting for me, berated me for hanging up on her.

"No more cliff-hangers!" she warned. "Ever."

"Sorry. Just some partiers from a place called Sweeney's across the bridge. Spooked everyone. It was session break. There was an anti-Halloween party in one of the rooms on the weekend."

"Disrespecting witches," she growled.

"Disrespecting the disrespectors," I said.

I thought of her orange clown hair, as fake as a Halloween wig, and how it became her. I wondered how long it could go on, this chaotic upcycling or becoming. I missed the old hag. I missed her more than I could say.

There were fewer callers than normal for this hour—maybe because of the Hunter. Or the fall in temperature. I overheard one of the Mades mention snow.

"So what have you decided?" I scraped silver paint from under my nails. "Will you help me with stories for the Gatherum?"

"Conjure is a heavy weapon. Him doesn't know how to use it yet."

"I can learn."

"Rich bitches are real wolves. Old story. Starving."

Starving. I smiled grimly. "I need you to throw me to those wolves, Narn. You can't protect me anymore. To be honest, you kind of suck at it."

The ravens sobbed. *Baiit. Baiiit.*

I belched, tasted punch. And the salt on Marvin's skin. My mood was turning ugly as the day.

"Hard to keep double-yolker safe from Boss," she protested. "Powerful trouble—no charm good enough. No charm firm enough."

"Tell me something I don't know." I saw a movement on the opposite bank, a phosphorescent glow in a clearing and then a spreading darkness like spilled ink.

But Narn could see my ugly and raise me. "Crappy twin doesn't know this: ravens saw bad sister show himself to crappy twin in stolen Made body."

I stared at the phone. "You knew about that? That I'd seen Tiff—the little snake girl—in the Blood Temple? Twice?"

"Once, twice. Bad sister sees crappy twin in itself. Double-trouble."

I felt a rising fury. I gripped the rail, the phone hot against my ear. "And did the ravens tell you that I didn't take the bait? Did they tell you what I did to that little bitch? How I sent her away for good?"

"Away," Narn said gently. "but not for good, that one. Never for good."

There was a long silence on the other end of the line. I heard rustling, the scrape of a match. Impossibly, I smelled burning sage and bone broth. My eyes hurt from the neon lights on the Corso, from all the misinformation. The palpating blue lights of the bridge were making me nauseous. I peered down at the bank. Some birds burst from the trees, shrieking.

"It will never be for good," I said. "Until it is."

"Why does Meera want this?"

I thought about it. "Justice?" I said. "Revenge?" I didn't know the difference. Maybe that's what I wanted. To find out if there was one.

"Conjure tales take no prisoners," Narn growled. "Conjure's cure more dangerous than his disease. Tales only work by leaving nothing safe."

"I don't know what I want," I said. "But when we get off the phone, you'll go to your cave and carve out penance on your skin, on your flesh. And Eric will cry and the ravens will shit and Mag will shoot something—and none of that will bring either of them back. Is it too much to ask for it to stop, Narn? That's all I want."

"Yes," she said. "The end is too much to ask."

Maybe it was the restless glowing movement on the riverbank, the desolate neon-lit bridge stretching into the mist or just my hangover roaring back, but before I could stop myself, I held the phone away from my ear and sobbed into the mic across the unspannable gulf between us: "You didn't follow your sister here because you didn't have the heart. To do what needed to be done. What still needs to be done."

Something splashed in the mud far below. Narn said something about how it wasn't a matter of the heart, and what would I know about souls anyway—it was time I started acting my age and not my shoe size, and I was all, fine, if I had a shoe size which I don't, never having had a pair of shoes to call my own, and whose fault was that? Narn asked. And we went back and forth like that for a while until finally, I gave up. "You knew Tiff had her eye on me, and you knew why—double-trouble. You knew that I'd put on her clothes and be able to put myself in her place, imagine what it feels like to be her—the criminal sister—imagine what I'd do in her place."

"So?"

"So, the Malemade told me about this thing called mind-hunting, Narn. Like, it takes one to know one. And it works both ways. The profiler becomes the profiled—hammy as that sounds."

Haaa-aaam, cried the ravens. And wafting on the breeze, a leathery smell like wet dog.

I said, "Remember when you made me pick something out of the trunk to wear to our last dinner together? You said how Tiff's clothes became me, fit me like a glove. And she saw me coming, witch—just as you dreaded, as you hoped. Well here I am."

"Couldn't throw filthy sister's rags away." She was crying. Deep old-woman sobs. "Cheap and cheerful . . . "

"Shhhh, Narn. We both knew this day was coming. No one is to blame."

We wept. No one took any notice—it was a bridge of tears. I knew what she'd do to herself in the cave, and she knew I punished myself every day just by being alive. Just by having survived. We all make our own scourges. We want it to end. And we want it never to end.

The silence between us grew thick, the miles short. It hurt to swallow, the past like broken glass in my throat. "The Gatherum is the bridge between sisters lost and found, Narn."

"Silence!" Narn said in a reverberant screech that made my knees buckle. I clung onto the blue-lit rails. "Bridge has eyes and ears."

The guards *had* begun pacing back and forth, each lap getting longer.

Advancing on us. Mades hung up, herded back like sheep, indigo shadows slouching behind them.

"Help me, Narn," I whispered. "Help me burn the bridge."

A branch cracked far below. A flash of queasy yellow. Narn said something that came out as a burble. The bridge emptied and the wind had died utterly. The guard clomped from around his post, jabbed at his watch with a fat finger.

Then slowly, tearfully, the burbling through the phone became deep. And grew deeper. It had no beginning or end. And somewhere in the formless depthless middle, the answer hurled itself after the question, breakneck for the finish.

No one knows that once...

CHAPTER 12
PLANNED OBSOLESCENCE

Snarling and spitting, the clown-haired witch presides over Kai's midnight burial behind a thicket of bloodwood trees, attended by the mute Mag who wields the shovel. I have been in the Starveling Hills for two days, battling the first of many sore throats that will plague me all my life. White blossoms chase the small enshrouded body down into the black hole—the blossoms stick to my face. I am surly, tearless. As unwilling to live without as with her, unwilling to see the merits in living at all.

Getting from the coast to the hut in the Starvelings is a blur—I know that the journey was long and that Mag was my shadow, but once I cut my sister down and gently pressed her remaining eye back in, I would not let them near her again. I had bundled her belongings into a pillowcase before we left Rogues Bay—her shoes and some dice, a deck of cards and her blue ribbon—and I would not let the twisted sister near these either.

"That freak strung her up," I observe coldly. "Like some weird ceremony."

"Old time sacrifice. Mag tried blood offering to the dead to take sister as its own."

Narn has gouged out an eye to match that which the ravens took from my sister in death. It is an affront to me. Kai is mine alone to mourn. Mine. I alone claim the right of atonement. And that of revenge.

"I don't care what it was. She's mine and you tried to take her."

Narn gibbers over the grave, as if to offer atonement by way of her own anguish and loss. Her grief is a torment to me.

Narn intones a little unconvincingly, "Mag summoned ravens to take twin's soul to proper dwelling."

Narn is clearly trying to defend her sister, but it is just as clear to me that it was not Mag's place to summon the ravens. However well-intentioned, this was an overstepping—the two weird sisters have been furiously arguing about this ever since our arrival. Narn's multiplying mutterings whirl and collide with Mag's defensive thoughtforms like a flock of birds driven off course in a storm.

The ravens were necessary, she tries to explain, to carry the soul to its proper dwelling. Mag only wanted to keep Kai's soul safe, she mutters and I throw dirt at their tattooed face and sob that keeping Kai safe was my job.

Mine.

Whatever agreement the sisters come to at last, excludes me. Like they excluded the dissenting Tiff when taking a new deal they knew she'd never agree to. I feel Tiff's rising fury. I feel it in my blood.

"You took her eye!" This I will never forgive, even if Narn gave her own eye in return. I will never forget. "I promised to get her out whole. Unhacked!"

The agony is blinding. It is the beginning and the end of me.

Narn mutters about blood justice, sacrilege for sacrilege. She points to the gore-filled hole on her face as if it settles the score. Trauma has drained her hair of its vibrant color—it is the old gold of a rotten peach. Her remaining eye is swollen with grief—in her gaze I see only that she wishes it was me being lowered into the ground instead of Kai.

That makes two of us.

The bleak silent Mag shovels too quickly. I rush to stop them, but Eric, snarls and stands between us. He looks like a regular thylacine with that stiff tail, the long face and body striped darkly crossways. But because of how he is the product of an unnatural union, his loyalties are divided. This is apparent in the prominence of his ribcage, an exaggerated musculature around the shoulders and a threatening mobility to the wide hinge of his jaw. Mag resumes, chastised and surly, peering out from under their hood at Narn whom they have displeased, and who will forgive—as is her nature now. This is something that I will learn living with these two—that nature isn't always as natural as you'd think.

I gather from Narn's incantations that my cutting my sister down will have—what did she call them—repercussions. Narn moves more slowly, is a little more bent than at Rogues Bay, and her eyehole smells infected. No wonder. I imagine her gouging it out with the same boline she uses to dig roots from the earth or trim candlewicks. I will drown in the terminal lake of Narn's remaining eye unless I say what cannot be unsaid:

"You killed her! You killed my sister because you couldn't have yours. Kai told me all about her, how she ran off because she couldn't stand you. Do you think I believe all that about the ravens keeping her soul safe? Safe from what? I think *they*"—I point to Mag—"offered my sister—*mine*—to your sister as a kind of barter, a balancing of the scales. Like if that bitch can get one of us on her side, then it's two against two." I clench my teeth, half ashamed, talking to myself more than anyone. "Like that'd ever happen! Do you think Kai'd go over to her side any more than I would? I'm going to find your shitty sister, I promise, and when I do, you'll be sorry. You'll all be sorry!"

Narn is staring at me with her clown mouth in a terrible stretched smile, a smile that circles her head. A magenta tear hangs off the edge of one eye. But there will be time enough for tears. We turn at once at the sound every Rim-dweller knows at the base of their spine. A one meter brown snake has slithered out from behind the bloodwood tree and is heading straight for my sister's grave. Eric is there in an instant and has the snake between his jaws, bites its head off, and Mag's shovel does the rest.

* * *

Narn's story broke me open, the indecipherable syllables and discordant music a deeper cut than I bargained for. Seeping into my bones so that my blood could make sense of the layered thought forms flying, even if my brain could not. And then, out of the flocking recall materialized the winged creature—the one I'd felt haunting me for weeks—atop the slated roof of the guard house. Two fierce eyes in a face across which scraps of blue cloud blew and Orion wheeled, a form so camouflaged against the firmament that you would never see it unless it wanted to be seen.

No one knows that once . . .

I would show Narn that I wasn't after all the crappy twin, and that she was right not to throw me away. Finding her lost sister as she had failed to do was one reason I needed her stories. But the real reason why she gave them to me was probably so I could make good on the most important promise of all—the one I made to myself. Either way it seemed to be enough for her, for a sense of justice for which she wasn't made, but which she had learned over time and at great cost.

I tore away from the bridge before I could forget. Translating the story as soon as I returned to my room: it began with a virgin who gives birth to a beaver covered in black feathers with a human mouth. The virgin holds the beaver-bird-baby in her arms and walks the streets, trying to work out how it happened, because maybe if she can find the source, the ravaging image that seeded such an abomination, she can *un*find it. The beaver-bird-baby rustles its feathers and gives her directions in a human tongue. But the destination was still fuzzy. To try and pass the time until it came to me, I opened my tablet to try and learn more about the Fearsome Gatherum and its mysterious curator.

Narn always said I had exceptional vision, that I could see through walls, but it just came down to knowing where to look. I read about Sasha Younger, but none of it really told me anything. I read that she was young, heir to some fortune, "unconventionally beautiful." I read that she took on the Dean for the right to hold the controversial reading series, and won. But most of what I found was about the series itself, as part of an underground movement:

~ *Which privileged subjective experience in all of its diverse shades of pain*
~ *Which didn't truck in shame*
~ *Which sought to put words back in the mouths of those whose tongues had been torn off, figuratively speaking, in the Blood Temple*

The readings worshiped fear in all its forms. Its manifesto stated that:

Fear is a human right. Fear makes us value our freedom. Fear returns to humanity the virtue of authenticity. Fear finds our truth.

But it comes at a price, the manifesto said. Sacrifices must be made. Leave your triggers at the door.

Over the next two days, I kept searching, following links, sidebars, cross-references. Even when I could find no answers, the more questions I asked, the more I felt my brain changing. The more I felt myself changing. On Saturday afternoon, I was deep in some discussion forum about the nature of fear, when Lara burst into the room. "I need to find Trudy. There's been another attack."

After several texts, Trudy was found safe at the indoor pool, training for the Village Games. Lara dropped her phone on the bed and collapsed beside it.

"I didn't sign up for this," she said, smoothing a chestnut curl. "It's not just the Redress Schemers who supposedly want to study our brains or turn us into weapons or slaves or whatnot—now there is this, like, this Ghost Hunter who wants to eliminate us with extreme prejudice. Like some kind of culling. Like what happened to the thylacines in the Rim. Is that what they want to do to us?"

I looked over my device at her. I thought of Eric, and my heart fluttered. Not everyone's guardian was a necromancer—in that at least I did get lucky.

Lara got to her feet and went over to the window, angled so I couldn't see her face. I could tell that she was looking not at, but beyond Wellsburg, to the south where we all came from, as if trying to work out how in the world to get back.

"It's like we're being punished for surviving," she said, "when *he* did not."

"Lara," I said gently. "The Father's dead. His own mutant ravens turned on him. They found bits of his body over a five-kilometer radius. He can't hurt us now."

She went to the bed and picked up her phone. At the door she stopped and turned. "Liar"

I averted my eyes, and she slammed out the door.

Being human is characterized by dread, the Gatherum manifesto continued. Without fear, life has no meaning. The comment thread was as instructive, at least to me, as the posts.

Life is triggers, @shiversdliver commented.

@shiversdliver your idea of a trigger is your vibrator, @made2break replied. *You've never been truly triggered or you'd know that these occur not as a response to life, but in the presence of anti-life; not at the prospect of mortality, but at the certainty of something far worse—the total impossibility of self-defense. That's fear, @shiversdliver. Not your bullshit Fearsome Humdrum.*

Get over yourself, @made2break, @shiversdliver replied. *Everyone else is.*

I read about how the reading series was a "safe space" for those who didn't wish to be triggered by trigger warnings. It was a safe space to learn that everyone is responsible for their own safety. To discover where you ended and the world began.

New members were welcome to apply. Any survivor able to make the proper expiatory sacrifices by way of the hefty membership fees, was also welcomed.

Welcome to make a sacrifice, @made2break dissented, *or to be one?*

Reading this gave me a cramp in my neck. It made my pulse race. Partly at the Gatherum's snarky dismissal of the unique terror of our reality. Partly at my own desire to believe it. My own desire to magic away everything that I survived into the realm of a good shiver designed to deliver its existential payload and nothing more. Give fear a name and you curse its power. *Once upon a time. No one knows that . . .*

Once was enough. Except when it wasn't.

As I tapped away at the computer, my mismatched eyes—Kai's blue and my brown—stared back at me from the monitor and I saw a bridge of code unreeling between them, fear and love, that two-faced bitched called fate.

The Father came to visit Kai in the infirmary. Took off his Akubra and spun it around on his finger, tears running down his ruddy cheeks. "You're the daughter I never had," he said, just like a real dad. "See you in Paradise."

What I wanted to find out was where the readings were held, so that I could time my arrival and departure. The old me would have been satisfied at having been invited to play a part, and waited for the details as Pagan saw fit to provide them. But I was not that me anymore. Pagan began to strike me as wrong—maybe it was what Marvin had said about her, or maybe it was how, whenever I thought of her now, I saw a statue come to life, a stone angel flown off a Wellsburg rooftop.

Except that I knew that Pagan was no angel.

The readings, I found out eventually, were held in a turret in Younger Wing, named after Sasha's founding family. During my searches, I came across news of the attack that Lara had told me about. The fourth, it reminded me. I'd lost count. The Made had been lashed across the back as had the others, chunks of flesh hacked from shoulder and buttocks, and was lying in the hospital wrapped in bandages and babbling about a giant killer-bat with prominent red nipples.

And just like that, whatever power memory had given me, it took away. Because it could.

CHAPTER 13
GATHERUM

Fearsome Gatherum was held on Sundays beginning promptly at eleven p.m. The witching hour. That was another problem, which Pagan breezily dispensed with in a text, saying that she'd arrange a special pass, authorized by Sasha Younger herself, for me to cross the bridge after curfew. My first trial was scheduled for tomorrow night. As promised, Pagan had ordered me a new outfit which arrived the morning before. I brought the box in from the hall and determined to return it unopened. But in a moment of doubt, I lifted the lid and there, folded in tissue was a silky black dress in my size. I closed the box and tried to forget about it, spending Saturday night alone with a cup of Narn's tea and my biology textbook. I selected my outfit from the clothes we had ordered together before I left the Starvelings. A clean skirt just short enough to pass for cute and a blouse with a collar I hated because it made my neck look too skinny. I hardly slept that night at all.

The next day I dressed and stood at the bathroom mirror. My hair out of control, dark puffy half-moons under my mismatched eyes. I heard a low hoarse giggle coming from the hallway or from under the bed, or maybe from somewhere inside my own head. I couldn't tell anymore. Whatever it was, I tore off my clothes, and lifted Pagan's gift out of the box.

The dress hugged my flat chest and followed the shy curve of my hips, ending in a split at the back that rose to just below my buttocks. There was more tissue in the gift box and I tore at it. Out came a mass of blue velvet. It was a voluminous coat, more like a cloak. It brushed my ankles. Spit gathered at the corners of my mouth. I had never come close to having anything as delicious. "Kai!" I couldn't help but say, "Look at me!" And I glanced over my shoulder in the mirror, and there she was.

There were shoes, too, platform brocade pumps in the oily midnight of a raven's ruff. Everything fit so perfectly that at the last minute I exchanged the brocade shoes for my sister's old brown blood-spattered boots. Their imperfection suited me better.

I liked the way they pinched.

It was dark when I crossed the bridge, my heart in my mouth. I ignored the guard's double take of me in my new outfit, concentrating on clocking the clawed smears on the bottom of the rails, as indelible as a shadow.

My thighs rubbed together beneath the tight black sheath, the clump of Kai's shoes like hooves ringing in my ear. I got to the Quad early and slipped behind the maple tree to avoid being seen, especially by Pagan. I watched one or two Regulars, dressed to party, slip into Old Dorm Hall. My heart was racing, incredulous at what I—crappy Meera—had agreed to. The maple's leaves were crimson and its roots were as ridged and lumpen as the scar tissue on Narn's back. A gleam of something caught my eye. It glinted in the reflected light of the lamps around the Quad. Unsteady in my tight dress, I bent down to have a closer look and even reached out my finger to touch it, recoiling in a revulsion all the more horrific for being familiar. It was not one but several pale snake skins tangled around each other in a ball. My skin grew cold, not at the seething knot of skins (impossible to tell where one ended and the other began) but at how they were the same milky white as the snaking braids of the Made being transfused in the infirmary all those years ago. The Made who was not a Made. And I knew that these ghostly sheddings were not from the garter snakes of Upper Slant, but something that slithered in a different place.

I stood up, the base of my neck tingling. I backed away from the snake ball, and I smoothed the grimace from my face, suspecting that I was being watched. Somehow I made it to the door of the building. Beneath a glowing cage light webbed in graceful ivy was a buzzer. I pressed it and a second later, the door clicked open. There was no elevator. I began climbing the steps, my footfall muffled on rose carpet that darkened to a sheep-heart maroon at the edges. Recessed sconces made my shadow flail. I held Marvin's notebook against my sweating ribs, the ending to Narn's story conjured from a scrap of dream.

I pressed another buzzer on a modern security console beside the door of a corner suite at one end of the fourth floor. It opened silently, and I was in.

The room was the most beautiful space I had ever seen, like all the Golden Book palaces come to life. Finally, my castle. The guests were all Regulars as far as I could see—all women, dressed in cocktail sheaths or clinging tights and exotic shoes. They lounged on velvet couches, stood in clumps around the oaken mantlepiece cradling golden liquor in cut crystal, or leaned gracefully against stone columns. Waiters moved silently bearing drinks. They had the same ready grins and peachy complexions as the officers from the weapons facility who came to sample the older Mades, the same ice in their stares. I took a glass of champagne from a tray, and it all but slipped through my fingers. Laughter and excited chatter filled the entire suite which looked to be many rooms, although there could not have been more than three or four. Mirrors and candles multiplied everything, including my own reflection—I didn't know myself in my dress-up clothes and messy lipstick. Through an open door, I glimpsed a four-poster bed piled with coats. I hung onto mine.

Logs popped in a wide stone fireplace. There was a marble bar in a corner and I made for it, exchanged the bubbles for a double vodka and immediately felt more like myself. An antique table was spread with hunks of rare meat at one end, fruit and soft cheeses at the other. Another table was loaded with cakes and crèmes and confectionary. Music played, something sweeping and unobtrusive that I didn't recognize. Candles everywhere made the walls recede and cheekbones pop. From beveled windows, the moon followed my progress through arches from one room into another until I found myself against a wine-colored wall in the largest room. Against the opposite wall and between two leadlight windows, stood an empty electric chair.

"It's a relic," said a voice behind me. I turned to see Pagan dressed in a black rubber unitard. "Sasha's old man bought it from a collector."

I nodded at the chair. "It's a lot," I said. The steel cap gleamed and the wooden arms were worn to a soft patina.

"Wait till you sit on it," Pagan said, her lipstick like some glossy dessert.

We clinked glasses and I noticed that she wore a large ugly ring. It was gold with a lustrous red stone in it, an opal or something similar, green and black markings across its face like an aerial view of a lake or an inland sea. I stared, taken aback at the resemblance to Narn's eye. Before I could ask about it, Pagan took a short breath and looked over my shoulder. I turned to watch a woman pass through the arches and stop to greet a group of guests. Her scarlet hair radiated light. The wide white planes of her cheekbones spread like wings, and her eyelids were so heavy as to look almost like a disfigurement, and all the more beautiful for that.

Sasha Younger, in the flesh.

She wore an oversized tweed suit, eight-inch heels and nothing else. The jacket fastened at the middle by a single button and gaped to reveal the curve of heavy breasts and a navel ring made of what looked like a tusk, or a tooth.

Sasha Younger. A recent Wellsburg alumna (recent enough), heiress, daughter of the wealthy benefactor Orrin Younger, himself son of a Wellsburg founding father. The notebook jumped from my hands onto the thick rug, and I felt time come to a stop. She had the same ugly ring on her finger as Pagan. Conversation and laughter became muted so that there was only the beating of a hundred hearts in my ear. The presence of this beautiful being made nonsense of my own in a way nothing had since my sister had died.

My thoughts turned to mush. My retrained brain failed me. I felt like I was falling backward. Pagan made hasty introductions while I was scrabbling on the floor for the notebook. And by the time I stood up they had both moved on.

Sometime later, Pagan moved toward the electric chair and tapped on her glass with the blade of a knife. Beneath the reverberating crystal ting, I heard her announce that the readings would begin. She welcomed and thanked everyone for coming and for their cooperation in the collection of their phones—one of the waiters moved among the guests, carefully collecting devices in a shallow tray. Pagan thanked the founder, Ms. Sasha Younger, and waited for the inevitable applause. She introduced the readers—I heard my name as if from a great distance—and the first one took her seat at the chair. Lights went out. Apart from the candles, and the moonlit rectangles of stained glass, the room was in darkness.

Shyly, the first reader offered a story about being turned inside out and pulled through her own navel. Used as a sail on a pirate ship, her ribs were the mast, her veins the rigging. I thought it was a good effort but I did not applaud because Sasha, now lounging on a leather chaise that had been moved in specially, also did not. The next story wasn't bad either but I forgot everything about it as soon as Pagan, smiling serenely, announced that it was my turn. I was surprised to hear her describe my story as speaking for and to all of the survivors present.

"And aren't we all survivors of something?" She pressed her hands together in *namaste* and mock-bowed in my direction. That is when I knew that I was not the only token Made in the room, and that part of me I'd never looked at directly, but had only seen reflected in the dead eyes of a lost witch, once again rose to the smell of a blood bath. To the challenge of a trial by ordeal. The electric chair beckoned. The branches of the maple tapped against the delicate glass, counting me in. Three-two-one.

I opened my mouth and began to read, noticing a Regular check her watch. Another pick a cuticle. Without warning, I heard the voice of my real sister say, "Read the room, idiot!" And in that instant I saw that the hostile bored, entitled faces around me were not my kind. They'd doubled the stakes and the odds were not in favor of a story of beaver babies born from the monstrous imagination of a South Rim virgin. I looked down at the words on the page, the words I'd scrawled after listening to Narn's story—they'd scrambled into a code I could no longer decipher. But my changing brain could and did, and from between its zeros and ones came something slowly, inexorably remade, a story conjured from my imagination uncoupled from the Father and conjoined, through Narn's babbled sorcery, to the memories of my dead twin.

"No one knows that once," I began . . .

There was a house haunted by a mean-spirit, a prank. The house and the prank were one. A joke house, floating above a lake lined with silvery trees. Vacationers rented it and vomited up their own half-digested souls. The joke was on them. A small reunion of college friends cooked and ate their feelings—the last member had none left—she ate herself. A ukulele group thought it would be radical to string their instruments with each other's guts until they were all strung out. The spirit of a dead serial killer crawled into the walls of the house. An author fell in love with him, wrote him out of the wallpaper and into her life. In return he killed her and shut her up in the wall and wrote himself off at the end. To be continued. Some drunken coworkers played truth or dare using a rubber chicken as the spinner. The chicken lost its head and became an axe—in the end the coworkers were all plucked.

My tongue felt strange. My voice had deepened and began from somewhere near the ceiling, instead of from *me*—the hearing and speaking of the tale just slightly out of sync. It told itself, doubled back and came out somewhere I didn't expect. The maple branches stopped their tapping. Regulars sat with varnished fingernails interlaced and their eyes in frozen *O*s. A token Made clamped her hands over her mouth and puke gushed from between her fingers as she wept silently. Pagan bit her lower lip with lipstick-smeared teeth making her look both goofy and grotesque. But I registered all of this only peripherally. My focus was on Sasha Younger. When her heavy eyelids narrowed to slits over her black contacts and she beckoned me to her with a dip of her head, I felt a kind of love. I left the electric chair, pardoned from my sins, exonerated from my crimes.

"Welcome," she said. And patted the seat beside her.

And fate laughed with both sides of her face.

* * *

It is two months before Kai digs herself up from beneath the bloodwood tree and wanders into the yard. I hear her before I see her. The ravens, silent since my arrival, begin their slit-throat cries and I look up from the porch and there she is. Limping out from a cloud of black feathers beneath a transparent sky that matches the blue ribbon I have tied in a choker around my neck.

"That's mine, sister."

If it weren't for a puckered eye socket and a begrimed shimmer around the shoulders, she'd look as alive as I do. The thylacine leaps to his feet and his striped hackles rise but he holds his ground—that rigidly pointed tail extended like a spear. I let the ribbon fall to the ground, unable to comprehend, to believe my eyes. Narn is on the porch in an instant, rolling up the sleeves of her tunic. Spittle and invocations fly from her lips. I side-eye Mag creeping around the hut with their shotgun. Kai calmly retrieves the ribbon from the dirt, demands a poultice for her eye. "One of your lungwort specials'll do the trick, witch." She twists her neck grotesquely. "Jeez, what a dump!"

Beneath the hysterical screech of the ravens, I am aware of Mag stealthy and watchful around the corner of the hut in their filthy oversized hoody and mud-caked sneakers. And perhaps that is what propels me into my sister's arms, like a baby, wrapping my legs around her waist. A maggot drops from her lips, and a watery ichor pools behind her toenails. But her hair smells like bloodwood blossoms. It has grown back coarse as a horse's mane. It is so long that I wind it around both of our necks so she can never leave me again.

* * *

I attended classes the week after the Gatherum, not seeking Marvin out but not deliberately avoiding him either. A misdirected sense of indignation stoked by my niggling sense of shame made me ask, why shouldn't I do whatever I wanted to? I was in a free country now. Wasn't I?

But I missed him. I missed our talks. I wanted to tell him about my success, to share it with him. But I was worried. Why could I remember the reaction my story caused, but nothing of the words themselves, or the plot, or characters . . . or anything? That was a blank, as though it had happened to someone else. I wondered if Marvin's coded indentations were responsible for that amnesia, and if so, I wanted to tell him that maybe he'd overstepped. My temples drummed with that old rage. I *wanted* to remember. I could see myself sitting in the electric chair, but I couldn't hear the words I'd offered for Sasha's protection. When I leafed through the notebook, the story seemed tame, even lame—the virgin eventually gave up the search for the image that had raped her, knowing that as soon as she destroyed it, she'd also destroy the bird-beaver-baby whom she'd grown to love—and I couldn't work out why it had caused the reaction it had. There was a part of me that couldn't yet acknowledge that although this was what I'd written in the notebook, it was neither the tale that Narn had told me, nor the story that I had "read" at the Gatherum.

I lay awake in my blue-stained Tower room searching my brain, reliving the evening, moment by moment, sucking nectar from the fragments of memory. I smiled in the dark. The triumph. The love. I felt like I was . . . remade. Behind my closed eyelids I conjured the gleaming throats and designer dresses, candle-light lapping at the louche cocktails, and above all Sasha Younger's approving nod—ever so slight—but a nod nonetheless. Alone in my room in the dark, I made her do it again and again. If the actual details of the tale itself were behind a psychic curtain—a fog of either Narn's sorcery, or Marvin's code or both, I didn't care. I'd found my place.

During my lunch break on Tuesday, there was a text from Pagan: *You're in.*

I texted back my thanks. *Same time this weekend?*

Every two weeks. Sasha doesn't want too much of a good thing. Keep them hungry, haha.

I texted back a laughing crying face.

She texted back, *So you'll be there?*

I checked my calendar. A week from next Sunday was just after Hallow-een—actual, not anti-Halloween. I recalled the way Sasha had moistened her lips with her tongue before asking me if I had more where that one came from. I knew Pagan was waiting for an answer but something held me back.

"Meera?" It was Marvin, standing behind me in the line for the salad bar at the student union.

"How did it go?" he asked. "I hear that you passed your trial. Survived the ordeal."

"Sink or swim," I said. "I think I knew that going in."

"Spoken like a true witch."

His smile was still sweet but his face was puffy and one of his suspenders was frayed. I plucked it playfully. "How's the mind-hunting research going, Marvin?"

"Well enough," he said. "So, you think you'll go back?"

I had guiltily pocketed my phone without answering Pagan's text.

"Haven't decided," I said, casually. "Term papers and all. I have to go back to FiFo in the meantime. I haven't been for a while."

I ladled greens onto my plate.

"FiFo? Let me know what the new TA is like," he said, popping a blueberry between his teeth.

"What happened to Jacinta?"

"Hunter got her." Marvin read something on his phone. "You didn't hear?"

I felt my legs grow cold.

"She's alive," Marvin shrugged and I got a faint whiff of eucalyptus—maybe some soap he brought with him from the Rim, using it carefully to make it last. "Now the cops are looking for a black-cloaked slasher."

That bothered me. "But the wounds are on their backs. So how do they know what their attacker is wearing?"

He scratched his stubble. "From what I gather from the reports and discussion threads, they are now considering the possibility that there are two attackers, and the one in black, an accomplice maybe, is who the victim sees?"

"Well you're the detective." I didn't push it. "Why all the fuss anyway, if it's just Mades?"

He wearily explained that a campus psycho on the loose wasn't a great look for a posh college trying to beef up its back-end with Redress subsidies. There had already been some withdrawals from the program—no funding cuts yet, but he imagined that there would be.

"I don't know how you find time to keep up with the latest and ace your grades too," I said. I took my tray and looked for a table for us, but Marvin asked for his in a box, blaming homework, and leaving me to eat alone. He acted nervous, like he couldn't get away from me fast enough. Was that the price I'd have to pay for being so . . . fearsome?

I doubled down and opened my bottle of soda. I chugged it thirstily, like there was no tomorrow.

CHAPTER 14
CHIMERA

Marvin was right about FiFo. During the weeks I'd missed, Jacinta had been replaced by another TA—a harried bearded Malemade who said his name was Corby. He was working on a PhD across the schools of media and environmental studies, about the role of heavy weather in film. He listened to our stories beneath the ticking clock—I added a jealous witch to the bird-beaver-baby story and someone said it was lame. Another student said they wanted to love it but found it derivative, and in poor taste considering the history of Wellsburg. Corby asked if the hybrid had flight feathers or a scaly tail, or both?

"And if its tail is flat and scaled like a beaver, one would assume that its feet are those of the Passeriformes order with three forward pointing toes and one backward, all joined at the level of the foot?"

"Yes and no," I said, eliciting a few laughs.

"It's your chimera, not mine." Corby lowered bushy eyebrows. "Although I have to say that I admire your vision."

A Regular gathered her books and walked out talking on the phone. "Don't let the door hit you on your way out," Corby said. No one laughed. Toward the end of the class he paused and looked around. "Do you know," he said, spreading his burly arms out on the scratched oaken table, "where this table is from?"

When no one answered he said, "At the edge of Wellsburg is an old graveyard. Some say it's haunted and there are even tours available. Outside the iron gates of the cemetery are some other graves, all women. The inscriptions are simple. 'Jody McCree, drowned.' 'Henrietta Cruickshank, hanged.' Seven of them in total. Seven graves, women between the ages of eleven and forty-two, all accused of witchcraft under the governorship of the town's founder, Captain Hermann Younger. All found guilty and put to death. There is a plaque to commemorate a famous seventeenth-century puritan and witch-hunter. It says something like, 'We shall soon enjoy halcyon days with all the vultures of hell trodden under our feet—' a quote from a sixteenth century witch-hunter. The Younger family donated this table from Hermann Younger's library."

Before he finished speaking, a shadow moved across the window, blocking out the star-sprinkled dusk. I was aware of the background clicking of phones and the rustling of sheets as my classmates packed their bags, but my focus was on the blue-limned form at the window—I couldn't make out where it ended and the actual night began, and maybe it was that—the way it filled me with itself and its strange uncertain shape.

"The past is never passed, right?" It was Corby and when I turned to see the reaction of the class, I saw we were alone, and that the bearded, blinking instructor only had eyes for me.

* * *

Dying seems to have galvanized my sister somehow. Given her a sense of purpose. Within days of digging herself out of the ground, she's taken over Narn's apothecary, sweeping piles of *Cladonia* into a container for compounding, sniffing blueish lobes of *Siphula* soaking in a beaker of urine.

"This has expired," she says.

"Takes one to know one," Narn mutters under her breath. Like me, she is unsure of how to take the rank return of her favorite, whatever deals she had to do to make it so. I watch Kai pick bugs from her eye socket. She wants Narn to make her a glass eye. Narn has made herself one from a rolled and polished agate, but has not yet been able to find a stone in the right shade of blue for Kai.

We regard ourselves in the mirror. Kai, willowy and empty-eyed, and me, stunted and wild, black hair frizzing out in all directions. My brown eyes gleaming with a love formless enough for the both of us. Strangely, we have never looked so . . .

"Identical," we say at the same time, and hook our pinkies in a broken promise.

Under Kai's instruction, I place orders for new beakers and test tubes, a heating mantle that won't set the whole hut on fire, a balance and a new scale—the ravens have made a nest in the old one. Kai completely reorganizes the whole lab so that like is categorized with like instead of just dumped and scattered into a shroomy unordered hodgepodge. It's like a game for her, I think—and she's all the players. Crucially, she finds all the cash and coin and IOUs from Narn's customers, locks everything in a box for Narn to hide in the root cellar. She counts out a small amount for errands in Norman, twenty klicks to the East almost all off-road.

Narn's hut, tucked along a narrow pass high in the uncharted Starvelings, is virtually inaccessible—Mag can immediately spot anyone moving along the canyon and Eric makes a better watchdog than he does a familiar. Narn and I go into town to make deliveries or pick up supplies, neither of us having much to say to each other. I get used to her mouth soundlessly moving, the gibberish coming from multiple discordant voices that fill the cab of the truck. I recognize the name of her lost sister Tiff and my found sister Kai and sometimes my own name Meera sliced uncomfortably in between. As we skirt the terminal lake, I turn to the window, feeling Narn's glass-eyed stare, but I am still too furious, too self-obsessed to admit what her sacrifice means. That she did it for me.

Her eye for Kai's soul—so I could have *my* sister back as Narn had not been able to have hers. I can't love her yet, but my gratitude, being nebulous, is also boundless. She saved me from the Father. She brought my sister back from the dungeon, saved her soul. I make a mental note to even the odds one day if I can—to find what's left of her sister's soul even if it costs me what's left of my own.

We jolt along through the slanted shade of the canyon, the abrupt emergence into dusty sunlight and the rough red road into town—kangaroos alert at the edge of shimmering paddocks, the high transparent sky that makes me feel as though across this entire restless land there is no place to hide except from where there is no return.

* * *

The guard was already blowing his whistle even though it wasn't yet nine o'clock. A dozen or so survivors had assembled—evening students like me, or casual workers from one of the Wellsburg bookshops or cafés. I was distracted by the memory of Corby's unnerving stare, the thought of those seven witches put to death and disremembered at the edges of some rich man's church.

"You lot are a pain in the ass," the guard said. "If you'd only just stay on your side, where you belonged, we wouldn't be having any of this trouble."

"That's a bit much," someone said. "It's not our fault we get attacked."

My heart in my mouth, the fleshy shadows beating at my back. I turned to the direction of music and laugher from the rooftop of Sweeney's Landing.

"Yeah," someone else said, "if it was a *Regular* getting attacked, they'd call in the army."

On close inspection the guard had the same ruddy smirk as the Fearsome Gatherum waiters, scions of the New World Order.

"Well this is all you got," the guard said, thumbing himself in the chest. "A little gratitude'd be nice."

I couldn't help but get all shrieky.

"The women lying unconscious in hospital after being mangled right under your noses are truly thankful," I cackled. "Forever and ever, Amen."

The guard took a step closer, eyed my wild hair and brimming mismatched eyes. I don't know why I was crying—Jacinta was nothing to me. "All dressed up and nowhere to go, Made? You look like trouble." He licked his lips.

"Double-trouble," a hammy purr floated out of the darkness. "Because by definition the system can't be held responsible for those it was never meant to protect."

The guard wheeled around. "You are?"

"Made to break," Marvin said from where he'd materialized beneath the arch. "It's the drinking hour, darlings, and I could murder a martini."

I had limited experience with unconditional friendship. By the second round at Dirty Bert's, it had brought on a fresh bout of tears, which I attributed to my errant period being due. But where Marvin touched me was real.

"Thank you," I said. "I'm glad we're still friends."

Marvin downed the cheap booze and made a gag-face. "If you were a real friend, you'd smuggle some twelve-year-old single malt out of Ms. Younger's next Gatherum-ti-dum."

I said I'd try and he said what, to get the high-end hooch or to be a real friend, and I said both. The bar was half-empty, the bartender distracted between his watch and repeated darting glances out the door. Drinkers huddled in nervous clusters or alone on their devices. Music played and I noticed Trudy and Lara at a booth, double-dating with Malemades. They were talking and laughing, the table littered with soggy fries and greasy glasses.

Resolutely, but with that halting confessional authority of his, Marvin said, "Back in the Blood Temple, I would lie in the dark prison of the bunkroom and listen for the drag of Master's sandals in the dirt outside the hut. He'd open the door, letting in the light. The terrible light."

"I know."

"The world outside the Blood Temple is an illusion, a mirage," he said. "It's hard to unsee our fate, Meera."

I didn't want to argue with him. "All I'm saying is that invisibility may not be the best choice. The Father, the Assistants, your Masters, they saw everything but us. Whenever they did to us what they did, they only saw themselves. That's invisibility—not fate, but choice. Theirs, by definition. Narn once told me that choice was just another word for fate flashing her heinie. That Paradise the Father wanted to go back to? It was Paradise to him only because it was hell to us."

"Okay," he leaned in, began moving a fry around the table to demonstrate his point. "How is being seen, stepping into the fearsome light, going to be any different?"

"Because I control it," I said. "I control the light."

But he was gone, staring into that space that I could, if I let myself, monstrously imagine. The abyss by definition: that which cannot in the end be fathomed. The bartender made a signal for last drinks. Lara and Trudy wove out with their dates, and Lara gave a little wave.

"I see you," I said when Marvin returned.

"I know."

"You're really Made2Break?"

"Aren't we all?"

We walked home through the eerily empty streets, our arms lightly touching. Steam plumed from our mouths. His hair silvery blue in the glow of the bridge.

"What do you know about a cemetery outside of town?" I said.

He shook his head. "I can't remember the last time I ventured across the bridge."

"The new TA, Corby, told us about the cemetery where the witches were buried."

"Maybe *he'll* take you there," he said, his smile not reaching his pussy-willow eyes.

I slept badly that week. I thought of the upcoming Gatherum and wondered if two weeks was long enough to be forgotten. Unable to face Corby again, I ditched FiFo on Wednesday, and when, on Halloween night, I tried to make my Thursday call to Narn the connection was so bad that we gave up. I barely slept, aware of Trudy sitting up in bed, her blue-tinged face fixed on her phone. I noticed that Lara's bed was empty and felt a weight on my legs and I dreamed that it was Eric.

A scream woke me in some dead hour just before dawn. Trudy sat up in the grainy dark, her eyes wide and a fist jammed in her mouth. I turned on my pillows and followed her gaze to where at the end of my bed sat the Hunter. He pixelated in and out from a curtain of static.

"Wretch," he said, the words not in sync with his lips. "Be gone, Vulture of Hell."

I lay paralyzed against the pillows, couldn't breathe.

He wore a hat like the Father's Akubra, caked with river mud. His broken face loomed out of the black and blue shadows—shreds of flesh hanging off a smashed, translucent skull. He lurched threateningly to his feet but I couldn't move. My arms and legs were leaden. I emitted a choked-off cry, but couldn't pull myself off the bed. A long black leather duster swung on his mangled frame. The static pulled at it, gave it wings. He clutched a curved hunting knife in one hand. In the other a pistol, which he raised with a jagged, pixelated hand and aimed at my head.

CHAPTER 15
FRESH MEAT

You'd never find our place high in the Starvelings unless you knew what you were looking for. The brown hills bunch at the edge of the desert, rising to an interminable prominence of rugged escarpments and sheer cliffs, below which rainforest canyons and inaccessible lowlands connect a network of underground lakes. But it is only one of many mountain ranges on this vast continent. Is it north or south? East or west? The Starvelings—a name spoken in whispers and never written—could be anywhere. Or nowhere.

The forgotten swaggie's hut is a steep climb up from any human civilization and is invisible behind a tangle of fern and vine, deep in the cleft of a vertical ridge. The people who come to call on Narn—who pay for her craft in coin or kind—walk, ride or drive a long dusty way, and their understanding of what, or where, the Starvelings are, varies according to their needs. There are plenty of places to hide in this vast southern land, as the Father discovered, where very little is worth the risk of being found. Narn's magic is one of those things.

Escaped Mades, survivors of other hells, bush people, dreamers, failures, fixers, elders and young blood, soldiers and castaways—they leave their humpies and tinnies and trailers and caves and cars and treehouses to slip through the secret byways—mainly for Narn's *Islandia* moonshine, eighty proof vodka distilled from wild-grown Iceland moss made with pure mountain water flowing from the myriad caves pocking the ridge. But they come too for her healing salves and poultices, her cures for boils and baldness, for pneumonia, warts, anxiety and ulcers. Her teas for insomnia and her candles for bad dreams and her powders for eating too much and drops for loving too hard. Trusted customers might get a spell or a charm thrown in, a sprig of pennyroyal for protection or snakeroot bundled with wattle for luck, or a pricey suspension of *Letharia* for hopelessness. My spine tingles to hear those who speak of a Made from the Rogues Bay camp, a raven-haired enchantress who spun bunkroom tales of magic so complete, so shimmering, that they conjured the very survival of all who listened to them. Narn's visitors speak sadly of the Made's inevitable unmaking, of the Father so jealous of how she loved her sister enough to die for her—that he had to kill her first.

When she first came back from the dead, Kai would brew a pot of tea for the customers, pick lemons from the gnarled tree over the vegetable patch. I'd discretely check both for maggots. But if Kai thinks that Eric will let just any stranger past the gate to sit under the cool of the veranda for a sip of homemade lemonade and a pipe, she is dead wrong. For reasons I cannot explain, Eric has taken a shine to me—he suffers Kai because he must, but it is my hand into which he presses his muzzle, and it is at my command that he rushes ahead of Narn to the gate, just in case. Narn in her gumboots is a picture of shuffling eccentricity, but there is a boline hidden in the folds of her tunic and even as her freckled hands extend for payment, her seeing eye scopes the still, pale treeline, and her dun lips mouth words of warning.

In the shadows cast by the lemon tree, Mag watches with her .303 trained on the customers.

Sometimes they stop for a while, whether born or Made, and sometimes they tell a story. Sometimes but not always their own. Heard maybe, or dreamed. Told standing up or leaning across the stone wall, and because of what they have forgotten, or never knew, the stories rarely start at the beginning and the ending is usually somewhere in the middle. Narn listens to their confessions and accusations, their excuses and lies, and helps stitch them together with her own, words they only pretend to understand, but which somehow help to make the stories, and those who tell them, whole again.

"Poor bitches," Kai says, from where we both watch behind the curtain. Her fingers leave a trail of rank slime. I swat away the flies.

Above the door is a .22, for snakes mainly. Or rabbits for the pot. Mag has shown me how to use it and keep it oiled and cleaned, just in case. The just-in-case-ness of our life in the hidden hut is something that gnaws at me, takes me away from my play and my chores. My sister's larger-than-life return is in opposite proportion to the decay that eats at her skin and makes a gluey strip slop off the inside of her arm and onto the worktable. Another batch of expensive betony oil ruined. But Narn doesn't scold her and neither do I—I go to paste her skin back on her arm like papier-mâché and she fondly slaps away my sisterly fussing. Kai's idea of a joke to "snap me out of it" is unchanged. She flicks a black fingernail in my tea, laughs like a loon when I spit it out in disgust. She pulls worms from her ear and leaves them on Narn's pillow, and Narn farts in surprise. But this *pretend* cruelty, the obsessive hoaxes and practical jokes, the love and fear that is pretend until its real—it is Kai as she was in life, so why not in death?

On dark days, she is quieter than usual, stinkier too. She fills out Narn's grimoire with pages of her round left-handed cursive, properly recorded measurements, equivalents and substitutions, the difference in properties between say, Witch's Hair and Wizard's Beard, between Hermes' Semen and Head of Snake. Narn's scattershot recall, her impatience with me, only goes so far. It is thanks to my twin's posthumous pedantry that I teach myself the science of lichenology. How for instance, to suspend *lithophiloides* dust in Baboon Tears, to evaporate it into a powder so fine that it feels like a lover's breath on your lips just before it kills you.

On these days it is me who tries to cheer her up. I buy a Scrabble set from the charity shop in Norman and I make the missing letters out of cardboard and bring it to her and she says, "How are we even twins?"

But she plays with me anyway. And she wins of course, by adding R-E-V-E-N-A-N to the "T" of my stupid word, ANT, managing, as she hoots triumphantly, to "get a seven-letter bingo across a Triple Word Square on my second-to-last move, a statistically impossible to prevent win except, you know, if one player totally sucks!"

I like to see Kai happy.

And if there is one thing that I am better at than her, that is scoping out botanicals for our stock in trade. Eric and I search lower in the canyon for exotic lichen, fragile stalks of *Xanthoparmelia convoluta* to stack in a corner of the apothecary, like broken bones. Kai brings it to her nose and sniffs it. "This is one of my favorite lichens," she says (I know), "because of how it just moves around in the wind."

"It's vagrant," I say. "It lacks rhizines to hold it down."

"Just like us," she says.

But however Kai has become philosophical in death, she has grown up somehow and there is damage in her empty eye.

"Is it hard?" I ask. "Being dead?"

She shrugs and I hear something crack. "Sometimes it just makes it easier."

Makes what easier? These are the things I don't like to ask. Because as much as I love having her back, I'm not sure I completely trust her. That she has been broken by the Father, and put back together by Narn in a place of darkness, makes me wonder what can crawl into the gaps or what maybe already has.

One day, coming back from feeding the chickens, I find a page from a notebook blown onto the path. The paper is not from the grimoire or from the cheap exercise book I use (at Kai's insistence) to record and observe my lichen findings. It's parchment, the skin of something. Thick and yellowed with age, and ridged with indentations. There are words written on the page, heavily scrawled—*ravelings, slavering, triangles, grievants.* The almost anagrams of the forbidden word march across the middle of the page in a horizontal strip, like a bridge, and another piece has been sheared off the lower edge, as if someone (else) maybe wrote (Starvelings) there and wanted to keep it for themselves, or keep it hidden.

The word is not to be written.

I don't tell anyone because Kai didn't write it. I know her southpaw script. And I know Narn's labored runic print. It wasn't either. I fold the paper up and throw it in the fire, and then I skulk past the brooding Mag to find my sister.

"We're lichenelicious," Kai says. "With your imagination and my memory, it's like we're two halves of the whole world."

Most of the time I happily admit the symbiosis of bacteria and fungus in lichen *is* like Kai and me—the living cohabiting with the dead. The righter of wrongs and the finder of lost things. She is the mind and I am the eye. Her memory is sharpened by death. My powers of imagination are heightened by life. I impress her by clocking a rusty bloom of *Caloplaca* a kilometer away. The weird creep of a *Cladonia* colony hidden under a fallen tree scrapes at that place in my heart that sees things hiding in the dark. The purplish *Pannaria* pops at the edge of my eye, and Eric and I bring it back to swing lazily from the roof of the porch, nebular, our very own universe—two twins, one brought back from the dead by the strength of the other's refusal to let her go.

* * *

The Hunter left a wet patch on the bed.

"Did he say wretch?" Trudy sounded on the edge of hysteria. "Or witch?"

I couldn't remember if the Hunter pulled his ghostly trigger before he lowered his gun. Before he turned and melted into the white noise from which he'd come. His outlines had become jumpy, nightmarish. I'd struggled against my paralysis but I couldn't move properly, until dawn had entered the room in his place.

"It'll never wash off." Trudy examined the bed, her rising voice shrill enough to break glass. "It looks like he shat himself. Look at the hollow left at the end where he was sitting. It's like a riverbed. Or a grave."

I brewed some calming tea for us both. Chamomile, valerian, nothing too magical. Sitting against her pillows she said, "I thought I was done with all that."

"Seeing ghosts?" I said. "We'll never be done with that."

Trudy frowned over her tea. Her tilted eyes were puffy. She'd had eyelash extensions and they clumped with her tears. "It smells of rotten eggs."

"River mud often does."

"Did you always have the Dead-See?"

"Yes."

"Even in the Blood Temple?"

"Yes."

"Me too," she said, picking a tea leaf off her lip. "I never told anyone."

"Me neither," I said.

"Why did he come?"

"I don't know."

"He could have killed you."

"I think we both know that isn't true."

"Is that why, d'you think?" she asked dully. "To tell us that he's not the one killing Mades?"

"Maybe."

"Maybe to say he's sorry, you know, for being such an ass about witches? Maybe to try and redeem himself?"

"That'd be pushing it."

"You're a bitch, you know."

We both smile.

"You're not going to tell anyone?" she asked.

"Neither of us are."

We looked at the pool of muddy goo on my bed.

"He was heavy."

"The things they carry," I say.

"Did he actually shit himself?" Trudy asked.

"Everyone does when they die."

"You can sleep with me?" She said it like a question and answer rolled into one.

My phone buzzed with a text that I knew would be Pagan with a second reminder about the Gatherum on Sunday, pissed that I hadn't replied to her first one.

"I don't think I'll sleep much."

She widened her black-smeared eyes in alarm. "You won't leave me alone?"

"I promise."

"Lara's still with her Halloween date."

"Yes.

"Can we tell her?"

"She won't believe you."

"No," Trudy said. "They never do."

She put the tea down and folded her hands in her lap. "After the Blood Temple, and back in South Rim when we were trying to survive, there were tales of three witches who brought themselves into being."

My flesh crawled. "I heard those stories too."

"Do you think . . ." she paused, trying to find the words. "Do you think that if witches conjure themselves into being, they can conjure themselves into unbeing too?"

I looked over at her, twisting her fingers around the bedsheets. "I don't think you have to be a witch to do that," I said.

"Does being able to see ghosts make us witches?"

I thought about it. "Does it matter?"

"It does if they ever go back to the old ways. I mean like before the Apology—when they'd hang us and dump our bodies outside the walls of graveyards—where we became ghosts. That's the how and the why of who we are—Made into ghosts."

I stared at her moving mouth. The graveyard, she said. Was that what the Hunter was trying to tell me with all that babble about wretches and vultures? Corby had quoted something similar from the cemetery where the witches lay—wretched. Vultures. Cursed.

But why?

I didn't really want to sleep on the Hunter's wet patch so I got into bed beside Trudy. I thought of the aspirin the girls had brought me, the term papers they'd written for me. How they took care of each other like real sisters. In a sense every Made was related. At one level we were all sisters from the same mister. Trudy curled on her side and fell asleep hiccuping. Maybe it was that which decided me. Which made me answer Pagan's text, finally. Because I knew there would be no going back.

I'll be there, I wrote.

I fell asleep wondering if I'd be able to get in touch with Narn tomorrow, and what she would come up with for the next story.

Reception was back to normal on the bridge Friday and my conversation with Narn was brief and businesslike. She'd barely finished gibbering her story at me before I hung up. There had been news of another attack on a Made and although it could have been a false alarm, crowds were still sparse. On the other side of the river, even Wellsburg looked chastened after its Halloween revelries, wet strips of toilet roll hanging limply from leafless branches. I labored through the night, trying to make sense of a variation on the eye-crushing raven-head tale that had triggered so much panic in the beginning. Again I struggled in the depths of it all—each scrap of unintelligible verse hiding another thought behind it. Each repetition ambushed by a hidden difference, each cadence rising, or falling to some screechy imperfection—forcing me to improvise, to make up the bits I couldn't fathom. I thought of the Father and his dream of sexless speciation and the seductive power that came with that. Narn, too, alone in the lab with her hell-broth, boiling and bubbling Kai and me into being. And now here I too sat alone in my Tower with my broken ghosts and amputated dreams, stitching them together with the blunt needle of my imagination and nothing else. Outside the window, the bridge glowed like an artery and the alien constellations wheeled. From the roof of the gatehouse the uninvited shadow that had clawed up from under the bridge, stood guard over my process. Because the fantasy of self-speciation was just that—fantasy, a contradiction in terms. By daybreak, I had what I needed, and slept.

On Saturday afternoon I read my story back and at the appointed time on Sunday, left my Tower and headed for the bridge.

Hunter frenzy had all but emptied the Corso, even for a Sunday night, when it was usually scattered with end-of-weekend die-hards. Despite all that had happened, my skin was tingling with anticipation. I'd unwrapped the new outfit Pagan had delivered, promising myself to repay her from my scholarship stipend, but as soon as I stepped off the bridge into Wellsburg in new red tights and a pink woolen dress with a bodice crisscrossed in black ribbon, all was forgotten. I felt a sense of crossing through a membrane into some kind of truth. One or two faces in the town nodded their recognition. The unsmiling photographer friend of Pagan's sat drinking in one of the taverns. He lifted his head as I passed. I expanded in his gaze, and in the gaze of this place. I was becoming more real, and everything else—the Hunter, Narn, the Blood Temple, the Starvelings (especially)—less so. I was beginning to feel free as if it were me cut down from that hanging tree instead of her. My soul, not Kai's, freed from the grasp of the restless dead.

But when I arrived in the turret room at eleven, I panicked to find only a scattering of guests, all but outnumbered by the dreadful hale waiters, waiting in a row with their hands hidden behind their backs. The food table was piled higher than usual, with plates of game bird and cheese and steaming plates of bloody meats. Orange cake in gooey syrup sprinkled with edible flowers.

But no guests. Surely Regulars had no reason to fear the Hunter, so why had they stayed away? Had they forgotten me? Or maybe they had heard about my story and been put off. Had I gone too far? What Narn had said about the conjure tales—had the story gotten away from me?

Had I blown it?

My reflection bounced back at me from the beveled mirrors and windows, from the green swell of the bottles and the crystalline stemware. There were dozens of me in the room—it was all Meera. My face in the reflection was doubtful, unreal, as if I had no place to be here, no place at all. Pagan hadn't showed. Sasha was nowhere to be seen. Here I was with no one but myself and a dozen sneering waiters, the corkscrews in their black aprons gleaming like scalpels.

I ordered another drink and kept my eye on the door. The barman slid a berry-red cocktail toward me, a Cosmopolitan. "On the house," he said. Meaning Sasha Younger. Eventually, the Regulars trickled in, even more extravagantly dressed up than before, the air sweet with perfume and the tinkle of precious metals, but with an edge to their talk, an anticipation that verged on aggression. They seemed to bare their teeth at me as they smiled. My armpits prickled, and I unsuccessfully tried to find my reflection in the crowd. Soon the turreted suite was even fuller than before, expectation crawling spider-like across the walls. More candles lit by an unseen hand. Pagan had arrived without me noticing, and shot me a thumbs-up from between a sea of sculpted shoulders, and soon, after the mandatory collection of phones, it was time to begin. My heart was in my mouth as I searched for Sasha in the crowd, but she was nowhere to be seen.

Three or four other girls—one a Made, I thought with a pang of bitterness—read their stories, all to muted appreciation. Then it was my turn. Dispirited by Sasha's absence, I took a seat in the electric chair, the cap lower than normal and pressing against my high hair. Once again, I couldn't feel my feet. My vodka-fueled confidence deserted me. A fat pregnant cat had chewed off my tongue. My mind was blank. As if everything had been erased. What bad joke was I the punchline to? I closed my eyes, that word scrawled on the Redress acceptance form flashed across my eyelids, and when I opened them and looked across the page, that is all I saw, the word *gni vrats* written over and over in the same indigo ink, a broken reversal that I couldn't place to save myself.

The cap squeezed my skull and time stopped. The joke-trial had grown old. My hands gripped the arms of the chair, and my body jerked. Heads turned in my direction, indulgent smiles at my "theatrics." I clenched my teeth—so far from *gnivrats* and never ever far enough. As long as I lived.

I closed my notebook.

The story told itself.

A swagman in a cloak made of raven feathers stalks a forgotten land, feeding on a rare species of pink moth that breeds in lost places, pulling off first their wings and then their little pink antennae and then their heads. He places the bits, like edible flowers, onto a boiling billy, and drinks it beside the fire, dancing to their tiny screams. He swirls their pain around his mouth, savoring it. Chew, swallow, repeat. He takes out his fiddle. Some real ravens from another world hear the shrieks from his bow, and swoop down on the swaggie, tearing off his imposter's cloak and then pulling strips of his skin from his body—his thighs and belly and face—until he is nothing but a carcass with a heartbeat, as flayed and glistening as a newborn. His torment is unimaginable. But the unimaginable has only just begun. The boss raven carefully places the strips of skin on the swagman's coals, while another holds open his mouth and two his eyes, feeding his own flesh to him piecemeal—for an eternity, or long enough for his skin to grow back—and they start all over again. And the more they feed him the hungrier he gets, until they don't have to pull his skin off anymore. He does it for himself. He has gotten a taste for it, and no other flesh will do for his hungers, but his own. He wants to stop. He begs for his hands to be tied, for a bullet in his brain. But the *Starving* Hills are nowhere, and no one hears his screams.

One guest threw up halfway through the reading. Another rushed into the hallway and began to sob. The token Made headed toward the river and was never heard of again. The Regulars stomped their feet and called for another. And another. But I knew the rules. No cliff-hangers. When I looked across the room, Sasha had appeared from nowhere. She lounged on her chaise, her lips parted, tracing lewd figure eights along her bare breastbone.

I tried to get up but my hair was caught in the cap of the chair. I tried to lift it off my head but that just made things worse, and my tears of pain and humiliation stung my eyes. As I struggled, I watched Sasha get up and, in that louche, swaying gait of hers, move off toward the bar.

When I finally managed to pull myself loose, I'd torn off clumps of hair left hanging from the cap. With a sinking sense of betrayal—this had clearly been the second part of my initiation—I made my way to the door. Sasha's reflection spiraled around the mirrored room like a brushfire. Even from here, I could feel her heat.

"Wait!" She came to me, her pure black irises half concealed by heavy lids. She wore a patchwork suit of beige suede. I searched her face, committing its wide mouth and low brow to memory the way Narn's customers would try to memorize the paths and byways to her hidden hut of stories and healing. But then something skittered across her eyes, and her parted lips transformed into a chasm, and I knew then that I too was lost.

"You're not going anywhere," she said. She pressed a drink into my hand, her long clawed nails scraping against my palm. Her voice scratched at the digital layer in my brain, my broken system registering the intrusion. "Come."

She took me to a quiet corner, sat down on a love seat and made some room beside her. The crowd had thinned but those who remained were drinking hard, crumbs on their fingers, lipstick-smeared mouths around loaded silver forks.

"I wasn't prepared for a second trial," I said, concentrating on not bringing a hand to my stinging scalp. "Pagan said I was in."

A wrinkle of irritation rippled, it seemed, not across Sasha's jawline, but under it, like a caterpillar. "My gatherum, my rules," she said with a heavy fluttering of her eyelids that restored her face back to its singular perfection. "One can never be too sure."

The candles dripped wax and the music had turned sultry. "Did I go too far?" I asked.

"Everyone here feels more alive than they have in months," she said. "Because of you. And it's only your second time."

She touched my wrist. The opaline eye on her ring ate the light. A waiter arrived with a plate of food on a tray. Sasha took it and stabbed her fork into a chunk of meat and delicately began to chew, a drop of red juice running down her chin. With her mouth full of food, she told me that she decided to have me read every week, not twice a month as originally intended.

"Every week?" I hesitated, thinking of Narn and how much that would ask of her.

"Can't have too much of a good thing." Sasha dabbed her chin with a napkin. "Don't worry about the scholarship. Or anything. You're Fearsome family now."

I didn't know what to say.

"Don't thank me." She put one of her unusually long fingers across my lips. "This reading's been starved of people like you. Do you want to know why I love Wellsburg? Not just because I was born and I will die here." The pressure of her finger forced my lips apart. "But also because Wellsburg's history is played on the battleground between hope and fear—when the only hope is fear. And vice versa. Without terror to unite us—we'll destroy each other." I felt my teeth break the skin of my lips under the pressure of her silencing finger. "That's what Fearsome Gatherum is for. It may seem like a game, and it is. But games are a metaphor for life. And for death. Hearts and minds, Meera. Losing either is not an option."

My lips were sufficiently open so I could, if I tried, have pressed the tip of my tongue against her finger. I felt glued to it, sutured to her like a bad graft, some scientific experiment gone wrong. I tried to pull away, but I couldn't. I tried harder, but my lips were stuck fast to her finger. Saliva pooled and over-flowed. I couldn't swallow—her eyes were black disks haloed in red, like a total eclipse of the sun.

"We needed to find a voice to bridge the gap between the 'fake' and the 'lore.' A storyteller for the age. Tales to conjure our deepest fears, only to vanquish them for all time. Like yours, in a word." A tendon throbbed on her pale neck. "And don't worry . . ."

She took her finger away, put it in her mouth and sucked it clean.

". . . if you go too far, you'll be the first to know."

That night, in spite of the pass Sasha had arranged to exempt me from the curfew, Pagan and some of the other Regulars walked me halfway across the bridge.

"Sasha's orders," Pagan said rummaging for a cigarette. "Oh, and as a regular performer, you get a waiver on membership fees, so there's that."

Performer. I liked that. She offered me a bag of her old sweaters—barely worn—and to send me a playlist of some of her favorite music, links to the trending blogs. "We're all sisters now," she said, smacking me playfully on the bottom. On this cold, clear November night, I actually felt that yes, it could be true. Sasha had revealed her shadowy side, but knew nothing of mine. I was unbreakable. We stood on the bridge, leaning against the illuminated railings. Ahead of us the Tower Village dorms glowed against the sky like hospitals or prisons. The stars swung from a low sky, black as pitch, and my mind flew to where meteors tore across the cathedral night and the bush was peopled with fleshy ghosts and ghostly flesh. But this is where I belonged now, on this bridge above the blue-veined mist with my *real* sisters. Narn had been right in sending me away. I *was* safer here. Eric and the ravens were one family, but this was another, bought with an exchange of fear for love. The mist over the river parted for a moment, and Pagan pointed at a yellow light moving far below and someone said, what if it's the Hunter, and someone else said that beavers still swam in the river—but you couldn't hunt them anymore. Someone else asked me if the beavers where I came from were as big, or as wet. And someone said they heard that beavers in South Rim had wings, like bats, and could fly. And we all made beaver jokes and I laughed and I heard my own laugh among theirs and I felt like I'd been made anew.

CHAPTER 16
STINKY SISTER

"Your round," Marvin said. It was two Fridays later at Dirty Bert's. I was late for happy hour, and he was already three drinks ahead of me. Seemed I was always running late these days. My stunted reflection left a blue smear in the thick glass windows of the village, as nightly, I tried to leave it behind. A runt in high hair and bespoke shoes (Pagan had sent me to her bootmaker), heads turned on the Corso as I passed. I told myself it was because it was easy, with a bit of effort, to stand out at a campus where everyone else tried not to. But another part, unspoken, hoped that the stares, the whispers, were because of how I was becoming beautiful. Like Kai.

"You're a vision," Marvin said. "Look at your hair. Like a black halo."

I blushed. I was still high from another triumphant Gatherum reading—the waves of applause, of sobs and gags still ringing in my ear. I chugged my drink and told him how Kai always said I could never read a room but that I thought I was learning. And it was true. Over the last couple of Gatherums, I *had* begun to gauge the muted clink of silverware, the slurp of rare meat soaking in the fragrant pools of blood. I read the discrete signal to a passing waiter for a quick tryst up against a bathroom sink. I eavesdropped on the texts Pagan sent to her dealer. But most of all, I had learned to read the collective inhale when I took my position in the electric chair. And when I opened the notebook, I heard the coded tap of the maple branches outside the window and I knew that someone out there was reading it too.

"Nothing like rising to the challenge," Marvin said, covering a yawn.

I told him about how the ghost of the Hunter had appeared in my room, but he just shrugged. "It was Halloween. What do you expect?"

"Well," I said. "He had a gun."

"You've always been good at finding lost things, Meera," he said through a desultory mouthful of crushed ice. "And they, you."

"How do you know?"

"You found me."

I leaned over and kissed him on the cheek. "You okay?"

"Can I read your latest story?" he asked.

"You can try." I pushed the notebook toward him, trying to avoid puddles of ketchup and melted ice.

He leafed through it—the black feather slipped out of the pouch and he absently tucked it back in. The pages were half-filled with what I'd scrawled with his blunt pencil. My handwriting had always been poor, made even more illegible because of Marvin's indentations—not that it mattered. Between Narn's unspooling and my retelling, I mostly knew the stories off by heart. And if I didn't, I had Kai's voice in my head telling me to wing it.

"I can just picture you," Marvin said, miming someone fluffing out their hair. "A vision in your finery, ironically strapped into the chair. Careful not to let the steel cap mess you up."

"I open the notebook, mainly for show, for the drama . . ." I said, playing along.

". . . to slow down time . . ."

". . . to read the room . . ."

". . . the bridge between you and them . . ."

". . . we meet in the middle . . ."

". . . and when you go your separate ways . . ." He passed the notebook back. ". . . you've forgotten who is who."

"They can't get enough of me," I said, "actually."

"*Is* there enough of you, actually?"

There was once, I thought. Once I was double.

"Are those new headphones?" I asked to change the subject.

"Did some casual work at the bookstore—they're a display set." He adjusted them and went for a moment to that secret place of his. It occurred to me that we could be falling in love. I felt a feathery lick of desire between my legs, my bits swollen with possibility. And suddenly he was back, pushed the headphones off, leaving his silver hair sticking out around his face.

"You know how you were raised by three sisters?"

"Two," I said. I was feeling drunker and flirtier than I should have been.

"Tell me about them."

Happy hour was over. "Narn's the leader, I guess. She's the one who got to be a witch, or who found enough that was witchy in herself to grow into that role. And my Aunt Mag—"

"So Narn's like the mother? I mean because you call the others 'Aunt,' so . . ."

I thought about it. "Yeah, I do. I guess it's because she brought us into the world. Got the eggs—two by mistake because her eyes were never great. And fertilized them in vitro, used her botanicals and who knows what else, and delivered us herself. Alone."

"Risky witch."

"The ravens kept watch . . . never mind. Where are you going with this, Marvin?"

"Tell me about the other one."

"Mag's the baby. They changed form, like Narn, either to mask their truth or to remember it. Tattooed a map of the underworld across their face so that they would never forget what hell was really like. Not a picnic."

"Neither is Paradise. So I've heard."

"They pulled out their own tongue so they could never ask anyone how to get back there, knowing they'd always be tempted." I'd never spoken of this. Not even to myself. I didn't know how I knew it. Or even if it was true.

"And what about the third sister?" he asked gently.

"MIA."

"But out there somewhere, right?"

"So what?" I tried to suppress my irritation with this line of questioning, or whatever it was. I heard Kai's voice in my head say, *Fuck him or forget him. You don't need a brother. You have . . .*

". . . another three sisters," he was saying. "I don't know if they're real—like yours—or just a myth. I don't think it matters. They come from a country further north called the Wastes. They were giants, originally. Like the ones who raised you, they change form over time. In some of the stories they're kindly. In others they're evil. Or malevolent, at least, harbingers—witness to or cause of bad intent, depending on the tale. They're known to visit newborns in order to either see or allot to each child their destiny."

"Fun fact. But what makes you think Mag and Narn were anything like that? Because they weren't. I don't think either had much of an idea what they were doing. Growing up I always had the feeling of something missing, that Narn was just making it up as she went along."

"Bingo. Because it should have been three," he said, eyes glassy. "Three is the last word on power. That something missing was the third sister."

"Meaning?"

"Meaning double-trouble's not the only game in town, Meera. Rule of threes is the killer." One-two-three with his knuckles in a puddle of booze.

I felt a great wave of exhaustion wash over me. Pagan was expecting me at a party across the bridge. "Marvin, why does the Gatherum's existential thrill-seeking bother you so much?"

"It's not theirs I'm worried about." He shrugged. "How can you afford such thrills? The membership fees are rapacious."

"Good word."

"Look, Dorothy. I don't mean . . ."

"I get a free ride, as it happens. Membership has increased since I've joined."

"So have the attacks," Marvin said.

I clenched my fists. "You think I have something to do with this? Is this a joke?"

"There was another one last night," he said tightly. "No joke."

"*I* made the Hunter real?"

"You tell me," he said.

I unclenched my hands, dark half-moons of blood on each palm.

"Look, it's not your fault, Dorothy. But just think about it. What if there is something in the combination of your stories, the Hunter myth, and some kind of ill intent that makes it all real?" He held up three fingers. "Rule of threes, remember?"

I got to my feet.

"Tell me something." I wiped the blood off my hands with the napkin, scrunched it up and dropped it into my glass. "Do you ever feel guilty for eating your twin?"

Once said never unsaid. Or taken back. My word-vomit flopped and squirmed between us and I saw It—how things could never be the same between us—and It could never be unseen.

He got up after a moment. He shouldered his bag, heavy with books, a wary sorrow to his movements that registered through my rage. "I'm sorry, Meera." His face inflexible and careful. "I didn't mean anything by it. I used to think like you do. Like I had it all under control. Like I could choose a mask, be the entertainment, distract the Regulars with my exotic shuffle while working on my next move. Exit Stage One. Until I realized that, yes it's true—the whole world is a stage, blah blah, and I was never going anywhere.

And I realized that the real reason I loved *them* seeing me is because I couldn't bear to look at myself."

At the next reading, instead of Pagan calling the session to order, it was Sasha who glided to the electric chair. The crowd froze with cocktails halfway to their lips, soft cheese melting in their mouths. She stood beside the chair in a white polyurethane pantsuit that hugged her Amazonian curves. Her feet were bare, heavy shackles around each fine ankle, and one around her neck. "I think we all know why we're here," she said.

All eyes turned to me. Pagan stood among them, her lips chipped as a cherub's. I tried to catch her eye, but she looked away. I put down my drink and took my place at the chair, with Sasha standing behind me. I opened the book on my lap.

"Close it," she said. And so I did.

She leaned in and brought her lips to my ear. "Start from the beginning," she whispered.

My legs turned to jelly. Standing at the precipice I felt her hand at the base of my neck, and I was terrified, but more turned on than I'd ever been in my life.

I was *on*.

"Once," I said in my best cracked voice, "there was a beast with no butt who wept tears of shit."

Behind me I heard a sharp intake of breath, and a soft moan like someone in the sweetest of pain.

Afterward, I sat alone at the bar thinking of Marvin, feeling ghastly. My brown eye radiated heat—the blue one a chilly indifference. The sound of Sasha's shackles jangled on my nerves. She shoveled cake into her mouth yet grew thinner every week, the striking contours of her face ever mobile, asking me about a plot point, a character. I thought it would make me feel safe, but it only made me invisible, my stories the mirror in which my patron would never see me, only herself.

Where was I?

Stories teemed in my head. How much of them came from Narn's incantatory babble and how much from me? Or Kai? I no longer knew. As the memories of my life in the Blood Temple grew stronger, as the scrappy recall of the dark years living with my dead sister conjoined itself to that of Narn's patients, to the drovers in the Five-Legged Nag and my own lonely imaginings on Narn's porch serenaded by the birds, I remembered more each day. I remembered the Father's slides of the Hairy Virgin, the Boy with the Upside-Down Face, the child broken on the rack of its mother's monstrous imaginings. I thought that if memory were a bird, it would be black of wing with an unlikely ruffle as rosy as the dawn, and how it would eat out its own heart with a sad-baby cry.

I clutched the notebook like a security blanket—my notes scribbled across Marvin's ones and zeros, the folded corners of pages that I wanted to come back to—I would carry it and never let it go, and the black raven feather stuck between the leaves would be all the protection I needed.

Against myself.

* * *

My dead sister stinks more and more each day. Gluey clumps of her scalp congregate in the bathroom sink. Bad-joke bugs crawl from her mouth and die on my pillow just like in Middles Bunk. Her hair is coarse and greasy and black as pitch. It is so long that she trips on it. Her good eye sputters like a bulb. I love her but I am scared of her. There is hunger in her gap-toothed smile, a need in her midnight caress that makes me want to blush and gag at the same time. She smooths the frizz from my pimply forehead and takes me in her arms.

"You're safe now, runt," she says. "No one can find us here."

She blows a raspberry on my neck and she is the twin sister she never was in the Blood Temple, the other half I always wanted. My dark heart. I turn around to face the windows partly because her breath smells like worms and partly so that she won't see me crying. It's meteor season in the Rim, and we watch the display for a while.

"Do you know why I came back?" she says in my ear.

"Because Tiff was there, waiting in the dungeon?"

"That bad-news junkie," Kai snorts. "I could smell her. Hear her. Railing about new wrong for ancient rights. I could hear her shriek on the winds down there, "Seize, seize, seize!" How it echoed on the walls of the dungeon. I was running from the fire of her breath, like a dragon. Oh it was terrible, Meera. I thought I was a goner."

"You made it," I say, trying to keep the doubt from my voice. "You're back."

She strokes my hair with her pulpy fingers, and my flesh crawls.

"I'd die for you, Kai. Don't ever leave me again."

"The old witch won't let me stay forever. Not even for you. It's too dangerous."

I want to turn around to look into her dead-sea eyes, but she has her arms wrapped so tightly around me that I can't move. Because that was the thing with calling something back into existence—surely I was just as responsible as Narn was for Kai. You make yourself inseparable from it, even indistinguishable—so fatal are the ties that bind you.

"What does Tiff want?"

"A sister," she says around a mouthful of my hair. "Two, actually. But she says one is better than none."

I hear her slobbering chew and then I hear her swallow.

CHAPTER 17

BIG MADE ON CAMPUS

Tower Village was emptying out as Mades fled and the college's reputation plummeted. Security became overwhelmed. Itinerants and dealers took up residence in the shadow of the village riverbank. A rumpled sleeping bag lay across the running track. The yoga studio closed down. Weeds grew at the edge of the mica along the Corso. At eight o'clock on Thursday evening, I was the only Made calling home on the bridge. It spanned ahead and behind me, the blue arches at either side eaten by rust that not even the illuminations could hide. I thought of how in the spring I might like to go down to the river, look for *Usnea* in the new growth—I had given my last batch to Lara for a cold sore.

The attacks seemed to follow the same pattern—each victim saved in the nick of time by something that scared the Hunter off. There was much speculation as to the nature of what exactly this was, and how much worse the damage, as they called it, would be without it.

I worried about Narn alone in the faraway hut with no one to help her in the apothecary, to tell her where she left her glass eye. No one to feed the birds or pull burrs out of Eric's tail. So when she picked up the phone, instead of asking for a story right away, I began with small talk. I asked after the thylacine and after the latest batch of moonshine. I asked about the weather. "So, I'm going to check out this cemetery tomorrow," I said casually. "Seven so-called witches are buried there."

"No apology can wash away the ghastly stain." She sounded old and tired. So much for small talk.

"People didn't know any better back then."

"People always know better."

She asked about the campus attacks. On the Wellsburg riverbank below, that livid streak I'd seen before began its inexorable inch through the undergrowth. The sting of sulfur tickled my nostrils. A guard came out and sniffed his fingers—a passing student hurried past, and the guard said, "Egg sandwich for lunch," and laughed but the student did not laugh with him.

"Another Made has been attacked outside Sweeney's Landing," I said. "Dragged down to the river, her back lashed down to her bowel."

"The doomsman's scourge?"

"You tell me." Saying it made me think with a pang of Marvin. The holes where I'd punctured the flesh of my hands with my fingernails had formed tiny crescent scabs.

She coughed and had to take a swallow of tea before she could continue. "Come home. Thylacine getting old."

I steeled myself. "The victim reports seeing a black cape or cloak, or something." I thought of the Hunter's black leather duster.

"Crappy twin bitten off more than it can chew." Her voice is laced with uncharacteristic quiet, the words spoken in a monotone like Marvin's when he left me standing at the bar.

"I'll be fine. Sasha gets some Regulars to walk me home after the readings. Like sisters."

"Rich bitches are fake sisters."

"I've run out of real ones," I said. "So there's that."

"Crappy twin is flesh meat."

"*Fresh* meat? Anyway, it's the stories they feed on, Narn. And while they're eating, I think I can feel Tiff getting closer."

"Could be anything," Narn said. "Or nothing."

And as I watched the undergrowth part for whatever it was that moved through it, I felt it again, that same tingling behind my ears, the lifting of hair on my scalp—that I'd always felt when things got out of control. Yes, it could be anything. Or nothing.

"Big Made on campus," Narn scoffed. "Too big for sister's shoes."

I was used to her bark—knew by now it was worse than her bite. But from the other end of the line, I heard her swallow a sigh.

"To be fair," I said, "the Gatherum's profits go to good works. Scholarships at Wellsburg for needy qualified students and such. Repairs and upgrades to the old buildings. So in a way, we're doing our bit to make the world a better place."

I heard Narn open the woodstove door with a squeal and slam it shut.

"Boss bitch buys power and influence. Pretend Queen—makes all the rules so him can break them too."

The bubble of something in that big, blackened pot. I salivated in spite of myself. How long since I'd had Narn's terrible cooking? I wanted to ask if she was tending to Kai's grave. If Eric still waited for me on the porch. But then something smashed. A jar of spice. A jug of moonshine. She cursed.

"Time's short," Narn said, as if to warn me against asking for another story. "Conjure tales cost too much."

What she was saying was how she would never admit to getting old—the least I could do was respect that. Those two missing letters in *Starv ing*—that was Narn and me. Caught between a lost sister who she'd never find and a found sister who I'd never escape. I *was* doing this as much for me as for her.

"There are baskets of roots in the cellar." I tried to keep the plea out of my voice. "And jerky. Mag and I worked hard before I left to build up the stores. Eric won't let anything happen to you."

"Brought that thylacine back from the dead," a great weariness in her voice.

"Yes and Kai too."

"Sometimes other stuff comes back," she grumbled. "Trash from the other side."

"Trash," I said. "But also the truth. When you brought Kai back from the dead, Narn, what you also brought back were answers. You know, like for a rainy day?"

Silence on the other end. Then finally, "Soon?"

"Soon," I said slowly, keeping my mouth close to the mic. "Whatever deal Tiff made with the Father—whatever code he wrote onto her for his own protection, and however hellish the powers she took in exchange—that's where I come in. Because if all she can do is steal, like when she stole the playground girl's body and then the Made's in the infirmary—I mean there are only so many skins a snake can shed, right?"

"Time running out for lost sister?" And there was a terrible catch in her voice.

Because we both knew—everything had to be running out for Tiff except her own impossibility. And we both knew this too: that there was nothing on earth or anywhere else so dangerous as a goner.

"What then?" Narn's voice suddenly as clear as if she was right there on the bridge beside me.

"She's got to go to plan *B*," I said.

"Plan B is . . . ?" As if she didn't know.

"Me," I said. "It's always been me."

When I looked down at the bank, the amorphous half-invisible presence was gone, leaving nothing but shriveled foliage in its wake. Narn started to drone, a singsong incantation but in a queer, flat tone that made my knees turn to jelly. Because now I could understand her speech as clearly as if I'd spoken it myself.

"Long ago goddess promised three sisters a future. No more dungeon. No more blood. No more fury. Anguish gone. Power in justice. No house could thrive without sisters' kindness. Accept it, goddess said, or be nothing."

I hung up without asking for a story that time. I had what I needed for a rainy day.

CHAPTER 18
WHICH WITCH?

A white November afternoon, stark with black branches and faded leaves. Marvin and I had already reached the outskirts of town where the old church was meant to be, and still hadn't found it. The signpost that I'd seen on the evening of my enrolling in FiFo was not where I thought it was. Nothing was.

I had called him to apologize about what I'd said about him eating his twin. I'd tried to explain how it should have been me. Me who was eaten. Blood on my hands and my feet too, twice as much as hers, and if I could go back and *be* her, I would. "I would sell my soul to go back in time and die for her," I'd sobbed, "instead of the other way around, but I can't get there. Marvin. I can't remember. No matter how hard I try, how many stories I try and tell—the beginning where she is alive and it is *me* unmade, never comes. It's the one thing I can't do. Be her. So now? I can only be this. Whatever is in the mirror is too much and not enough but it's all I have. All I am."

He said that was good enough for him, but just to be sure, just to get him back to me, whatever I was, I'd appealed to the criminal in him and also the detective, the profiler and the profiled.

"What you said about those three sisters," I began, "Mine are the only ones I know. Between the beginning and the end, there's a bridge called the middle sister. And I have to find her, before she can do any more damage."

"You think she's connected with the attacks?"

I waited.

"And?"

"And I need your help," I'd said, which was a first. "Come with me to the cemetery."

Marvin stopped in his tracks and blew on his gloves. The small stone church huddled in a little clearing down an unnamed dirt road. A spire peered over the trees. As we got closer, I saw that the building was bigger than it first appeared, sprawling at the back and surrounded by a high stone wall. We entered through an iron gate, past a mottled sycamore. The stone wall enclosed overgrown grounds beyond which the forest encroached.

"The main cemetery will be around the back." Marvin had dyed a tendril of his hair a blue-black, and it squiggled out of the silver mop like a tentacle. His fingers were misshapen from chilblains, and the circles under his eyes were purplish in the frigid light. He took off in long strides around the west side of the church through lichen-stained graves and piles of fallen leaves, the woods watching us all around.

I hesitated, looking up at the leadlight windows. "Wonder why they closed it in the first place."

Marvin was bent toward the woods, the breeze tugging at his clothes. "A witch-hating past is not a good look for a progressive all-girls school like Wellsburg," he called over his shoulder, beginning to sound more like his old self. Maybe things could be right between us again.

A homemade sign offered tours of the grounds, with a website address underneath. I felt uneasy so close to the blackened walls, the stern stone angles. Its windows depicted religious scenes in stark leaden outline that we learned about in the Temple—it was the same unease as I'd felt near the church in Norman. The windows looked identical—the glass stained ruby and gold and unearthly blue.

"Looks aren't everything," I said under my breath and ran to catch up. The ground was frosty beneath Kai's shoes. I didn't want to stand alone in this place.

We arrived at the rear of the church, stopped short at the edge of the cemetery. Unnumbered rows of gravestones, their edges blackened by time and spotted with crustose lichen, pale green scales growing in the engraved names. Markers all but drowned in kudzu listed against the stone wall like broken teeth, and beyond that stretched arcades of moss-hung tree trunks and watchful pines.

I stopped at a large family plot. In its center was a stone crypt, caked in bird shit and guarded by an angel with broken wings. Across the slate door, *Psilolechia lucida* picked out letters that said *Younger. Hermann Younger, b. 1649 d. 1722*, and beneath his name, *his beloved wife, Louisa Isabel*, and beneath her name, *Nicholas, b. 1660 d. 1661*, and others, more recent.

At the very lower edge of the plot, was a brass plaque half sunk into the earth: *We shall soon enjoy Halcyon Days with all the Vultures of Hell, Trodden under our feet.*

The words were barely legible—the metal had been scratched over by a sharp instrument, the name of whoever the quote was attributed to covered in dirt. But from Corby, I knew what it said. Clustered around the crypt was the Younger family plot. At the marble gravestone of Sasha's father, Orrin (beloved husband to Mary Younger and father to Sasha Younger), someone had placed a bunch of wilted flowers.

"They must still be putting Youngers in the ground here." I thought of Sasha as she might have been at the start of all this, and suddenly understood what weight of history possessed her, at least in the beginning, to found the Fearsome Gatherum, what debt she felt she owed to the false memory of a past that never was, to keep it intact (unhacked) forever and ever, amen.

But Marvin had gone ahead and was marching through the graves until he got to a broken chunk of wall. At the edge of my eye, something plummeted to earth but when I turned it was gone. My feet could not feel the ground beneath them—I flew wingless after him over the tumbled stone blocks, through the wall and into desecrated ground, ankle deep in fallen leaves. In a clearing, the trees halted at a distance of about twenty meters, some small plain stone markers lay among the piled brown leaves. Despite the distance of the trees, no sun fell here. The smell of decay was suffocating. I struggled to breathe. It was the smell of the Hunter.

April B. Hobbes, 1680–1903, Pressed to death.

"Is that a human turd?" Martin said, pointing to a collapsed pile of feces above the name.

The distraught sound of his voice made me want to cry.

There was another one. *Mary Goode, 1703–1712, Hanged. Pansy Osmon, 1692–1730, Hanged.* And another, and another.

The dead leaves flung their spores of rot and grief up at us, until it was Marvin who sneezed and finally wept. We held each other and I could smell beer in his tears. Set off apart from the seven sad markers was a broad fallen log, hewn with a flat surface as if for a seat. Lobes of fungus grew between the softening layers of heartwood. Marvin's square shoulders slumped in defeat. He sobbed the faint words crudely scratched across the flattened surface.

I am innocent. Wronged by HY.

"Hermann Younger." I sunk down onto my knees. "The founding father."

Tufts of bright yellow-green lichen grew at one end of the log. *Letharia vulpina.*

"It's pretty." Marvin sniffed and squatted beside me to touch the lurid stalks.

"And lethal." I told him how the South Rim settlers had used the poisonous wolfsbane to cull foxes and wild dogs and thylacines, lacing fresh sheep carcasses with a mixture of powdered *L.vulpina* and broken glass that would shred the thylacine's stomachs and ensure faster absorption of the poison.

"Narn found some thylacine bones in her cave," I said.

"What did she do with them?" He hiccuped.

"She made herself a familiar, is what she did. She tried to make one for Mag, too, but that one didn't make it."

"From what you've told me about your aunt, maybe it didn't want to be made."

He pulled me to my feet.

The woods were silent the way winter forests are in this part of the world, the thick drifts of damp brown leaves scattered with crimson and yellow, the haggard branches, and monumental pines, imprisoned in this yearly ritual, this dark almanac.

Marvin wiped his nose on his sleeve. "You okay?"

"All this witchy stuff is pretty close to home," I said. Again, that jagged downward movement from the corner of my eye, and a low sob, half animal, half something else. I narrowed my eyes. The silence so thick. I thought of death. Of how the problem with anything brought back, was that it wasn't ever itself, not entirely. Never as fully committed to life and to the living as you hoped—like Kai. Always looking back over her shoulder to where she came from and where she mostly still wanted to be, the longer she wasn't. And probably where she wanted to take me too, out of spite maybe or just so we could both be together again forever and ever, hold the amens.

At that moment the trees shifted and my head spun to where I could see, as sure as anything, a parting of the branches. Nothing there but the spiteful dead.

"Do you think"—Marvin moved in closer to me and took my hand, so I knew he could see it too—"it's the Hunter?"

"It's me it wants."

"Who?"

"You'd make it to the wall in time," I said. "Go!"

He didn't move but *it* did, cutting a wide swathe through the trees, leaving a gelid streak of evanescence behind it. The canopy agitated, and the air grew gluey in the wake of the thing. We stood there together in some terrible grinding dream, with the woods spinning around us. We rotated on the spot, our sweat mingling, trying to keep up with the movement of the branches, low one moment, high the next. Birds shrieked. The canopy shifted, but when I looked to where I thought it should be, it was somewhere else—and somewhere else again. Branches cracked and fell, and the air hummed.

It was never in the same place.

"Hey!" Marvin yelled at it.

"Don't," I said. "You don't know what it is."

"And you do?"

The canopy in tumult, reek of graves—like the smell had taken form, cold and real enough to smash my head open. Even if we could get to the wall, the church blocked our escape on one side, the woods on the other. In the punishing silence, only the thunder of my pulse in my ears. Marvin's shallow breaths coming quicker.

"What are you?" Marvin called.

Brave boy, Kai said. *Brave brother from misbegotten mother.*

Dead leaves whorled. A tree howled as it fell. Leaves and debris spun closer, a whirlwind forming itself into tails, nine slithering lassoes that sliced my hands and face. Marvin's neck lashed in red. He screamed.

No! Not him, I howled above the wind, my breath pluming white against the spinning debris. I heard my voice amplified and shrill through my foghorn of fear. And Marvin heard it too. His eyes bulged as he stared at me.

And then I heard a rumble, distant like thunder.

It came from under our feet, a thudding that I felt in my bones. It grew louder and closer and the woods drew back. "What is that?" Marvin rasped. The rumble grew thunderous in the false silence of the woods, and then, with a final crack, it stopped.

We were still holding hands. We were still bleeding.

The sharp snap of a branch underfoot made me wheel around to face the church. From around a corner came a broad-shouldered man wrapped in black—in his hand he held some kind of weapon. He moved toward us through the graves. I watched as the man reached up and drew off his hood, except . . .

"A bike helmet?" breathed Marvin.

Big biker boots beneath which cracked the frost.

He came to a stop and glared, and I felt something give in me. "Corby?"

"Meera? From class?" He was holding a small tire iron, so I knew it was he who had defaced the Orrins' plaque. "I heard someone scream."

He looked at us clutching each other. But mostly he looked at Marvin, and so, in a kind of awe, did I. Behind the steam of his breath, the lacerations on his neck were gone, or going, tiny threads of crimson across his throat and under his ear, dissipating as I stared. Too small for anyone to see unless they knew what they were looking for. I brought my hands to my own face, then stared down at them. Minute gashes across my knuckles and wrists wriggling back under my skin until with a final blink, they were gone.

"I'm sorry," Corby said. "I didn't mean to interrupt. I come here to pay my, um, respects to the witches." He moved the tire iron to behind his back.

Marvin dropped my hand. His face chalky white.

"Marvin, this is Corby—my new TA in FiFo."

Corby pulled off a leather glove and extended a burly hand to Marvin. I looked past them to the woods beyond and could see no hooded being, nothing. The stinky air overlaid again with pine and I closed my eyes, partly to breathe it in and partly not to impolitely stare at how their hands stayed joined in the handshake for just a beat longer than was absolutely necessary.

* * *

One day, in our second spring in the Starvelings, my sister and I head off with a flask and sandwiches to our favorite place to play, even though she is dead and I am too old for games. The lichen-striped outcrop is toward the mouth of the ridge and spiky with grass trees whose spears we use in our games. Kai's inky hair swooshes back and forth and the flies buzz, and the ravens flap and caw their sad-baby cries. Goannas spit at us in wary boredom. It is Kai who spots the stranger first, a shadowless speck working up through the canyon, so that by the time the birds have gone silent, and the goannas have slithered behind deadfall, the speck has become a man, crawling hand over hand onto the outcrop like a giant spider. He finally stands there and his eyes flick down to our flask and back again.

"The Assistant," Kai says, in a percussive witchy baritone. "Looking for his . . . thi-i-i-ing!"

But the unmanned Assistant looks from my aura of stunted frizz to my sister with the missing eye and her hair standing up from her head, chalk-skinned after death with a map of fiery veins you can follow right to her heart. The Assistant licks dry, flaked lips and then with a hand not as steady as he might wish, more like a moth than a spider, he points to me and then to her and then back again.

"Twins," he says. "Non-identical."

I feel I've turned a corner onto a winter morning. I refuse to look, refuse to face the empty space where my sister has been, an emptiness I always knew was coming again, just not when. Because this is the day that begins and ends with a lesson more important than anything Narn has been trying to teach me with her potions and her spells:

You can never forget who you were. Or what. Because it will never ever forget you.

CHAPTER 19

SWEENEY'S

I was hurrying everywhere these days. A darting runt with two-faced eyes, my misbegotten stories writing themselves—lost fragments of conjure that found each other in the retelling. Fingers in the silverware drawer, webs crawling with spider-hands, vampire babies who suckled blood from witch's tits, a computer that solved the year of your death through backward reasoning, zombies cursed with eating their own children . . . The stories kept coming, telling themselves anew just in time for Gatherum. I would need a new notebook soon.

Campus life in the Tower Village had ground to a halt—Mades were fleeing to wherever they were from, anywhere safer than here—forfeiting their Redress Award money, forfeiting a tomorrow that was no better than yesterday. Fear spread like a virus. Thanksgiving had come and gone, and as agreed, I'd joined Lara and Trudy at the Thanksgiving party in the student union but it was so poorly attended that we left. The three of us had walked arm in arm back to our room and shared what I had left of Narn's shroom brew between us.

In contrast to the Village, Fearsome Gatherum numbers were up. Regulars joined by the dozen, lured in by Pagan's blogged promises of "transformative" readings, of "being lost in a forest of no return," of "our very own resident survivor holding a mirror up to your darkest fears and hidden desires," of "fairy tales spun by a 'born' storyteller from the land that fairies forgot," "unspeakable tales conjured by a fearsome enchantress." Of discounted membership fees subsidized by the already generous donations of Sasha's inner circle. The readings were standing room only.

You're the big Made on campus, now, Pagan texted.

That night there was another attack in the woods. Three others had already been airlifted from the college clinic to hospitalization in unspecified locations. I felt the creature stir under the bridge, the pump of vast wings through the midnight clouds. The press had caught onto the whole Hunter hysteria and the Dean had been asked to step down. But between struggling to keep up my grades and my fearsomeness, I didn't have much time to think about the

Hunter. I lived for midnight in the moonlit suite of my beautiful, rich patron, who gave me clothes that smelled like oak moss and whiskey. Sasha got Pagan to open a bank account for my, quote, *cut*, most of which I wired to Narn through the post office in Norman. Marvin and I hatched up a scheme to anonymously recruit the services of a private security company to provide added protection for Mades at both entrances to the bridge. It worked for a while until a couple of their men got beaten up by some of the more territorial lowlife along the banks, and the firm pulled out. A few days later, there was another attack. I asked Marvin to meet me at Dirty Bert's to talk about it.

No time, he texted back.

Instead, he said he'd met someone and why didn't we all have lunch in the student union the next day? I read the text over and over again, wondering what "someone" meant, feeling things flying out of control, a twinge at my temple that soon manifested as a dull headache. Finally, rather than meet Marvin and his new someone, I went over the bridge looking for the photographer friend of Pagan's. I sat alone at a freezing café, sipping chocolate that I didn't want and ordering new underwear. I felt a return of my chest infection, the flutter of panic that wouldn't lift. At dusk, I wove back across the bridge in velvet oxfords that made no sound. Kai's bloodstained shoes were in my locker. I was alone on the bridge but didn't feel alone. My keen eyesight picked up a shadow behind me, too far back to see when I turned around, but unmistakable in hindsight. What did it want with me? What did it want with any of us? I tried to phone Narn while I was there. It wasn't our scheduled night and she picked up in confusion, not knowing who I was. I hung up without telling her.

To spare Narn, I decided to write my own story for the next Gatherum. I told myself I had plenty of unused material—that her words had sunk in at varying depths for me to plumb at will. I thought of it as a game, like shuffling a deck of cards. I rose to the challenge. I was the big Made on campus, after all.

On my way back to the Village, the never-ending pulse of the bridge reflected in the multiple gaze of the Towers, I ran into two Mades I didn't know. They were weeping, on their way to the campus clinic where one of their friends lay fighting for her life, the latest nameless victim of the Hunter. Maybe it was that. Or maybe it was my reflection in the ascending elevator, as desirable as I had ever wanted to be—friendless, sisterless, shameless. But not gutless, no. Never again. Sasha must love me as I am, or not at all—I'd seen enough of a glimmer of possibility that she would. More than a glimmer. She owed me after all. Without me, she'd be ... Or maybe it was just that old fiend, self-sabotage, rearing its misbegotten head. Whatever it was, when I sat down to write my story, for the first time, it was me. Just me and my twin, the dead blank page.

But when I got to the high turret room the next Sunday, all the self-confidence I'd conjured deserted me while I waited for my turn in the chair. As the headliner, I always went last. I felt out of control. Spinning, netless in a Big Top of my own making. Deathly white faces all around to watch me fall. I was about to leave with some excuse about a headache, when Pagan came up behind me. "Coming to Sweeney's afterwards?" I must have blanched, because she reached out and tucked a loose curl behind my ear. "Sasha said to put you on the List."

I'd had a Plan B just in case I lost my nerve—a tale of twin demonic princesses, but Pagan's invitation disorientated me. I sat under the electric chair's terrible cap and opened my notebook. Without meaning to I recited my recklessly scribbled story about a demonic medical doctor who collected lady-bits in a cabinet of curiosities he called a matrix.

A row of candles blew out. A waiter belched.

"Boo," someone jeered.

"Boring."

Sasha's eyes were unreadable slits. She said something from the chaise where she lounged. But in my anxiety, I couldn't hear her. I could just see her mouth move. The maple branches scratched a distress signal on the window. Short short short long long long short short short.

Remember!

I looked at Sasha and for a moment she was unrecognizable to me. She looked as yellowed and brittle as the fake vellum of my notebook, as drained of life.

Imagine!

"And then ... the lady-bits turned to snakes and jumped onto his eyes and wormed their way into his soul and took it down to hell."

"How," someone drawled, "did the snakes jump out if they were in jars?"

I wasn't used to hecklers.

Wing it! Kai said. *Show some guts!*

So I did.

"The doctor had an assistant, who wasn't really his assistant, but an ancient avenger who dwelled in the underworld. Instead of punishing him for his crimes against blood, as was her right, she asked him to teach her everything he knew.

They made a deal—in return for his hell powers, she'd bring him back from the dead to avenge his blood enemies."

My voice felt like it was speeding up. My tongue twisted around the truth. The maple branch screeched against the window, and I registered the collective murmuring of concern, hostility even. But it was too late to stop now. I slowed my voice to a crawl.

"Except that when she emerged to begin her reign of terror, the world had moved on, and she could not. Blood vengeance was no longer a thing—change would not bend to her will and she, being a goddess of rage, of fury, could not bend to its. What kind of world was this, what trick had the universe played on her, when the ancient laws were all undone? And the night was winged and the winds of change were bane to her shriveled lungs, and the hunter, unshepherded, became the hunted?"

The applause was sporadic. Uncertain. "What's the answer to the question?" someone called out. "What happened in the end?"

"To be continued," I sat back in the electric chair. And my smile was the rictus of the doomed.

Sasha was gone.

* * *

The Assistant never makes it past the property gate. The thylacine is an airborne blur of stripes and teeth, gets the intruder to the ground, goes for his face first, pulling it off by the lips. The Assistant gets his hand around a fallen branch, uses it to break one of Eric's ribs—the yelping draws me from the outcrop at a dead run. By the time I get to the porch, the Assistant has lurched to a stand, reaching for his pistol. A central strip of skin hangs from his chin like a bloody beard, nose bone and tongue gaily flapping, eyes bulging from bony sockets. Eric regroups and tears at his crotch—where Kai stomped his man-thing off.

From close range on the porch, I shoot the pistol from his hand. Eric finishes the Assistant off, burying his muzzle in the soft flesh of his right breast. He gets his teeth around the heart and tosses it, still beating, to the ravens, followed by intestines, bladder, stomach, and lungs. Proudly arranging them in a spreading circle, barking like a lunatic as if to entice the victim to the game of his own dying.

It is only when the ravens swoop, Eric called to heel, that I notice Mag hunched off to one side, their hood pulled back high above their face so that I get a full view of the inky scrawl. It is a labyrinthine map—delineations of geographical features familiar yet strange—and it covers their entire face and what I can see of their hands and the patch of ankle above their sneakers. Their entire flesh a topographical atlas of a forgotten world—place names and lakes and rivers and dark meadows. Narn stumbles past, blood pouring from her good eye and all around us that hellbound hum.

"Never safe," Narn moans. "Nowhere safe from Father."

"How did he find us?" I yell after her. "Your lost sister told him, didn't she? Because the only one she's lost to is you!"

Narn looks at me in rage and Mag leads her away, bearing what's left of the Assistant's hand. They disappear for days, leaving me finally alone in the kitchen with lichen gone blighty and nothing to eat but what I dig from the vegetable patch, the air filled with orgiastic reverb from the cave as the scourge rips flesh down to the bone. This time Kai does not come back. And there is no one to explain it to me. I sit alone at the kitchen table in a patch of sunlight, and I eat a tomato and wait for something to happen. Eric clicks back and forth across the porch, bewildered totem waiting just as I wait, for nothing.

"I hate you," I call out.

"Witches," I shriek. "Hags!"

I leaf through the parchment grimoire looking for a curse, but I can't make out enough of the words. What language is it in and where did Kai learn it, and why had I not? I sweep the kitchen table clear of piled lichen and bundled herbs and Eric whines at the crash of precious vials onto the floor. I light a match and watch it burn down to my thumb, Eric's undead gaze never leaving the flame.

I tie a rope around my neck and head to the bloodwood tree but the thylacine cuts me off snarling—he has been to the land of the dead and it is not my place. I sink down on the ground, the rope still around my neck. He comes close, leans into me. Presses that marsupial muzzle into my neck. We stay like that for a while—one beast as unviable as the other.

And still the tears don't come.

He leads me back to the hut and I throw up. Then the tears come. And they don't stop until I throw up again. I don't want to live this way, but I don't want to die, so what else is there? It doesn't occur to me yet that death is not the only way to leave this place. It doesn't occur to me yet that as a failure at both living and dying, I will have to find another way.

I light every candle in the hut.

A confusion of tongues fills the night.

You left while my back was turned, Kai. *I had to—the Assistant found us. I have to make sure he isn't followed.* By whom? *You know who.* I didn't get a chance to say goodbye. *I said it for both of us.* Kai? *Meera.* It should have been me. *It is you, Meera. It was always you . . .*

I look over my shoulder in the first manifestation of a tic I will have all my life, just in case she's twice-returned.

. . . to find me to see me to be free.

* * *

Despite my disgrace, I went with my new sisters to Sweeney's Landing, the oldest inn in Wellsburg, built onto the riverbank, and famous for its rooftop parties.

But it was not to the roof where Pagan led me.

Lichen-sprayed columns at the street level entrance disguised the old pub's age, the dazzling decrepitude inside. Beneath a dusty crystal chandelier, I felt unattractive in what I was wearing—some ill-fitting cast-off of Pagan's. I had a bitter taste in my mouth about where Sasha had gone, and how she had refused to look at me before she disappeared, Pagan explained, to prepare for a reception tomorrow.

"She's donating some money for repair of the clock tower," Pagan said. "What came over you tonight, Meera?"

"I don't know," I said and it was the truth. "I'm not myself."

"No kidding," Pagan said, leaning against the marble bar. "Are you having a panic attack or something? Here, have one of these." She passed me a pill from her purse. "What *does* happen in the end, by the way?"

I washed the pill down with spit. "A good ending is hard to find." But she was right. I was panicking because I'd failed to read the room. Everything depended on that. Everything I needed to be.

Her chapped lips curled. "If you're lucky she'll give you a second chance. But there won't be a third."

She ordered two dirty martinis and then led me down flight after flight of stairs on the river side of the pub, carpeted at first and then just the bare boards. From the window of each landing I could see the oily strip of river, until finally I couldn't.

I gripped the railing with one hand, the papered wall with the other.

"Coming?" Pagan said, looking up at me from where I had begun to hang back behind the group.

"Not a fan of dungeons," I said.

"You'll be a fan of this one."

The stairs narrowed as we descended, the disrepair hazardous, toothy holes in the risers snapping at my new shoes. I began to sweat beneath my dress.

Ahead of me, Pagan pushed open a door. Music throbbed. Bodies moved in the jewel-box night.

I had an impression of thick black columns around which were wound garlands that glistened stickily like entrails. A deceptive space both small and vast. The décor down here was plain enough. It was the guests who sparkled. Eyes glittered and earrings swung and long pale necks strobed black and blue. The bar was circular in the center of the room, like a naval. I followed Pagan toward it but she veered off to the dance floor, and then I felt a hot hand on my arm. Got a whiff of chocolate and cologne. It was the unsmiling photographer. I felt his man-hand hot around my arm.

"Let's dance," he said.

CHAPTER 20
THE BRIDGE

The Father is everywhere.

I, Tiff, am owed. I am owed unto eternity. They had no right to exclude me. I see the fury of my sameness, the sameness of my fury. My unchanging beauty—bought and paid for. The Father—oh my Father—so taken with it, that in me he saw no one but himself. We were made for each other. He in me and me in him.

I am so hungry that my vision tunnels and I am too wobbly to dig in the dirt of the garden. I go back to the house, still with the noose around my neck, still with the .22 in my fourteen-year-old hand. A crescent moon has risen above the branches and the sky is blood orange. The tears come and go. A rabbit stands stock still in the yard—an easy target. I shoot it, skin it, and drop it into the big pot on the stove. Eric flops on the dirt, matter is feathered across his pouch. I burn some tree-fern bundles for cleansing and I wash him clean of the dried blood and filth, picking the bones from his pelt and saying the magic words Narn says when something needs to be purified on the outside as well as in. Then we eat rabbit stew on the porch. It is terrible, undercooked and chewy, but it's better than Narn's. I eat ravenously. The ravens flap and sob, daring me to do what I know must be done.

To be free.

You promised you'd always be with me.

I am.

I got you out. I got you across the water. All of you. Not one bit of you in a jar.

You did, Meera.

And then they took your eye.

You can't always finesse everything, Meera.

I wipe my mouth and get up. Voices divide and multiply. Eric pants at my heel, and I see myself through the eyes of a raven as unnatural as I am. Their neck ruffles are black with a rose iridescence and they angle their heads to watch me pass. I creep past the still and the shed and past the graveyard beneath the slanting blossoms, the rifle cocked. I make a hard left toward the cave deep in the hollow beneath the overhanging rock, where I am forbidden to go, where Eric is forbidden to go, where even the raven children are silent and keep well back. My breathing is a runaway train. I want blood. I want justice. Seize! Seize! It is not enough that Narn brought us here. She failed to keep us safe. Not enough that she offered to pay for Mag's overreaching by bringing Kai back to me. She left behind her own treacherous sister who brought death to our door.

Tiff is not my real name, just saying. They had no right. I am owed bigtime. They took everything and left me with nothing. Without the key to change. Small wonder that the Father came in me and me in him.

Narn will never forgive herself.

Can I forgive Narn?

My heart. For my Kai, I demand justice.

Narn not its real name, either. Never speak it. Don't need real name now. Had to make the ravens sleep. Boss sees what him wants to see, no more. One twin named Kai because it means Key, and the runt twin named Meera—means Wonder, because it survived against all odds, and is its sister's keeper.

I demand a sacrifice, some pound of flesh for everything I have lost. Something is wrong with me. There are thoughts all around me, not from inside myself but from somewhere further away. I mouth words in a speech that makes my blood go cold. In a language from deeper in me than I dare go, so deep it shoots rhizines from my feet out my eyes and ears and mouth, I find all the wrong words. I am not a witch. I am an avenging angel. Forget the angel part.

Suffer unto truth. After we became the Kindred, we, Mag—a name as blunt and ugly as ourselves—could do nothing but suffer. We tore out our tongue because we would not speak of it again—that place of lapping gore—and there was nothing else to say.

I near the forbidden cave.

From it flows a sluggish keen, undercut by that mannish hum. A spider skittles out onto the lip of the cave as big as a hand. It is man-muscle and tendon, with fingernails filed to a point. Four fingers on each side of a flayed man-hand, two bloody thumbs for mandibles. The greasy lap of candlelight spills into the night. There is the whoosh of something whipped through the air, a splat as it connects with flesh.

"Kill her," the hum says. "Blood for blood. Burn the witch."

We, Mag, remember. We did what we could. We do what we do. We are bound to protect not to avenge. To be loved and not feared. That is our power now.

"Wicked sister knew Assistant would seek vengeance for his lost thing," the spider-hand says. Gooseflesh ripples down my buttocks, and I feel the hot rush of urine, cooling as it runs down my legs.

Not even death, the Father promised . . .

I, Kai, came back because I wanted to find a way to ask your forgiveness for lying. For making you feel small. For thinking, even for a while, that I was the chosen one. I could never bring myself to say sorry. What I'm going to do next, Meera—what I'm going to do to the Father, I will do it for you. And you will be with me. We will be heroes, like in a Golden Book. And maybe then you will forgive me for what has been and what is to come.".

That slows me down a little. Kai's voice in my head, just when I don't need it. Just when *listening* is the last thing I want to do.

"Hero shmeero!" I yell. "Narn is still the worst witch in the world. Don't let the door kick her on the way out."

We, Mag, remember. This is the story of us—Megaera, Alecto and Tisiphone, conjured from the blood of an unmanned god. Three sisters given a second chance to bridge the old worlds and the new, not with fury but with compassion.

I take another step toward the cave, eyeing the Assistant's arachnid hand. Another spell gone wrong? Another demon who slipped the coop? Old crone be losing her touch. I think how I will take ugly old Mag out first, a kill shot with the .22 if I'm lucky. If they've got the big rifle, I'll use that to take Narn. Then me. I've hefted the .303 once or twice when Mag wasn't looking. I can handle it, I think, being stronger than a normal fourteen-year-old. I think how it will be an act of kindness. Put us all out of our misery.

Sisters of second chances.

A mercy killing.

Here I come Kai.

My hand trembles round the barrel. I face the hungry black mouth of the cave. Abruptly the incantations stop. A heavy silence, the moon a gutless crescent. Beneath the silence is a mouth breathing, my senses alert to each new terror. I step over the threshold. Candles sputter from recesses in the stone walls. A distant trickle. The trapped echo of a sob lost somewhere in a cave system twisting down to hell.

And back.

I, Tiff and the Father—we're birds of a feather. Those damned ravens got him in the end. But we had a deal. Basically, eternal life for infernal vengeance. Sweet deal—mutualistic as hell, you could say. He liked to play rough. In the Dungeon of the Damned—bizarre name—he got what he wanted. More than he wanted. The game a little much for him. "Tisiphone, my little vulture," he said. "This is a lot." So long since I'd fed—nothing looked good on me anymore. I was wasted, goo dripping off bones, my phosphorescence the color of pus, my face melting, dripping poison back into my mouth. "It's a look," the Father said. "What happened to the vast wings and tiny waistline, the snakes and erect nipples? You look like if Salvador Dali and Martha Graham had a baby." I contained my fury—that was the deal. I'd pieced the Father together from what the birds left behind—everything but his head. I said, "Daddy, have you looked in the mirror lately?"

Narn lies curled on the dirt floor near some soiled sacking, her dress pulled up over her buttocks. Her shoulder is lashed, the scourge in the other hand. Blood slowly glugs from where the blade of her boline has hacked her wrist to the bone.

I turn my head and throw up. The incantations resume and I look to their source. They are coming in from all directions.

I, Tiff—the cute sister—made him howl. He howled for his head. For vengeance. I sucked at games but I knew how to play rough. Not sure I can take it, he said. So I sucked harder. But I am not what I was. The world has become a strange thing. Where is my kindred? The world twists and the ages take their toll. Twin sisters to replace the ones who betrayed me—it's not much but it will have to do. A good chimera is hard to find.

Mag stands in the shadows against a wall dripping and slick, naked to the waist, black nipples as big as bullets, their voluminous hoody pulled back from their beastly face until I see that it's not a hoody at all, but leathery wings furled and pointed. That unbearable hum emanating from a toothless maw, and because their hood is down and pulled away from a scarified and stricken face, I can now see that instead of hair, their scalp is slick with squirming gore—snakes coated in blood. They turn their inked face to me, bare black gums and begin to growl. They are unarmed.

We are Mag. We etched a map of where we came from upon our flesh. We cut with ink and with blood so that we will never forget the thirsty dust. Suffering and madness. Famine and drought. The pain we wrought. What we were—vultures, carrions from hell. Forged from a bloody law so ancient and corrupt that it fed on itself and became monstrous.

Maybe it's that. Or the wings. This growling passive carrier of death, their face charted in runes of loss, their eyes dripping grief. Maybe it is just the growing awareness that I lack the courage to sacrifice myself because . . .

I, Tiff, demand the last word.

. . . because I am double.

So maybe it's that demon-hand, transformed into a spider from unsourced nightmares creeping ever closer. Or maybe it's knowing that Narn blames herself for letting Kai stay as long as she did, the end in the beginning, and that she did it for me.

I pivot and pull the trigger just for the satisfaction of seeing the spider-hand shredded. Bats burst from the roof and I am on Narn in a heartbeat, wrestling the scourge from her animal grip before she can bring it down upon herself again.

"Draw the knife out," I command Mag, "After all she's done for you, batshit crazy sister."

Mag lifts her hands palm up to the cave ceiling, and their growls rise to a roar as they magic the knife from Narn's wrist. It clanks on the stone floor. Narn screams and blood spurts from the wound. Torn veins squirm like firehoses. Her hand flops, the bone cracked and protruding. I seize some sacking from the floor. It smells like ordinary old-lady shit and puke, and I wrap her in it and carry her in my arms out of the cave. Through the woods, past the flowers raining down on a restless grave.

The runt is stronger than she looks.

The kitchen reeks of rabbit stew, which I put on to heat, the whole place warm in minutes with wood glowing in the stove and water on the boil. Narn has lost too much blood so I fashion an emergency transfusion from my memory of the infirmary and from material Mag and I find in the apothecary—a length of rubber tubing, clamps, two gel ice packs (one for blood, one for saline) that I empty and sterilize. Mag retrieves some hypodermic syringes and needles still in their cellophane packaging from when a nurse exchanged them for some of Narn's aphrodisiac candles. All that seems like a lifetime ago.

After the transfusion, I bathe the old woman from top to tail in bucket after bucket of fresh water fetched by Mag, and apply her rarest healing poultice to the wrist, deaf to the eternity of regret and fury and futility that pours from her mouth, and to the blood and tears from her eye for an eye.

Now it is only my voice in my head, the same but different.

"Blood vengeance is complicated," I say, "especially when you take it out on yourself."

"Kai?" Narn says. "Meera?"

"Yes," we say.

Mag brings me a splint hewn from the bloodwood tree. I attach it to Narn's wrist with clean white muslin wound in a tight cast. I give her some *Pannaria lucida* for the pain, and brew her some lemon myrtle tea and put her to bed, leaving a steaming cup and some stew out on the porch for her sister.

There we are, just before dawn, sitting on the porch. A girl of fourteen with a bandage around her arm and a bird's nest for hair. The thylacine's head rests on my bare feet. Mag is on point, hidden in some place of their choosing. I sip from a bottle of Narn's moonshine, a rifle across my knees.

CHAPTER 21
DROWNING

I'm worried about you, I texted.

I'm not the one who almost blew my chances with the cool crowd, Marvin texted back. I was making my way back to Tower Village at daybreak, filling him in on my recklessness the night before.

Sasha is giving me a second chance, I said. *She's shown her hand.*

Well played.

Not perfect. But Kai would be proud of me, I thought. That winged shadow yet lurking at the edge of my eye.

Depends. Perfect play can be either the fastest method leading to a good result, or the slowest that leads to a bad one.

Perfect play can be the best way of putting off the inevitable?

There was a pause and I watched the ellipses run across the screen as he composed his reply.

The game is solved either way . . .

More ellipses. He wasn't finished yet. *Takes guts though.*

Yes, it had taken guts. But what more would it take—another Made? Had I thought about the riskiness of my reckless cliffhanger? Mad doctors and lady-bits—how could I speak of such things? I didn't know any more. The morning-after crash hit me like a tidal wave.

The mid-December morning wasn't particularly cold, but it was bleak and an unfamiliar smell blew up off the river. I shivered in my velvet coat. Marvin was sitting on our bench near the giant chessboard. He didn't take his headphones off. Bent over his device, he shoveled ketchupy fries into his mouth from a box, and swigged cold coffee. At first I wasn't sure he heard me. I leaned forward and was about to tap on his headphone when he jabbed a finger at his screen and said, "Look!"

I jumped. I leaned over his shoulder to glance at an article on an archived page about a gang war that had happened several years ago in New Dip, a hundred and fifty kilometers to the southwest. "A family basically wiped out," he said. "This guy"—pointing at the fuzzy image with a bitten fingernail—"was the last to die, tortured in some motel basement."

"He was who?"

"A billionaire investor in tech and big pharma who a decade or so ago pulled out at the last minute from guess what?"

I shook my head.

"Investing in a company called AnamNesis, which got behind a lot of genomic and pharma startups. Anyway, apparently he was related to the CEO of AnamNesis and it caused a lot of family friction. But guess who the CEO was?"

The smell of the fries was making me hungry and queasy at the same time. "You're talking Greek to me, Marvin."

He pulled out a handkerchief and sneezed wetly into it. Stuffed it back into the pocket of his jacket, just managing to catch his device before it slid off his bony knees.

"He was the Father's partner. The guy that everyone knows the Father killed to get his share. Or had killed. Remember?"

A lump of frustration was rising in my throat. The mist from the river wasn't good for my hair, but I was trying to be a better friend to Marvin since the day at the cemetery. "I don't remember, Marvin. I want to but I really don't."

"Sorry." He shut his laptop. Swiveled around to face me. The dead river at his back and the bridge arcing up behind him in the dreary light. He faked disapproval. "Is that makeup from last night?"

I'd staggered out of Sweeney's around dawn. Grabbed a croissant from the kitchen and ate it as I walked across the bridge, my ankles wobbling in their dancing shoes.

"The Father had a partner who put up the cash to buy up all that land in the Rim for Paradise. Ring a bell?"

"A faint one. Rusty and jangly," I said.

"So the partner was attacked by some tribe members in Rogues Bay, supposedly, while picnicking by a waterhole with his date. Also who died. Flayed, basically, both of them—which the tribal group denied, but their men ended up in death row for it, anyway. And now, well a couple years ago, the rest of this AnamNesis guy's family is killed in a city less than a day's drive away from here."

"How were they killed?" I asked slowly.

He took a deep breath. "Let's just say that a cat-o'-nine-tails was involved."

"Bane," I said. "Another word for scourge."

Marvin chewed salt off his lips. "The point is that not very far from here, someone was still taking out the Father's enemies—even after his death—in the same way as they did in Rogues Bay."

Further along the walkway the giant chessboard was missing most of the pieces. A dealer leaned on a rook and counted his cash.

"You okay?" Marvin tossed the remainder of his fries to the pigeons. "I mean you asked me to help you find your aunt. So ... your guardian's gut instinct that she'd still be in Upper Slant was probably right."

"In which case," I said, "you're in danger now. You need to leave, like on the next pod."

"Not without you, Dorothy." He checked his watch. "Oh shit. I gotta go." He unfurled from the bench. "Can you smell that? Coming from the river? Snow—it'll be here soon."

And then he was gone, making his long-legged stride up the path and back toward whoever waited for him in one of the Towers made for tomorrow.

My hangover beat against my temple. Some man's seed sticky between my legs. Sleep tugged at me. If Marvin's detective work was any good, then I had to find a way to convince him to leave, whoever he was now staying for. Because I was no longer so sure that it was me.

I stopped at the vending machine on our floor and bought a Coke. Lara was sitting on my bed beside the hollow left by the Hunter.

"Lara?"

She didn't look up. She was humming some pop tune, and rocking back and forth. I took her by the shoulders and only then did her eyes partially focus. Her face was blotchy from crying. She said, "If the Hunter was a ghost, how come the rug is still damp?"

I looked down at the wet patch on the carpet and knew that it would never dry completely. "Ghosts always leave a snail trail."

"Trudy's in the hospital," she said. "He got her."

"What?" The shock was too much to take. "Why didn't you say so?" I swayed on my high heels—an ankle gave way with a stab of pain.

Lara reached up to grab the blue velvet of my coat, like a lifeline.

I texted Marvin. He didn't reply. There were daily pods now departing from the rooftop of the Bibliotheca to get Mades away from Tower Village. Away from the Hunter. Maybe try and lose themselves in some place whose name could not be spoken, make sure this time they were never found. I quickly packed a bag for Lara and tried to convince her to get on the next pod. She refused—not without Trudy. They'd take her to a clinic, she said, and find only one way to fix her, and Lara couldn't let that happen.

I pulled off my shoes and limped into the bathroom, stared at my mismatched eyes ringed in makeup that wouldn't wash off. Who was I kidding? I could write over the past with all the present I wanted. It wouldn't erase it any more than my curated bespokery would erase the ones and zeros etched in my brain.

"I'll always be with you," the Father said.

And also with you.

And suddenly I saw a room not unlike the Father's womb room, except this room was shiny and new and maybe it was in some kind of Brain Dynamics Center built with endowment funds on a campus just like Wellsburg. And instead of jars like in the Father's womb room there were tiny drawers, thousands of them, and in each drawer a tiny piece of neocortex, the piece that merged with the Father's chip. Numbered and named according to the unfixable Made from whom it had been removed.

No. I did not want that for Trudy. For any of us. It had to stop.

Marvin finally texted back.

A male got attacked too. Kudos for the equal-opportunity Hunter.

You could be next, I said.

There was a hissing sound now, according to media posts about the attacks. Some victims reported sounds of slithering.

Game over.

* * *

From the day that I bring her back to me, an understanding, delicate and strong as bone, will bridge the gap between Narn and me. Between self-made and unmade, failed witch and crappy twin, there is a kind of peace. Over time it will even grow into love. But I will never stop wondering if Narn wishes it were Kai who made it across Rogues Bay instead of me, if the old crone wished she'd thrown me in the trash after all. Sacrificed *me* to the god of blood vengeance so that the hunt for her own dangerous and disappeared sister would be lucky.

"Sometimes," I say while changing her bandages, "sisters just want different things."

"Maybe not the same sister anymore. Maybe Father got to him."

"Her," I say. "I'm pretty sure Tiff is a her."

"Not anymore," Narn said. "No way of knowing what it is."

From the shadows of the porch, Mag puts a tattooed finger over their lips and I stick out my tongue, regret it instantly. Narn mutters something, trying to ladle a spoon of rabbit stew into her mouth with her left hand and dropping it onto her lap instead. I go to help her and she gibbers at me. I step back and fold my arms, and Eric's heavy tail thumps on the floor.

"You'll be fine," I say. "We're all going to be fine."

I stop growing—by the time I'm eighteen I am just over 153 centimeters tall and although I eat enough for two, my weight hovers just below the forty-seven kilogram mark. My coarse hair is another story though and Narn has to cut a tangled inch from it every month with a pair of hedge trimmers, the effect always lopsided due to having to learn to use her left hand. The only thing that helps my vicious periods is a drop or three of *Pamelia*—shield lichen—mixed in coffee or moonshine, and often both. My eyes are too big for my face, but so is my nose, which makes me hopeful that no one will try to make me pretty, that no one will try to make me anything ever again.

I'm already made.

Narn is selective in what she teaches me. "Some magic cannot be taught," she says. "Because already here." She brings her bandaged hand to my heart.

Every evening after my chores are done, Eric and I sit on the porch together, a bottle of *Islandia* brew between us and the rifle over my knees, and we wait for the inevitable. I am ready for whoever, whatever, will follow in the wake of the Assistant, and Eric is readier. But slowly I will learn that the inevitable and the unexpected are as mutualistic as bacteria and fungi in lichen, and as easily confused.

CHAPTER 22

LAST CALL

Power outages at this time of the year were not infrequent in an old town like Wellsburg. The bridge became a dark wind tunnel. I thought about my "Aunt" Tiff and how wherever she was that was all she knew. *Maybe if she were a twin,* Kai whispered at the end of the tunnel, *maybe then she would know what she doesn't know.*

Sasha *had* given me a second chance.

But I couldn't do it alone. Even if my scheduled phone call with Narn was now less to get a story—I had more than I needed—than for us to check up on each other, I needed the connection more than ever. Surrounded by lies and uncertainty, Narn was my only truth. I stood on the bridge, eerily unilluminated, the restive mist over the river below and the vertical coffins of the Village Towers blocking out the stars. On the other side, the façade of the old campus slumped against the night. Disembodied voices from the Corso collided with stray scraps of music and laughter from Wellsburg. The glow of a lantern here, the white arc of a phone flashlight there. The power out for hours at a stretch.

"Another Gatherum?" Narn said groggily into the phone. "Fearsome bitches can't get enough."

She had gone early to bed. I pictured Eric lying across her feet. There was a drought, she said. Cattle dying in the fields, birds falling out of the sky. Fewer travelers passed through the Starvelings. The last time she'd been to town the post office was closed. The dry had shriveled the golden-eye on Kai's grave.

"Tower Village is half-empty now," I said. "Mades are leaving in droves. Scared off by the Hunter and taking their subsidy money with them."

"Power back in old hands now. Old money, old blood—"

"Yeah well she needs me more than I need her. She's shown her hand."

"—boss bitch will get the last word."

Maybe Sasha *was* the surly counter-revolutionary face of old-school alumni that Marvin had told me about weeks ago. Maybe her faction *had* voted against

Wellsburg participating in the Redress Scheme. But I couldn't help myself. A part of me still loved her. Longed for her. Owed her.

"You can't think the Hunter is . . . convenient for Sasha? Seriously?" Too late to take back the defensive wheedle in my voice.

"Working together maybe. Power like lichen," she said. "Oldest thing in the planet. Has to feed itself or it dies."

"Feed itself? Or feed on itself. Because they're two different things, Narn," I said like the know-it-all I would never be. Truth be told, I just wanted to make this call last forever.

"Redress justice and old justice serve one power—play both sides. Kill Zone."

"Okay, but the Gatherum—Sasha, the whole movement to beef up Wellsburg's coffers—it needs us. It still needs our stories. Pagan's office is filled with activist literature—she believes in it, at least."

And I felt that to be true.

Narn blew a derisive raspberry that sounded like thunder in my ear. "Whole world turned its back on Blood Temples, on witches' purges and Mades' suffering." In my heart, I knew this also. How even before the self-serving activism, witches in the Rim had tried to circulate secret atrocity footage. Underground groups, dark web interviews with escapees, marches, graffiti, memes—"them rich bitches knew and did nothing."

"Still, I doubt even Sasha'd resort to hiring someone to scare off Mades just so they can have Wellsburg back the way it was. For one, they need our fakelore. Where would the Gatherum be without it?"

She sighed. "Not all lore is fake."

"Tell me," I said.

"Already told."

"Tell me again."

So she did. How after Tiff ran off, she and Mag needed a third sister to make up the magic number—to be whole again so they could fulfill the bargain they made with the goddess. Having searched for Tiff from one side of the planet to the other, Narn followed her south to the Rim and into the hinterland, to the Blood Temple, where she had disappeared. She suspected that the Father and Tiff had discovered each other, found an infernal mutualism that couldn't be denied. Made a deal against which Narn and Mag alone would be no defense because the chain was broken—the triple charm undone. So Narn decided to make a third sister from scratch.

"That's where Kai and I came in," I said, because it never gets old.

"Only in bringing number back to three, could sisters be a match for two—Tiff and the Bossman," a partnership forged not from godjizz but from man's own hellish grasp.

"So you chose one egg from the Father's supply, fertilized it but put a special lichen extract into the dish to give it some protection it from the Forever Code."

"Not enough. Never enough."

"Then you said some conjure words. And maybe they were the wrong words, or maybe not. But they conjured two eggs from one!"

"A double-yolker good for rainy day. Eggs grow. Plenty conjure for both and power shared is power doubled."

"An eye for an eye, a sister to avenge your lost Tiff—eaten alive by darkness."

Before implantation in the surrogate, Narn continued, she noticed that one egg was too small. Again, she decided to dispose of it so it wouldn't drain the nutrients from the good egg but when she took it to the sink, something happened. The good egg started to bleed.

"Blood in dish. Couldn't let good egg die. Talked to Mag—wrote conjure on paper to put bad egg into surrogate with good. Broken eggs need each other. Broken eggs fix each other."

"And we did. Tell me everything else."

"Don't remember."

"Tell me anyway."

The wind tunnel on the bridge was a crescendo of sighs. "Didn't tell surrogate about twins inside her. Made ravens sleep, sent Assassins—"

"Assistants," I said.

"Sent them from lab, Matrons too. Strong twin came out first, alive. Runt second, not breathing. Not moving. Left to die and cut cord of strong one—started to scream. Good twin wouldn't stop, wouldn't breathe until runt breathed."

"So you said some words to bring me back from the dead."

She had only spoken of my stillbirth once before.

"No one sees. No one knows. Narn puts twins side by side in nursery, wouldn't be separate. From then on, twofer was one."

Students trickled by, angled against the wind. I slid down, collapsed against the rails, my face bathed in neon sky. "And the end?"

"Twins work together like stories. Conjure protection and protect conjure. Nature of the beast."

There was movement again on the opposite bank. It was dark but in the reflected light of the river, I made out an amorphous shadow. It changed shape, leaving a snail trail of phosphorescent green. It crawled slow as a sloth, then sped up like a nightmare, shapeless, but with an indelible impression of bones, of haunches and gaunt ribcage.

Narn said something else, or sang it, but it was in the old tongue that I couldn't decipher above the sound of the sobbing wind, crying like I was twelve years old again and Kai's head was in my lap and her eye was half in and half out, and I didn't know how to fix it and didn't know if I wanted to.

That was our last call.

CHAPTER 23

SWEET SIXTEEN

It is a chilly June on our sixteenth birthday. One of Narn's customers comes to the fence with news from the Blood Temple. It is the woman who gave us the first aid kit. She is an escapee from the mainland. It took her a year to cross the desert. "Hard to find the place unless you know what you're looking for," she'd said.

She was a surrogate and at first believed the Father's lies about Paradise until she'd wandered, doped and in a panic into one of the labs. There she saw the robot surgeon hunched over a petri dish, Assistants in white coats watching a screen displaying what looked like the curvature of the earth mapped with delicate crimson tributaries. Tiny blood vessels, they were, beating to the rhythm of her own heart, she said, the robot hunched over the embryonic brain—"could have been one of mine"—inserting the Father's code into it on the downbeat. She tells us how she still wakes up in the night with that pulse in her head. *Badoom-BOOM. Badoom-BOOM.*

"After that I knew there was too much I didn't know," she says. "About the Father. About everything."

No one went to the authorities because of the ravens. Staff and surrogates were fed stories of how the ravens were the Father's eyes. His brain. His children. Everyone was terrified of the ravens—no one dared to go against the Father.

Narn laughs so hard she cries. "Ravens not Bossman's children," she screeches. "Ravens be witch's eyes."

The woman has a heart condition. She takes the moonshine and shield lichen from Narn and tells us news of how the Father's pet raven attacked him.

"Dani?" I say.

Dani, Kai giggles. *What a rush.*

I step away from the porch and go down the path so I can hear her better.

"The other ravens joined that big bird in pulling him to bits. By the time the Matrons had set the place alight, like the Father made them promise to do, the Assistants had made a run for it. They knew they were done for. Authorities took Mades, the ones who hadn't escaped or fled, into state care. Arrested what Assistants they could, some already in their pods."

The cloud of ravens, a kindness of *Corvus* rising toward a winter sun in a shitting screeching rage of rose-stained plumage, each with a piece of the Father in their beaks. Dani, his pet with the biggest piece of all.

"The Father's head hung from the beak of that huge bird," the woman recalls, shuddering, "by a dirty blue ribbon."

"She did it," I say to Eric. "My sister, Kai."

The bloodwoods rain blossoms down on her grave, and I don't have to look to know that she is now really there, in soul as well as body. The ravens sing "Happy Birthday to you," and the property rings with the sound of their song.

* * *

No one knows that once . . .

The stories had kept coming.

Until they didn't.

From my window in the high dorm where I was finally alone, I gazed down at the bridge, blue as an eye, blue as a lie. Expensive new clothes lay scattered across my bed. Sprigs of *Letharia vulpina* dried on the windowsill. Fearsome Gatherum had grown so large that Sasha would not hear of me having a weekend off, not even to spend time with Trudy. The membership was growing, and the stories *had* to deliver. No more cliff-hangers, Pagan warned me over coffee. No more chances, remember? She reminded me of how Sasha had pulled me out of the wilderness. She reminded me of all the clothes and money, and protection. Especially from the Hunter from whom I was safe even if my Made sisters were not.

"But you're not like them," Pagan said. "You're more like us."

Trying to get that straight in my head was exhausting.

"We're like the Three Graces—get it?" she said. "Sasha Younger, Pagan Case and Meera Made."

It all rang gloriously true in my ears. Thanks to my stories, the Gatherum was much more than the sum of its parts, she said. It was a real movement now, a force for change. Changes that will trickle down to the survivors, too, enable them to re-enter the world on a whole new footing. I wanted to believe her.

"It's fearsomely awesome and awesomely fearsome," she said. "It's the future."

I couldn't wait to tell Marvin—surely this would convince him that the Gatherum-ti-dums weren't all bad. But we were both busy. He had other friends, people I'd had no time to meet. Plus he was writing his term papers—as I should be now that I didn't have Trudy and Lara to do it for me. Finally I bribed him with lunch on the pretense that we could talk about what we were both planning to do in the break.

The student union was less than half full. Decorations festooned the Corso and a Christmas tree had been put up and strung with tinsel in the dining hall. I picked him out from the sparse crowd but at first he looked right through me. Then he shook his head like someone waking from daze.

"I didn't recognize you," he said lightly. "You look different."

I brought my hand to my hair. "It's straightened," I said. "Sasha got a two-for-one deal at her salon."

"It's not just the hair. Found the missing sister yet?"

I said I felt her close.

"You sure you're not lost in the chase, Dorothy? Gone native?"

"We couldn't go native if we tried." I tried to keep my voice even to hide my doubt. "It's you I'm worried about."

We'd loaded our trays with tacos and found a table by the window that looked out on a rainy strip of the Corso. The bookstore across the way was advertising a sale.

"You're really staying? It's not safe," I said. "You should leave with the others."

"Where would I go?" He sprinkled hot sauce onto his plate.

"Back to the Rim," I said. "Don't you have anyone there?"

"Not anyone who'll have *me*."

After a silence, I told him what Pagan had said about the future, and how it was fearsome.

He wore his unkempt look well—the Goodwill sweater beneath frayed suspenders, the tousled silver hair that he cut himself.

"I see him here, Meera. I feel him in the air. In the attacks. In the empty Corso, I see his ghost."

"The Father?"

"Who else?"

Because there was someone—the Father was not working alone. If he were, I reasoned through my hangover and need for sleep, the Mades he attacked would all be dead.

No, he wasn't quite himself after all. The bridge glowed its lies. I had to get it right. There'd be no second chances.

After the afternoon class, I went up to my room to work on a new story. Marvin's notebook was almost full and I ran my hands over the faux vellum cover that had once felt so icky, but which I now carried like a second skin. Once I had the bones of the tale, I decided there was enough time to visit Trudy in the clinic before coming back to try and catch up on class work. On my way to the infirmary, a movement in the distance on the track beside the river caught my eye. I stopped to peer between the Towers. It was two figures walking toward each other. The reason they caught my eye was because one of them wore a Goodwill sweater too large for him, and had an unmistakable shock of silver hair, and the other carried a bike helmet under his arm. They met almost smack in the middle distance between the two buildings and then they continued together around the peninsula out of sight. You didn't need eyesight as good as mine to see that they were holding hands.

When I got to the college clinic, the nurse told me that Trudy had been transported to another hospital, the whereabouts of which she was not at liberty to disclose.

CHAPTER 24

THREE WAY

One late afternoon, almost two years after the Blood Temple has been dismantled, I am in Norman making a delivery and I stop for a beer at the Five-Legged Nag. There is another pub in town, the Excelsior, but it's not for the likes of me. From his place behind the bar, Three Way tells me about an arrangement between South Rim and Upper Slant offering cult survivors scholarships to undertake study at select liberal arts colleges. The tuition part of the scholarship alone was worth forty thousand dollars.

The pub has gone silent, all eyes on me.

"Why would I care?" I ask.

"Just in case, on account of you being one of them bitzers. It's a good deal for the likes of you."

"Not cool, Three Way," warns a bush elder.

"Who you calling bitzer?" I get to my feet, accidentally knocking over a chair.

The men laugh and make way for us, wiping beery hands over wife-beaters, fat tongues lolling in the heat.

"Half-human, half-computer. Which part of you is which?" Three Way says, grabbing at his crotch.

"I'm no more a bitzer than you. Or you. Or you." I lurch around the room with my arm extended like a truth or dare spinner. The bush elder's father is First Nations. His mother's Archipelaga. A sales rep with a case full of sunglasses is half Upper Slant, half Old Sumneun. The cook has a titanium knee and hair extensions. "And you, Three Way, your old man's a front row forward and your mother is a Merino-cross."

The pub erupts in laughter, and Three Way's fleshy face reddens. It's a small town.

"This is your chance, darlin'," he says later, after shouting me a pint. He tells me how after the cult closed down and they seized all the evidence and the embassy was flooded with extradition requests, NATO suggested Redress as the best way forward.

I say, "If I gave a shit, you'd be the first one I'd give it to, Three Way."

But this time, I'm lying.

"The government shut down the weapons testing base. And there's a federal inquest, ongoing, into how a cult like this—for ten years—a whole generation of kids, could have happened right under the government's nose. Who looked the other way? Who was in on it? No secret that a major cash injection would have been a way for this shitty little country in the middle of nowhere to stand out and be counted."

Like Narn's jealous, bitter middle sister, I think, castaway between the devil and the deep blue sea. I haven't been following all the developments—why would I want to? The Father is dead and that is all that matters. But I pick up news whenever I come into town, or whenever Narn's customers talk about it. The elder chimes in how survivors of the unlawful and inhumane Augmented Reproductive Technology have been guaranteed refugee status under the terms of the War Convention. All refugees from the Blood Temple Paradise Cult are encouraged to seriously consider the Redress Scheme. "Not to be viewed as exiles in any sense," the elder says. "Safe return to country of origin also guaranteed under the terms of the convention."

He adds that the whole country's in turmoil after the revelations. "You'd think they'd have learned by now." The bush elder shakes his head, shaded beneath the brim of his hat.

"Also I heard that the safety of any survivors who don't take up the offer won't be guaranteed," the cook says, leaning through the pass window to reach for her cigs.

"Cause of what they reckon will be a backlash," Three Way says, "Copycat cults, paranoia and the like." He points to an article in one of the tabloids about how the greatest danger is in "remoter regions where the law is less readily enforced, and where vigilante mentalities are easily fostered at the frontier of change."

"Vigilante?" I say.

"That's government-speak for dumb as fuck and dangerous as hell."

"Free money, anyways," the cook says. "You ask me."

When I go home and tell Narn about it, she says, there is no such thing as free money and she doesn't need some limp dick to tell her what vigilante means.

"I'm not going," I say. "I'll never leave you."

* * *

I sat in the dorm that third December Sunday with Marvin's bitten-down pencil and the notebook open to the last blank page. Here the coded indentations were faint, but I knew it didn't matter. Enough of Narn's conjure had seeped in to shield my chimeric soul from the corruption within and without. To bring me to this point. To this page. I closed my eyes, waiting for scraps on the cutting-room floor of my memory to reassemble themselves into a story. A spin-off. A sequel or a prequel or a tie-in. Don't panic, I told myself, it will come back. It always does.

And it did.

The last story I "read" from my notebook at the Gatherum was a killer—at the end of the world, two little pink fairy princesses hold hands and with their passerine claws they cut each other into pieces and eat each other all up until there is only a morsel left, a tiny crumb of poison princess for a demon bird to find. The demon bird of memory.

Regulars stood in the hallway outside the turret room, craned their heads to hear, to see me. The applause was deafening. Even Sasha came to the after party at Sweeneys, stayed for one drink and to watch me dance. The strobe light turned us all into ghosts, and from somewhere in the shadows another watched too, and I also danced for her and for lost sisters everywhere. And when the music stopped, they were both gone.

It ended, as it began. In FiFo.

The last days before the holiday were passing in a blur, between classes and end of term assignments. In the empty windows of the Yoga studio, I caught a glimpse of my tamed hair—on Pagan's advice I'd found a moisturizing conditioner that worked wonders—and my newly purchased push-up bra gave me curves that became me. I was thin as a reed, beak-nosed, one eye like broken glass, the other like river mud.

Of all the classes I had regularly struggled to attend, the worst was FiFo. It was Corby—his relationship with Marvin made it too close to home. I didn't think either of us could be objective. But I needed a pass in all my subjects to get my B-plus average or I'd get kicked out of the program—couldn't risk that now that I felt so close to finding Tiff. I wasn't sure how much time it would take and I couldn't let another Made go down. Narn had given me all she had—it was what I did with it now that mattered. A part of me thought that Sasha would pull some strings, but Marvin warned me against taking her for granted. "What fearsomeness giveth, fearsomeness taketh away." So for this last class before the break, I'd cobbled something together in my notebook that I figured would get me a pass. I had no choice but to go.

I crossed the Quad. If Hunter fear had emptied the village, Wellsburg had gotten the spoils. Sasha's Gatherum was now an official patron of the arts at the university, responsible for what was being referred to as the Wellsburg Renaissance. Repairs to the clock tower were underway. A new Institute for Brain Studies was planned near the Founders Church. The site already being cleared for construction, the air ringing with fallen trees. Sasha Younger pictured everywhere donating to this or that cause. The youngest alumna ever to sit on the Board of Directors. The youngest majority shareholder of Wellsburg itself.

And all because of me. A humble Made, whose stories were the new heroin, the bloggers gushed, except perfectly legal!

A bejeweled Christmas tree rose two stories high between the fountain and the central arches of the Quad. I had never seen one like it—freshly cut from the forest along the river, fragrant and dripping with light. The sheer wonder of it made my jaw drop. I remembered the tree in Norman. A moth-eaten artificial they dragged out every year and decorated with faded baubles and strands of LED lights from the supermarket. A beer-can star on the top buffeted by the dry summer winds.

The Writing and Culture Office was shut. I could hear Pagan rustling around inside, her cold voice on the phone and the clink of a fork, something scraped into the trash. I climbed the stairs past the leadlight window of Adam planning to knock Eve up as soon as they got out of Paradise. For her sins.

Corby sat in brooding profile at the oaken table. His bike helmet was on the floor beside his backpack and he appeared to be wrestling a legal pad with two bearish paws. Seven or eight students sat around the table, reading through their pieces or tapping on their phones. Notebooks open and at the ready.

I emptied my backpack. My notebook wasn't there.

"A writer's soul is in her words, her humanity on the page," Corby said. "It comes from here"—he tapped his head—"and here"—he tapped his heart. "And this"—he tapped the legal pad with his pencil—"is the bridge between the two."

"I can't find mine," I piped up. The last I'd opened it was at the Gatherum. He ignored me. "Stories are the bridge. Write about a fatal injury."

Someone wagged their wrist back and forth in a jerking-off gesture. Glances were exchanged in confusion. A few walked out. The remainder reluctantly turned their notebooks to a blank page and began to write.

"Wait." I grew hot in my new angora sweater. "I must have left it somewhere."

Where? In Sasha's turret? At Sweeney's? I began a kind of spinning chair-dance, ducking under the table, pivoting to the wall, checking my satchel. The thought of my scribbling, my weapon, my conjure—Dani's feather—exposed! To my dates! To Sasha! It was unthinkable. I needed that notebook. I was literally lost without it.

"Write on this." Corby tore off a sheet of yellow paper and slid it across the table to me. Kept his big brawny hand on it for a moment before letting it go. "You don't have much time. None of us do."

CHAPTER 25
LAST SUPPER

Once my application to Wellsburg's Redress Scheme is accepted, time literally flies. The sky is a shifting schematic of migrating cockatoos, Eastern Koels and curlews. Narn wants to have our last meal together in Norman. I don't think it's a good idea. There have been a number of vigilante attacks against Mades, some rapes. With impregnation impossible, the repercussions are even less than they are with regular women. But there are uprisings on both sides. Marches accusing the government of not offering enough protection. Religious uprisings calling us abominations. Witches.

I say that I just want us to be together at home, at the little kitchen table as always. Narn knows I love her now, that we are a family—her, Mag, Eric, even the hungry-baby ravens—but that it is Kai who is hardest for me to leave. Maybe that's why she says, "Easier in town."

"Will we go to the Nag?" I say doubtfully.

"Excelsior!" she says.

I wasn't expecting that. The Excelsior is the fancy pub. For white men and loose women. But Narn says every time she has one of Three Way's frozen pies at the Nag, she has to eat nothing but blackberry root for a week afterward. There is an Old Sumneun restaurant at the Excelsior. She has never had Sumneun food.

"Might be fun." I don't want to deny her this. Like me, Narn hasn't been the same since Tiff led the unmanned Assistant to us, sniffing out vengeance. The news of the Father's death perked us up, but that doesn't change the fact that she's getting old, and must cut me loose.

We take the truck. It is a warm evening and we leave Mag and Eric to guard the place. Narn has at least one knife concealed in her tunic, and on the jump seat is a preloved 20-gauge I exchanged with a customer for two rare Golden Seal roots. Vapor trails bloom across the indigo sky like the rarest foliose lichen.

Norman is a zig-zag main street that melts into sand plain at either end. There is a post office, a feed 'n' seed, a gun store and hardware store, a few scattered shacks, two pubs and a chemist-cum-grocery store with a petrol pump to one side. The worst thing about the town is an old wooden church, and a cemetery which contains a scattering of limestone and granite markers overgrown with *X. borealis* and less rare Rim lichens. Some witch-hunter from bygone days has graffitied "Vultures from Hell" across the peeling boards.

The Excelsior is a fine sandstone palace from the settler days when the idea of exterminating all the children of an alien god was still better than sex. We climb honey-colored steps and enter a wide lobby. There is a TV blaring and men sit in a public bar. We pass a ballroom with papered walls and a grand piano. A sepia-tinged chambermaid with a crimson slit across her throat flicks a feather duster at the keys. Her feet don't touch the floor. Further down the hall, outside the bathroom, an Archipelaga girl in a wedding dress sits with her legs spread pulling a ping pong ball in and out of herself, and I can see the flocked wallpaper through her tiny perfect body.

"So many ghosts," I say.

A middle-aged man comes out of the poker machine room and there is a bullet hole above his temple and the back of his head his missing. My scalp itches, my legs feel cold. I can hear music from the Nag, where a band is playing. Why didn't we just go there? A pretty barmaid with green hair is doing a crossword puzzle behind the counter. She smiles at us and points to the dining room upstairs.

"There," Narn says. "Not all ghosts."

"But what do they want . . . with me?"

"To see their stories."

I try to dismiss my resentment, but years of begrudging Narn's insistent multi-tasking makes that hard to do. I'm here for a night out, not to babysit the dead.

Apart from the clink of silver and the tinkle of glassware, the Excelsior dining room is silent. The tablecloths are the same faded blue as Kai's hair ribbon and I feel like I might be sick. Diners stare at the one-eyed witch with her dusky ward. We find a table by a window overlooking the street. At Narn's insistence, I have dressed for the occasion in some of Tiff's cast-offs—low rider jeans and a tight ribbed top with a sweetheart neck. This is the first time I have worn Kai's brown shoes because they finally fit. There are still dark patches on them from the blood of the Assistant, and they remind me of what I could have been. Should have been.

Dead.

I've oiled and braided my hair into a frizzy crown at the top of my head. I feel like crying.

"Come. Make the best of it," Narn says, eyeing the food that the waitress brings us.

I poke at a gray dumplings and sip some watery tea, my thoughts flying to our little porch that smells of jasmine and rabbit stew.

Narn chomps down a dumpling and clear fluid dribbles down her chin. "Crappy twin brought back from the dead at birth—not long enough for death to get hooks in but long enough to give twin Dead-See."

This is the first time she has referred to my stillbirth. I poke at a plate of what looks like stick figures from a game of Hangman.

"Chicken feet," Narn says.

I push the plate away.

"You can see the future, Narn."

She shrugs.

"Don't lie," I say.

She spits out the bones with pointy teeth. "Most times."

"So you knew Kai would be the one to kill the Father?"

She nods. "Hoped but didn't know."

She blows on the cup of tea cradled in tremulous hands. Her left works just as well as the right one now—neither perfect but good enough. There is a jagged scar across her wrist from where she tried to hack it off.

"And what did you hope for me?"

For a moment that stretches into much longer, her lips are a grim line.

"Crappy twin would protect brave sister. Keep him alive."

"Well I failed spectacularly at that."

"Father too strong."

A cleaner wearing a hairnet slops liquid into a bucket, swishes a mop around.

"Why was he so strong, Narn?"

"Turbo charged." She shrugs. "Father has extra power."

"Tiff you mean."

Power of a goddess and power of a man, power to the power of power.

A lady in white comes up to the table and asks if we've seen her children. She isn't speaking English, but there is no mistaking the meaning of her words, the urgent flow of her tears. Her breasts sag with milk gone bad, and lacerations swell across her translucent brown back.

I give my chicken foot to an emaciated ghost dog skulking at our feet.

"Kai changed," I say. "She was different when she came back. Like she wanted to tell me something but couldn't. Like she was afraid."

She sucks her teeth, stalling. She's smoothed down her clown hair for the occasion and Mag has smeared pink lipstick across her mouth.

"Death was in her then," Narn says. "Blood isn't everything."

"If your sister came back"—I top up our teacups from the chipped pot—"what would you say to her?"

She spits gristle into a napkin, blinking both eyes—the real agate one and the fake one. She is trying not to cry. Neither of us want to cry. "Would tell sister, sorry."

It's not what I was expecting. "If Kai came back, I would tell *her* the same thing."

She gets up to find the bathroom. Narn's depth perception has been getting worse, and I watch her bang along the walls toward a door at the opposite end of the big silent dining room. The light is watery, the color of tears. The cleaner has started to drag the mop across the floor. Coarse black hair wisps from her hairnet. A skin-crawl begins beneath my belly, works its way up. She bumps into the table, and Narn's empty chair jumps on its legs. I look away, anywhere but at the cleaner. She pulls off her hairnet.

"Look at me."

"Kai?" I am appalled at the baby weakness in my voice.

It is and isn't my thirteen-year-old twin sister, deathly pale and heart-stoppingly lovely. Her black hair is tied back in the faded ribbon and falls down her shoulders and her deep blue eye flashes like an electrical storm.

"You're all grown up," she says reading my mind. There is a cruel set to her mouth, a tearful hardness. "You turned out pretty tough."

Her speech is muffled and I don't know if she says "pretty tough" or "pretty enough."

"And you don't stink anymore."

She looks at the chair as if unsure of whether to go or stay, as if unsure what she should do. "I don't feel up to much," she says. "I can't remember how I got here."

"That's not like you."

"I'm not like me. I think I'm more like you now."

A lump rises in my throat—pushes the horror back a little. "Is it you? Really?"

"In the not-flesh," she says, miming a grotesque twerk.

The ghosts cock their heads to listen in. "Maybe that's because the memory of who *all* of you are exists in those you left behind," I swallow painfully. "I've kept you alive."

"Thanks. I guess." She wrinkles her chalky brow. "Remember killing the Father? That was—"

"I wasn't—"

"—a total rush!" She sits down, and if I focus with one eye, I can't see the lines of the chair through her body. "It was all winged vengeance, the world gone red. I'm Dani and not Dani. I am a bird!" She looks at me with both wonder and triumph, like someone who pulled off the unthinkable and doesn't quite know how they did it. "Seize! Seize!" she caws.

"How did you do it?"

"Dani let me in. I became her. But me too. Power from the ravens, the whole murder of us—just pure feathered fury. And power from you, Meera. You killed him too!"

She leans forward so her pale see-through hands are almost touching mine, and I will not pull away from their fiery chill. "You ate his eyes, Meera. They popped like grapes between your—"

"Beak?" I finish off.

"He's gunning for you, college girl. Be careful."

We stare at each other and then smile. It's hard not to.

"How will I know what to do?"

She flicks her hair from her shoulders. "Muscle memory. Up here." She points to her head.

"If I don't? If my brain-muscle misremembers? I don't want to keep failing."

She leans in confidentially, and I smell blossoms on her breath, but that can't be right because she isn't breathing. "Then here." She touches me on the breastbone. "That muscle never forgets."

Where she touches me, on my heart, it stops. I open and close my mouth like a fish. No air. I look down at my chest, at Tiff's sweetheart neck. I can see the shadow of my heart through my skin. It looks like a clenched fist. My vision begins to darken at the edges. Then abruptly my heart unclenches. I gasp and draw in hard gulps of air. "Neat trick," I finally say.

The pretty barmaid from downstairs has come in on her dinner break and walks to a table. Kai swivels and grins blackly. "We play Scrabble sometimes. She isn't bad."

"I missed you."

"I missed you more."

"Will I see you again?"

She winks, mimes *I-C-U*. Then she reaches above her head and unties her ribbon. "I want you to have this," she says.

"No way."

"It's not really your style is it?" She looks doubtful and shoves it across the table. "Keep it for a snowy day."

I run my finger up and down the ribbon. It's faded and the silk feels impossibly warm.

"Why are you here now, Kai?"

She looks confused. She fades and jerks back into form, her head bent so low that her hair drags on the table.

"Last supper and all," she says in a voice at the wrong speed. "Three's company."

I looked at my uneaten food. "You hate dumplings."

She lifts her head and lets her tongue hang out in a gag-face. Behind that curtain of hair she says, "Meera, you need to find that bitch-sister and put her out of our misery. Everything depends on that."

"Tell me how. Something's missing, Kai. I feel like there's this gap, this breakage between what I am and what I need to be. I can't get there. Stay. Stay and help me."

But her empty eye looks right through me, and she starts to speak but I can't hear more than a frustrating whisper just below range. I lean in.

"I can't hear, Kai. I can't begin the end until I know what the middle is. You came back to tell me, and then you went away again, and this is my last chance."

"Third one's the charm. I'll give you that."

"Please?"

She has all but faded except for her hands riven with thick black veins—without warning she pounds these down on the table. "It was your fault! You shouldn't have hero-worshiped me like that. You thought I was like an angel or something. You didn't see me. You only saw yourself. Your sad and lonely self."

I grab both of those terrible familiar hands in mine. I pull with all my strength, holding her here with me. "What is the middle bit? You need to tell me what I need to know. If you leave without telling me now, you'll just be lost forever. I don't want you to be lost, roaming, stuck in some middle place." I lower my voice. "That must be hell for you."

She struggles against my grip but I am the stronger one now.

"What was so important to this whole thing, the story of you and me, that Narn brought you back from the dead to tell me? Save yourself, Kai, please. Because I can't."

I'm concentrating so hard on keeping her with me that at first I don't notice Narn shuffle back to the table, and pull up a third chair. "It's time," she nods, "for middle bits."

Narn's words bring Kai back but so distorted and monstrous at first that I yelp and drop her hands. Her shoulders slump until her neck is stretched and extended like a raven's, her chin almost on the table. Her too-blue eye ratchets open and closed. "I was going to leave without you, okay? When I started to bleed, and I knew that I had the bad lady-bits, I knew that the game was up with the Father, pardon the pun. Narn had told me about the secret place where she and her sisters were from and I begged her to get me out of there or I'd tell the Father that she was a spy. I was scared. So scared."

"You were going to leave without me?" My voice is shrill with disbelief.

"I didn't care. All I cared about was myself. Some twin, eh." She sits up straight and she is Kai again, beautiful liar, a horror.

"You didn't know, though," I beg. "You didn't know we were twins."

Nightfall darkens the windows. The Excelsior ghosts have taken their places in the dining room, scattered at tables, undone and expectant.

"I knew." Kai rocks back and forth on her chair. "I always knew. Didn't you?"

Hadn't I known that the teller of those bunkroom tales was intricately, intimately bound to me? Like seeking like, and even then, how proud I was of her, clever gutsy Kai, even before I knew that I had a reason to be.

"Yes," I whisper. "I always knew."

Narn is snoring gently.

"I thought you were weak enough to pass for a normal Made. That the Father wouldn't harm you if he never found out." Her voice drops to a low percussive whisper, like a snare drum. "I told myself I'd come back for you."

Narn lifts her mutilated wrist, holds up two fingers in the peace sign. "Truth or dead."

"Is that all?" I say. "Is this what you needed me to know? Because it doesn't matter. I would have done the same."

"No you wouldn't."

No, I wouldn't.

"No more lies!" Narn howls, and the ghosts cower. "Truth or dead!"

Kai does not cower. She unfurls, as if having come to a decision, or having one come to her. She stretches black lips in a squishy smile. "But then everything changed."

"What? When?"

"You know. The Assistant that time in the Blood Temple." She sticks her finger in her mouth and fake-gags. "The way you fought him off when he tried to turn you into a specimen."

"What?"

"It was intense. Such fury. Such rage. You kicked him with your bare feet and kept him down and kept kicking. Extreme gore between your toes—the evidence. But you didn't care. You just kept kicking where it counts. That's when I knew I could never leave you."

I feel my chair lurch. The dining room bulbs flicker. Narn rattles from her throat.

"No! It was you. It was *you* who brought him down. With *your* heavy brown shoes." I kick the leg of her chair under the table. "*You* who saved *me*."

She wobbles her head and smiles sadly. "You saved yourself, sister. Didn't need shoes. You were always the strong one. The dangerous one."

"Shhhhh," Narn surfaces from her dreaming pool. Her painted mouth serene as a bronze goddess.

"I stomped him? With my bare feet? I was like, twelve years old."

"Almost thirteen. And look again."

I lift the tablecloth, slip one of my feet out of the brown shoes. Oh horror! The passerine talons—engineered for perching, retract as soon as I look at them. I get a glimpse of a stumpy hallux. My mouth hangs open. Narn watches me from behind a slitted eye. Kai looks away, bloodlessly whistles.

"Why haven't I noticed before?" I can barely speak. Weightless with shock.

"Maybe because you haven't known what to look for." Kai points to where in the place of her missing blue eye, there is now a new brown one. It's bigger than the blue one, and it looks wrong—like a human eye on an animal, or a cat's eye on a dog.

"Why didn't anyone tell me?" I look between them. "All this time I thought I was . . ."

"Crappy twin," Narn says between stagy snores.

"Because then I knew you'd do something stupid and heartfelt because that's who you are. That's what makes you a danger. You live in how you feel." Kai brings her hand to her heart again. "I live in how I think." She points to her head. "You *do* first, ask questions later. And I couldn't let you *do* anything that would make you dead meat in a jar."

"But you could have been instead. That was . . ."

"Brain dead," Narn wheezes and wakes up suddenly.

"I took the blame because the shoe fit." Her white face darkens and there is a note of doom in her confession, like the slamming shut of a cage. "When we first started playing boardgames, it was a novelty, but then he began to see my noncompliance, my non-perfectibility, as the original sin. I knew that if I took the blame for what you did to the Assistant, he'd see that he had seriously blown it. He'd created a monster, and he wouldn't be able to forgive me anymore than he could forgive himself. That was the only thing that got me through the unmaking. It *did* hurt him more than it hurt me. Almost."

"Men!" Narn says something else in her language, and it sets my teeth on edge.

"Besides," Kai says with a dread coyness. "I knew you'd save me."

"Why don't I remember?"

"Why do you think?" Kai makes a finger-gun and shoots herself in the head. "The Father's Forever Code—memory wiped clean as a whistle."

She begins to whistle that song she started. When I ask her, she says it's from a different time, a different place. "*Like birds of forever,* " she hums in perfect pitch, "*to be or not, yeah yeah.*"

Now it is Kai who is crying. The three of us are holding hands.

"Do I have to be dead for my memory to come back?" I ask.

Ghostly tears run down her face. "It helps but I wouldn't recommend it."

I wiggle my toes to make sure they've gone back to normal.

"Sorry," Kai says.

"I told you she'd forgive you," the witch says, and both Kai and I stare at her. It is the first time we have ever heard Narn use the correct pronouns.

And then Narn does that clicky thing in her throat and my sister is gone.

* * *

I headed to the bridge after the last FiFo class, thinking I would retrace my steps to find the notebook, when a text came in from Pagan.

You left your little book behind. S will return to you next Gatherum. X-mas party afterward at Sweeney's—you're coming!

CHAPTER 26

LOST AND FOUND

For the rest of the week, I went to every class. I comforted Lara—helped her arrange her flight and we said tearful goodbyes.

On the Sunday evening of the last Fearsome Gatherum before the Christmas break, I texted Marvin and said I was going to get a drink. I didn't wait for him to text back. I dressed without really thinking about it. I laced up our old brown shoes. From the windowsill, I took a yellow sprig of *Letharia vulpina* and ground it carefully into powder using the handle of my hairbrush. I mixed the wolfsbane into some water in a plastic bottle small enough to fit into my coat pocket. In my locker, I rummaged for the little purse and the tips of my fingers touched something hot and slick. I pulled it gently out. I went to the mirror and tied your blue ribbon around my crown of frizz. It was time. I'd made a promise. And the story had to deliver. Narn taught me how to do that, just as she taught you.

"And we flock in fury together," I hummed, as off-key as your ghostly pitch was perfect. *"No word of a lie."*

Leaves had gathered along the Corso and the trash bins were overflowing. The bookshop clerk stared sadly out of the window. Bicycles rusted in their stands. Sasha, it seemed, had won. The Redress Scheme looked doomed.

I went into Dirty Bert's, empty except for a couple of older Mades. I ordered two beers and two shots before Marvin texted that he had a big day and would see me another time. I checked my watch. Just after eleven p.m. The readings in Sasha's turret would begin soon. It was a special Christmas session with everyone asked to write a holiday-themed story and a big party afterward with the select few moving on to Sweeney's. The beer at Dirty Bert's was even more watery than usual. A text came in from Pagan. I ignored it. Another one came in.

Where are you?

I ignored that too.

You're up next.

You missed your spot.

Sasha pissed.

Halfway across the bridge, I called Narn. Someone picked up but said nothing. Into the silence I said, "I think I've found your sister. She's killing Mades to avenge the Father. They had a deal, I guess."

After another pause, "What do you want me to do?" I said into the silence.

"You know," the silence said. "You always knew." The silence was in me. It had always been in me. It was your blue eye, and the blood on my shoe. It was how I could imagine and forget. It was my fear and your love.

"Are you sure?"

The silence was answer enough.

I hung up and leaned on the rails of the bridge. The miasma shifted above the impenetrable forest below. The bridge breathed its neon blue gasp. I turned toward Wellsburg. This would be my last play. The bouncer at Sweeney's let me in. "You're early," she said. I ordered two dirty martinis—and then I began to descend.

The basement was already crowded. A sea of strobing shoulders obscured the dance area. I sat at the black circular bar and waited. When the photographer arrived, I took him to an empty storage room in the back.

Afterward, he asked me my name.

"Kaimeera."

"What does it mean?"

"It means an individual made of genetic material from two or more different organisms. A creature assembled from mismatched parts."

"Like in myth—that she-goat thingie?" He was looking it up on his phone, showed me a picture of a tripartite beast with the head of a lioness, out of its back the head of a goat and from its rump, the coiled tail of a serpent.

"Like that."

"Wow." A text came in on his phone. He read it and giggled.

"Truth or dare," I say.

We were lying on my coat. He reminded me of a shearer from the Nag whose name I also would never ask.

"That chick that brought you here—Pagan Case? She and I dated for a while. Nothing serious. She was the one who said that you might have an itch needs scratching. Being what you are."

"It's okay. I get it," I said. "And I do."

A while later he continued his confession. "She gave me a small remuneration.

She got me on the List at Sweeney's. Nothing to sniff at. It's not that I don't like you, Kaimeera. It's just that, you know. I want to be a father one day. And the girls from the cult can't reproduce. I mean you could always adopt and such. But no one knows how you'll age, or even if. Not being full human and all."

"Kiss me," I said.

"Your turn," he said. "Truth or dare."

I dared him to take my picture for his collection of monsters.

* * *

Narn says she wants dessert but not here so I shove Kai's ribbon into my pocket, and we pay our bill and step out into the Norman night. The streets are empty and I remember alighting from the train six years ago, with my dead twin in my arms. We stop at the grocery store to get ice cream, but it's closed. In the window is a poster for a two-for-one deal on superseded phones. Narn stops and points.

"A good one that one."

I stare at her. "You want a mobile phone?"

She points at the deal. "It's a twofer."

I tell her I'll pick them up in the morning. She makes me promise to call once a week from college, and I say only if she promises to call me back.

"No more fighting," she says.

"No more fighting." I take her arm, navigate the sidewalk cracks.

"What were you like when you were my age, Narn?"

She looks at me sideways, and seems to think about it for a while. "Fast," she says, "and furious."

Easy to imagine: Narn and her two sisters tearing through hell, chasing the bad guys. "Even afterward," I say, "when you moved to the surface, started to fix things. Broken things?"

She shook her head. "Slower then. Fixing takes more time than breaking. Baby sister Tiff had no time for fixing. Big fight."

"I know all about that."

"Maybe. Maybe not. Lots of power in blood vengeance. Sinners pay with their souls. Lots of riches. Plenty souls. All too much power for one sister."

I look around, not remembering where we've parked the truck. I thought it was closer than this. "Would you forgive her if she asked?"

"Trick question."

"Not all power is bad, Narn. The power to change. The power to heal. To create. You of all people know this. Those stories you gave to Kai in Middles

Bunk. They gave her a kind of power, but she shared it with the Mades, didn't keep it for herself. Your stories, in her words, gave them the power to imagine a world outside of Paradise. Power is a door. You just can't let it kick you on the way out."

She pulls me to a stop. "Where's the truck?"

I tell her it is just around the corner. She knows I have no idea.

Narn wraps her birdlike fingers around my arm. "Meera?"

"Yes, Narn." Cars drag out on the highway somewhere.

"Some lost things never be found. Important to know not every game can be solved. Some take the player with him, never comes back."

"Okay." Because all I can do is try and choose my words, if not my destiny. "So what should I do? Stop playing?"

"Start looking. Already it sees you."

I feel it too. I always have. The gone-but-not-forgotten malevolence of the world that made us. That eye for an I, that total commitment to sameness.

"There's the truck. Just past the chemist."

"This day was always coming." Narn's breath is labored, her lurching gait pulling me to a stop. "Narn has truths too."

"About what?"

"About lies. Narn conjured two sisters, *not* by accident. On purpose." She grips me harder. "Always. Witch wanted both—one to kill Father, another to find sister. Needed two, yes, but then loved both the same—from the beginning."

I guess that this too is something I have always known, even if I have not always felt it. "Does it matter who does what—me or Kai?"

"Same difference. Look."

We are outside the chemist. She pushes me toward a mirror fixed atop a sunglass display. At first I don't notice anything. I bring a hand up to my twisted bun that is already coming undone. My heart quickens. I blink. My eyes are different! One is still my own brown eye, a little large for my face. The other is smaller, more almond and it is an impure blue.

My sister's eye.

When did it change? At the same time I saw the talons on my feet retract in the dining room? Did one need to happen so the other could? I guess I'll never know. I touch my eye, just under it, tenderly. It's my best feature.

We continue walking down a street that after all looks not much different behind mismatched eyes than it ever did. I was hoping that the band would still be playing at the Nag but it is closed and the curtained windows along Main Street glow with pee-colored light or flicker from television screens. The bush is awake though and the cry of the night creatures is an orchestra. In the distance a ceremony is underway to awake the ancestors, a song that carries Narn and me along on this night of beginnings—which is also a night of ends—all the way home, to the middle.

* * *

I left Sweeney's through the kitchen door on the river side that opened onto stone steps hewn out of the rock bed. I took the steps down to the river, glad that I'd put on our old brown shoes. What began in an old goddess's dream as two for one was now one for two.

Kai's ribbon burned like a crown of fire.

The woods were all around. So thick that from this side the spider eyes of Tower Village looked dim and far away. The bark of the trees shimmered with blue from the bridge—I smelled that alien smell and when I looked up, it was snowing.

A weight lifted from my chest. I smiled, almost laughed. I wished Narn could see it. There were ravens here in the North, but they weren't Narn's ravens and they couldn't show her the snow. More important, they couldn't protect me—no one could—and for the first time in my life, I felt cut loose. Weightless.

I found a path that skirted the riverbank into denser forest, and I kept to it as best as I could. The snowflakes drifted down like the white blossoms above my sister's grave, and the form my life had taken in Wellsburg suddenly made sense. It had all led to this, had been leading to this ever since I'd been born to die for her.

I was you. And you were me. *It won't be long now.*

Something invisible moved ahead in the snow. But the growl, when it came, was behind me. I wheeled to face it. The snow fell faster, melting as soon as it touched the black earth. I caught a smear of livid green like a stain and then just the dark.

"Come out, come out wherever you are." *Whatever you are.*

Again that abject arrowing streak. Beastly. Impossible.

"I can see you, Tiff. Always could."

Branches crunched behind me. I turned again. No one. I began to walk deeper into the forest. The further north along the bank I went, away from Wellsburg, the denser it became, with thick-trunked old-growth trees, the ground spongy with rot. And behind me a smell, that meaty perfume.

"Meera."

I swung around.

"You missed the Gatherum."

"Sasha?"

"You look like you've seen a ghost."

I almost didn't recognize her. She came out from under a low blue-washed bough. She wore a leather duster, a hunter's cap. She looked . . . suddenly so hammy that I had to laugh.

"It's you? The Hunter? Is this some kind of joke?"

Loose tendrils of her hair jumped from beneath the base of the cap like flayed snakes.

"You tell me, Meera. You're the joker."

"What are you doing here?" I faltered, my blood turning cold.

"Same as you, I expect. Hunting."

Narn had been right after all. My face burned with shame and I felt Sasha's deception like a knife in the heart. But I had to process this quickly—had to keep my focus as long as I could.

"Why would you want to be killing Mades?" I asked, my voice hitching. "Why go to all this trouble, when the Redress Scheme will eliminate us anyway?"

"For shits and giggles," she said. "Bait and switch."

"A distraction?" I shook my head idiotically. "I, I thought you loved me. Like a sister?"

"I could have. Maybe I did. If you'd followed the rules." She cocked her chin defiantly and twisted her joker's lips. "That whole Redress thing lowered the tone. Wellsburg is my place. My rules."

The voice was out of context. Out of the cozy turret room, something else had caught Sasha's louche, breathy tongue—something petulant, exhausted. She suddenly looked her age, the jawline lumpier than it should be. Pins and needles crawled up my arms. "If the shoe fits. *Slasher* Younger—of course."

"Anyway, it wasn't killing them so much as scaring them off—reminding them of their place, in truth, and that Wellsburg isn't it. That this place doesn't belong to any Scheme except that which founded it. Never will."

I had to think about this for a minute. The signs were all there, but I hadn't seen them, or maybe I had, and I'd loved her anyway. Grief and terror crashed over me, washed away and left me clean and unvarnished enough to see the truth and raise it. I pitied her, oh how I pitied her and that in itself was almost a relief. "Do you have my notebook, *Sasha*?"

She wrinkled her brow and for a moment her hairline lowered like a beast's, and I took a step back. She rummaged in a leather satchel slung across her body, casually brought out a cat-o'-nine-tails in one hand and my notebook in the other. I continued to back away.

"Truth or dead," she said, and lunged.

I ran. Chased by the smell of blood and shit and bitter bile. The steps behind me were lumbering, the way you'd expect a being facing its own extinction to sound, so desperate to survive it would do anything except change. Slowing, I took out the bottle filled with crushed wolfsbane and I drank it down.

"Was it worth it, Sasha?" I swung around to face her, my arms to either side like I was flying. "Selling your tiny soul to an old has-been in return for the power to have your pathetic 'burg back?"

I talked to confuse her. I ran to exhaust her. But mainly I ran to speed up my metabolism so that the *vulpina* would enter my blood as quickly as possible. The first cramp came at the same moment as a white bolt of pain took me from behind. Tiff—for it *was* Tiff in there somewhere—Tiff's scourge ripped through the back of my coat and brought me to my knees. Another lashing loosened my bowel.

She got me on my back with maximum force, the wind knocked out of me, nothing but the overwhelming panic of not being able to breathe, choked by my own upchuck. Tears springing and snot flowing as I tried to crawl away through drifts of leaves, brittle with frost. One of Kai's shoes had come off in the woods and I felt the cold on my bare foot, just like before. Just as it caught me I kicked at the demon with my clawed feet. I ripped it where it hurt, in the guts. Gore squished between my passerine talons, now fully extended, heel and toe. Just like that time with the Assistant, Kai—what a rush!

It felt good to be together again, finally.

Behind the mask of the young heiress, the old goddess (no less a chimera than I was) took my foot in her paw and crushed every bone in it and I screamed. I may have blacked out. *Shhhh. Not long now.* Then she leaped on my chest all shrunk down to the size and shape of a little bitty girl, with a bouquet of fiery snakes in one hand and my notebook, my soul in the other. She bit the snake heads off one by one with pointy teeth, her maw aflame. How perfectly the snowflakes sat on her scarlet hair. She chewed and chewed on the viper heads, and grew and grew until she was Sasha Younger again, riding my chest, my ribs cracking under her larger-than-life weight.

"You found me," she said, "like I always wanted you to."

I felt crushed beneath the weight of her rage.

She spread her legs wide and blood seeped from behind her black contacts and brimmed from her eyes.

"You tricked me," I said.

Sasha-Tiff pouted scornfully, triumphantly. "You loved me. Not in spite of what I was but because. Just like you loved—"

"Tiff!" Grief gave way to rage—at myself yes, but also at her. The terror she inflicted on those Mades. My sisters. A collective scar that will never heal.

"You just opened the door and let her walk right in, Sasha. Sold yourself cheap, you stinky skank. Took the double and lost to a pro."

"Takes one to know one, runt."

"I'm not . . ."

"The gutless sister. Always were, always will be."

Tiff-Sasha's lids closed over her tarry eyes and she opened her abyssal mouth and began to laugh. Cracking up, she began to change. Endangered species, desperate enough to possess the soul-starved body of a witch-hunter's heiress—oh the irony—and desperate enough to take a dead Father's blood money to pay for it.

The blue glow of the bridge rose above the trees. To the west the Towers sparkled and I thought of Marvin and how I would have liked to have seen him one more time.

"That was you who tortured that AnamNesis guy?" I said. "Aunty Tiff? Why so much trouble for the Father's enemies?"

She shrugged, not laughing now.

"Money?" I said. "You have plenty."

"I did it for you," she said in a siren's voice. "You belong to me."

"I thought I did," I said, trying to throw her off me. "Just like you think you belong to the Father, Tiff. Or whoever you are after all this time. I know you're in there somewhere, sister, deep under the skin, the tissue, the bone of a body you'll toss—whatever. Either way, Sasha, *you're* dead meat. Tiff won't need you soon, boohoo. That's why Mag could never get to you in time, not that they didn't try to stop you hurting Mades. But they were sniffing for familiar blood, their own kind not the stink of old money in new flesh. Such banality threw them off, at first. By the time the fury in Mag found its prey, you were already gone but Tiff's scourge had done its damage—not deadly but may as well have been. You're right. It killed the Redress scheme, if not the Mades themselves, which isn't bad for a running game, eh, Tiff? A strategist like yourself'd have to be happy with that."

In that she's like Kai.

She'd stopped laughing. Legs akimbo across my chest, she held up two elongated, turgid fingers in a peace sign.

"Double or nothing. One, daddy loves me. And two, he's coming back."

I grimaced, turned my head away from her crotch. I managed to roll out and start crawling away before the next sting of the lash. I may have blacked out. When I came to, she had me in a headlock.

"You're mine, little sister, perfect for a rainy day. Hostage to hold over an old witch. Insurance against . . ."

"The Father?" I coughed, and gagged on the poison, careful to swallow it back down. "Good luck with that."

I kept talking. Telling stories. Stories about how it wasn't any of that. It was jealousy. Jealousy over her sisters' powers. Jealousy over their capacity to change, even though change was her poison. "You take and destroy, over centuries, the bodies of others—hunter, Made, witch-hunting heiress—while your sisters look deep inside their own selves. Find scraps of consciousness they can keep, pieces they can let go of in order to change. To become not less, but more of themselves. You think you can jump from hot body to hot body forever, but every time you throw one of those bags of meat in the trash, a piece of you goes with it."

I trembled to think that the next hunk will now be mine. And the shivers delivered a hot flash of poison through my blood.

"My sister sent you to feed me," she growled. "She wants me back. She'd do anything, even sacrifice her twofers—most heinous sin of all."

"Narn didn't send me to feed you," I said through the pain, the falling snow. "She sent me to kill you."

"Kindred ones!" she shrieked. "No kin to me."

It was working. She was changing. Still Sasha on the outside, but Sasha as she really was, behind the mask of beauty and art that blinded me to her charms— withering, rotting before my eyes. Something skittered in the trees—getting as far away from this as it could. The Lots River meandered more freely here. I could hear the faint rush of water.

"I was the beautiful one," she wailed. "My fury drove men to madness."

"Men like the Father?" I was beginning to falter, the poison working in me. "I wouldn't brag about it."

She brought down the lash again. It cut me across the breast, broke my nose and ribs. I turned my head so I wouldn't choke on my tongue. Not yet.

"I'm starving," I gurgled. "Aren't you?"

"I would bend the chase to my will, never bending to its."

"Let me know how that works out for you," I said, gagging on blood and teeth. "I got a little lost in mine."

"My sisters gave power away!" The Tiff-thing snarled, baring pointed yellow teeth. "Without consulting me! Seduced by the younger gods. What do the younger gods know from blood? What does the law know about mother-killers, and father-slayers? The law is blind. It sees everything and nothing."

I see you see me.

My stomach doing forward rolls as the poison coursed through me. "Your sister told me to tell you she was sorry."

The effect was instantaneous. Whatever remained of the Fury's purloined humanity fled at those words. Rearing out of Sasha's form emerged the real Tiff, flayed abomination, older than old, sister from a no-good mister. Massive, fluid, she crouched over me on all fours, half obscured by shadow. Trails of luminous decay ran down her limbs. Rank heat plumed from a fanged mouth. Her breasts swung and snakes reared from her head. The snow swirled.

"Look at you," I panted. "All those years of taking the law into your own hands, truthfully? That was just an excuse, like any other bid for power. You're like the Father—he sees himself in you. And when that happens you're a goner."

She took my notebook and tore it in two. Pages fluttered against the dark branches.

The goddess bayed. "I'll hound him down. Scorch him with reek of fire, waste him!"

Again I braced against the roller-coaster lurch of the poison. "You'll rot and fester, Tiff. Slow and ugly. Toxic sludge splashing around the Forever Father's dumpster. Oh Kai." The pain was white. I tried not to puke. I did puke.

She raked her talons down my chest, brought my flesh to her mouth and messily sucked the blood off. Of course, I screamed. It seemed like the right thing to do.

"Eat," I panted—buying seconds with my words, a language I didn't know I knew, my tongue twisting around the clicks and glottal. "Feast, sister." The snowflakes unfurled like blossoms. Talking was too hard so Kai had to do it for me. "*Mag knew one broken word that spelled home—S-T-A-R-V-E-L-I-N-G—it would lure you here even as it triggered Sasha, the two of you made for each other. Then, acting alone as the extreme situation demanded, they magicked themselves here and crawled up from under the bridge in their true form—at first Meera didn't know it was them. But you did. And Mag scared the hell out of you, Tiff—the only being in any world that ever could, because they are multiple, fluid, a murder, a kindness. And there is power in that beyond anything you will ever know. And so you ran. Because it's the only game you know.*"

"But Mag can't save the Made this time, Tiff. It's too late. You have to be quick. Eat. You must be starving."

So finally the beast sunk its teeth into my chest. I screamed in agony and it ate, my flesh its food. And it wasn't Tiff anymore. And it wasn't Sasha.

I smelled him before I felt him.

The Father. Three's a crowd. Tiff in Sasha, the Father in Tiff. Of course. With my final shreds of thought I remembered Marvin's detective work. The Father's nemeses eliminated with extreme prejudice. Paving the way for his return through a goddess's futile lust for eternal life. Coded on her atrophied soul, her endless memory. He'd digitally entered her—I guessed some kind of Forever Code on steroids—and sent her to the Slant as insurance should anything happen to him. Like a flock of killer ravens.

And now I had him. Oh Father.

"He becomes you, Tiff! And not in a good way."

My dying heart pumped for joy. I panted for blood—the pain was a trip because the creature was eating for three.

"Oh my Father, beware Mades bearing gifts."

Snowflakes on my face, so cold. So cutting. So perfect. Are you seeing this Narn? Me, the crappy twin! Unmaking the Father who'd already unmade Tiff who'd consumed Sasha—three *is* the charm. And I'm doing it—just like you hoped I would. Don't be sad, witch. I do it for you—because I love you and you saved me—and I'm going to see my sister now. I'm going to be . . .

Kaimeera.

I felt, and it seemed almost funny now, the Father's white teeth in another's head—not having one of his own—gnawing, tearing, hungry, so hungry. He couldn't get enough, knowing that if he ate me, he'd become me, Meera, and then he'd go back to the Starvelings and destroy everything I'd ever loved. Never, Father, because a Made's love is the Maker's poison. My shame its food. How my scrawny flesh wobbled in those teeth, blood dribbling down its chin. Funny, I thought. Funny how the bait takes longer to work when it's working for two. And funny now, the frothing at its mouth, the vermillion spume. Funny, the roar of surprise, the eyes cracking at the corners, the black tongue lolling. Unholy spasm as the wolfsbane crosses the brain barrier and funny the spray of the yellow-green bile. Are you seeing this Kai? How it eats? And eats?

The last thing I knew was Mag's huge wings beating above me, too late finally to scare the ravening mister-sister off, and too late to save it too. The demon as furious in death as in life—the death-rattle and the way the red light pulsed and then faded from its two-faced eyes. And I lay in a lake of my own poisoned blood, while Mag knelt beside me. The snow slanted down and the world turned white. They took my hand and tried to explain with shrieks and sobs—the tattooed markings forming and reforming across their face—how the three sisters' timeless fury against blood crimes tragically transformed into a crusade against one of their own, a twisted sister gotten too big for her boots.

ANAMNESIS

Marvin isn't a god. But he makes a good witch. The bush people like coming to him because for one, he doesn't sic Eric on them, and two, he's always up for a chat. He's a quick study. He has even managed to decode Narn's grimoire, in which he's already made several new entries. After my long recovery, we spend hours hiking on the lookout for rare lichen. Sometimes we stop at the rocky outcrop to share a bit of lunch with the goannas and the watchful ravens.

He and Corby live in Narn's old room. I have the bed I shared with my dead sister, and Mag still hunts for our food and sleeps wherever they sleep, and together we tend the graves, taking turns to scrape the golden-eye lichen off Kai's and the raven shit off Narn's. I'm sorry, I say to her. I wish that we hadn't had to kill your sister in order to kill the Father. I hope you can forgive me for it, love me for it even. I hope that in the end you were glad you didn't throw me away. When a fresh gust of blossoms blows down from the bloodwoods like an impossible snowfall, I tell myself she's heard me, worlds away, like she did on the bridge. Because when I listen very hard, I can hear her too—the flowing waters of that ancient song—always changing, always new.

I have never found the words to thank Mag for trying to keep up with Tiff's Father-fueled rampage against the Mades in Wellsburg, for infusing the poison from my veins, and for their silent doctoring back in the Starvelings. The scars on my back and belly are my pride.

Lately Mag has taken to stepping up onto the porch of an evening to take a swig of moonshine. I watch them settle onto the seat beside me, adjusting the sharp angles of wings beneath the high hood, a sorcerer's headdress. I put the rescued notebook down—the stories miraculously rearranging themselves to make room for more—and slide the pencil in its ring. The cover is permanently sticky. There are torn and missing pages, words overwritten so thickly that they look to be floating above the page. Eric sits on his haunches, his ears pricked and his spear-tail patchy with mange.

"You knew your lost sister would find her way home if she could," I say above the song of the cicadas.

Mag lifts the jar and I get a glimpse of black wing.

"And you couldn't let that happen because she wasn't your sister anymore. She was mostly the Father by then."

They nod.

"That's why you scrawled out Norman and put the real place on the form, right? To draw her out—what was left of her?"

Mag passes me back the jar and rummages in a pocket. They pull out a scrap of lined yellow paper and a small begrimed wooden case. From it they take one of three ink-stained reed pens and a block of dried ink. Mag scrapes the tip of the calamus into the block of ink and on the paper carefully writes something and passes it to me.

"*Starvelings,*" it says in the same dark hand as on the Redress Form, and as the self-inked map that covers every inch of their body.

Mag sits back in the chair. Eric unhinges his oversized jaw in a yawn and settles down with his muzzle on my feet.

"It's okay to write it down now?"

They shrug. The sister of second chances.

"That map all over you. Can you do one on me maybe one day?"

They look at me in disbelief.

I laugh. "Okay. It's a lot. Maybe a mini version. Just so I can find myself next time I get lost, too."

Mag nods and we sit there for a while, the old thylacine watchful between us. We have two now. He has a sister—Marvin's first successful experiment with necromancy. Eric is slowing down but I know I can never replace him.

Sometimes I drive into Norman to have a drink at the Five-Legged Nag. The Excelsior has shut down. Haunted they say. The green-haired waitress and I play word games from the newspapers lying around the pub and she says I remind her of someone but she can't say who.

"Memory is tricky like that," I say, because she reminds me of the same person.

She spells out a nine-letter word from the grid: "ANAMNESIS."

When I ask her, she counts out the possible meanings on three fingers. In medicine, she tells me, it can refer to the history of a patient's immune response. In religion, to a tripartite ritual remembrance, and in philosophy, she says, "To the closest human reasoning can come to knowing the previous existence of the soul. Your turn, Meera."

I think about it as I ponder the grid. I wonder aloud if the reasoning that can know that, is really human or maybe something else?

"Maybe both," she says.

We agree it's a question for another day.

Three Way's saving up to buy the Excelsior to take people through it, like those witches' burial grounds in Upper Slant, or our very own Blood Temple if it had not burned down, or any other man-made structure haunted by the hungry ghost of shame.

It'll eat you alive if you let it.

ACKNOWLEDGMENTS

Thank you to my agent Matt Bialer and my publisher and editor, Tricia Reeks of the mighty Meerkat Press.

The Bridge was born from a short story I wrote a couple of years ago, and I'd like to thank the Thorbys Writers Workshop for their initial feedback on both the story and the work as it grew. Likewise to Sarah Klenbort and Seb Doubinsky for reading early drafts and especially Angela Slatter for her generosity, her game-changing criticism and ongoing support. At the eleventh hour, Jack Breukelaar jumped in to help with proofreading, to weigh in with boardgame and plant taxonomy expertise and to him I send love and thanks especially for his sustaining late-night pep talks.

Thank you to H. Morgan-Harris and everyone at The Aerie for providing me with the shared solitude I needed to complete this project. I would also like to gratefully acknowledge a grant from CreateNSW for conference attendance and readings—much-needed support and flexibility during these weird times.

I would like to acknowledge Marie-Hélène Huet's 1993 analysis of maternal fancy, *The Monstrous Imagination*. I bumped up against this work while finishing my dissertation in 2007, and knew that it would one day find its way into my fiction. To it I owe the Father's sections ascribing prodigal births to an adulterous female imagination seduced by false imagery. Behind my twisted triplets, Narn, Mag and Tiff, readers will recognize the myth of the Furies conjoined to a bunch of other Wyrd Sisters—the Three Graces, the Valkyries, Gorgons—the whole concept monstrously stitched together with whatever I thought I could make up and get away with.

The inscription in the Founder's Cemetery, "We shall soon enjoy Halcyon Days with all the Vultures of Hell, Trodden under our feet," belongs to Cotton Mather, and can be found in his 1693 treatise, *The Wonders of the Invisible World: Observations as Well Historical as Theological upon the Nature, the Number and the Operations of the Devils.*

I paraphrased Kai's conjuring salvo, "The soul confessor of my tale of dread has passed. No one knows that once . . ." from Mary Shelley's 1831 short story, "The Transformation."

One more thing. In the box of material I compiled for this book there is a cutesy picture of my two sisters and me mugging before the Three Sisters, a rock formation in the Blue Mountains of New South Wales, shortly after we moved here. It is one of my most treasured possessions. Partly because our mother took it and partly because behind our adolescent smiles there is grown-up damage in our eyes.

Finally, thank you to my family—John, Isabella, Jack and Troy, always and forever. Honestly, I pinch myself every day.

ABOUT THE AUTHOR

J.S. Breukelaar is the author of *Collision: Stories,* a 2019 Shirley Jackson Award finalist, and winner of the 2019 Aurealis and Ditmar Awards. Previous novels include *Aletheia* and *American Monster.* Her short fiction has appeared in the *Dark Magazine, Tiny Nightmares, Black Static, Gamut, Unnerving, Lightspeed, Lamplight, Juked,* in *Year's Best Horror and Fantasy 2019* and elsewhere. She currently lives in Sydney, Australia, where she teaches writing and literature, and is at work on a new collection of short stories and a novella. You can find her at thelivingsuitcase.com and on Twitter and elsewhere @jsbreukelaar.

DID YOU ENJOY THIS BOOK?

If so, word-of-mouth recommendations and online reviews are critical to the success of any book, so we hope you'll tell your friends about it and consider leaving a review at your favorite bookseller's or library's website.

Visit us at www.meerkatpress.com for our full catalog.

Meerkat Press
Asheville